HE SEALED HIS MOUTH OVER HERS....

A shimmer of fear shot through her. What was he doing? Why wasn't he just taking her? He slid his tongue into her mouth. Tingles of excitement shot through her as he brushed his thumbs over her nipples, making them hard and taut.

"Why do you want to torture me?" she whispered.

"I don't want to torture you," he said, caressing her cheek. "I want you to want more than a mindless coupling to satisfy your lust."

"But there isn't supposed to be more than that," she said plaintively.

"And that's exactly why there has to be more."

"I don't understand, Sebas—"

He cut off her words by settling his lips over hers as his tongue met with hers in a slow, seductive dance. "You will...."

Touch of Lightning

Carin Rafferty

A TOPAZ BOOK

TOPAZ
Published by the Penguin Group
Penguin Books USA Inc., 375 Hudson Street,
New York, New York 10014, U.S.A.
Penguin Books Ltd, 27 Wrights Lane,
London W8 5TZ, England
Penguin Books Australia Ltd, Ringwood,
Victoria, Australia
Penguin Books Canada Ltd, 10 Alcorn Avenue,
Toronto, Ontario, Canada M4V 3B2
Penguin Books (N.Z.) Ltd, 182–190 Wairau Road,
Auckland 10, New Zealand

Penguin Books Ltd, Registered Offices:
Harmondsworth, Middlesex, England

First published by Topaz, an imprint of Dutton Signet,
a division of Penguin Books USA Inc.

First Printing, January, 1996
10 9 8 7 6 5 4 3 2 1

PUBLISHER'S NOTE
This is a work of fiction. Names, characters, places, and incidents either are the
product of the author's imagination or are used fictitiously, and any resemblance
to actual persons, living or dead, events, or locales is entirely coincidental.

BOOKS ARE AVAILABLE AT QUANTITY DISCOUNTS WHEN USED TO PROMOTE PRODUCTS
OR SERVICES. FOR INFORMATION PLEASE WRITE TO PREMIUM MARKETING DIVISION,
PENGUIN BOOKS USA INC., 375 HUDSON STREET, NEW YORK, NEW YORK 10014.

For Orysia Earhart, a great friend.
Thanks for always being there for me!

The Talisman
and the Guardian

✣

SALEM, MASSACHUSETTS — 1692

Ragna Morpeth slid stealthily to the edge of the bed. When her mate, Seamus, suddenly stirred she froze. As Ulrich Morgret, the coven's high priest, had instructed, she had slipped Seamus a sleeping potion. But what if the dose wasn't strong enough? What if he awakened?

At the thought, her pulse began to pound and her entire body trembled in fear. If Seamus realized that she was about to betray him . . .

She forced herself to draw in a deep, calming breath. Ulrich had cast a shielding spell over her, so even if Seamus awoke, he would not realize her perfidy. All she had to say was that she was going to check on their infant daughter. The worst that would happen was that he'd grumble about her overprotectiveness.

No, the worst that will happen is that he'll make love to you, and if that happens, how will you find the strength to do what you must do?

Ragna closed her eyes tightly against the pain that wrapped around her heart and squeezed. Seamus was her mate, and although he had changed, she would love him until the day she died.

She couldn't go through with this, she decided,

opening her eyes. She had to wake Seamus and tell him Ulrich's plans. They would take their daughter and run away. They would go where no one could find them. They would . . .

Ragna gave a sharp shake of her head to stop her ridiculous fantasizing and climbed out of bed. Even if she managed to wake Seamus, he'd never run away. He'd insist on fighting Ulrich until one of them was dead, and that battle would create a new dilemma. If Ulrich died the entire coven would be lost. If Seamus died, then she would have lost him forever. At least this way, Seamus would have a chance to survive, and she'd much rather lose him to banishment than to death.

After she dressed, she looked at Seamus and made herself see the reality of what he'd become rather than the image of the warlock with whom she'd fallen in love. His dark hair was tousled, but that was the only softness to his countenance. There was a sinister sharpness to his features, and even in sleep his mouth had a cruel twist to it.

When they'd mated, he'd been a kind and loving warlock. Granted, he'd had the same pride and vanity that plagued all warlocks, she admitted. But how could he have changed so drastically? How could he have become this . . . monster?

Unfortunately, she knew the answer, and she lowered her gaze to the silver talisman resting on his bare chest. It consisted of two large triangles that had been molded together to form a six-pointed star. The star was centered in the middle of a circle that was delicately engraved with symbols commanding the dark forces of nature.

As she regarded the magical object, a wave of hatred washed over her. When Seamus had inherited the talisman upon his father's death, it had changed him. Made him evil.

The talisman only enhanced what was already there, Ragna, Ulrich Morpeth murmured in her mind, using the old language—the secret language—of their race. *For it to create evil, the seed of evil must exist inside its possessor. Now, it is time for you to do what you must do. For yourself. For your child. For the coven. And most of all, for Seamus.*

Ulrich's voice was so clear, Ragna jerked her head toward the bedroom door, expecting to see the high priest standing there. But he wasn't there. He waited outside as they'd planned, and he couldn't enter her home until she invited him in. If he couldn't enter, he couldn't cast the spell over Seamus that would render him immobile and allow Ulrich to safely remove the talisman from around Seamus's neck. Nor could he cast the spell that would take away all but a modicum of Seamus's powers so he could banish him into the wilderness.

She returned her attention to Seamus. If she just waited until the sleeping potion wore off, she could talk with him. She would persuade him to give the talisman to Ulrich. Once he no longer had it, Seamus would revert to the warlock he had once been, and he wouldn't have to be banished. They could remain together and raise their child. They could—

Ragna, you know that is wishful thinking, Ulrich interrupted impatiently. *I've already explained that once the talisman has corrupted its possessors, they remain changed forever. Seamus is lost to us. He must be banished so he can bring no further harm to us or to the mortals.*

Touch the minds of the sleeping Pilgrims, Ragna, he urged. *Look into their nightmares—their dreaming cries of witch! We must take care of Seamus now. We must flee before dawn. If we don't, we will all die, Ragna. All of us. Including your child!*

No! Ragna screamed in silent denial, even as her mind raced from mortal house to mortal house— mortal mind to mortal mind. By the time she was done, she had to accept what he said. The witch hysteria hovered over the community like a death pall. Though Ulrich had tried to curb the hysteria, his spells had done no good. The Pilgrims' fear was too strong, and in the past few months, innocent mortals had been accused, condemned, and killed as witches because of what Seamus had done.

Now every mortal mind was centered on the members of the coven. The talisman had done its work well. It had corrupted Seamus—made him plant the seeds of the witch hysteria into the Pilgrims' minds—and if he wasn't stopped tonight, the talisman would be well on its way to its final goal.

Ragna shudddered as the full impact of that goal suddenly clarified for her. Now that the talisman had created the witch hysteria and given the mortals a taste for violence, it was focusing their attention on the coven members. Once the coven was destroyed, there would be no one with the power to stop the talisman. It would continue to use Seamus, giving him increasingly more power to destroy until, through him, it had wiped out the human population on this continent. Then it would find a way to move him to the next continent, and then the next, wreaking death wherever he went.

Ragna pressed her hands over her mouth to hold back a keening wail. If she betrayed Seamus, she would surely die. But if she didn't betray him, all of humanity could die. She knew she had to obey Ulrich, but how would she find the strength to do it? How could she see Seamus banished and not go with him? How would she live with herself if she never knew if he was alive or dead? And she wouldn't know, because once Ulrich cast the banishment spell, no one within the coven, not even herself, would be able to connect with Seamus.

Ragna, you must do this. You have no other choice.

You are wrong, Ulrich, she mentally argued. *You can give Seamus an amulet or some other object that will give me the power to know whether he lives or dies.*

I wish I could do as you ask, Ragna, but now that Seamus has changed, the only magical object that will work for him is the talisman. There is nothing else that will let you connect with him.

Ragna shook her head, refusing to accept his words. There *had* to be a way for her to maintain a link with Seamus. Involuntarily, her gaze returned to the talisman, and she knew the solution to her dilemma.

There is a way for you to give me what I ask, she told Ulrich. *You're going to break the talisman into three pieces. Give a piece of it to Seamus, and let me have the coven's piece. It will give me the power to know whether he lives or dies.*

You know that's impossible, Ragna. The talisman gains its powers from the energies of the moon and the sun. Once it is broken up, only one piece can remain in our possession. The other two pieces must be buried

*far apart, so there will be no chance that the talisman
can be resurrected. To allow two pieces to remain
above ground could prove catastrophic.*

*You are wrong again, Ulrich. Seamus will be forced
to go into the wilderness and live far away from here.
When he dies, his piece will surely be buried with
him. So the odds of all three pieces surfacing are next
to impossible. You must give him a piece so that I can
be connected with him.*

*Ragna, even if I did what you are asking, your only
contact would be nothing more than the knowledge of
whether or not he lives,* Ulrich rebutted. *Because of
the banishment spell, you won't be able to communicate with him or know anything about his life. You
must let him go. Keeping two pieces above ground is
too dangerous!*

And what you are asking is too cruel! she countered. *If you want me to invite you in, you must agree
with my terms. Give Seamus a piece of the talisman
and let me have the coven's piece. He is my mate,
Ulrich. I cannot let him go without a way of knowing
if he is alive. Give me what I want, or find another
way to stop him.*

Ulrich was silent for so long that Ragna wondered
if he'd left. Then his mind again connected with
hers.

*All right, Ragna. The urgency of our predicament is
too great for me to refuse. I just pray our descendants
will not live to regret my decision.*

Ragna refused to contemplate his dire words. Instead, she bent and pressed a quick kiss to Seamus's
lips. Then she ran out of the room and to the nursery. Gathering their daughter into her arms, she hurried to the front door.

When she flung it open, Ulrich waited on the other side. She looked at him for a long moment before saying, "You may enter my home, Ulrich. Just remember our bargain. A piece of the talisman for Seamus, and the coven's piece for me."

She didn't wait for his answer, but rushed past him and headed for the other members of the coven, who were gathered nearby. When Ulrich finished, they would flee, their sacred belongings protected by spells until they had finally relocated. Then, through magic, they would transport the objects to their new home.

She hadn't quite reached the security of the coven when lightning rent the sky. As she watched the ominous bolts gather into an electrically charged circle, terror swept through her.

Instinctively, she gathered her baby closer to her chest and refused to look at the lightning, even when she heard it striking the ground close behind her.

Ragna, how could you do this to . . . ! Seamus suddenly screamed in her mind. Before he could finish his accusation, the lightning disappeared.

At that moment, Ragna knew Ulrich had succeeded. He possessed the talisman, and she would never see Seamus again. But at least they each would have a piece of the magical object, and that would keep her connected to him. She also knew that the day Seamus died, she would take her own life—her final punishment for betraying him.

* * *

BLACK HILLS, SOUTH DAKOTA, 1975

Shaman Leonard Night Wolf shivered violently, but it wasn't from the cold. He felt as if someone, or rather *something*, were spying on him, and he glanced around his small encampment fearfully.

Other than the circle of trees illuminated by his fire, all he saw was the impenetrable darkness of a cloudy, starless night. He tried to tell himself that he was sensing an animal, but he couldn't quite convince himself that it was true.

As he had every winter for the past forty-five years, he'd left the Lakota Indian reservation and trekked deep into the mountains. His journey was a spiritual quest. A time to reaffirm his beliefs, a time to feed his soul. But this year, the trip wasn't soothing him. He felt as if the spirits were out of harmony, and that frightened him.

Huddling under the blanket wrapped around his shoulders, he anxiously fondled the silver triangle hanging from a chain around his neck. He had just celebrated his fiftieth birthday, and he knew it was time to select the new guardian for the triangle. It was one of the dilemmas he hoped to resolve on this trip.

Deciding to quell his apprehension by concentrating on the problem, he stared thoughtfully into the fire. There were several promising young braves within his tribe, but he hadn't found the one that struck that special spark of recognition inside him.

But was it really the spark that was missing? he asked himself. Or, as his wife claimed, was he too filled with self-importance to relinquish his hold on the triangle? Not that he'd be relinquishing it soon. It would take several years of training to make his successor ready to assume that duty, and he couldn't put off the selection much longer. If he died before the new guardian was prepared to take over the triangle, it could mean annihilation for his tribe.

He shivered again, but this time it wasn't due to unseen eyes. It was from the legend of the triangle, which had been taken from the evil *wicáhmunga*, Seamus Morpeth, nearly three hundred years before.

As the gruesome details of Seamus's time with his ancestors tried to surface, Leonard forced back the memory of the story. Now was not the time to remember the past. It was time to think of the future—to choose a new guardian who would protect his people from the curse Seamus had placed upon them just before his death.

"The triangle gives me my power," Seamus had told them. "And it is the triangle that will exact my revenge. It will join with its other pieces, and then your tribe will be no more."

And that was the guardian's onerous duty. To make sure the triangle never joined with its other pieces. But every guardian who touched it found himself drawn into a war with evil. That's why the selection was so important. The guardian had to be so pure of heart that his goodness would overcome the evil that the triangle tried to wedge into his soul.

Yes, it had to be someone special, Leonard acknowledged, and he wasn't convinced that any of the young braves vying for the honor was that pure.

"That is because none of the braves is meant to be the guardian," a strange, hollow-sounding voice announced.

Leonard jerked his head up in disbelief. When his gaze landed on the man standing on the other side of the fire, his heart began to race and his mouth went dry. He was looking at a fierce-looking brave dressed in full battle regalia of centuries past. How had he sneaked up on him?

"Who are you?" Leonard asked, studying the man's face and determining that he'd never seen him before.

The warrior didn't answer. He simply summoned Leonard to follow with a wave of his hand. Then he turned away from the fire and walked—or rather glided—toward the trees.

At that moment Leonard realized he wasn't looking at a man but a spirit, and he shuddered in terror. Did this mean his time was over? Had the spirit come to claim his soul?

Every self-protective instinct he possessed screamed at him to run in the opposite direction as fast as he could. He couldn't die until he chose the new guardian! So why did he feel his body rise of its own accord and follow the spirit?

Before he could ponder the thought, his mind filled with the image of a young and beautiful woman standing in profile. She was tall, and her black braided hair, familiar features, and dark complexion told him that she was a member of his race. But then she turned her head toward him. When he saw her gleaming, golden eyes, he realized she was a half-breed. No full-blooded Native American had eyes the color of the sun.

Suddenly she raised her arm, and he gasped in alarm. A rattlesnake curled around her arm from wrist to shoulder. He shuddered again as he watched it bury its head into the crook of her neck, as if it were settling down for a nap.

Although he was astonished by the snake, he was shocked to see that she wore a triangle identical to his. Who was she? And where had she gotten the triangle? Was this a portent that Seamus Morpeth's curse was about to come true?

As the questions arose, her image faded from his mind. He was dismayed to realize that not only had the spirit disappeared, but he had continued walking into the forest. When Leonard glanced over his shoulder, all he could see was blackness.

How far away was his camp? Could he find his way back?

"My friends and I have been waiting for you."

Leonard let out a startled yelp and swung toward the sound of the childish voice. At first he couldn't see anything, but then an eerie light began to glow beside a nearby tree.

As the light brightened, Leonard's mouth dropped open in shock. Beneath the tree sat a four- or five-year-old girl dressed in a thin, white T-shirt and a pair of white panties. In her lap lay a baby rattlesnake, and she stroked its head as if it were a kitten.

Behind her stood the spirit Indian, his body bowed over her as if protecting her from the cold. And perhaps he was, Leonard realized, because he couldn't see any sign of goose flesh marring her skin.

"Who are you?" he questioned in wonder.

"Sarah," she said, raising her gaze to his. "I am the new guardian."

As he found himself looking into her large, golden eyes, Leonard shook his head. But it wasn't an act of denial. It was one of recognition. The spark was there, and he knew that she spoke the truth. She was the new guardian. He also knew instinctively that this child, whom he'd just envisioned as a beautiful young woman, would be more than the triangle's guardian. She would be the one tasked to fight the curse Seamus Morpeth had cast upon his tribe nearly three hundred years ago.

Part One

Your eyes shall be opened,
and ye shall be as gods,
knowing good and evil.

—The Holy Bible:
Genesis 3:5

1

Evil Resurrected

"Supercilious bitch!"

As he spoke, archeologist John Butler III slammed down the telephone receiver and glared at the pictorial calendar tacked to the wall above the phone. The photograph was a trite rendition of the ocean, its waves ruthlessly battering a rocky shore. As much as he hated the unimaginative depiction, it was a good reflection of his life. He felt like those rocks, stuck in position while the world—or, more exactly, Dr. Lois Layton, the head of the archeology department—pummeled him.

How could she do this to him? The dig in the Middle East was his! If it hadn't been for his meticulous research, she wouldn't even have known about the site. This was his discovery, his chance to finally make a name for himself. She wanted to take it away from him, just as everyone always took the prestige away from him. He had to make her change her mind, but how?

Calm down and think! he ordered himself, while drawing in a deep breath and letting it out slowly. When he finally reached a measure of calmness, he walked to the window. As far as he was concerned, the scene outside was as insipid as the oceanic photograph. Acres of meadowland stretched before him, complete with witless, grazing sheep.

His temper stirred at the sight. He shouldn't be stuck on a deserted farm outside Salem, Massachusetts, supervising a half dozen undergraduate students, who were excavating what amounted to a garbage dump generated by the damn Pilgrims. He should be heading for what promised to be the biggest archeological discovery in fifty years!

With a curse, he swung around and looked at the room. He'd seen more habitable slums. The old farmhouse hadn't been lived in for ten years, but The Bitch hadn't cared that it was filled with mice and bugs, that the roof leaked, the plumbing didn't work, and portions of the building were structurally unsound.

"You're an archeologist. Be thankful you even have a roof over your head," she'd told him in a maddeningly deprecating tone. "I'm not wasting money on a motel when the team can stay at the farmhouse for free. Make the best of it, or I'll find someone else who will."

He'd known her threat was real, so he'd made the best of it by placing a plank of wood on two sawhorses to create a makeshift desk. A laptop computer sat in its center, surrounded by a half dozen buckets that caught the rain during a downpour, which seemed to be occurring every other day.

He continued his survey of the room. More makeshift tables were scattered throughout it to accommodate the findings from the dig. So far they'd uncovered nothing more than some potsherds and a few rotted pieces from wagon wheels. In a far corner lay his sleeping bag, which he rolled up tightly every morning to make sure that the bugs and mice stayed out of it.

Yes, he had made the best of it, but now he wondered if he shouldn't have told her to find someone else. If she had to talk to him face to face, she might not be able to deny him his rightful position as head of the Middle East team.

As her words repeated in his mind, he ground his teeth. "You're too volatile, John. This is an unstable area of the world and inappropriate behavior could endanger the lives of the entire team. I need someone who can maintain his composure at all times."

Her explanation had angered him, but her intonation had infuriated him. She'd sounded as if she were lecturing a recalcitrant child, and he knew that her attitude was fostered by his small stature. If he were six foot tall and built like a linebacker, she wouldn't give a damn about his volatility. But even with heel lifts he barely measured five feet seven, and years of weight lifting hadn't added significant muscular bulk to his spare frame. If anything, it had made him look skinnier.

He turned back to the window, bitterly deciding that it wasn't his temper destroying his career. It was his appearance. She wanted someone who'd look good on television interviews and magazine covers. She wanted a Harrison Ford clone, and he didn't fit the image of a rough-and-tumble Indiana Jones. He was a small man, and in the eyes of the world, a small man wasn't a man at all.

"Dr. Butler?" a hesitant female voice said behind him.

Startled, John spun away from the window and stared at the young woman standing in the doorway. With her lank brown hair and dull brown eyes, she had the vapid looks of a cow and a personality to match. Indeed, she was so unremarkable that he couldn't even remember her name. The only reason he'd let her be on this project was that she was one of The Bitch's pets.

"Why aren't you at the site?" he snapped, cursing himself when she eyed him fearfully. *Dammit!* He had to get a handle on his temper, or he would never make it to the Middle East.

"Michael sent us back," she said, a quaver in her voice. "Something . . . weird is happening at the dig, and he doesn't think it's safe for us to be there."

John scowled at the mention of his nemesis, Michael Forest. The man wasn't an archeologist, but a rich bastard who'd recently retired and turned his business empire over to his grandson. Then he'd made an obscenely large donation to the archeology department and persuaded The Bitch to let him work on a dig. Unfortunately, John had gotten stuck with him, and he'd come to despise the old man. Forest was constantly usurping his authority, and more than once they'd had words about it.

Maybe that was why The Bitch had decided to keep him off the Middle East project. He'd bet the old man had complained about him, and with the kind of money Forest had, she'd take his word over John's. Hell, he wouldn't be surprised to learn that Forest was financing the Middle East excavation, and in exchange, he would be a part of the team. The son of a bitch would share in the fame, while John remained stuck in obscurity.

"Dr. Butler?"

The young woman's anxious voice jerked him out of his angry speculation. He started to tell her to go tell Forest to go to hell. Luckily, his common sense surfaced. If Forest was behind The Bitch's treachery, he couldn't give him more ammunition.

"What is this 'weird something' that's going on?" he asked.

A look of terror settled on her face. "Lightning."

"Lightning?" he repeated, sure he'd misunderstood her. There wasn't a cloud in the sky. How could there be lightning?

She nodded and began to wring her hands. "It's the scariest thing I've ever seen."

John arched a brow, unimpressed by her pronouncement. She looked like the type who'd be afraid of her own shadow. He opened his mouth to question her further, but she said, "Michael said you're to come to the site immediately."

Forest's dictatorial summons reignited his temper. He stalked past her, determined to have it out with Forest once and for all. It was time the old man understood that he may have been a captain of industry, but on this project he was nothing more than a lackey. If it cost John the Middle East project, so be it. He was tired of being pushed around.

When he arrived at the excavation site, however, all thoughts of confrontation disappeared and his mouth dropped open in shock. As he'd already noted, the sky was cloudless, but an intricately entwined wreath of lightning bolts hung above the pit they'd been excavating. The lightning circled so rapidly it made him dizzy. It also made no sound.

He switched his gaze from the phenomenon to Michael Forest. He stood on the edge of the pit, staring up at the lightning with a rapt expression, unaware of John's presence.

Look at him, standing there like some god surveying his kingdom. Doesn't that prove he's the one behind

The Bitch's decision? He wants to destroy you. Are you going to stand by and let that happen?

Hatred surged through John. Forest was at least thirty years his senior, but despite his shock of silver hair and the slight paunch that came with age, he looked more vibrant—more *manly*—than John ever had or ever would. And because of his bottomless coffers, Forest was buying his way into the world that John had fought tooth and nail to enter. Now the old goat wanted to take that world away from him.

Stop him, and you will be rewarded. Remember, glory goes to those who protect themselves.

The word "glory" vibrated through John. It was what he wanted—what he deserved—and people like Forest and The Bitch always stole it from him. Well, he was *not* going to take it from them any longer.

He glanced around the site, confirming that they were alone, before leaning down and grabbing a shovel used to place discarded dirt from the pit into a pile. Then he crept up behind Forest, who continued to stare at the lightning as though hypnotized by it. John knew instinctively that that was exactly what was happening to the old man. He also knew he had to take care of him before the spell broke and he realized John was there.

When John was a couple of feet behind Forest, he hefted the shovel into the air. Letting a lifetime of anger and frustration fuel him, he brought the shovel down on the back of Forest's head. There was a satisfying crack of metal against bone, and Forest teetered for a moment before toppling into the pit. As he fell, John dropped the shovel and stepped into the same spot where Forest had stood.

Staring down into the pit, he noted that the old man's head was bent at such an angle that, when he'd fallen, he'd probably broken his neck. But broken neck or not, he was obviously dead.

As the gravity of that hit him, a shiver of fear crept up John's spine. "My God, what have I done?"

Vengeance is thy right, and glory thy reward. Everything thou desireth will now be granted.

As the words echoed in John's mind, a lightning bolt broke free of the wreath and struck a spot near the center of the pit. Excitement stirred inside him. The lightning was showing him the way to his reward, and whatever lay buried at that spot would help him achieve his glory!

He scrambled into the hole and hurried to where the lightning had hit. All he saw were clumps of earth, still muddy from a recent rain, but then a gleam of silver caught his eye. Dropping to his knees, he dug with his fingers until he uncovered a dirt-encrusted metal object about six inches in diameter.

As he lifted it into his hands, another bolt of lightning broke free of the wreath and struck the object. John felt his body convulse from the electrified charge, and he screamed in agony as metal burned into his hands.

He didn't know how long he suffered from the excruciating pain. All he knew was that one moment he was sure he was going to die, and the next moment the pain had vanished.

In its place came a flood of knowledge, and he suddenly knew secrets he shouldn't have—*couldn't have*—known. But he did know them, and their significance was profound.

He shook his head in disbelief. He held a piece of an ancient talisman, which had been broken apart centuries ago. This piece had been buried, and the other pieces taken away so the talisman couldn't be made whole again. If he recovered the other two pieces, he would be the most powerful man in the world.

"But how do I find the other pieces?" he asked in confusion, running his fingers over the circle. It was no longer encrusted with dirt but gleamed like newly polished silver. Delicately engraved symbols, unlike anything he'd ever seen, ringed its edge.

All thou must know will be revealed. Now thou must escape, for others come.

A nagging voice in the back of John's mind said he was crazy. He was talking to a piece of metal, for God's sake! Worse, he thought it was talking back.

Uneasily, he glanced over his shoulder. When his gaze landed on Forest, he shuddered both in revulsion and fear. He'd just killed one of the richest men in the world, and even an insanity plea wouldn't save him. He had to get out of here!

With a mumbled curse, he leaped to his feet, hurried to the side of the pit, and scrambled out of it. When he saw a group of students approaching in the distance, he cursed again. Forest had told them to stay away, so why were they coming back?

Recognizing that the question was moot, he ran toward an outlying stand of pines. He had no idea where he was going, but as panic tried to surface, an inner voice told him there was no reason to be afraid. The talisman would protect him, and it would tell him everything he needed to know.

As he entered the woods, he burst into exhilarated laughter. He was finally going to have the glory he deserved, and no one would ever take it away from him again.

* * *

SANCTUARY, PENNSYLVANIA

Sebastian Moran warily studied the glowing silver triangle, linked to a delicate silver chain. The triangle measured about four inches long and three inches wide at the base. Both it and the chain were sealed in a small glass dome. The dome was in a glass display case filled with crystal and gem amulets.

"How long has it been glowing like this?" he asked Shana Morland-Alden, the caretaker of the coven's repository, where the triangle was kept. She had summoned him, declaring that something "strange" was happening. As the troubleshooter for the council of high priests, who ruled all the covens around the world, it was Sebastian's job to handle unexplained phenomena.

"I don't know," she answered. "I haven't been in here for several weeks. I wouldn't have come in here today, except . . ."

"Except what?" Sebastian demanded when she fell silent.

She shook her head and frowned. "It was as if I felt an undercurrent of magical energy that I couldn't pinpoint."

"And you hadn't felt the energy before today?"

When she shook her head again, he returned his attention to the triangle, disturbed by her answer. He'd felt the same undercurrent for nearly a month, and he also hadn't been able to pinpoint it. Now he knew the source, but what was making the triangle glow? And why hadn't Shana, who lived in the house, felt the energy before now?

Because the triangle wants you.

Sebastian started. Where had that thought come from?

"What?" he said, looking at Shana, who had spoken at the same time the thought had arrived.

"I said that unless you need me, I'm going upstairs to look for the journal that will tell us about the amulet."

"Fine," he murmured, resuming his inspection of the object. For an amulet, it was unusually plain. There were no gems attached to it, nor was there any engraving. Of course, there might be something engraved on its back, but he'd have to take the dome out of the display case to find out. Instinct told him that he should remove it only as a last resort.

He turned to search the room for a reason for the triangle to glow. It was the first time he'd been in the repository, which was located in the center of Shana's house, and he surveyed it curiously.

The room was circular and a good twenty-five to thirty feet in diameter. A pentagram was built into the center of the floor, and a brick fireplace filled one wall. Scattered around the room were more display cases and tables cluttered with objects, ranging from crystals to weaponry and everything in between.

He knew that some of the articles were sacrosanct, but most were stored here because they had been created under the Old Ways and involved the dark forces of nature. Sebastian recognized that it was an important safety measure to keep them here. More than two hundred years ago, the council of high priests had banned the practice of the Old Ways. Many of these objects could unleash dangerous powers that, without the knowledge of the Old Ways, the coven couldn't control.

He continued his survey of the repository. On the wall opposite the fireplace was a staircase. He let his gaze follow it upward to a balcony on the second-floor level, where he saw Shana searching through what appeared to be thousands of books in built-in bookcases. She was awash in a rainbow of colors. Where was the color coming from?

Looking for the answer, he turned his attention to the staircase leading from the second-floor balcony to the third-story level. It contained more display cases and tables. Finally, he raised his gaze to the ceiling, and he found the origin of the colors. The ceiling consisted of a stained-glass pentagram mirroring the one on the floor. Early-morning sunlight flowed through the glass, creating a dazzling show of vibrant hues. Was that what was making the triangle glow? Was it nothing more than a reflection of light?

No, he quickly concluded. The display case was tucked into a dark corner, and even if light could get to it, the triangle would be reflecting colors, not emitting that strange white-hot light.

"How much longer is it going to take you to find the journal?" he called up to Shana, who was no longer in sight. He knew he shouldn't harass her, but he was uneasy with this entire situation. He wanted answers, and he wanted them now.

She appeared at the railing. "It could take a few hours. The journals are grouped by object, and there's a listing in the front of the book that gives a physical description of each item entered. But you've seen how many amulets are in here. If you want to leave, I'll contact you when I've found it."

"Don't be ridiculous, Shana," he grumbled. "I'm not leaving until I find out what's going on."

"Then I suggest you sit down and relax."

She disappeared before he could respond, and he turned to look at the triangle. Though he still found it disturbing, he had to admit that its glow was rather pleasant, particularly with the jewels from the other amulets sparkling in its light.

He moved closer to the display case and leaned down to get a better look. When he did, he felt an overwhelming urge to remove the triangle from the dome, to hold it in his hand. Would it be warm or cool? Warm, he decided, and if he put it on, it would make him the most—

"I've found it!" Shana declared excitedly.

Startled, he spun around. She was coming down the stairs with a large, tattered book clutched to her chest. As he watched her descent, he frowned. She looked different, but he couldn't define the change in her appearance. Then it hit him. Her long, brown hair was in disarray and her clothing wrinkled, as though she'd been working for a long time.

Instinctively, he glanced toward the stained-glass pentagram and an apprehensive shiver crawled up his spine. He would have sworn that he'd been talking to Shana only moments ago, but the angle of the light indicated that a good two hours had passed.

But that's impossible. How could I lose track of that much time?

You know how. The triangle wants you.

As the answer reverberated in his mind, Shana sat down at a nearby table and said, "The reason it took me so long to find it is because it isn't an amulet. It's a piece of a talisman."

At her announcement, Sebastian's anxiety grew. The differences between an amulet and a talisman were significant. Depending on the physical properties of the material from which it was made, an amulet provided passive protection for everything from bad luck to illness to evil. A talisman, however, had magical power, and it transferred that power to its wearer. The trouble was, the powers it imbued were often tinged with evil.

He cast an uncomfortable glance toward the triangle. Now that he knew it was a piece of a talisman, the fact that it was sealed in its own glass dome took on new importance. Whoever had put it in there had wanted to make sure that it wasn't easily accessible. That alone assured him that he was dealing with something potentially dangerous.

"What kind of talisman is it?" he asked, as Shana opened the book and began to read.

"This is written in the old language, so it's going to take me a minute to figure it out," she said.

Sebastian wanted to snatch the book away from her and read it himself, but he knew it would take him longer to interpret the old language. Because of her job, Shana had occasion to read it more frequently.

As she turned the page, she began to grow pale. When she finally looked up at him, her eyes were wide with terror.

"What is it?" he asked, alarmed. A few months before Shana had fought an evil spirit witch. After that harrowing experience, he knew it would take a lot to frighten her.

She raked a shaking hand through her hair and

said, "Around the year 1000 A.D., a young warlock named Aodán Morpeth disappeared from his coven on the Norwegian coast. Five years later, he returned with a silver talisman. The talisman was made up of three pieces. A large circle and two triangles molded together to form a six-pointed star. The triangles were centered in the circle, which was engraved with thirteen symbols, four of which were unknown to the coven."

She paused and ran a finger down the page, as though needing to verify what she was about to say. "Aodán couldn't remember where he had been or what had happened to him. He was also terrified of the talisman, though he didn't know why. He locked it in a box, where it remained, because every family member who inherited it had an instinctive fear it."

Sebastian took a moment to mull over the information before saying, "Obviously someone wasn't afraid of it, or we wouldn't have just a piece of it. What happened?"

This time, she turned the page. "In 1691, Seamus Morpeth inherited the talisman upon his father's death. According to his mate, Ragna, he didn't know about the talisman until he went through his father's things. She claimed Seamus was afraid of it, but he was also beguiled by it and he put it on. Once he did, the talisman began to change Seamus."

"How was he beguiled by it?" Sebastian asked, ignoring the urge to turn around and look at the triangle again. Was that what had happened to him? Had he lost track of time because he'd been beguiled by it?

No! he told himself firmly. He was the troubleshooter, which made him the most powerful warlock alive. If the entire talisman were here, it might be able to enchant him, but there was no way a piece of it could affect him that strongly.

"The journal doesn't talk about his beguilement," Shana answered. "I'm surprised it even tells as much as it does. Generally, there's nothing more listed than what the object is, who made it, and what it was used for."

"Does it say anything else?"

She nodded, her expression grim. "The coven's high priest, Ulrich Morgret, was convinced the witch hysteria that began in Salem and spread throughout Massachusetts was caused by Seamus."

Sebastian blinked at her in disbelief. "*Seamus* caused the witch hysteria? Because of the talisman?" When Shana nodded, he said, "This is the first time I've heard that theory."

"That's because Ulrich ordered the few people who knew about it to keep it a secret," Shana replied. "Seamus's actions endangered the entire coven, and they had to flee Massachusetts and go into the wilderness to escape persecution. Ulrich didn't want the other coven members turning against Ragna Morpeth and her daughter because of what Seamus had done."

"That makes sense. But why wasn't the information reported to the council? They should have been informed about what happened."

"Maybe they were informed."

He shook his head. "Something that significant would be passed down to the troubleshooter, so if it had been reported, I would know. What happened to Seamus and the talisman?"

"Ulrich researched the symbols on the circle," Shana replied, again referring to the book. "He determined that it was inherently evil, and that it would look for evil in its possessor and corrupt him. He also concluded that the talisman's sole purpose was to destroy humankind."

Sebastian gaped at her. "That's impossible. A talisman with that kind of power would *have* to be reported to the council."

Shana gave a helpless shrug. "I'm only repeating what's in the journal."

"What else does it say?" He risked another glance toward the triangle. What she was saying couldn't be true! But if it were . . . He refused to complete the thought. The ramifications were too horrible to even contemplate.

"According to this, Ulrich knew the talisman couldn't be destroyed. He did, however, ascertain that it gained its energy from the moon and the sun. He concluded that if its three pieces—the circle and the two triangles—were broken apart and one of the pieces buried, it would lose its power.

"He decided that it would be even better if two of the pieces were buried far apart, making it more unlikely that it could be resurrected," she went on. "But first he had to get the talisman away from Seamus and exile him, because he had also determined that once a person is corrupted by the talisman he can't be rehabilitated."

Sebastian shuddered. He'd heard of magical objects so pernicious they could forever corrupt their possessor, but this was the first time he'd come into contact with one. Assuming, of course, that everything in the journal was true. He still had his doubts. It seemed inconceivable that something this ominous had not been reported.

"How did Ulrich get the talisman?" he asked next.

As Shana told him about the night Ragna betrayed her mate and demanded that both she and Seamus be allowed to keep a piece of the talisman, Sebastian walked closer to the display case. Was the triangle glowing brighter? Or was his imagination working overtime because of this bizarre story?

When she was done, he said, "When Ragna died, why wasn't this piece buried? That would have ensured that all three pieces would never be above ground at the same time."

"It wasn't buried because of the unfamiliar symbols engraved on the circle," Shana stated. "Ulrich didn't recognize them, but he was sure they had to do with the earth. He was afraid that if all three pieces were underground, they might be able to connect through the earth energies and cause natural disasters. Since there was a good chance that Seamus's piece would be buried with him on his death, when Ragna died, Ulrich had the triangle sealed in that dome and stored in the repository."

"And until now it has never glowed?"

"I'll check out some of the other journals to make sure, but I doubt it. If it had, it should have been recorded here."

Sebastian began to pace. "So we have to assume that it's glowing because all three pieces are now above ground."

Again, Shana nodded, and she placed both hands over her abdomen in a protective gesture. Sebastian recognized the significance of her action. She was nearly four months pregnant. Her first instinct would be to protect her child. But how did you protect an unborn child, or anyone else, from what was purportedly a doomsday device?

Since it was his job to do just that, he'd have to find a way, and fast.

"What are you going to do, Sebastian?" she asked.

"There's only one thing I can do," he stated grimly. "Take the triangle off coven land and put it on. If all three pieces are above ground, then it should draw me to the other two."

"Wouldn't it be better to just bury this piece? That would deactivate the talisman."

Sebastian shook his head. "It would deactivate it for now, but what if the other two pieces end up buried somewhere down the road? If Ulrich was right and it connects underground, no telling how much damage would occur before we figured out what was going on. The best way to stop it is for me to get the other two pieces and bury them myself. Then I can return this piece to the repository for safekeeping."

"I suppose you're right," Shana allowed. "But why do you have to take it off coven land? Wouldn't it be safer for you to put it on here—on consecrated ground?"

"Safer for me, maybe," he admitted. "But not necessarily safer for the coven."

When she looked confused, he explained, "Since the triangle is only a piece of the talisman, if I'm off coven land, the energy barrier encircling Sanctuary will protect the coven from any malevolence. If I put it on within the coven boundary, it may be able to penetrate the energy barrier. Until I know what I'm dealing with, I can't take any chances."

"But what if it . . . corrupts you as it corrupted Seamus?" Shana questioned hesitantly, fearfully.

"That isn't going to happen. I'm the trouble-shooter, remember? I'm incorruptible."

He knew his answer was flip, but he wasn't about to admit that her concern was valid. It appeared that the triangle had made him lose time. If it could do that to him while sealed in a glass dome, what would it do once he put it on?

He wanted to reassure himself that it couldn't corrupt him. But if the journal was right, the talisman had corrupted Seamus Morpeth, a warlock who had both a mate and a child. His very nature would have demanded that he sacrifice his life to protect them both from harm. Yet the talisman had made Seamus go against his nature—to put not only the coven but both his mate and child at risk.

As the import of that hit him, Sebastian felt unadulterated fear rush through him. How could he, a warlock with no mate or child to enhance his primal protective instincts, fight against such insidious evil, when Seamus had had both and had failed?

Knowing that he couldn't afford to think about the issue, Sebastian opened the display case and lifted out the glass dome. He had to believe that he was stronger than Seamus.

He told Shana goodbye and walked out, praying that he was strong enough to defeat the talisman. If he weren't, he might be responsible for the annihilation of the human race.

* * *

LAKOTA SIOUX RESERVATION, SOUTH DAKOTA

This wasn't like her normal dreams. It didn't have the strong echoes of the past or the insubstantial vibrations of the future. It felt immediate—real—and a frisson of unease slid through her. She *never* dreamed of the present.

As she glanced around her surroundings, she

frowned. She was in the woods, but it wasn't the familiar forest of the sacred Black Hills. This place didn't have the stark, soaring mountains to which she was accustomed, and there were more leafy trees than conifers. The ground was also different. It was thick with undergrowth and brambles, but what disturbed her was the strange golden barrier that shimmered in front of her. It stretched from ground to sky, and no matter how hard she tried, she couldn't see through the barrier.

When a man suddenly strode through it, she could only stare at him in awe. He was extraordinarily tall and dressed all in black. But it was his breadth she found astounding. His shoulders were so broad she was sure that if she stood in front of him he'd block out the sun. As her gaze roamed down him, she noted that he carried a glass dome. She tried to see what was inside it, but it emitted a blinding light.

Who was he? she wondered, returning her gaze to his face. His features were too austere to consider him handsome. He had hollow cheeks, a hooked nose, and a jawline and chin so sharply defined they looked as if they had been chiseled from granite. His shoulder-length, dark-brown hair and glittering dark eyes gave him a dangerous, predatory look, which was enhanced by an aura of raw power. She felt drawn to him, yet repelled by him. The conflicting feelings made her shiver, though she wasn't sure it was from fear. There was something else stirring inside her. An emotion she had never felt before and couldn't identify, but it made her feel hot and weak and trembling.

Warily, she watched him set the dome on the ground and kneel in front it. Then he raised his hands and began to speak. She tried to hear his words and wanted to curse in frustration when she couldn't. Who was he? What was he doing?

A moment later the dome burst open and she watched him quickly grab whatever was inside it. When he did, a strange wreath of lightning appeared in the sky. It circled above him with dizzying speed, and then a bolt of lightning broke free from the wreath and struck the object in his hand.

His body violently convulsed, and his hands smoked as if on fire. She cried out in horror, sure he was going to die. When the lightning disappeared, however, he didn't fall dead to the ground. He remained kneeling, and he tossed back his head and opened his mouth, as though in exhilarated laughter. Then he raised his hands and dropped whatever he'd taken from the dome around his neck.

When it settled against his chest, she could finally see what it was. Panic ripped through her. He wore a triangle identical to the one she guarded. That could only mean that he was a *wicáhmunga*—a magician. Since he possessed the triangle, he had to be like Seamus Morpeth, who had tortured and slaughtered her people, and then placed the curse upon them nearly three hundred years ago.

Fearfully, she returned her gaze to his face and was startled to find him staring at her. She assured herself that it was a coincidence. She wasn't really here but having one of her dreams. There was no way he could see her.

That didn't alleviate the unnerving sensation that he could. Nor did it alter the transformation of his visage. Before he'd put on the triangle, he'd looked harsh and uncompromising. Now he looked cruel

and maniacal, almost inhuman, and his glittering
eyes seemed to delve into her soul.

As she stared into his eyes, she could perceive
the evil uncoiling inside him, and she knew that
even if he couldn't see her, his malevolence was
directed at her. Unmitigated fear enveloped her, and
she forced her way toward consciousness to escape
him. As his image faded, she heard him say "Sarah."

Terror shot through her. His voice was soft, almost a caress. It was also the most menacing sound
she had ever heard. Instinctively, she knew he
wasn't just saying her name. He was letting her
know that he knew who she was. She also knew
that he would come after her, and when he found
her he would kill her.

Sarah Many Dreams bolted upright in bed. Her
entire body trembled, and her heart raced so fast
that she pressed a hand to her chest. When she did,
her fingers brushed against the silver triangle resting
between her breasts. It felt white hot, and she
jerked her hand away.

"It was just a dream!" she told herself, frantically
clutching the covers to her chest.

But she knew she was lying to herself. She never
had "just a dream," and never would. The *wasičun*
world called her psychic; her people called her
wakan—holy. She hated both descriptions. They
made her different, and because she was different,
she was ostracized by both the non-Indians and the
Lakotas.

She thrust a hand through her tangled hair, trying to alleviate the remnants of her terror, but the
painful pull against her scalp didn't help. The
wicáhmunga knew who she was, and he would

come after her. When he did, she would have to defeat him. This was her destiny—what she'd prepared for her entire life. She shouldn't be frightened.

"Of course you should be frightened, Sarah. To be otherwise would be foolish, and you are not foolish," a deep, ethereal voice announced.

"Wanága!" Sarah gasped, as a mystical glow appeared at the foot of her bed.

She watched her spirit guide take form. As his body appeared, she marveled at his beauty. He sported a leather headband, with an eagle feather tucked over his left ear. His long black hair flowed down his back. His eyebrows arched across his forehead, and emphasized the upward slant of his dark eyes. His face was narrow; his nose long and straight. His lips were thin and unsmiling, giving him a ferocious look.

Automatically, her gaze dropped to his compact, muscular body. Wanága had two wardrobes. One was full battle regalia; the other, which he appeared in tonight, consisted of nothing more than a leather breach clout covering his slim hips. Except for the feather in his headband, his only adornment was a necklace made of small seashells.

Several years ago, she'd asked him where he'd gotten such a necklace, since seashells were not indigenous to South Dakota. He'd replied, "When it is time for you to know all, you will understand."

Over the years she'd grown used to his cryptic statement, though it still frustrated her. Even his real name was a mystery, because *wanága* was the Lakota word for ghost. She was also sure that he knew who she was and where she had come from. But no matter how much she begged for the information, he answered with that maddening, "When it is time for you to know all, you will understand."

"Who am I, Wanáġa?" she suddenly demanded, even though she knew that, under the circumstances, it was an irrational question. She should be asking him about the dream and the *wicáhmunġa*. She should be ascertaining the best way to fight him. Her identity was unimportant when mortal danger loomed over her people.

But how could she defeat the *wicáhmunġa* if she didn't have a sense of who she was? She needed that knowledge to ground her, to make her spirit stronger. Unfortunately, it was an argument Wanáġa wouldn't understand, or at least he'd pretend he didn't understand it. She had used it with him before to no avail.

Wanáġa arched a brow. "Why do you ask me such a question now, Sarah?"

"Because if you don't tell me, I may never know the answer."

"Why would this be?" he asked, regarding her in bemusement.

"You know what I saw in my dream," she said, deciding to use an argument he couldn't deny understanding. Over the years he'd picked up contemporary language, but he was still from the past. A past rich with mysticism and ritual that he ardently observed. "You also know the danger I face. What if I die? How will my spirit know where to go if it doesn't know where it came from?"

"I have guided you in this earthly world. Do you believe I would abandon you in the spirit world?"

"In other words, you refuse to tell me what I want—no, *need*—to know," she said angrily, though it wasn't anger provoking her temper. It was fear. No matter how hard she tried, she couldn't get the *wicáhmunga's* menacing voice out of her mind. He knew who she was, and he would come after her. She had sensed his raw power, and it was stronger than anything she'd ever known. How could she possibly defeat him?

Wanáǧa opened his mouth to respond, but she interrupted, "Withholding that information isn't fair, Wanáǧa. I have accepted the role of guardian, and I am willing to risk my life to do what must be done. I don't think it's too much to ask for my identity in return."

"You already know your identity. You are Sarah, and you are the guardian."

"Why are you doing this to me? Why won't you just tell me who I am?" she cried in frustration.

"Because it is not knowledge you seek. You have seen a part of what is to come, and you are frightened. You want to escape, but you cannot escape. Look at the tipi, Sarah. Look at it. Touch it. Learn what you must know."

Sarah shuddered at his instruction. Tipi was the Lakota word for tepee. It was also the word Wanáǧa used when referring to the triangle she wore around her neck. Until now, she'd managed to ignore it, even though she'd been subliminally aware that it was so hot against her skin that it burned.

Closing her eyes tightly, she whispered, "I don't want to look at it or touch it. I saw what it did to the *wicáhmunga*. It summoned the lightning, and it burned him!"

"Fear lies in ignorance, Sarah," Wanáǧa chided. "Look at the tipi. Touch it. Learn from it, and then you will no longer be ignorant."

Every self-protective instinct Sarah possessed

screamed at her to ignore Wanága. But after twenty
years, obedience was too deeply ingrained in her.

She opened her eyes and looked down at the triangle. It was glowing so brightly that she felt
blinded. Hesitantly, she raised her hand to it. When
her fingers brushed against it, she heard a soft rustling sound overhead. Anxiously, she glanced toward
the ceiling, only to confirm her worst fear. The
wreath of lightning circled above her bed.

She started to jerk her fingers away from the triangle, but a bolt of lightning broke free and struck
it. Pain shot through her with such intensity that
she knew she was going to die. She could feel her
body convulsing and smell the singed flesh of her
fingertips. But when the pain became so unbearable
that she couldn't stand it a moment longer, the
lightning disappeared.

The feelings that next flooded through her were
euphoric. She felt more alive than she'd ever felt before, and she tossed back her head and laughed at
the exhilarating sensation.

But then her mind filled with images that made
her laughter die. She was having another vision, but
this one had the familiar echoes of the past, which
meant it had already happened.

She saw the wreath of lightning spinning above a
pit, and she gasped as she watched a small, feral
man hit an older man over the head with a shovel.
She knew the older man was dead; she saw his
spirit ascend from his body. Then she watched the
small man climb into the pit and dig up an object.
When he did, he was hit by the lightning, and his
name flashed through her mind—Butler. John Butler III, an archeologist.

She no more than completed the thought than, as

in her dream with the *wicáhmunġa*, the small man started staring at her. He too knew who she was and would be coming to kill her.

But as she looked into his ice-blue eyes, she didn't experience fear at the evil she perceived in him. She felt mesmerized by it. Drawn into it. Would it be so bad to give in to it? To let herself be consumed by it?

"Let go of the tipi, Sarah," Wanáġa suddenly commanded. "Let go of it *now!*"

Wanáġa's voice was so urgent that she instantly released the triangle. Then she collapsed onto the mattress, feeling as if she'd been drained of her life force.

"I'm going to die," she sobbed, tears rolling down her cheeks. "They are going to kill me, and my people will be lost."

"There are different kinds of deaths, Sarah," Wanáġa said, placing his palm on her forehead. Until she felt his cool touch, she didn't realize she was burning up with fever. "Your duty will be to choose the right one."

"What does that mean?" she asked weakly. "I don't understand."

"When it is time for you to know all, you will understand."

2

Evil Perceived

✥

As Sebastian Moran neared the top of the mountain he was climbing, he stopped walking and warily surveyed his surroundings. Moments ago he'd been listening to the scurry of small animals. Now all he could hear was the sigh of a summer wind through the spruce and pine trees encircling him.

While he scanned the moonlit woods, using both his eyes and his mind, for a reason for the animals' sudden stillness, he considered how he'd ended up in a remote area of South Dakota's Black Hills. Early this morning he'd learned about the talisman. When he put on the triangle, he'd immediately learned about the mortal woman who had the other triangle. Although he hadn't been able to mentally connect with her, touching the triangle had provided her name—Sarah. It had also given him her location—Rapid City, South Dakota. A plane had brought him to Rapid City by early evening, and a rental car to the base of this towering, granite mountain about an hour ago. All he had to do was touch the triangle, and it showed him where to go to find this Sarah.

That's how he'd gotten here, he concluded, but it didn't explain the animals' odd behavior. He frowned. Something was wrong, but he hadn't picked up on anything that could be a personal threat. So what was going on?

He considered casting a spell to find out, but decided it would be a waste of time. Spells rarely worked on wild animals, because they were incapable of reasoning. Or at least the kind of reasoning that humans could decipher, he amended.

Instinctively, he touched the triangle hanging around his neck. His mind immediately filled with the image of Sarah. She sat beneath a large pine tree, but he couldn't determine its location. Frustrated, he tried to connect with her mind, but that didn't work, either.

Releasing the triangle, he muttered a curse. He knew she was close. The triangle had been glowing softly for the past several minutes, and he was sure it was a reaction to the other triangle. So why wasn't it showing him her location? It had, after all, led him this far. And since she was nearby, why couldn't he touch her mind?

He didn't have the answers, so he decided to finish climbing to the mountaintop. Maybe from there he would see something that would lead him to her.

He resumed his trek upward, constantly searching the shadows. When he still didn't hear any animals, he mumbled, "They're just afraid of me."

But if that were the case, he would have encountered the silence all the way up the mountain. Something was definitely wrong, and he felt damned uneasy.

A few minutes later he heard a soft, slithering sound behind him. He instantly halted. There was only one animal that made that hair-raising sound. A *snake*.

He shuddered. Because of slight physiological

differences between his race and mortals, the bite
of a nonpoisonous snake would make him critically
ill. The bite of a poisonous snake was so lethal that
even antivenom couldn't save him. Snakes were also
one of the few living creatures that couldn't be
spellbound, which meant he couldn't control them.
Worse, because he hadn't picked up on anything
threatening, he hadn't cast a protective spell over
himself.

How could he have been so damn stupid? Even if
he hadn't picked up on the snakes, he should have
realized there would be some out here. He was in
the middle of the wilderness, for pity's sake!

He considered casting the protective spell now,
but he knew he had to determine the snake's location first. The spell-lightning might startle the reptile and make it strike. He had to make sure it was
far enough away for the spell to take hold before it
could get to him.

Cautiously, he turned around. When he did, he
heard the slithering again. This time it came from
his right. He pivoted his head in that direction. Before he could focus on the area, the sound came
from his left, and then from behind him.

That's why the animals were silent, he realized in
horror. This part of the mountain crawled with
snakes!

He no more than completed the thought when he
heard the first rattle. It was followed by another and
another and another until the air vibrated with the
clatter.

Terror coiled in his gut, and he broke out in a
cold sweat. These weren't just snakes. They were
rattlesnakes, and they had him surrounded.

"Well, *wicáhmunġa,* as you can see, my friends and I have been waiting for you," a woman said.

Startled, he swung his head toward the sound of her voice. He knew it had to be Sarah, but he couldn't see her. Recalling that the triangle had shown her sitting beneath a pine tree, he concentrated on the trunks. Finally, he spotted her, though she was nothing more than a faint silhouette against the darker outline of the tree.

Why hadn't he sensed her? he wondered in confusion, again trying to connect with her mind. When he failed, he was even more baffled. He also recognized that, under the circumstances, his inability to touch her mind was irrelevant. He had to find a way to protect himself from the snakes.

He glanced at the ground. He couldn't see the serpents, but they had stopped their rattling. That didn't ease his trepidation. The rattle was a warning. Did their silence mean they were preparing to strike?

"What's the matter, *wicáhmunġa?* Cat—or I guess I should say *snake*—got your tongue?"

Sebastian switched his attention to Sarah and frowned. She was baiting him, so he didn't bother responding to her taunt. Instead, he considered her claim that she and her *friends* had been waiting for him. She had to be referring to the snakes. But that implied she controlled them, and that was impossible. If he couldn't control them, there was no way a mortal could do so. But what else could explain what was happening?

Nothing, and as fantastic as it seemed, he had to conclude that she was capable of communicating with the repugnant reptiles.

Deciding to take the offensive, he said, "Hello, Sarah. My name is—"

"I don't need to know your name," she interrupted curtly as she stood. "I already know everything I need to know about you. You're a *wicáhmunga,* and you're here to fulfill the curse."

"Curse?" Sebastian repeated, bewildered by her unexpected charge.

"Yes, curse," she said, stepping into the moonlight.

Sebastian gaped at her. A rattlesnake curled around her right arm from wrist to shoulder, with its head nestled against her neck. As if sensing his scrutiny, the vile creature swiveled its head toward him and flicked its forked tongue.

Sebastian instinctively took a step back. When he did, the snakes on the ground resumed their rattling. He froze.

"Careful, *wicáhmunga,*" Sarah drawled. "Otherwise this battle will be over before it has a chance to begin."

Sebastian dragged his attention from the snake to Sarah's face and cursed inwardly. Since he couldn't read her mind, he needed to see her expression. But she was too far away and standing with her back to the moon, so her face was shadowed.

"Obviously, you've mistaken my intentions, Sarah. I'm not here because of any curse, and I'm certainly not here to do battle with you," he told her. "All I want is the triangle."

"What triangle?" she said, reaching up to stroke the snake's head. Sebastian barely managed to repress a shudder. How could she touch something so repulsive?

"You know what triangle," he said. "What you don't know is that you're in grave danger from it."

She continued to stroke the snake. "I really hate to point out the obvious, *wicáhmunga*, but you're the person in danger right now."

Unable to dispute her words, Sebastian balled his hands into fists, furious that he'd gotten himself into this mess. He had to get out of it, and the only way to do so was to cast a protective spell. Did he dare take the risk?

Yes! an inner voice cried. But he knew it was his pride talking, and his mission was too important to let his ego dictate his actions. Besides, he was sure he could persuade Sarah to cooperate with him.

"How did you get the triangle, Sarah?" he asked.

She stopped petting the snake. He still couldn't see her expression, but he could feel her tension. "What triangle?"

"Sarah, denying that you have it is ridiculous," he chided. "The moment I put on my triangle this morning, I connected with you. Obviously, your triangle also connected you with me, or you wouldn't have set up this ambush."

When she didn't respond, he went on, "It's apparent that you perceive me as a threat, but I'm not the threat. The triangle is, and it's more dangerous than you can even imagine. It's important—no, *critical*—that I get it. If you don't give it to me a lot of people, including yourself, could die."

"You dare talk to me about death?" she said in a low voice that quivered with rage. "You are standing in the very spot where your ancestor tortured and slaughtered my people. If you listen, you can still hear their screams. If you look hard, you can see their lost spirits wandering this ground, because he gouged out their eyes so they couldn't find their way to the spirit world."

She paused and drew in an angry breath. "I don't perceive you as a threat. I see you for what you are—the evil *wicáhmunga*, who has come to finish what Seamus Morpeth started. But my ancestors destroyed him with the snakes, and now I'm going to destroy you with them!"

Sebastian stared at her, stunned by her diatribe. Just the thought of a warlock performing such atrocities was inconceivable. It went against the very doctrines of his race.

But Seamus had been corrupted by the talisman, he reminded himself. And if he had needed proof of just how evil the object was, he now had it. He also had to convince Sarah that he wasn't her enemy. Considering her feelings toward Seamus, that wouldn't be easy, particularly when she knew how deadly the snakes were to him. Although he recognized that Seamus didn't deserve pity, he couldn't help feeling sympathy for the agony he would have suffered while dying from several rattlesnake bites.

"What Seamus did was unforgivable," he told Sarah. "But I am not like him, and I swear to you that I am not here to harm you or anyone else. Can we sit down and talk? Once you understand what's going on, you'll know that I'm telling you the truth."

"I'm not stupid," she said derisively. "You're trying to trick me into calling off the snakes, but I'll make you a deal. You give me your triangle, and I'll let you live."

Sebastian shook his head. "I can't do that, Sarah. You have no idea what you're dealing with, which is why we need to talk."

"So talk."

"It's a rather long and involved story," he hedged. He had to make her get rid of the snakes. Once they were gone, he could cast the protective spell. Then he'd figure out something to tell her that would make her give him the triangle. He couldn't tell her the truth. To do so, he would have to reveal the existence of his race, and even though she knew about Seamus, he knew instinctively that whatever *wicáhmunga* meant, it wasn't warlock. No, the truth was out of the question.

It was as if she read his mind, because she said, "I am not calling off the snakes. So I suggest that you either tell me your story or give me your triangle."

Sebastian wanted to rake a hand through his hair in frustration, but he refrained. He didn't want to startle the snakes. He also couldn't believe that a mortal had trapped him like this.

He studied her for a long moment before saying, "And what if I refuse to do either?"

"I'll walk away and leave you to the snakes."

"That would be murder, Sarah."

"No, *wicáhmunga*. That would be smart. So what's it going to be? The story or the triangle?"

"Neither. If you're going to murder me, then do it," he answered, deciding to call her bluff. At least he was fairly sure it was a bluff. He hadn't had much contact with mortals, but he'd had enough to realize that most women were not violent by nature. It took a lot to provoke them into killing, and even then most of them couldn't do it.

Since her face was still shadowed, he couldn't see her reaction to his demand. When she didn't respond right away, he knew he'd regained the upper hand.

A moment later, however, he gaped at her in shock as she stated, "Have it your way." Then she turned and disappeared into the forest.

Sebastian, realizing that he'd backed himself into a deadly corner, quickly murmured the incantation for the protective spell. But when he circled his hand and flicked his fingers nothing happened.

He stared at his hand in horrified disbelief. His magic wasn't working!

The moment Sarah was out of the *wicáhmunga's* sight, she collapsed against a nearby tree and closed her eyes. Her entire body trembled, and she couldn't remember ever feeling so frightened. She also couldn't believe that she'd captured him so easily. After a lifetime of training for this moment, it was almost a letdown.

"Why haven't you ordered the snakes to strike, Sarah?"

Her eyes flew open at Wanága's voice. She hadn't seen him since before dawn, when she'd had the visions about the *wicáhmunga* and the archeologist, John Butler. She was surprised that Wanága still appeared in his leather breach clout. She would have thought he'd be displaying his full battle regalia for this momentous occasion. She also couldn't believe that he had deserted her at a time like this.

"Where have you been?" she demanded, purposely ignoring his question. She knew she had to give the order to the snakes, but she kept hearing the *wicáhmunga* accusing her of murder. But this *wasn't* murder. It was the survival of her people. The justification didn't make her feel any better. "I could have used your help."

"You did fine without me," he said. "But why haven't you given the order to the snakes?"

"Have I ever told you that you're like a dog with a bone?" she snapped.

"Many times."

"Well, I'm telling you again," she said, pushing herself away from the tree.

When she did, her pet rattlesnake, Willow, flicked its tongue against the side of her neck. She automatically petted the reptile's head. Then she eased the snake off her arm.

As she watched the snake uncoil itself and slide to the ground, she shivered, feeling unexpectedly chilled. Though she knew many people had an almost pathological fear of snakes, she'd never felt a moment of alarm around them. She'd always known they were her friends and would protect her.

Only now, as they waited for her to give them an order to kill, did she recognize their menace.

She could feel Wanáǧa watching her, and she slowly raised her gaze to his face. She expected him to be regarding her in disappointment, but his expression was one of concern.

"You always talk to me like this when you're afraid, Sarah," he said. "But there is no reason for you to be afraid. You've trapped the *wicáhmunǧa*. So why haven't you told the snakes to strike?"

Sarah sagged back against the tree and rubbed her hands across her face, the word *murder* echoing in her head. Dropping her hands to her sides, she looked at him and said, "I know I have to do it, Wanáǧa, but . . ."

"But?" he prodded when she stopped speaking.

She shook her head in confusion and whispered, "It feels wrong." When he didn't respond, she sighed heavily and said, "I wish Leonard were here. He'd understand."

At the thought of Leonard Night Wolf, tears filled her eyes. He'd found her in these mountains when she was five years old and taken her into his home, making her a member of his family. He'd claimed he was only doing it because she was the new guardian and it was his duty to train her. But she knew he had loved her as much as she loved him. When he died two years ago, it had devastated her.

"What would Leonard understand that I cannot understand?" Wanáǧa asked.

"My reluctance," she answered, as she again pushed away from the tree and began to pace. "I know you've told me I must kill the *wicáhmunǧa,* but—"

"I have never said you must kill him," Wanáǧa interrupted. "I have only said that you must protect your people from the curse."

"But you've implied that his death is the only way to do that," she rebutted as she came to a stop and frowned at him.

He shook his head. "No. I showed you the way to achieve his death with the snakes. You are the guardian, and only you can decide if that is necessary."

"And just how am I supposed to make that determination? Toss a coin into the air?" she countered, angry that he would choose now, of all times, to change the rules on her. And regardless of his claim, he *had* implied that the *wicáhmunǧa's* death was her only option.

"If you feel that tossing a coin is the best way to make your decision," he stated.

"You're impossible!" she cried, resuming her pacing. "Damn! I wish I could read the *wicáhmunga's* mind. Then I could figure out why I feel this reluctance."

"But Sarah, one of the reasons you are the guardian is that you are capable of reading his mind. Why would you think you couldn't do so?"

She shot him a frustrated glare. He'd been with her for more than twenty years, but he hadn't picked up the subtle nuances of modern-day language and took everything she said literally. Most of the time it amused her, but this was not a humorous situation. It was a matter of life and death—a question of murder.

"I didn't mean I was incapable of reading his mind," she said. "I was just pointing out that I can't risk doing so. He's a *wicáhmunga*, remember? If he connects with my mind, he's capable of controlling my thoughts. I can't let that happen."

"Then, what are you going to do about him?"

"You're the spirit guide, so why don't you guide me and tell me what to do?"

"I cannot do that, Sarah. You are the guardian, and only you can make the decision."

"Then why are you even here?"

She wanted to scream when he said, "When it is time for you to know all, you will understand."

She stopped pacing, perched her hands on her hips and glared at him. "I'll tell you what I understand, Wanáǵa. I have captured the *wicáhmunga*, and now I don't know what to do with him. The only one who can give me advice is you, and all you do is talk in riddles. In the meantime, he's standing in a circle of snakes. Eventually he or the snakes are going to make a move, and when that happens, the decision will be out of my hands."

"Then I suggest you make a decision before that happens."

"That's easy for you to say. You aren't the one who has to take responsibility."

"Responsibility is not mine to take. I am not the guardian."

"No, you're a spirit guide who doesn't know how to guide!"

"You're angry with me."

"Gosh, what was your first clue?" she snapped.

"It was when—"

"Dammit, Wanága! Don't take everything I say so literally," she broke in impatiently. When he opened his mouth, she held up her hand. "Please don't say anything more. I need to think."

"No, Sarah. You need to feel," he replied.

"Feel?" she repeated dubiously.

He nodded. "You said that destroying the *wicáh-munga* felt wrong. Explore those feelings."

He vanished, and Sarah grumbled, "That's just like a spirit guide. Always disappearing in a crisis."

Even as she voiced the complaint, she knew Wanága was right. She was the guardian, and she had to make the decision about the *wicáhmunga*.

Reluctantly, she walked back through the trees until she could see him. He was still standing where she had left him, but he was actively searching the ground. She suspected that it wouldn't be long before he'd try to make a break for it. Maybe she should just let it happen. There was a chance he could escape the snakes.

But if he escaped and he was as evil as Seamus Morpeth, he'd be back. Next time he'd be prepared for her trap, and he might succeed in destroying her. However, there was a chance—albeit a remote one—that he wasn't evil. If he wasn't and he died from a snake bite, then she would be guilty of murder.

But you know he's evil. In the vision, you saw it when he put on the triangle.

That's what was nagging at her, she realized as she shifted her weight from one foot to the other. She had perceived the evil *after* he'd put on the triangle. She knew that everyone had a dark side to his personality. She also knew from personal experience that the triangle enhanced and fed on that darkness. For years, she'd fought against its insidious power. Only when she'd become immune to it had Leonard officially declared her the guardian and given her the triangle permanently.

Since the *wicáhmunġa* had just come into possession of his triangle, it was possible that he was engaging in that struggle between good and evil.

She heaved a forlorn sigh, torn by her dilemma. If the *wicáhmunġa* were caught in that struggle, she couldn't destroy him before he failed the test. Yet she couldn't let him go until she knew the outcome. That meant she'd have to keep him here until the problem was resolved. But how did one keep a *wicáhmunġa* captive against his will?

"I'll think of something," she mumbled as she walked toward him. "But whatever it is, I have to resolve this situation before John Butler arrives. It would be too dangerous to battle both of them at the same time."

Why isn't my magic working? Sebastian wondered in bewilderment as he again tried the spell to no avail. Is the triangle causing the problem?

But he knew it couldn't be the triangle. He'd

been wearing it since early morning. If it was going to interfere with his magic, it would have done so before now. He also knew he had to concentrate on the immediate problem—getting away from the snakes. And the safest way to do that was to locate them. Then he could gauge their proximity and plan an escape route.

He began to search the ground, and he cursed when a cloud chose that moment to drift across the moon. As the darkness deepened, his survival instincts started screaming at him to run. He quelled the impulse. He'd already made one foolish mistake by not casting a protective spell before starting up the mountain. He couldn't compound it by charging blindly into a pack of deadly rattlesnakes.

Instead, he glanced toward the sky to watch the cloud, while listening intently for movement on the ground. As long as the snakes were still, he wasn't in danger. It seemed to take forever before the cloud finally passed. When it did, he resumed his search.

He was so absorbed in the activity that he started when Sarah said, "Even if you escape, the snakes will come after you. Are you sure you can outrun them?"

He looked toward the trees, so relieved that she'd returned, he couldn't speak. He also decided that he'd cooperate with her. He'd tell her some story that would make her call off the snakes. Then he'd persuade her to give him her triangle and get the hell out of here.

Before he could speak, however, she said, "Take off your shoes and socks and throw them to me."

He blinked, sure he'd misunderstood her. "What?"

"I said, take off your shoes and socks and throw them to me."

"No," he said with an adamant shake of his head. At least with his boots on he had a chance of surviving.

"I'm not giving you a choice, *wicáhmunǧa*. I'm giving you an order."

"If you think I'm going to obey you, you're crazy."

She crossed her arms over her chest. It was then he realized she was no longer holding the snake. *Damn!* That meant there was another one of the bastards on the ground.

"A smart man would at least find out why I'm issuing the order before he decided to disobey it," she said.

He glared at her, deciding that if she was standing next to him, she wouldn't be so blithely questioning his intelligence. Compared to witches, who were tall, she was a small woman. The top of her head probably wouldn't reach his chin. He flexed his fingers, wishing he could get his hands on her. He'd throttle her for treating him so disdainfully. *Dammit!* He was a warlock and deserved to be treated with respect!

"I don't care why you're issuing the order," he rasped. "Only a fool would remove his shoes in a situation like this, and I am no fool."

"Believe me, *wicáhmunǧa,* I don't consider you a fool. You did, however, say that you wanted to sit down and talk. I've decided to listen to what you have to say. However, I do not intend to place myself in jeopardy while doing so. So, if you'll give me your shoes and socks, I'll tell the snakes to back off. Then we can go somewhere and talk."

He regarded her for a long moment, then said, "I

have no intention of harming you, Sarah. But if I did, I don't see how giving you my shoes will protect you."

"It won't. But if you want to get off this mountain, I'll have to tell the snakes to let you go. If you harm me, I can't do that, and there is no way you'll get past them barefoot."

"And why couldn't I just kill you and put my shoes on?" he shot back, growing more incensed with her. He'd come here in peace, and she was declaring war. Worse, she was winning the battle.

"I'm no fool, either," she said. "I'll hide your shoes before I call off the snakes."

Sebastian frowned in angry frustration. "And how do I know you're not asking me to take off my shoes to make sure the snakes kill me?"

She shrugged. "You'll just have to trust me."

Sebastian arched a brow in patent disbelief. Trust her? When surrounded by vipers? Not in a million years.

He opened his mouth to tell her that, but she said, "Considering the history my people share with Seamus Morpeth, I have every reason to believe you're as sadistic and deadly as he was. I also have you trapped, and to even think of giving up that advantage is crazy. Prove that I'm not crazy, *wicáhmunǧa*. Please. Give me your shoes and socks."

At her compelling plea, Sebastian felt torn. He'd be insane to do what she asked. Yet he couldn't fault her logic. After what Seamus had done, she had every reason to distrust him. But how could he possibly trust her?

He couldn't, but how else was he going to get out of this lethal trap?

"Well, *wicáhmunǧa*?" she said.

"I'm thinking," he replied, taking one last look at the ground. When he spied one of the snakes, he couldn't believe it. He quickly scanned for more and spotted a second one to the right. There wasn't much distance between them, but it was enough to run between them. If they struck, his boots were ankle high, and he was wearing heavy denims. At the speed he'd be moving, it was unlikely they'd hit a vulnerable spot.

Of course, he'd still be in danger from them, he reminded himself, and since his magic wasn't working, he couldn't cast a protective spell. To his chagrin, he also realized that Sarah had made a valid point. He didn't have any idea how fast a rattlesnake moved, so he didn't know if he could outrun them.

And since when has the most powerful warlock alive started running from a fight? an inner voice sneered. *Even without your magic, you're both physically and intellectually superior to mortals. Are you going to let a small woman best you?*

At the gibe, Sebastian's temper flared and he again balled his fists at his sides. The voice was right. He *was* the most powerful warlock alive, and it was time he showed her that.

Don't be a fool! another voice rebutted. *You're here so you can stop the talisman's pieces from coming back together. Run! Once you figure out what's wrong with your magic and fix it, you can cast a protective spell and come back. You can't risk your life—not to mention the entire human race—just to prove you're superior.*

It's better to die a hero than a coward, and only cowards run, the first voice countered.

"I'm losing patience, *wicáhmunga,*" Sarah said, interrupting the argument taking place inside him. "What's it going to be? Your shoes or the snakes?"

He cast another quick look at the ground, confirming that the snakes were still at the same spot. Then he raised his gaze to Sarah and calculated the distance between them, deciding that both voices were right. Giving her his shoes could be suicidal, but running was only advantageous if he knew for sure he could outdistance the snakes.

Since he didn't know that for sure, he had only one smart option. Run to Sarah and physically overwhelm her. Then he could threaten her with bodily harm if she didn't call off the snakes. There was no way she could know he wouldn't carry out the threat. Then, once the snakes were gone, he'd sit her down and talk to her.

"Well, Sarah," he said, as he tensed his muscles in preparation for flight, "I think . . ."

He didn't finish the statement, but sprinted toward her. When something brushed against his pants leg, he shuddered, but didn't look down to see what it was. Instead, he focused his attention on Sarah, telling himself not to slow down—or look down—until he'd reached her.

When he got to her, he was going too fast to stop, so he grabbed her arms and propelled her toward the tree behind her. By the time her back came up against its trunk, he was able to stop. He immediately released her arms and reached for her throat, knowing that action would frighten her the most.

As his hands curled around her neck, however, he felt something cold and rough fall against the back of his neck. He reached up to knock it away, but it wrapped around his throat, and a snake's face popped up in front of his. He gasped in horror as the viper opened its mouth wide and bared its fangs, its rattle vibrating next to his ear.

He couldn't believe it when Sarah said, "Well, *wicáhmunġa,* are you a betting man? If so, I accept your chokehold and raise you one prairie rattlesnake."

3

Evil Revealed

Sarah decided that if brains were ants, she wouldn't have enough to pick up a bread crumb. The *wicáhmunga* had his hands around her throat, and though he wasn't choking her yet, she could feel the strength in his fingers. He would probably break her neck before she could order Willow to strike. Why had she taunted him with that crack about being a betting man?

Because she was always flip when she was afraid, and when he'd unexpectedly charged her, she'd been terrified. Thankfully, Willow had come to her rescue. But rattlers couldn't climb trees. How had she gotten up there? *Wanáǧa*.

"You can relax, *wicáhmunga*," she told him, projecting a bravado she didn't feel. But maybe if she acted as if she were in control, he'd think she was. "Your life isn't in immediate danger, so why don't you let me go? I suggest you do it slowly, however. Willow doesn't like to be jolted, and I'm sure she's upset enough about falling out of a tree. I'd also recommend that you don't speak. She isn't fond of men's voices, either."

She felt his fingers flex around her neck, and she was sure he was going to kill her. But he released her, and she quickly scrambled away from the tree.

When she put some distance between them, she took a good look at him. Willow's face was only inches from his, and his expression was a combination of fear and revulsion.

But it wasn't fear Sarah sensed emanating from him. It was fury. Bewildered, she took another step back. She could understand his anger. He was a *wicáhmunǧa*, and not only had she trapped him, he'd failed to escape. But with Willow around his neck, fear should have been his overriding emotion. So from where was all that anger coming?

Instinctively, she lowered her gaze to the triangle hanging around his neck. The object was glowing red, and she gulped. She knew from her own experiences that it only became that color when it was feeding on intense rage, forcing the evil inside a person to surface. But was it true evil it had found inside the *wicáhmunǧa*, or was the triangle trying to poison his soul?

There was only one way to find out. Remove Willow from around his neck and see what he did. But first, she had to make sure he was in a place where he couldn't escape. To her distress, there was only one place close by that fit the bill. She had to take him to her special cave.

Dispiritedly, she said, "Follow me, *wicáhmunǧa*. We won't be going far. And don't try to run away. Even if you manage to get rid of Willow, the other snakes are still around."

Turning into the trees, she didn't bother to see if he followed. She was too busy fretting over taking him to her cave. It had been her sanctuary since childhood, and no one, not even Wanáǧa or Leonard, had ever entered it. It was the one place where she could escape the demands of being the guardian and pretend she was a normal person.

But now the *wicáhmunǧa* would enter it, and the echoes of his presence would remain within its walls forever. The cave would no longer be a sanctuary, but a reminder that she could never lead a normal life.

When she arrived at the cave's mouth, she stopped and glanced back. The *wicáhmunǧa* was a short distance behind her and walking so cautiously he looked as if he were moving in slow motion. Evidently, he'd taken her warning about jolting Willow to heart.

"Just come into the cave," she told him, ducking into the dark interior before she could change her mind.

She paused inside to fish an old cigarette lighter out of her pants pocket. When she pulled it out, she rubbed her thumb over its worn surface. The lighter had belonged to Leonard. Normally, just touching it made her feel close to him. Tonight, however, it reminded her of her aloneness.

When she felt the sting of tears, she impatiently blinked them back and flicked on the lighter. Now was *not* the time to indulge in a bout of self-pity. She was the guardian, and she had a job to do.

Cupping her hand around the flame, she walked purposefully toward the firewood she'd laid earlier in the day. When she reached it, she dropped to her knees and lit the kindling, which was so dry it immediately caught fire.

Sitting back on her heels, she watched the small flames spread to the brittle bark of the logs. As larger flames flared, she heard the *wicáhmunǧa* enter behind her. She pivoted on her knees to look at him.

As her gaze landed on him, she gasped. She'd known he was big, but standing inside her small cave, he looked like a giant. Indeed, his shoulders were so broad they blocked the opening. Even Willow, who was more than four feet long, was dwarfed by his size.

Cautiously, Sarah raised her gaze to his face. There was no longer fear in his expression. It reflected unadulterated fury, and the glitter in his dark eyes was so malevolent that she trembled in fright.

But the wave of terror that washed over her wasn't due to his expression or his eyes. It was caused by the vision forming in her mind. She and the *wicáhmunǧa* were making love!

She gave a frantic shake of her head, refusing to believe the vision. But the harder she tried to deny it, the more distinct it became.

Their naked bodies were entwined, and she cried out as he flexed his hips and entered her urgently, ruthlessly. But her cry wasn't due to physical pain. It was caused by a raging storm inside her—a spiritual agony that she knew would destroy her. But no matter how hard she fought against the storm, it continued to rage until—

No! she screamed inwardly, cutting off the image. It isn't true. I would never make love with the *wicáhmunǧa*. To defeat him I have to remain pure!

Although she didn't want to accept what she'd seen, she knew that all her visions came true. And there was only one way to stop this one from happening. If she didn't, the *wicáhmunga* would win the battle and her people would be lost.

Closing her eyes tightly, she mentally ordered Willow to strike.

Strike! As the word reverberated in Sebastian's mind, he reacted on instinct. Just as the snake opened its mouth and extended its fangs, he reached up and grabbed it behind the head.

It struggled violently as it tried to get at him, and he shuddered as he jerked it from around his neck. Its scaly body felt like sandpaper scraping against his skin, and its coldness was a grisly reminder of how close he was to death.

Holding the viper at arm's length, he glared at it. It flailed against his hold with such force that, even over its deafening rattle, it sounded like a whip slashing through the air.

When its tail whisked against his abdomen, he grabbed it and grinned in grim satisfaction. With a little fancy footwork, he should be able to swing the snake and smash its head against the wall. Then the bastard wouldn't be a threat to him or anyone else.

No! Don't hurt her!

Shocked, he jerked his head toward Sarah. She was mentally communicating with him, and he hadn't initiated the connection. In fact, every time he'd tried to touch her mind, he'd failed. What in hell was going on?

Before he could consider the question, she surged to her feet and held out her hand in a supplicating gesture. "Please! Willow was just obeying my command. If you'll give her to me, I swear she won't harm you."

Sebastian glanced back at the snake. It had stopped struggling, but its mouth was still open and its fangs bared. He returned his attention to Sarah and regarded her through narrowed eyes. Her acute anxiety was palpable. Obviously, the snake was important to her. But was it important enough for her to give him the triangle? There was only one way to find out.

"I'll make you a deal," he said. "You give me the triangle and guarantee me safe passage to my car, and I won't kill your snake."

She looked at the snake and her lower lip quivered, but when she returned her gaze to him, she said, "What triangle?"

"Why are you being so damn stubborn?" he yelled as his temper snapped. "I know you have the triangle. Why else would you have demanded that I give you mine?"

When she mutely stared at him, he tried to touch her mind. He couldn't get a glimmer of her thoughts, and that baffled him. She'd connected with him, so why couldn't he connect with her? Her triangle must be imbuing her with a certain amount of power, he concluded. But if that were the case, why were his powers malfunctioning?

He didn't have the answer, so he ordered, "Give me the triangle and safe passage, Sarah, or I swear I'll beat this snake against the wall so hard that you'll be picking up pieces for a month."

Again, her lower lip quivered, but she lifted her chin a defiant notch and repeated, "What triangle?"

Sebastian's entire body trembled in fury. He knew that mortals could be arbitrarily stubborn, but why would she continue to deny the existence of the triangle when it was obvious that she had it?

Her behavior was so ridiculous it went beyond the absurd.

He also didn't have time for this. He needed her triangle so he could find the talisman's circle before someone else found it. And he was sure that no one had found it yet. If they had, he would have connected with them, just as he'd connected with Sarah.

"You're wrong, *wicáhmunga*," Sarah said. "Someone has found the circle. His name is John Butler, and . . ."

She closed her eyes and tilted her head, as though listening to someone talking. A moment later, she opened her eyes and went on, "He's trying to get here, but he killed a man and the police are after him, so he can't just get on a plane like you did. But he's working on a plan, and I suspect he'll be here in twenty-four to forty-eight hours."

Realizing his mouth was hanging open, Sebastian closed it. He wasn't sure what he found more astounding. The proof that she was reading his mind, or her claim that someone already had the circle. The latter was more important, but, if it were true that this Butler had the triangle, why hadn't Sebastian connected with him?

Because his magic wasn't working, and he couldn't fix it until he was out of danger.

He returned his attention to the snake. It had finally closed its mouth, but as he stared into its cold, unblinking eyes, he knew it was just waiting for an opportunity to strike. He needed to settle this problem, and then he could move on to the Butler issue, assuming Sarah was telling him the truth about the man.

"Oh, I'm telling you the truth," she said, confirming that she was still reading his mind. "I'm also willing to declare a truce. If you'll turn Willow loose, I'll tell you everything I know about John Butler and his circle."

He frowned at her. "I'll turn the snake loose on two conditions. One, that you guarantee you'll order every snake on this mountain to leave me alone, including this one. Secondly, that you give me your triangle."

"I can easily grant your first request," she replied. "I can't, however, give you what I don't have, and I don't have any triangle. If you don't believe me, search me."

Until now, Sebastian had been too worried about survival to take a good look at her. Of course, he'd known what she looked like. Whenever he'd touched the triangle, he'd seen her, but it was as if the object had revealed her in a one-dimensional image.

As his gaze swept over her, he noted that she was definitely three dimensional. Her long black hair was plaited into a single braid that hung over her left shoulder and dropped below her waist. Her face was a perfect oval, and beneath delicately arched brows, her large, eerily golden eyes were slanted like a cat's. Her nose was small and straight, and her cheekbones high and prominent. As he stared at her exotic face, he felt an unexpected tug of desire.

Startled by his physical reaction to her, he lowered his gaze. She wore a fitted, long-sleeved leather shirt that laced up the front and clung to her full breasts. Fringe hung from its sleeves, and the shirt nipped in at her waist, which was so small Sebastian was sure his hands could completely encircle it. Denims, worn almost white, molded to her slender hips and legs.

An image of those shapely legs wrapped around his hips flitted through his mind and he snapped his head up, irritated. What the hell was wrong with him? Now was *not* the time to indulge in sexual fantasies. For pity's sake, he was holding a rattlesnake that was determined to kill him!

As he stared at Sarah, he noted her heightened color and downcast eyes. Realizing she'd been reading his mind during his inspection of her, he muttered a curse. It was bad enough she'd been one step ahead of him from the time he arrived. For her to know that he'd felt a momentary flash of desire for her was intolerable. It also made him mad as hell.

He told himself to ignore the matter. After all, if he'd been able to read her mind, he might have picked up on some personal thought or emotion that would have been equally untenable for her.

But his common sense seemed to have gone on vacation, because he heard himself say, "Strip."

Her head shot up and her strange, golden eyes were as brilliant as two suns as she gasped, "What?"

"I said strip," he repeated, lifting the snake slightly. "As you can see, my hands are full, so I can't search you."

"I'm not going to take off my clothes!"

He flashed her a vindictive smile as he drawled, "As you so aptly put it when we were arguing over my shoes, I'm not giving you a choice. I'm giving you an order. So, what's it going to be, Sarah? A striptease or a dead snake?"

"I swear that I don't have the triangle, and making me take off my clothes to prove it is . . . inappropriate," Sarah argued frantically. After the vision she'd seen of them making love, she wouldn't take off so much as her moccasins around him.

"*Inappropriate?*" he repeated derisively. "I suppose it was *appropriate* for you to order me to take off my shoes while surrounded by rattlesnakes."

She shifted uncomfortably from one foot to the other. "That may have been a little extreme, but I was trying to protect myself."

"From what?" he challenged. "You can read my mind, so you knew I wasn't a personal threat to you. That means you purposely set out to make a fool of me."

Sarah opened her mouth, but closed it when she realized she didn't know how to respond. If she denied reading his mind earlier, he wouldn't believe her. Even if he did, it wasn't going to make a difference. She'd wounded his pride.

She cast a quick glance at his triangle and gulped. It was blood red and glowing so brightly it was practically pulsing. With the combination of his anger and bruised ego, it was having a veritable feast. Did he realize what the triangle was doing to him? she wondered, raising her gaze back to his face.

His vengeful expression assured her he wanted retaliation, but his mind didn't reveal if it was a conscious or unconscious act. *Damn!* How could she deal with him if she couldn't determine if he was being willingly controlled by the triangle?

"What's the matter, Sarah," he drawled, breaking into her agitated musing. "Cat, or should I say *snake*, got your tongue?"

At his taunt, she switched her attention to Willow, and her heart skipped a beat. He was squeezing her pet so tightly that if she didn't do something fast, he wouldn't have to beat Willow against the wall. He'd strangle her.

Why did I let him know I could read his mind? she railed at herself.

Because, between the vision of her making love with him and her fear for Willow's safety, her mental barriers had dropped and her mind had automatically connected with his. How could she have been so stupid as to let her emotions get out of hand?

"Stop ignoring me!" he suddenly yelled.

Sarah jumped, startled by his unexpected outburst. Clearly, the triangle was pushing him to the edge. For Willow's sake, she had to make him calm down before he went over it.

"I'm not ignoring you. I'm trying to figure out a compromise that we'll both find satisfactory," she said, cursing the slight quaver in her voice.

His gaze slid down her body in blatant, lascivious perusal. When he returned it to her face, he drawled, "It takes a lot to satisfy me, but I'm willing to let you give it a try. So, strip, Sarah, and let me see your ammunition."

Sarah felt her cheeks flame. "I am *not* going to undress for you!"

"I thought you said you wanted us both satisfied. I can't possibly do my part if you're dressed."

As she picked up the sensual images flooding his mind, her cheeks grew hotter. The things he was imagining doing to her body were worse than the vision she'd had!

Don't you mean better than the vision?

Ignoring her traitorous conscience, she angrily declared, "Stop it!"

The *wicáhmunga* widened his eyes in a parody of innocence that made him look positively demonic. "Stop what?"

She glared at him. "You know what. You're playing mind games with me."

"As soon as you strip, I'll gladly make them physical," he replied in a suggestive voice that sent shivers down her spine. To her irritation, her reaction was not due to fear but to a strange heat stirring deep inside her.

Confused by the feeling, she again glanced at his triangle. It had taken on a deep purple sheen, and she suddenly understood that the object had taken a new tack. It hadn't been able to push him over the edge with anger, so it had resorted to using his libido. She gulped again. She knew how to fight anger, but her experience with sex was limited to one chaste kiss.

"I realize you're angry with me," she said, raising her gaze back to his face. "And I can understand your feelings. But you aren't looking beyond the immediate situation. It's true that I don't want you to harm Willow, but if you do, what will you gain? Certainly not my cooperation, and I'll summon the rest of the snakes. You might be able to kill a few of them, but you won't be able to kill them all. Then who's going to handle this urgent mission you're on?"

Lucien. The name flashed through his mind, and Sarah blinked in surprise when it was immediately followed by the image of two babies, who couldn't be more than a few months old. Even more startling were the strong feelings of remorse that erupted inside him at the image.

Why was he feeling remorse about the children?

Had he harmed them in some way? The thought was too disturbing to even consider, so she looked at the triangle. It was fading back to silver, and she knew that this might be her only chance to regain control of the situation.

She looked back up at him and said, "You said you aren't like Seamus Morpeth, so prove it. Give me Willow, and I'll declare a truce."

As Sarah spoke, Sebastian glared at her, unable—or, rather, unwilling—to believe that she'd wrested control from him again. But as much as he abhorred admitting it, her argument was sound. Other than the satisfaction he'd derive from killing the snake, he wouldn't gain anything.

He glanced down at the reptile. It was now as passive as a rope, which was why he'd all but forgotten he was holding it. He knew, however, that the moment he released the rattler it could—and probably would—turn on him. To let it live would be insane, but if he died, Lucien would have to take over his mission until the council of high priests found another troubleshooter. Sebastian knew he couldn't place that burden on his cousin. Lucien was a powerful warlock, but he didn't have the powers that the troubleshooter possessed. He was also a new father—he and his mortal wife, Ariel, had four-month-old twins. If Lucien took over this job, there was a good chance he'd be killed. Sebastian couldn't risk that. Lucien and his children were too important to the coven's survival.

"Please, *wicáhmunga*," Sarah said, breaking into his thoughts. When he looked at her, she took a step toward him and extended her hand. "Trust me."

He cast a quick glance at the snake, which was

still passive. Returning his attention to Sarah, he made one last effort to connect with her mind. When nothing happened, he cursed. It went against his very nature, but he knew his only chance at survival was to trust her.

"Take the vile beast," he said before he could change his mind.

She quickly reached for the snake. When she took it from him, the serpent immediately bared its fangs at him and began to rattle. As Sarah lifted its head to her face, she murmured something low and unintelligible. The snake swiveled its head toward her and flicked its tongue against her cheek.

Sebastian grimaced in revulsion, then scowled when Sarah gave him a tentative smile and said, "Thank you."

He wasn't feeling gracious, so instead of telling her she was welcome, he stuffed his hands into his pockets and asked, "When are you going to call off the rest of the snakes?"

"I've already done so," she replied as she bent to set the rattler on the floor. It slithered toward the shadows at the back of the cave. "You're safe for now, *wicáhmuṅga*."

"My name is Sebastian, so stop calling me *wicáhmuṅga*," he snapped, not sure he believed her about the snakes but not about to admit it. "And what the hell is a *wicáhmuṅga* anyway?"

"A literal translation is magician," she said as she stood upright.

"And a nonliteral translation?"

She regarded him for a long moment, and Sebastian found himself mesmerized by her eyes. There were only two eye colors within his race—a silvery blue from birth until the age of sixteen, and brown thereafter. He knew there were more color variations within mortals, but he also knew that Sarah's strange golden hue would be considered an oddity even for them.

She gave him a wry look and shook her head. "Only a *wasičun* would ask for a nonliteral translation."

"*Wasičun?*"

"Literally, it means white man, but it applies to all non-Indians."

"And you don't like *wasičuns?*"

"I think it would be more fair to say they don't like us. But you aren't here to have a philosophical discussion about the trials and tribulations of my people," she said, gesturing toward the fire. "Let's sit down and talk about why you are here."

Sebastian knew he should do as she asked, but he still smarted over the fact that she'd bested him. So instead of sitting down at the fire, he glanced around the cave.

It wasn't that large. Maybe twenty-five or thirty feet deep and about twenty feet wide. He glanced toward the ceiling and noted it was only a few inches higher than his own six feet, five inches. He turned his attention to the items stored within the cave. There was a rolled sleeping bag, some cast-iron pots and pans, and a few dishes. There was also a wooden trunk, and he suspected it stored clothing.

"You live here?" he asked, glancing back at Sarah.

"Do I look like a cave dweller?" she replied dryly.

Sebastian automatically flicked his gaze over her, and he experienced another surge of desire. Irritated, he returned his gaze to her face. When her beautiful features came into focus, he forgot to breathe.

Ever since he'd donned the triangle, he'd been trying to connect with Sarah's mind and failed. But now, as he stared at her, his mind meshed with hers without any effort on his part.

But it wasn't her thoughts he latched onto. It was a vision so powerful that he had to lock his knees to keep from falling.

They were making love, and the sensations were so intense—so *real*—that his entire body was instantly aroused. They lay naked on the sleeping bag in front of the fire. He could feel the softness of her smooth skin against his hair-roughened flesh. Her full, pliable breasts were crushed against his chest; her pebbled nipples exciting him to even greater heights of desire.

Suddenly, she wrapped her legs around his hips and arched toward him, and he entered her urgently, roughly. He groaned. Being inside her was like nothing he'd ever felt before. She was so tight. So hot. So wet. Then he moved inside her, and she responded with such passion that he had to fight to maintain control. But he almost lost it when she mentally wailed. *Sebastian! Please!*

He wanted to prolong their lovemaking, but he couldn't ignore her plea. He began to thrust into her rapidly, latching onto the storm of her desire—letting it sweep him away until—

The vision ended so abruptly that Sebastian felt as if he'd fallen into a bottomless abyss. His entire body was taut and trembling, and his groin was heavy with the ache of unfulfilled desire.

He closed his eyes and tried to regain control. But the lovemaking images began to repeat in his mind with such clarity that he knew Sarah was replaying them in her mind. He also knew instinctively that she would again end them a moment before climax.

Isn't it interesting that this is the first time you've been able to read her mind, and she's tormenting you with visions of unfulfilled sex, an inner voice murmured. *She knows you're stronger and smarter than her, so she's using seduction to manipulate you. And once she has you weak and begging for completion, she will destroy you.*

As Sebastian's eyes flew open, he noted that Sarah's eyes were closed tightly. Her face had a sensual flush, and as he lowered his gaze to her heaving breasts, his temper exploded. If she thought she could destroy him with fantasies of sex, she was in for one hell of a surprise!

Prove that to her. Show her that when she incites a warlock's passion, she can't deny him fulfillment. Make her the one to beg, and then give her what she wants.

At the voice's prodding, Sebastian crossed the short distance between him and Sarah and dragged her into his arms. As he crushed her against him and lowered his lips to hers, another voice cried, *You can't do this. Stop and think. There's something wrong with this picture!*

He shut out the voice. He didn't want to think.

He wanted to feel, and he listened to his body, which was demanding he assuage the lust that had him so hot he was sure he was about to burst into flame.

4

Evil Tempted

✛

Desire. Sarah had always thought it would be a sweet, tender yearning. But as her mind again filled with the vision of her and the *wicáhmunga* making love, she realized there was nothing sweet or tender about it. It was a hot, consuming need that centered low in her abdomen and raged throughout her body with the violence of a thunderstorm.

Instinctively, she knew that succumbing to passion would destroy her, and she fought frantically against the vision. Thankfully, she stopped the images before the moment of climax. To her horror, however, that didn't end her torment. The vision merely began to repeat itself in her mind, causing her desire to escalate.

She knew she wasn't strong enough to stop the vision a second time, and she mentally beseeched, *Wanáǧa! Help me!*

If he heard her, he ignored her, and she closed her eyes tightly and renewed her frantic struggle against the vision. If she refused to let it reach its natural conclusion, then maybe she could keep it from coming true.

And I have to keep it from coming true. I have to. I have to. I have to! she chanted urgently.

When she felt the *wicáhmunga* pull her into his

arms, she thought it was a part of the vision. Then
he lowered his lips to hers. She didn't have to open
her eyes to know that this was real. His kiss was
ruthless, bruising, but it didn't cool her ardor. It
made it flare higher, hotter, until she felt as if she
was aflame.

Bite him! Claw him! Kick him! her self-preservation
instincts screamed. *You have to escape him!*

But he chose that moment to crush her body
against his. When the hard length of his arousal
pressed against her abdomen, she gasped. He took
advantage of her parted lips to slide his tongue into
her mouth.

As he plundered her with his tongue, she told
herself she had to fight him. She raised her hands to
push him away, but she felt her body mold to his
and her arms rise to wrap around his neck. When
he rocked his hips against her, the sensual friction
made her entire body tremble.

Wanáǵa! Please! Help me! she again pleaded.

There was still no answer. As the *wicáhmunǵa*
continued to ravage her with his kiss she moaned,
but she didn't know if it was from fear or from the
ravenous need growing inside her.

*Open your mind to me, Sarah. Let me feel what
you're feeling,* the *wicáhmunǵa* encouraged. *Let me
show you what you're doing to me.*

No! she responded desperately, closing her eyes
tighter. She knew if she gave in to the temptation of
what he asked she'd be lost forever.

She'd been reading minds for as long as she could
remember, but she couldn't recall ever hearing mental laughter. But that was the response she received
from the *wicáhmunǵa's* mind at her denial. However, it wasn't a mirthful resonance. It was a low,

scornful sound, immediately followed by the onslaught of intense, sexual emotions that rocked her to the core.

She shivered in alarm. What was happening to her? Where were these emotions coming from?

The wicáhmunġa. He was making her feel what he felt—projecting his own desire into her mind!

She again told herself to fight him, but his passion swamped her, irresistibly drawing her into his unrestrained lust. The heavy need in his groin made her womb contract with wanton need. When he swept his hand down to cup her buttock and pull her even more intimately against him, the searing wave of desire that swept through him made her knees buckle. If she hadn't had her arms around his neck, she would have fallen. Instead, she sank slowly, bonelessly, to the floor.

He sank with her, his mouth never leaving hers. When they were kneeling, he grasped one of her arms and pulled it from around his neck. Then he lowered her hand to the front of his trousers.

She started at the shock of touching him so intimately and ordered herself to jerk her hand away. But she couldn't stop herself from exploring him. He was so big. So hard. And the shuddering wave of passion that raced through him at her touch filled her with a beguiling sense of power.

Ah, Sarah, power is such an illusion. Just when you think you have it, it's stripped away from you, the *wicáhmunġa* taunted.

Before she could assimilate his pronouncement, he slipped his hand between her thighs. As he began to stroke her, he moved his tongue in and out of her mouth in a parody of lovemaking.

Her body quivered—her heart racing and her

pulse pounding at this new sensual torture. She couldn't think. She couldn't breathe. All she could do was feel, and the sensation was exquisite pleasure.

Open your eyes, Sarah, Wanága suddenly ordered.

No! she answered, knowing that if she obeyed him the magic would stop. And that's what this was. Magic so wonderful that she wanted the *wicáhmunga* to keep kissing her, touching her, forever.

Sarah, open your eyes. Now!

She mentally shook her head, but she slowly opened her eyes. She was so engulfed in the haze of passion that it took a moment for her mind to register what she saw. When it did, she blinked in shock. She could still feel the *wicáhmunga's* lips on hers, his tongue plundering her mouth. She could still feel his hand between her thighs, touching her, stroking her into mindless passion. But he wasn't kneeling in front of her. She was staring at his knees!

A shiver of horror crawled down her spine, dispelling all remnants of desire. When he'd first pulled her into his arms, she knew it had been real. His kiss had been too rough to be anything else. So when had reality turned to fantasy?

Obviously, when she'd sunk to her knees, and she cursed herself for falling for his lies. He'd made her believe that his magic wasn't working, and when she'd let her defenses down, he'd taken control of her mind. He'd made her think he was making love to her, but outside of that initial kiss, he hadn't even touched her.

She felt the heat of humiliation stain her cheeks. She'd been right about him all along. He was as evil as Seamus Morpeth, and he'd use whatever means

of torture necessary—even sexual torture—to get
what he wanted from her.

Warily, she leaned her head back to look at him.
He towered over her, his hands braced on his hips.
The triangle was again glowing red, but it was his
eyes that made her shudder. They were alight with
a strange, pulsing glow, and she knew it wasn't a reflection of the fire. The light came from somewhere
inside him, and it was so brilliant it was almost
blinding.

Suddenly, he murmured some unintelligible
words and circled his hand. She let out a yelp and
scrambled backward as small flashes of lightning
flared from his fingertips, encircled him, and then
disappeared.

If she'd had any doubts that he was a *wicáhmunga*, they were alleviated by that show of magic.
Seamus Morpeth had also had the touch of lightning, and he'd used it mercilessly during his brutal
slaughter of her people. She had to escape before
the *wicáhmunga* used his lightning touch on her!

Unfortunately, she was still on her knees, and he
stood between her and the cave's opening. By the
time she got to her feet, he'd be prepared to stop
her flight. She considered summoning the snakes,
but she knew intuitively that he was now immune
to them.

Damn! This was Wanága's fault. If he hadn't suddenly changed the rules on her, she would have destroyed the *wicáhmunga* when she had the chance.
Now there was only one final option left to her. No
one knew where the triangle was but her, and if he
couldn't get the location from her mind, he'd never
find it.

She leaped to her feet and took a couple of running steps forward. As she'd expected, he immediately moved to block the opening. When he did, she spun around and ran toward the back of the cave, mentally ordering, *Willow. Come!*

The snake slithered out of the shadows, and the moment Sarah reached her, she bent and snatched her pet up with her hands.

Bringing Willow's head toward her, Sarah raised her chin, exposing the pulse point at her neck to her pet. Then she commanded, *Strike me!*

When Sarah raced toward the back of the cave and grabbed her snake, Sebastian smiled smugly. Mortals were so damn predictable. He'd known she'd rely on the rattler for protection. What she didn't know was that the reptile was no longer a threat to him. As inexplicably as it had disappeared his magic had returned, and he'd already cast a protective spell over himself.

You also won another major victory, that inner voice chimed in. *You turned her seduction against her and taught her the consequences of playing sex games with a warlock.*

Sebastian frowned, uncomfortable with that observation. It wasn't that he'd turned the tables on her that bothered him. It was that he'd carried the act too far. It was as if some primitive part of him had taken over, and the need to debase her had overridden all other thoughts. Such a deed was not only wrong, it went against his nature. So why had he done it?

He was so busy contemplating the issue that when Sarah mentally ordered the snake to strike, it took him a moment to realize her intent. When it

registered that she planned to kill herself, he gaped
at her, stunned.

But as he watched the rattler's mouth open and
its head bob toward Sarah's neck, he was jarred into
action. She was too far away, so there was no way he
could reach her before the snake struck. He also
didn't have time to cast a protective spell over
Sarah, but, hopefully, he could stop the snake from
biting her.

Murmuring a quick incantation, he flicked his
fingers toward the viper. Spell lightning shot across
the room and enveloped the snake just as its fangs
began to sink into Sarah's flesh. The viper went
limp, its head dropping to loll against the back of
Sarah's hand.

Sebastian caught his breath, not sure if the spell
had taken effect in time. If it hadn't, he didn't know
what he'd do. He suspected that Sarah didn't have
any antivenom, and even if she did, he doubted it
would work. She'd directed the blasted beast to an
artery. If any poison had gotten into her blood-
stream, it had already pumped through her body. A
full dose would have killed her immediately. How
long would it take a small dose to take effect?

He let out his breath in a relieved rush when
Sarah suddenly spun toward him, her golden eyes
flashing with fury as she accused, "You killed Willow!"

Her anger reassured him the snake hadn't bitten
her. If it had, she wouldn't have the energy to be
railing at him.

"I didn't kill your damn snake. I stunned it," he
said, not bothering to explain that the only reason
he hadn't killed it was that type of spell would have
taken longer. Hooking his thumbs in the waistband

of his jeans, he scowled at her. "But if you make another stupid suicide attempt, I will kill the damn beast. Just what in hell were you trying to prove?"

Ignoring him, she looked down at the limp rattler. Then she knelt and gently laid it on the floor. After stroking her hand along its length, she looked up at him, her expression one of hatred as she said, "I don't know if you're telling me the truth about Willow, but I do know I should have destroyed you when I had the chance. But you haven't won yet, *wicáhmunga*. You can't get anything from a dead person, and I'll find a way to kill myself before I ever give it to you."

At her words, Sebastian rocked back on his heels and drummed the fingers of his right hand against his hip. He didn't have to ask what "it" was. He was also baffled by her determination. Why would she be willing to sacrifice her life for the triangle? It didn't make sense.

He tried to brush against her mind to discover her reasoning. When he found himself again unable to connect with her, he became more baffled. His magic was back, so he should be able to link with her at will. Granted, she had strong psychic abilities, but even psychics were unable to barricade their mind against a member of his race. If she wore the triangle it might be able to imbue her with that much power, but he knew she didn't have the object on her person. So why couldn't he connect with her?

He didn't have the answer, and he decided that his best offense was to keep her talking until he could figure out what was going on.

"Well, at least we're making some progress," he

said. "You're finally admitting that you have the triangle."

She didn't respond, but climbed to her feet. After stepping over the snake, she stood in front of it like a sentry—her legs braced apart and her arms crossed over her chest.

As she stared at him in belligerent silence, he heaved an irritated sigh and said, "Sarah, I can understand why you're frightened of me. But as I said before, I am not here to harm you or anyone else, so you don't need to even consider taking your own life."

"I'm sure you'll understand if I don't lend much credence to your claim," she said. "Even a fool would realize that it's to your advantage for me to stay alive until you can get what you want."

At her words, his temper flared. He wanted to go to her and shake her for being so damn stubborn, but he knew that would only make matters worse. So instead of acting on the impulse, he opened his mouth to argue with her. He stopped, however, when she lowered her gaze to stare intently at his chest.

Automatically, he glanced down to see what had caught her attention and frowned. The triangle had a rosy hue that began to fade the moment he looked at it.

As it returned to normal, he told himself it was just a reflection of the fire. But he hadn't moved, so if it was a reflection, the color shouldn't have faded.

He shrugged uneasily, recalling that the triangle had been emitting a strange, white-hot light in the repository. When he'd stared at it he'd lost track of time.

This isn't the same. Not only was the color differ-

ent, but I didn't lose any time. It was probably just a reflection of the fire, and a breeze made the flames shift, which made the color disappear.

The pep talk didn't alleviate his apprehension. He hadn't felt any breeze, and with the fire in the center of the cave, it would have taken a strong gust to stir the flames. Also, he didn't know the magical properties of the triangle, and since it was a part of the talisman, it had to have some mystical function. To ignore any aberrant behavior would be foolish, but if he didn't know what it meant, how could he counteract it?

He couldn't, but instinct told him that the triangle was a threat. The longer he wore it, the more vulnerable he would become. He needed to get Sarah's triangle so he could stop the talisman before it could do any damage.

Returning his gaze to Sarah, he noted that she regarded him with suspicion and fear. He cursed inwardly. As long as she feared him, she wasn't going to cooperate.

Sarah, I am not going to harm you, he thought compellingly, hoping that she could still read his mind. Maybe if she received the thought telepathically, she would believe him.

When she didn't even blink, he raked a hand through his hair. Either she couldn't read his mind because his magic was back, or she was refusing to acknowledge his thoughts.

He considered casting a spell to make her reveal the triangle's whereabouts, but he quickly dismissed that option as too dangerous. Generally, mortals could easily be spellbound, but extreme fear made them impervious to normal magic. To bypass her fear, he'd have to use a potent spell. The mortal psyche was fragile, and there was no way he could determine exactly how much power she could handle. Instead of getting the triangle from her, he might end up destroying her mind.

So what in hell am I going to do? he wondered in frustration. Unfortunately, there was only one safe solution. He had to tell her the truth. Or as much of it as necessary to make her understand the danger her triangle presented. And the first step in doing that was to make her feel at ease.

He walked back to the fire and sat down beside it. Knowing that asking her to join him would be fruitless, he stared at the flames for a moment before glancing up at her.

"Look, Sarah, ever since I arrived, we've been playing a game of one-upmanship, and the situation is getting out of hand. One of us has to stop fighting and start talking before someone gets hurt. Since I'm the stranger here and it's clear that you distrust me—for valid reasons—I'm going to be that person, okay?"

He hadn't expected her to respond, but it still irked him when she didn't. As the troubleshooter, he was accustomed to having people do whatever he wanted without question. Pride insisted he wait her out until she at least gave him the courtesy of an answer. But he knew that if he did that, he'd just be wasting time. He needed to resolve this issue so he could move on.

"I'll assume that your silence means you're willing to listen," he stated. "So I'll begin by explaining why I'm here. Do you know what a talisman is?"

When she still didn't reply, he thought she was going to continue giving him the silent treatment. Then she surprised him by saying, "It's an object that grants supernatural powers or protection to its possessor."

He arched a brow, impressed. Most mortals wouldn't know the purpose of a talisman. Indeed, they'd think it was a piece of junk jewelry and scoff at the thought that it might have supernatural abilities. But Sarah had not only known the definition, she obviously believed in the mystical. Otherwise, she would have said something like, "It's *supposed* to grant supernatural powers."

He didn't know why he was surprised that she believed. She was a Native American, and from what he'd read, many of their beliefs were grounded in the occult.

"You're exactly right," he said. "And our triangles are pieces of a very dangerous talisman."

He paused, waiting to see if he'd aroused her curiosity sufficiently for her to finally start participating in the conversation.

Again, she didn't speak right away, but finally she asked, "Just how dangerous is it?"

"I don't know the exact extent of its power," he hedged. It wasn't a lie. He didn't know for certain that the talisman was a doomsday device. "What I do know is that it was in Seamus Morpeth's family for about 700 years. When Seamus's father died, he inherited the talisman.

"Apparently, until Seamus came into its possession, no one in the family had ever worn the object. But Seamus put it on and it corrupted him—made him evil. According to the records, he caused the death of several innocent people where he lived. After what you've said about his activities here, I have to believe those accounts are true."

"So how did he end up here?" Sarah asked next,

still standing in her militant position in front of the snake, although her wary expression had relaxed somewhat.

Sebastian rubbed a hand against the bridge of his nose. This was where the story would start to get tricky. He had to tell her enough to satisfy her, but he couldn't reveal the existence of the coven.

Dropping his hand to his lap, he said, "Seamus's wife and . . . a friend of the family realized that Seamus had become dangerous. They drugged him so they could take the talisman away from him. Then they broke the talisman into three pieces—the two triangles and a circle—so it would be powerless. They buried the circle, and gave one of the triangles to Seamus, who was then banished into the wilderness. They thought that when he died, his triangle would be buried with him. With the two pieces buried so far apart, they were sure no one would ever be able to reassemble the talisman."

He started to say more, but Sarah interrupted, "Let me get this straight. Seamus killed several people. But instead of turning him over to the authorities to be punished, they give him a piece of this evil talisman and send him out into the wilderness to terrorize the Indians with it?"

Sebastian frowned. Damn, he hadn't handled the explanation well. The trouble was, he wasn't sure how he could have explained it any other way without revealing too much.

"It wasn't exactly like that, Sarah."

"The hell it wasn't!" she declared, dropping her arms to her sides and balling her hands into fists. "I don't know why I'm surprised. After all, it's just a new twist on the same old story. What does it matter if a few hundred Indians get tortured and killed?

In the *wasičun* world they were—and still are in many people's minds—just a bunch of savages with no social value."

"A few *hundred*?" Sebastian gasped in horror. When she'd told him what Seamus had done, he'd thought she was talking about a handful of people. Seamus hadn't been evil, he'd been positively malevolent!

"Don't bother pretending to be shocked, *wicáh-munġa*," she drawled contemptuously. "You wear the triangle, so you know how it feeds on violence. You also know that the more it's fed, the more voracious its appetite becomes. And that's why you want the second triangle, isn't it? Your triangle's appetite has become so big that you can no longer satisfy it. But to give it more sustenance, you need more power, and the only way you can get that is to gain another piece of the talisman.

"Well, you won't get my triangle," she went on before he could reply. "I am the guardian of my people, and I vowed to protect them from Seamus's curse. I failed them by giving you the benefit of the doubt instead of killing you when I had the chance. But just because you manipulated yourself out of my trap doesn't mean you've won. I've put my triangle where no one can find it, and no amount of torture will drag that information from me."

She paused to draw in a deep breath before finishing, "So if you want more power, go after John Butler and his circle. At least you'll both be far away from here and forced to prey upon your own kind for a while. By the time one of you has destroyed the other and comes back here to finish the annihilation of my tribe, they will be prepared for you. You may end up winning, but you'll be in for one hell of a fight before you do. That's one thing we *savages* know how to do. Fight, even if it is a losing battle."

As Sebastian listened to her diatribe, a few pieces of the puzzle began to drop into place. He now understood her willingness to die for the triangle. She said she was a guardian and had vowed to protect her people from Seamus's curse, which, evidently, was that her tribe would be destroyed.

However, that piece of information was irrelevant when compared to her alarming reference to John Butler. Although she'd mentioned the man before, so much had happened that Sebastian had forgotten it. Now, however, he recognized the chilling importance of what she said.

If this Butler truly had the circle, Sebastian's mission was not only more urgent but also far more dangerous. All those years ago, Ulrich Morgret had felt the circle was the talisman's major energy source, which was why he'd chosen to bury it instead of one of the triangles. With all three pieces now above ground, the circle wouldn't need to be physically connected to the other two pieces to start its swath of destruction. And if it fell into the wrong hands . . .

He quickly cut off the thought. The conclusion for which it was heading was too frightening. Sarah *had* to be wrong. If Butler had discovered the circle, Sebastian would have connected with him, just as he'd connected with Sarah. But why would she lie to him?

Because she wants the talisman for herself, that inner voice proposed. *Think about it. She has Seamus's triangle, and she's probably known all along it was part of a talisman. But she didn't know where the other pieces were, so she couldn't do anything about* it. *Then you connected with her, and she realized that if she got your triangle, she could locate the circle. She doesn't know the true purpose of the talisman. She just wants the power. Why else would she have been prepared to kill you the moment you arrived?*

Because of Seamus's reign of terror, Sebastian answered.

Do you really believe that Ulrich would have let Seamus live if he thought he was capable of such violence?

As he studied Sarah, who stared at him with hatred, Sebastian shifted uncomfortably on the ground. The voice had a valid point. If Ulrich had suspected that Seamus was capable of such atrocities, he never would have let him live.

But if Sarah was lying to him to get the pieces of the talisman, why had she tried to kill herself?

It was a scheme to throw you off guard and gain your sympathy, the voice answered. *Your magic had returned, and she knew she was powerless against you. You proved that to her during that little display of fantasy lovemaking. To make you release her from your power, she pulled the fake suicide stunt, counting on you to save her. If you hadn't reacted, she would have simply called off the snake, or it's possible that she's immune to their venom. But even if she isn't immune, she controls the rattlers, and that particular one is her pet. You can't honestly believe it would have really bitten her.*

Now she's making up this Butler so you'll focus on him—or rather the fabrication—rather than on her, the voice went on. *Face it. She's made a fool of you again. You'd better resign as the troubleshooter and give the job to a warlock who can't be manipulated by powerless mortal women.*

Sebastian clenched his fist at that last gibe, and his temper charged to the surface with the speed of a launching rocket. The voice was right. She had made a fool of him again, but she wouldn't have another opportunity to do so. He'd get the triangle away from her tonight if he had to throttle her to get it.

You're letting your pride override your common sense again, a more rational voice nagged. *You have no proof that Sarah is lying. Until you do, you must move cautiously with her, because if she is sincere, she might kill herself, and then where will you be?*

Getting the proof is easy, the first voice rejoined. *Touch the triangle. If this Butler really does exist, you'll connect with him.*

Sebastian immediately raised his hand toward the triangle.

Why didn't I kill him when I had the chance? How could I have been such a fool? Sarah railed at herself as she watched the *wicáhmunǧa.*

He hadn't responded to her suggestion that he seek out John Butler for the circle. She wasn't surprised. Why should he go looking for Butler when the man would eventually show up on his own? Then the two of them would battle over the talisman's pieces, and whoever won would destroy her people.

As she stared at the *wicáhmunǧa,* a hard knot of hatred formed in the pit of her stomach. Yet as much as she despised him, there was a traitorous part of her drawn toward him. She didn't want to give that part a name, but she knew that to defeat it, she had to face it. Lust.

The triangle's final temptation, Sarah, Wanága suddenly whispered in her mind.

As the import of his words hit her, Sarah felt the color drain from her face. He *couldn't* be implying what she thought. She'd faced all the triangle's temptations and beaten them. If she hadn't, Leonard never would have made her the guardian. Besides, she wasn't wearing the triangle, so there was no way it could tempt her.

She started to tell Wanága he'd lost his mind, but she suddenly noticed the *wicáhmunga's* triangle was turning red again. Warily, she glanced from it to his face and gulped. Not only was the triangle changing color, but his eyes took on that strange, inner light.

Suddenly, a strong wind swirled around the cave, and Sarah trembled in terror. According to legend, Seamus had used a wind against anyone who angered him, and it had been forceful enough to slam them into walls and trees, breaking their bones. Then, when they lay there, crippled and helpless, he'd—

The thought was interrupted by a familiar and frightening rustling sound. Sarah jerked her head toward the roof of the cave, and her blood ran cold. Circling above the *wicáhmunga* was the lightning wreath.

She quickly glanced down at him and gasped in horror. The triangle glowed red hot, and she could see thin wisps of smoke rising from where it rested against his chest. As the smell of burning flesh reached her nose, he suddenly raised his hand toward the triangle.

"No! Don't touch it!" she yelled at him, sensing

that he didn't even know what he was doing, but she was too late.

As his fingers closed around the triangle, lightning shot from the wreath and struck the back of his hand. When it did, Sarah saw a flash of light fly toward her, and her mind filled with a vision so horrible, so bloody, that she started screaming and couldn't stop.

5

Evil Confronted

Sarah's mind was filled with the image of an unfamiliar bedroom, but it was the body on the bed that held her attention. Although she didn't know the dead woman, it didn't make the gruesome details of her death any easier.

As she continued to scream, Wanága ordered, *Calm yourself, Sarah. You have been brought here for a reason, and you cannot learn that reason if you are not calm.*

If Sarah hadn't already been hysterical, she would have burst into frantic laughter at his words. How could she possibly be calm when faced with such butchery? It was impossible!

You are the guardian, Sarah. For you, nothing is impossible. Now find out what is going on. If you don't, your people will die, and their deaths will be worse than this.

Sarah shook her head in disbelief. Nothing could be worse than this, and she wanted to close her mind down completely, crawl into the black hole of oblivion forever, rather than look at this scene a moment longer.

But even as she considered a mental escape, she knew she couldn't do it. If she closed down now, she'd not only forsake her people, she'd let Leonard down. He'd trusted her to carry out her duties as guardian with the same dedication he had carried them out for more than fifty years. Leonard would have been sickened by this carnage, but he would have never sought to escape from it.

She drew in a deep breath, forcing her hysteria to subside, although it still rested dangerously close to the surface. Then she made herself examine the scene analytically.

A woman sat on top of a bed. Her legs stretched out in front of her, and her back rested against an ornately carved, wooden headboard. The hem of her black skirt was smoothed down over her knees, and her hands were folded in her lap. The primness of her posture made the inhumanity of her death that much worse.

The white lace coverlet beneath her was drenched in blood, and Sarah drew in another deep breath before raising her gaze from the woman's lap to her face. When she did, she tasted bile. The woman's throat had been cut, but more horrifying for Sarah, her eyes had been gouged out.

It's the same type of torture Seamus performed on my people! she thought, her hysteria threatening to overwhelm her again. *How will that poor woman find her way to the spirit world without her eyes?*

I will guide her, Wanáġa said.

Soothed by his words, Sarah managed to curb her rising hysteria. Then she looked around the room. Until now, she'd been so focused on the body, she hadn't noticed anything else. When she saw John Butler, she caught her breath in horror. He stood at the woman's mirrored dresser, pawing through her jewelry box, his hands dripping blood. Sarah watched him lift necklace after necklace, gazing at each for a moment before tossing it to the floor.

Normally, sound didn't accompany her visions, and Sarah started when she suddenly heard him whistling. The tune was off key, and it took her a moment to identify it. When she did, she again tasted bile. It was "Whistle While You Work."

A moment later, he lifted a necklace and said, "This will do. A little dainty, but what the hell."

He opened the clasp and slipped a small silver ball off the chain. When Sarah heard the tinkling sound, she recognized it as a harmony ball, which was supposed to bring harmony into the possessor's life.

Obviously, John Butler also knew what it was, because he let out a low, maniacal laugh and turned toward the bed, tossing the ball toward the dead woman. As it landed in her lap with a discordant clamor, he said, "Well, Bitch, you thought it was a harmony ball, but it was really a disharmony ball."

He looked at the body, cocking his head as though listening intently, before continuing, "What's wrong? You don't find my little joke funny? That was always your problem. No sense of humor. Unless, of course, it was directed at me. But I had the last laugh, didn't I? You stole the Middle East project away from me, but you gave me a better opportunity without even knowing it. I am going to be rich and famous beyond belief."

He swiveled to face the dresser and lifted the circle. After threading the chain through the eye on the circle, he put the chain around his neck and fastened it.

When he turned back around, he lifted the circle, as though showing it to the woman. "This is my

power, Bitch. With it, I can do anything. Be anything. And if anyone gets in my way . . ."

He stopped speaking and swiveled his head toward Sarah. She told herself that he couldn't see
her, but a slow, sinister smile stretched across his
face as he drawled, "Why, Sarah, you've come to
view my handiwork."

Leave, Sarah. Now! Wanáǵa commanded.

Sarah barely heard him. John Butler stared at her
so compellingly that she found herself drawn into
the depths of his ice-blue eyes against her will. As
had happened the first time she connected with
him, she perceived the evil inside him. It was pulsing, growing, and it mesmerized her. She again
wanted to give in to it. Be consumed by it.

Sarah, leave! Wanáǵa repeated urgently.

"Stay, Sarah," John Butler whispered, his voice
low and alluring. "Let me show you the future."

She heard the rustling sound of the lightning
wreath. At the sound, terror writhed inside her,
screaming at her to end the vision. But she was
trapped by his gaze.

Bolts shot from the wreath, striking the circle in
a hypnotic, strobelike rhythm. He seemed unaware
that his fingers smoked, that the tips were becoming charred flesh.

"Look at the future, Sarah," he whispered.

The room whirled at a dizzying speed, and when
it finally stopped Sarah let out a keening wail.
She was back in the Black Hills, standing in the
very spot where she'd captured the *wicáhmunǵa*—
the spot where Seamus had tortured her people—
and everywhere she looked, there was carnage. Old
men. Young men. Women. Children. Even swad-
dled babies. And all of them were the people she

knew and loved, the people she'd been tasked to protect. They had been brutally slaughtered, but worst of all, their eyes were gouged out.

"This is the future, Sarah. This is what the *wicáhmunǧa* will do if he gets all three pieces of the talisman. But I will help you, Sarah. Together we will stop him," John Butler said.

"You don't want to help me. You're evil. I must destroy you. I must!" she cried frantically.

"But you can't destroy me, because I have the circle, and that is the true power. I know everything you think, Sarah," he whispered, his voice low and insidious. "I know everything you do. I even know where you buried the triangle, and you will never be able to hide it from me.

"Help me destroy the *wicáhmunǧa*, and we'll rule together, Sarah. Fight me, and not only will your people die, I'll make you the instrument of their destruction. You'll be the one to gouge their eyes and mangle their bodies. And you'll love every moment of it, because you are just like me."

"I am *not* like you," she said, clapping her hands over her ears to shut out his voice. It didn't work.

"Of course you are," he crooned. "That's why you aren't afraid of me, because what you see inside me is what is inside yourself."

"No! It's not true. *I am not like you!*" she screamed.

"I'll be there soon, and I'll prove to you that I speak the truth. I'll be inside you, Sarah, and you'll welcome me, because we share the lust."

The word *lust* hit Sarah with a staggering force, and she gave a frenzied shake of her head. She felt horror and disgust toward John Butler, not lust!

"There are different kinds of lust, Sarah, but in

the end, we'll share the lust of the flesh, too," he said with a lecherous chuckle.

What he said was too horrible to contemplate, and Sarah yanked her mind from his and fled into the dark abyss of oblivion. She knew it was the coward's way out, but it was the only way she could save her sanity.

As awareness returned, Sebastian felt as if he were caught in a whirling vortex. When he felt himself teetering on the edge of unconsciousness, he struggled frantically to keep himself anchored to the present.

It seemed to take forever, but he finally stopped whirling. When he did, an agonizing pain shot through his chest and hand. He groaned. Why did he hurt like this? He tried to look at his hand to see what was wrong with it, but his vision blurred. He blinked a few times, but when his eyes remained unfocused, panic mushroomed inside him. Why couldn't he see?

I have to remain calm, he told himself, forcing back the panic. There has to be an explanation for this. What's the last thing I remember?

Closing his eyes, he tried to think, but it was an effort. He felt drained, as if he'd undergone some extreme physical exertion. If he hadn't been in such pain, he would have just lain down and gone to sleep.

Forcing himself to concentrate, he remembered sitting down beside the fire and giving Sarah a sketchy story about the talisman. She'd told him Seamus had killed hundreds of people, and then she'd made some reference to the circle, but what had she said? The remainder of their conversation was as fuzzy as his eyesight, and he still had no idea how he'd gotten hurt.

Slowly he opened his eyes, relieved that his vision was clearing. He immediately looked at his hand, and he gasped when it came into focus. There was a quarter-size burn on the back of it, and from the blackened edges, he knew it had to be a second- or third-degree burn. How in hell had that happened?

The triangle.

As the statement reverberated in his mind, dread crept through him. Still staring at his wound, he tentatively raised the other hand and touched the aching spot on his chest. It lay beneath the cool metal of the triangle.

But how had it happened? More importantly, *why* had it happened? he wondered in bewilderment.

Sarah.

He pivoted his head toward the spot where Sarah had been standing, and he gasped again. She lay sprawled on her back on the ground and, to his horror, the rattler lay curled in the center of her chest. Dammit! While he'd been out of it, the stunning spell had worn off, and Sarah must have given the snake another order to kill her!

Surging to his feet he started toward her, but froze when a man said behind him, "Don't touch her, or I'll have to harm you."

Warily, Sebastian turned to face the man, and his jaw dropped. The man's face was painted in yellow and red stripes, but he didn't look comical. He looked damn ferocious.

Sebastian's gaze flicked over him, taking in his attire, which was almost as bizarre as the face paint. A feather headdress wrapped around his head like a bonnet. His hair was long and split to hang over his shoulders like braids, but instead of being braided, it was wrapped in some type of furry animal skin. His chest was covered with a bone breastplate, and his hips with an unadorned breach clout. Leather armbands and leggings, quilled with triangular symbols, covered his arms and legs. Buckskin moccasins disappeared beneath the leggings.

Sebastian didn't see a weapon, but that didn't ease his wariness. Instinct told him this man wouldn't make a threat unless he felt he could carry it out.

"Look, I don't know who you are, but all I want to do is check on Sarah. I think the snake has bitten her."

"The snake has not harmed her."

"And how do you know that?"

"Because I know."

"Well, I'm sorry, but that isn't good enough for me," Sebastian stated impatiently. "I'm going to check on her."

"You have already put your mark on her, *wicáh-munga*. If you touch her before she wakes up, you may kill her."

Sebastian blinked at him. "What the hell are you talking about?"

"Look at her right hand."

Not about to turn his back on the man, Sebastian risked a glance over his shoulder. Sarah's right arm stretched out on the cave's rock floor, and he let his gaze follow it down to her hand. When he reached it, he stared at it in disbelief. She had a burn identical to his own. Did she also have one on her chest?

He winced at the thought. He had a higher pain threshold than mortals, and even though he'd forced most of the pain to the back of his mind, he'd almost passed out before he'd gotten it under control. If she suffered the same agony, no wonder she was unconscious.

"What did you do to her? To us?" he demanded, swinging his head back around and glaring at the man.

The man arched a brow. "I have done nothing. It is your mark."

"I'd never do something like this to myself, let alone anyone else."

"When rage becomes us, we become rage."

"What the hell is that supposed to mean?"

"If you are meant to know all, you will understand. Do not touch her before she wakes up."

The man disappeared. As Sebastian gaped at the spot, he felt the hair on the back of his neck bristle.

"I must be hallucinating," he mumbled. "Men do not just disappear. Even if he were a warlock, an invisibility spell takes longer than that."

But Sebastian knew he wasn't hallucinating. The man's presence had been too real. He also knew he hadn't been dealing with a warlock. He instinctively balked at the only other answer he could come up with, but he knew there was only one thing that could disappear that fast. A spirit.

But if he were a spirit, why didn't I pick up on the energy displacement that a spirit causes? he asked himself. And for a spirit to take such a solid form, it would have had to be one hell of a displacement.

He could think of only one reason for him not to have recognized what the man was. His magic was malfunctioning again.

With a feeling of trepidation, he murmured a

short, nonsensical spell and flicked his fingers. When nothing happened, he cursed.

Suddenly, he heard an ominous rattle behind him, and he felt the blood drain out of his face. If his magic were gone, so was the protective spell. That meant he was trapped on the mountain with the rattlesnakes, and as long as Sarah was unconscious, she couldn't control them.

He slowly turned to confront the rattler. It still lay coiled on Sarah's chest, with both the tip of its tail and its head raised. As he and the beast stared at each other, it rattled again.

Sebastian automatically took a step back. "Nice snake," he said.

At his words, the snake flicked its tongue and, to Sebastian's surprise, lowered its tail. When he took another step back, it lowered its head. Sebastian understood it wasn't threatening him, but warning him to stay away from Sarah.

"No problem," he told it. "I have no intention of bothering you or your mistress. I'm just going to go sit by the fire until she wakes up."

Cautiously, he walked to the fire. The snake never took its eyes off him, but it didn't move.

When he sat down, he stared at Sarah. He couldn't hear her breathing over the fire's crackling, but he could see the gentle rise and fall of her chest. That reassured him that she was alive.

Now that he was sitting here with nothing to do, he again became aware of his throbbing wounds, and his gaze drifted to Sarah's hand. As he stared at her burn, the spirit's words reverberated in his mind. "It is your mark."

That was impossible. He would never burn someone! But he knew a spirit never lied.

Unless he's an evil spirit.

He frowned. He hadn't sensed evil. Of course, his magic wasn't working, and that could have distorted his instincts. Then again, he'd confronted enough evil as the troubleshooter that he was sure he would recognize it even without his magic. But if the spirit weren't evil, why was he here? Spirits didn't just pop up for no reason. They always had an agenda.

Since the spirit had materialized to protect Sarah, she had to be the connection, and it was probably her involvement with the talisman that had brought the spirit here. Was he one of Seamus's victims, and with the resurfacing of the talisman's evil, would he come back?

It's the most logical explanation I can come up with, so why do I feel as if I'm missing something important? Impulsively, he closed his eyes and re-created the spirit's image in his mind.

"That's it! The quilling on the spirit's armbands and leggings were triangles! But it has to be a coincidence," he said, opening his eyes and frowning at the fire. "The talisman originated in Europe. There is no way it could be connected to a Native American. He has to be one of Seamus's victims, and he either has a strong need for revenge, or he feels responsible for what happened and has a karmic need to make amends."

Satisfied that either reason would explain the spirit's presence, he moved on to their conversation, focusing on the spirit's statement, "When rage becomes us, we become rage."

Of course he understood the concept, because it was intrinsic to his race. Warlocks had volatile tempers, and their anger manifested in a wind. From childhood, they were trained to control both their temper and the wind, because if they were angry enough, their rage had the potential to destroy everything around them. In other words, if they let themselves become enraged, they became a dangerous force.

But what did that have to do with his and Sarah's burns? And why did the spirit claim it was his fault? What had happened? And, dammit, why couldn't he remember?

The burn on his chest chose that moment to throb, and he cursed. The answer was so obvious. Why hadn't he seen it before now?

It had to be the triangle. It had made him lose two hours in the repository, and he had no memory of what had happened during that time. It had to have also caused the burns and his new memory loss.

Fear slithered down his spine and he shivered. If the triangle could make him harm someone without realizing it, then the talisman had to be gaining power. And it could only do that if someone had the circle.

Memory stirred at the thought, and he remembered Sarah telling him that a man by the name of John Butler had the circle. Suddenly the floodgates to Sebastian's mind flew open. As he relived the moments of their last conversation and remembered the inner voice prodding him into anger and then into fury, his blood ran cold.

When he hit the point where he had reached for his triangle to verify she wasn't lying about Butler, his memory again disappeared. No matter how hard he tried to push it further, he couldn't remember anything beyond that point.

"But I don't need to know more," he said. "The voice was the talisman, and it knew exactly what buttons to push to manipulate me. It took control of me without my even realizing what was going on."

Horrified, he glanced toward Sarah, whispering, "What did it make me do to you?"

His gaze returned to her burned hand. He felt both aghast at and ashamed of hurting her. His only consolation was that he had suffered the same pain.

Suddenly he saw her hand twitch, and he realized that she was waking up. He also knew that the longer he was around her, the more danger she'd be in. He decided that the moment she woke up, he would tell her everything, even if it meant revealing the coven, so she would give him her triangle and he could leave.

It is time for you to come back, Sarah.

As Wanága's voice intruded into her unconsciousness, Sarah tried to burrow further into the haven of darkness.

His voice merely followed her. *The curse has started, Sarah, and you are the guardian.*

I don't want to be the guardian! she cried, stubbornly clinging to the darkness.

But Wanága's invasion had disturbed her sanctuary, and she became aware of a hot, searing pain. It was so intense that she almost retreated back into unconsciousness to escape it. She knew, however, that Wanága would just come after her again, so she used the mental techniques Leonard had taught her to manage pain.

When she had eased it to a dull ache, she let her mind follow it to its source. It was in her hand, and she carefully flexed her fingers, trying to determine the cause.

Her eyes flew open when the *wicáhmunga* said, "Sarah? You moved your hand. Are you awake? Are you okay?"

She was startled to find herself looking up at the cave's roof. *How did I end up on the ground? Of course. I collapsed when I closed down.*

Is that what's wrong with my hand? Did I hurt it when I fell? She started to raise her hand so she could look at it, but she stopped when she felt something move on her chest.

A moment later, she felt Willow's tongue against her cheek, and she gasped, "Willow! You're all right!"

"Of course she's all right. I told you I just stunned her."

Raising her uninjured hand to pet the snake, she rolled her head so she could look at the *wicáhmunga*. He still sat beside the fire, but there was something different about him.

Before she could pinpoint what it was, he asked, "Are you in a great deal of pain?"

"No," she answered, realizing it was his expression that was different. He looked solemn, almost contrite.

"Are you sure?"

When she nodded, he said, "Thank heavens. How did I burn you?"

She blinked at him. "Burn me?"

"Your hand," he replied. "How did I burn it?"

Bewildered, she raised her hand to look at it. When she saw the burn, she stared at it in disbelief. No wonder it hurt so badly. It was one of the worst burns she'd ever seen!

Easing Willow off her chest, she sat up and glared at him. "You did this to me?"

He looked down at the fire. "Yes."

"Why?" she demanded angrily.

"I don't know," he answered, still looking at the fire.

"You burn someone, and you don't know *why* you did it? What kind of a monster are you?"

His head shot up, and he scowled at her. "I'm not a monster. I . . . Dammit! I don't know why I did it. I don't even know *how* I did it, and if it will make you feel any better, I have the same burn."

He held up his hand, and when Sarah saw his wound, she frowned in confusion. Why would he burn himself? It didn't make sense.

"Do you also have a burn on your . . . chest?" he asked hesitantly.

She automatically pressed a hand to the front of her shirt. When there was no pain, she drew in a relieved breath. After releasing it, she said, "No."

"Good," he replied, as his own hand rose toward his chest.

As Sarah watched it hover over the triangle, her mind flipped back in time. Just before her vision of John Butler, the *wicáhmunga's* triangle had been glowing red hot, and she'd seen wisps of smoke rising from his chest. She'd also smelled burning flesh, and lightning had struck his hand when he'd touched the triangle. That must have caused the burn on his hand. But how had she gotten burned?

"You don't remember anything about your burns?" she questioned.

When he shook his head, she wasn't surprised. When he'd touched the triangle, she'd sensed that he didn't know what he was doing.

She started to tell him about the lightning, but then she recalled the horrible vision of her people's slaughter. John Butler said it was what the *wicáhmunga* would do if he got all three pieces of the talisman. She wasn't sure if she believed him. The *wicáhmunga* had shown a propensity for evil, but John Butler was the one who had gouged out eyes, she noted with a nauseated shudder. But if John Butler was right, then she'd be foolish to give the *wicáhmunga* any information about the triangle.

Instead, she closed her eyes and relived those few moments when the *wicáhmunga* had reached for the triangle, trying to figure out how she'd been burned.

I called out a warning, she thought, but I was too late. As his fingers curled around the triangle, my mind was thrust instantly into the vision of the dead woman.

Except that wasn't exactly true, she realized, as the scene finished playing out in her mind. Just before she'd been caught up in the vision, she'd seen a streak of light coming toward her. Now she realized it must have been a bolt of lightning.

She opened her eyes and stared down at her hand in bewilderment. "But what does it mean?"

When it is time for you to know all, you will understand, Wanága replied.

Dammit, Wanága! If you can't give me a better answer than that, don't say anything at all.

Of course, he didn't respond, and she glanced up at the *wicáhmunga*. He was staring at her with such a look of contrition that her heart went out to him.

She quickly reeled it back in. Until she could prove otherwise, she had to consider him a threat, and she was going to have to figure out whether he was friend or enemy fast. John Butler said he'd be here soon. Before he arrived, she had to either destroy the *wicáhmunǧa* or make him her ally.

6

Evil Explored

Sebastian had resolved to tell Sarah everything, but as they stared at each other over the fire, he couldn't decide how to begin. Unaccustomed to being at a loss for words, he rose and walked to the cave's opening, startled to see it was still night. So much had happened since his arrival that he felt as if he'd been here for days. But when he looked at the moon, its position assured him it had only been a few hours.

He tucked his uninjured hand into his pants pocket and braced the other hand against the opening's granite arch. When a breeze touched him, he was surprised to feel gooseflesh spring up on his arms. It was midsummer, but compared to the humid torpor of Pennsylvania's summer nights, it was cold here. He found the coolness refreshing, however, and he drew in a deep breath of the clean, crisp air, redolent with the scent of pine and earthy, virgin forest.

Releasing the breath, he knew he had to start communicating with Sarah. Since he still wasn't sure how to begin, he decided to just start talking.

As he continued to look outside, he said, "I haven't been completely honest with you, Sarah."

"Why, *wicáhmunga*, are you saying you lied to me?" she mocked.

At her sarcasm, his temper stirred. He quickly tamped it down. A show of anger would only alienate her further and delay him from his goal, which was to get her triangle and get the hell out of here.

"I didn't lie to you. I gave you a condensed version of the truth," he said, turning around to face her. "I told you that I don't know the exact extent of the talisman's power, and that's true. There is, however, a strong possibility that it's some kind of a . . . doomsday device, that its purpose is to destroy humankind."

She blinked at him, her expression incredulous. "That's absurd. What would this talisman possibly gain by destroying everyone?"

He smiled grimly. "You're applying humanistic qualities to an inanimate, albeit magical, object. It isn't out to *gain* anything. It is simply fulfilling the destiny for which it was created."

"That's even more preposterous," she stated, frowning at him. "Why would someone create an object that would destroy mankind? What would *they* hope to gain?"

"I have no idea, Sarah. The talisman is almost a thousand years old, if not older, so who knows what its creator planned when he made it. But how the talisman came into being isn't important. What matters is stopping it, and the only way I can do that is to gather all three pieces and dispose of them appropriately. That's why I've come for your triangle. I need it to disable the talisman for good."

"Forget it, *wicáhmunga*. I'll *never* give you my triangle," she responded vehemently.

"Why not?" Sebastian gasped in disbelief. He'd anticipated her questioning him, even arguing with him, but he hadn't expected a flat refusal.

"Because you've just confirmed that Seamus Morpeth's curse is true," she replied. "He said that when his triangle joined with its other pieces, my people would be no more. To keep that from happening, I have to make sure the pieces never come together."

"Dammit, Sarah!" he yelled, his temper snapping, despite his resolve to hold onto it. "We're not dealing with an issue that just affects your people. We're dealing with a potentially catastrophic magical object that must be stopped forever, or every man, woman, and child on the face of the earth may die!"

Instead of responding, she lowered her gaze to his chest. With a feeling of trepidation, he also looked down. Again, the triangle had taken on a rosy hue that began to fade the moment he looked at it. This time, he knew for sure it wasn't a reflection of the fire. So why was it glowing?

He thought back to when the phenomenon had occurred before and realized he'd also been angry with Sarah then. That's why it was glowing! It reflected his mood, and magical objects always displayed anger as the color red.

He jerked his head up when Sarah declared, "Your triangle has its hold on you, *wicáhmunga*, which is another reason why I won't cooperate with you. You can't be trusted."

"You don't know what you're talking about," he said impatiently. "The triangle doesn't have a hold on me. It's just reflecting my emotions, and that's a common trait among magical objects."

She eyed him dubiously. "And is it common for magical objects to burn their possessor?"

"Of course that's not common," he stated, growing more impatient. He didn't have time to discuss the complicated idiosyncracies of magical devices. "But we aren't dealing with an ordinary object."

"My point, exactly," she said. "I also have to wonder why you continue to wear the triangle. Common sense says you would take it off to protect yourself from further injury. So why haven't you done that, *wicáhmunga*? Is it because the triangle won't let you take it off? Or is it because you're in collusion with it?"

"Neither," he snapped, although he wasn't as irritated with her as he was with the situation. He couldn't believe he was having to justify his actions to a mortal. "I can't take it off before I've stopped the talisman, or it will automatically return to Sanctuary."

She blinked again. "Sanctuary?"

"It's a town in Pennsylvania."

"You're telling me that if you take off your triangle, it's going to go back to Pennsylvania on its own? As in, poof, it's gone?" When he nodded, she frowned. "I don't know what kind of game you're trying to play, *wicáhmunga*, but as I keep telling you, I am not stupid."

"I know you're not stupid, Sarah, and I'm telling you the truth." She still looked skeptical, so he said, "If you don't believe me, read my mind."

"So that's what you're up to," she gasped angrily, as she surged to her feet. "You want me to read your mind so you can control me again. Well, forget it, *wicáhmunga*. I *never* make the same mistake twice."

"What in hell are you talking about?" he asked, bewildered.

She crossed her arms over her chest and glared at him accusingly. "You know exactly what I'm talking about, and I assure you, you will never have the opportunity to humiliate me like that again."

At her reference to humiliation, he realized she was talking about the fantasy lovemaking. He felt a guilty flush crawl into his cheeks. He'd never treated anyone so callously, so why had he debased her like that?

The voice made you do it.

He raked a hand through his hair, wanting to deny his conscience's charge, but it was true. The same voice that had prodded him into fury, causing him to somehow burn Sarah and himself, had also taunted him into carrying the fantasy lovemaking to the extreme.

His stomach churned at the admission. Was Sarah right? Did the talisman have a hold on him?

Again he wanted to deny the charge. He had to allow, however, that the talisman had a strong influence over him or it wouldn't be able to manipulate his emotions.

Was that how it had corrupted Seamus? he wondered, a frisson of alarm racing through him. Had it started with a subtle exploitation of his feelings, gradually poisoning him with its evil until he was beyond salvation?

Sebastian knew it was probable. He also knew that since the talisman was able to influence him, he should take off the triangle and let it return to Sanctuary. But if he did that the coven would think something had happened to him, and with his magic gone, he couldn't tell them otherwise. Once the triangle appeared, Lucien, as high priest, would take on the mission. Like Sebastian, he'd put on the triangle to locate the other pieces, and he'd fall under the talisman's influence.

No, he didn't dare send the triangle back until his magic returned and he could contact Lucien. But if he stayed with Sarah while wearing the triangle, he could be placing her in jeopardy. The talisman had already made him burn her, and he suspected that when it came to the object, that was a minor transgression.

Feeling torn, he studied Sarah, who continued to glare at him accusingly. Although his logic insisted he had to go before he inadvertently harmed her again, his instincts said he'd be placing her in more danger if he left. What were his instincts picking up on that he wasn't consciously aware of?

Unfortunately, he didn't know, and he wasn't about to leave until he did, because he always trusted his instincts. He also knew that if he stayed he had to address Sarah's grievance about his sexual debasement of her.

He felt another guilty flush heat his cheeks, and he heaved a sigh before saying, "I apologize for treating you so . . . crassly earlier, Sarah. It was unconscionable, and I assure you that it won't happen again."

"I've already said that, *wicáhmunga*," she muttered.

"So you have," he replied wryly. "Since we've finally found something that we agree on, do you think you could call me Sebastian?"

"No."

"Why not?"

"Because my people consider names blessed, and we do not bless our enemies."

Sebastian started to reiterate that he was not her enemy. He stopped himself, however, realizing that if he were in her place, he wouldn't believe him. After all, he'd threatened to strangle her when he escaped from the rattlers. He'd threatened to kill her pet snake. He'd sexually demeaned her and he'd burned her hand. He was lucky she hadn't pushed him off the nearest cliff.

Stuffing his hand back into his pocket, he said, "Look, Sarah, I realize that we haven't had the most propitious beginning, and I accept the majority of the blame for that. We do, however, share a common goal—to keep the talisman from destroying our people. Can't we find a way to work together?"

"No," she replied firmly, irrevocably, as she tightened her arms over her chest.

"Dammit, why not?" he yelled, his temper again getting the best of him.

"Because I'm a proponent of history," she replied. "And, historically, every time my people have trusted a *wasičun*, they've lived—or, rather, died—to regret it."

"But I'm not a *wasičun*," Sebastian snapped. "I'm a . . ."

He cut himself off, realizing he was about to reveal his race's existence.

"You're a what?" she prodded.

Sebastian frowned. He'd already decided that if he had to tell her about his race to get her cooperation he would. But was it truly necessary at this point?

Again feeling torn, he turned to face the cave's opening and stared outside. One part of him—the part that had had secrecy instilled in him since infancy—insisted he couldn't tell her. Another part, however, pointed out that he wasn't getting anywhere with her. Maybe if she knew about his race, she'd relent and give him her triangle.

"We have more in common than you think, Sarah," he said, turning back to face her. "Both of our races have been massacred by your *wasičuns.*"

"What are you talking about?" she asked warily.

"I'm not a magician, Sarah. I'm a warlock, and my race has been persecuted for more than a thousand years."

Warlock? Sarah gaped at the *wicáhmunǧa* in disbelief. She didn't think he could have said anything that would have stunned her more.

Yet oddly enough she wasn't that surprised by his claim. Indeed, it answered a question about Seamus Morpeth that had troubled her all her life. She'd never been able to fathom his senseless butchery of her people. Now she understood that it must have been a witchcraft ritual, probably designed to call up demons or other hellish denizens. Had he accomplished his goal? Had her people lost their souls to some eternal damnation that would deny them their rightful place with the gods?

She shuddered in horror at the thought and mentally cried, *Wanáǧa, why didn't you tell me what he was?*

It was not time for you to know.

Sarah couldn't decide which shocked her more. His admission that he'd known the truth about the *wicáhmunǧa,* or the variation in his familiar refrain.

But I am not trained to fight witchcraft, she informed him frantically. *How could you keep this se-*

cret? If you didn't want to share it with me, why didn't
you tell Leonard? If Leonard had known, he would
have trained me differently!

*Leonard could not train you, Sarah. Your power
comes from inside you, and only you can bring it to
life.*

What power? she questioned in bewilderment.

*When it is time for you to know all, you will under-
stand.*

She wanted to scream. Why did he insist on talking in riddles? Why couldn't he just give her a
straightforward answer? She wanted to demand that
for once he explain himself, but she knew he'd ignore her. She also didn't have time to argue with
him. She had to escape from the *wicáhmunga.*

But before she could do that, she had to get him
away from the cave's door. Then she'd run, and once
outside, she would head deep into the wilderness.
He'd follow her, of course, but at least she'd be
leading him away from her people. With any luck,
she'd again be able to trap him with the rattlers, and
this time she wouldn't hesitate to tell them to strike.

You cannot run away, Sarah, Wanága suddenly
said. *You must stay and listen to the wicáhmunga. You
must learn from him.*

She gave a firm shake of her head. There was no
way she was going to stay with a practitioner of
witchcraft, and nothing Wanága said would change
her mind.

Evidently the *wicáhmunga* thought she was denying his claim of being a warlock, because he said, "I
know it's hard to believe, Sarah, but I am a warlock.
Because of our persecution, my race has been in
hiding for centuries. It's the only way we've been

able to survive, and even now, we're on the brink of extinction."

"You should be extinct. You're evil!" she blurted out, taking a fearful step back.

"No," he declared adamantly. "We're different from you, but we are not evil and never have been."

"And just how would you describe Seamus Morpeth?" she demanded, anger stirring at his claim. She welcomed the emotion, encouraged it, because without anger, she knew she'd be over-whelmed by fright. How could Wanága have done this to her? How was she supposed to fight witch-craft without the proper training?

There has to be *something* I can do to fight him, she thought desperately. But no matter how hard she racked her brain, she couldn't come up with one idea.

"Seamus was not representative of my race," the *wicáhmunga* said, interrupting her thoughts. "He was corrupted by the talisman."

"And is that your excuse for John Butler?" she shot back, growing more angry. How could he stand there and exonerate Seamus's abominable actions? Did he have no regard for life? Of course, he didn't. He was a warlock.

He frowned at her. "Whoever this John Butler is, Sarah, he is not one of us."

She let out a harsh laugh that, even to her, sounded suspiciously close to hysteria. "He's not one of you? Then why does he kill in the same man-ner as Seamus Morpeth? Why did he gouge out that woman's eyes?"

"He what?" the *wicáhmunga* gasped, his expres-sion appalled.

"Oh, don't look so horrified," she said contemptuously. "I thought you were innocent when you touched the triangle, that you didn't know what you were doing. But that was before I knew what you are. You knew exactly what you were doing. You summoned the lightning wreath, and you made the lightning strike me. And, worst of all, you did it so I would see what John Butler had done so you could frighten me!"

"Sarah, I don't know what you're talking about, but—"

"You *do* know what I'm talking about!" she interrupted furiously. "The two of you are working together, aren't you? You're trying to scare me into telling you where my triangle is, but it isn't going to work. I have it safely buried, and—"

Before she could finish what she was saying, the *wicáhmunga* sprinted across the distance separating them. He moved so quickly that before she even realized what was happening, he had a punishing grip on her arms.

As she stared up at him, she shivered in fear. His eyes were taking on that strange, inner glow, and his voice was as low and sibilant as a snake's hiss as he said, "What did you just say?"

She had to gulp several times to find her voice. It still came out as a squeak, when she replied, "I said you know about John Bu—"

"No!" he broke in, giving her a hard shake. "I don't want to know about Butler right now. Tell me what you said about the triangle!"

"I . . . I said . . . it was . . . safely . . . buried," she stammered.

"In the ground?" he questioned harshly, his hands tightening on her arms so hard she winced.

"Yes."

"You're sure?" he demanded, shaking her again. "Don't lie to me, Sarah."

"It's . . . in the . . . ground."

"When did you bury it?"

"Early this . . . morning."

He muttered a particularly vile curse and released her so abruptly she almost fell. By the time she regained her balance, he'd already moved back to the cave's opening. He stood staring out it, and she jumped when he suddenly raised a balled fist and slammed it against the rock wall.

Several seconds passed before she found the nerve to ask, "What's wrong, *wicáhmunġa*?"

"My name is Sebastian!" he yelled, spinning around to face her. "If you can't call me that, then don't call me anything at all. Have you got that?"

With a gulp, she nodded. His eyes were still glowing, but when she glanced down at his chest, she was surprised to see that the triangle hadn't changed color. Why? Obviously, he was angry, and it should be feeding on the emotion.

Before she could consider the oddity, he said, "You said earlier that this John Butler has the circle, and he's on his way here. Is that the truth?"

She eyed him warily, trying to figure out what he was up to now. She was sure he knew about John Butler, so why was he pretending he didn't?

Suddenly, Wanáġa said, *Answer his question, Sarah.*

No. It's some kind of trick!

Answer him, Sarah.

She instinctively balked at Wanáġa's command, but she said, "Yes, it's the truth. John Butler has the circle and he's on his way here."

The *wicáhmunġa* muttered another vile curse and

strode purposely toward her. She immediately backed up, panicking when her back came up against solid rock. Although she knew she was trapped, she glanced from side to side, trying to figure out a way to escape him.

When she caught sight of Willow, who was coiled about five feet away and watching her expectantly, she considered summoning her pet to the rescue. A quick glance toward the *wicáhmunga*, however, changed her mind. His eyes were glowing again, and his expression was so dark, so foreboding, that she knew he'd probably kill Willow before she could even strike.

Sarah's knees began to quiver when he came to a stop in front of her and said quietly, menacingly, "I want your triangle, Sarah."

"I . . . told you. It's . . . buried," she whispered hoarsely.

"I want you to get it for me. *Now.*"

Her throat was so dry, she couldn't speak, so she shook her head. She let out a yelp when he suddenly grabbed her arms again, jerking her up so that she was standing on tiptoe. Then he lowered his head so that their eyes were level.

As she looked into them, she shuddered in terror. They were now glowing so brightly it was like peering into the high beams of an oncoming car. She also became aware of a strong wind swirling around them, and she knew he was causing it. He was probably going to blow her body around the cave, smashing her into the walls and breaking her bones, just as Seamus had done to her people. Then he would—

He interrupted her morbid thoughts with, "There are things going on here that you don't understand;

things that I don't have the time to explain. But I need your triangle, and I need it now."

"No," she managed weakly. "I can't—*won't*—give it to you. I am the guardian, and—"

"Dammit, Sarah!" he bellowed, jerking her up higher, his grip so hard she yelped in pain. "I am *not* going to risk my own life, as well as the rest of mankind, so you can play guardian. Now, you *are* going to get your triangle for me. The only question is, are you going to do it voluntarily, or am I going to have to make you do it. Believe me, if it's the latter, you aren't going to like it."

Sarah wasn't sure what incited her temper. Perhaps it was the painful grip he had on her arms. Perhaps it was the fear his glowing eyes instilled in her. Or, perhaps, it was nothing more than the tone of his voice. He was furious, but he talked to her as if she were some doltish, ineffectual child.

All she knew for sure was that she had never been so infuriated, and her anger was like a living, breathing thing inside her.

"Let me go, *wicáhmunga*," she stated softly, warningly.

"I'm not letting you go until you tell me if you're going to cooperate," he answered, his voice a determined rasp.

"I said, let me go!"

"And I said—"

She didn't wait for him to complete the sentence. She closed her eyes and latched onto her anger, centering it inside her. Then she mentally thrust it at him.

"What the hell!" he yelled as she felt him release her arms.

Her eyes flew open, and her jaw dropped as she

watched him fly across the cave and smash into the
far wall.

"What did I do?" she whispered in disbelief as he
slid to the floor in an inglorious sprawl.

You brought your power to life, Wanáǧa answered
in a tone that sounded full of pride. Then it
changed to warning as he added, *But that is the easy
part. Control will be more difficult.*

Sebastian stared up at the cave's ceiling, dazed.
He felt as if he'd just been run over by a truck.
What the hell had happened?

Suddenly, Sarah appeared above him, gasping,
"Are you all right?"

As memory came rushing in, he blinked at her in
disbelief. She'd thrown him across the cave! Not
physically, of course, because he easily outweighed
her by a good hundred pounds. She'd done it mentally, and he couldn't have been more shocked if it
had been a physical accomplishment.

"How did you do that?" he demanded, pushing
himself into a sitting position as she dropped to her
knees beside him.

She sat back on her heels and nervously rubbed
her hands against her thighs as she mumbled, "You
made me mad."

Sebastian opened his mouth but closed it when
he realized he didn't know how to respond. Raking
a hand through his hair, he stared at her. Who was
she? More importantly, *what* was she? As far as he
knew, only a witch or warlock was capable of such
a feat, and he knew she wasn't a witch.

Or was she? he wondered. Could she be Seamus
Morpeth's descendant?

He quickly dismissed that theory. A warlock

could only father one child during his lifetime, and a witch could only bear one during hers. Their limited procreation was one of the reasons his race was almost extinct. And Seamus had fathered a child with Ragna Morpeth before his banishment, so he couldn't have fathered another child. So who was Sarah, and why did she have the power?

She interrupted his musing by again asking, "Are you all right?"

"Yeah," Sebastian muttered, although it wasn't exactly true. Every bone in his body felt bruised, and no wonder. He'd hit the wall with enough force to cripple an ordinary man. Thankfully, he was a warlock, and his body could withstand more abuse.

"I'm sorry," she said, glancing toward the ground. "I didn't mean to hurt you, but—"

"I made you mad," he finished dryly when she stopped speaking.

She glanced up at him and looked quickly away. "I don't know how I . . . I've never . . ."

"You don't know how you did it, and you've never done it before?" he guessed, when she again fell into silence.

She nodded.

"Who are you, Sarah?" he prodded encouragingly.

She shot to her feet and began to pace, stating, "I am the guardian. My duty is to protect my people from Seamus Morpeth's curse."

Sebastian frowned. That wasn't what he meant, and he knew she knew it. What was she hiding from him?

He refrained from asking, knowing that she'd probably lie. Instead he said, "Well, you may be the guardian, but it's going to take more than the mental ability to throw a man across the room to defeat the talisman."

She stopped pacing and regarded him warily. "And what, in your opinion, will it take to defeat it?"

"Until a short time ago, I thought the solution was simple," he answered, deciding he might as well tell her the truth. "According to our records, all we had to do was bury one piece, and the talisman would be stopped. But you say you've already buried your piece, and it's apparent that the talisman is still working. So if you're telling me the truth, I don't know how to stop it."

7

Evil Denied

Stunned, Sarah stared down at the *wicáhmunġa*, who still sat on the floor. What did he mean he didn't know how to stop the talisman? Was he implying that the three pieces didn't need to come together to fulfill Seamus Morpeth's curse?

At the thought, the image of John Butler and the dead woman formed in Sarah's mind's eye, and she knew that was exactly what the *wicáhmunġa* meant. Shuddering, she rubbed her hands against her upper arms, feeling chilled to the depths of her soul. John Butler was coming after her, and he might start butchering her people, just as he had that poor woman. To ensure that didn't happen, Sarah knew she had to lead him away from here.

But what should she do about her triangle? Butler had said he knew where she'd buried it and she'd never be able to hide it from him. Since he'd specifically used the word *buried,* she had to believe he did know, so she didn't dare leave it behind. But he'd also said that if the *wicáhmunġa* got her triangle, he would cause that horrible vision she'd seen of her people's deaths. Although the *wicáhmunġa* still hadn't exhibited the evil Butler had, she knew she couldn't discount the claim. When Seamus had first come here, he'd also seemed harmless. So she couldn't chance digging up the triangle while the *wicáhmunġa* was here, either.

Recognizing that she was at an impasse, she started to call on Wanáġa for advice, but the *wicáhmunġa* said, "Sarah, we're both in extraordinary danger. I know I'm being redundant, but would you please sit down and listen to what I have to say?"

She frowned down at him, automatically ready to deny his request. Then she remembered that Wanáġa had told her to listen and learn from him. Now, she understood why. The *wicáhmunġa* knew more about this talisman than she did, and the more she knew, the better chance she'd have to stop it.

"I'll listen. Let's sit by the fire," she said, quickly walking toward it before he could object. Leonard had always told her that if she wanted to know what was really in a man's heart, she should look into his eyes while he talked. Since she didn't dare read the *wicáhmunġa's* mind, she wanted to make sure she could see his face, which was currently obscured by night shadow.

But more importantly, if she sat in front of the fire, he would have to sit behind it. That would give her clear access to the cave's opening and an opportunity to escape.

She reached the fire just as he levered himself to his feet, and she was again amazed by his size. When he walked toward her, she shivered, but it wasn't from fear. It was from a strange, hot restlessness stirring inside her. As he drew closer, she found herself wanting to reach out and touch him, to explore the breadth of his shoulders and chest.

Appalled by the impulse, she gestured him toward the other side of the fire. Then she tucked her hands into her pants pockets to keep them out of trouble.

At her gesture, he hesitated, glancing from where she stood to the cave door. Obviously, he knew what she was up to, and she expected him to object. He surprised her by walking past her and sitting down without uttering a word.

As soon as he sat, she knelt in front of the fire, leaned back on her heels and said, "Okay, talk."

"Tell me about John Butler."

She blinked, startled. She wasn't sure what she'd expected him to say, but it wasn't that. Regarding him warily, she said, "Why?"

He drew up a knee and rested his forearm on it. "Because he's the enemy, and to fight him, I have to know about him."

"And why should I believe that he's the enemy?"

"Come on, Sarah," he chided. "A little while ago, you said he gouged out a woman's eyes, and when I was wrestling with your damn snake earlier, you said he couldn't hop on a plane because he'd killed a man. I was too busy trying to keep from getting bitten to give that any thought. Then, everything else started happening, and, quite frankly, I forgot it until you mentioned the woman's eyes. But the moment you told me Butler had killed a man, I should have realized what was going on."

"And just what is going on?" she asked warily. If he really didn't know anything about John Butler, she wasn't sure she should tell him anything.

"I've already told you that. The talisman's goal is to destroy mankind."

"You said you didn't know that for sure."

"You're not going to make this easy, are you?" he grumbled.

She shrugged. "It's been my experience that when people want you to make things easy, it's because they have something to hide."

"I'm not trying to hide anything from you," he denied impatiently. "I'm trying to clear up some questions so I can come up with a plan. So please, Sarah, tell me about Butler. Specifically, how do you know about him? Do you know how he got the circle? What, exactly, has he done since he got it? What does he look like? How close is he? I need to know everything."

Answer him, Sarah, Wanáǧa urged.

"I know about Butler the same way I knew about you," she said. "I saw him in a vision."

"A vision?" he repeated, his expression skeptical.

She didn't know why his disbelief irked her. Few *wasičuns* believed in her abilities. For some inexplicable reason, however, his skepticism particularly rubbed her the wrong way. "Look, *wicáhmunǧa,* if you're going to doubt my veracity—"

"I asked you not to call me that," he broke in, frowning. "I am not a *wicáhmunǧa.* I'm a warlock. And I don't doubt your veracity. I've seen enough of your . . . talents to believe you have visions. In this instance, however, I'm questioning your terminology. A vision is psychic foresight or hindsight. I suspect that what you experienced with me and Butler was in real time, which makes it a mental link, not a vision."

Sarah gnawed on her bottom lip as she considered his words. Finally, she said, "You're partially right. The vision I had of you was in the present, which confused me. My visions are always of the past or the future. But my first vision of John Butler had the familiar echoes of the past, and I knew it had already happened."

"Are you sure it was in the past?" he asked, leaning toward the fire and staring at her intently.

His scrutiny made her uneasy, and she rubbed her hands against her thighs as she replied, "I'm positive. Why?"

"I need more information before I can answer that. Who did you connect with first? Me or Butler?"

"You."

"Tell me what happened," he stated. "I need to know exactly when you connected with me."

She hesitated, and Wanáġa suddenly said, *Tell him.*

Reassured by Wanáġa's approval, she told the *wicáhmunġa* about envisioning an unfamiliar forest and seeing him walk through a golden barrier. He looked surprised when she mentioned the barrier, but he didn't interrupt until she reached the part about the lightning wreath appearing after he put on the triangle.

"You saw a lightning wreath?" he asked incredulously.

"You saw it too," she replied. "When the lightning struck you—"

"Lightning *struck* me?" he repeated, looking so dumbfounded that she knew he wasn't faking it.

"You don't remember the lightning?" she questioned, wondering if she should tell him it had struck him a second time right here in this cave.

She cast an uneasy glance down at her burned hand, and her jaw dropped in shock. The burn was almost healed. But that was impossible! She quickly looked at the *wicáhmunġa's* hand and frowned in concern. His wound wasn't healing. If anything, it looked worse, and she switched her attention to his chest. His triangle covered that burn, but she saw a small trickle of blood oozing from beneath the silver object. Raising her gaze to his face, she saw that he too was comparing their hands with a puzzled expression.

"You need to tend to your wounds," she said. "They must be painful, and you should protect them against infection."

He glanced up and shook his head. "I can control the pain, and I rarely get infections. It's one of the benefits of being a warlock. Let's get back to when you first connected with me. What happened after the lightning struck me?"

"You laughed," she replied. "Then you seemed to look at me—which, of course, was impossible, because I wasn't really there—and you said my name. It frightened me, and I ended the vision."

"And then you connected with Butler?"

"Not immediately," she hedged, recalling that Wanága had forced her to do that. When the *wicáhmunga* didn't respond, she continued, "A few minutes later I touched my triangle, and that's when I had the vision of John Butler."

"But it wasn't in real time?"

"No. It was definitely a vision of the past," she said, staring at a spot on the wall behind him and shivering as she called up the memory. "The lightning wreath circled above a pit, and John Butler sneaked up on an older man and hit him over the head with a shovel. I know Butler killed him, because I saw the man's spirit ascend from his body. Then, Butler climbed into the pit and dug up an object. Lightning struck him, and . . ."

"And?" the *wicáhmunǧa* prodded when she didn't continue.

She shivered again, recalling how John Butler had also looked at her. As she'd gazed into his ice-blue eyes, she'd felt drawn into his evil, mesmerized by it. She'd wanted to be a part of it, and . . .

Sarah, answer the wicáhmunǧa! Wanáǧa commanded sternly.

She blinked, ending the memory, and said, "And he seemed to look at me and said my name, just like you did."

"When he said your name, did that also have the feeling of the past?"

As she considered the question, she frowned. "Yes and no. When he said my name, that felt real, but the sense of the past didn't change. Does that make sense?"

"Unfortunately, yes," he muttered, leaning away from the fire and rubbing a hand over his face.

"Why unfortunately?" she asked, alarm sparking inside her.

He dropped his hand to his lap and stared at her pensively. Several tension-filled seconds passed before he murmured, "Who *are* you, Sarah?"

"I am the guardian."

"No," he said, shaking his head. "You're the talisman's power source."

"I don't understand what you mean," she said, her spine stiffening as her alarm flared toward fear.

"It's very simple, Sarah," he said, leaning forward again. "I put on the triangle because, under traditional magic, it should have connected me with the other two pieces and led me to the people who possessed them. But I've never connected with this

John Butler. I only connected with you, and you connected with me *before* I put on the triangle."

"So?" she said in confusion.

"So you shouldn't have known about me until *after* I put on the triangle."

"I still don't see how that would make me the talisman's power source."

"The key is in the vision you had of John Butler," he explained. "You came to me in real time, because you had to verify that all three pieces were in position to come together. Once you confirmed that I was in possession of the triangle and would bring it to you, you had to connect with Butler so he would bring you his piece."

She opened her mouth to object, but he held up his hand. "Let me finish, okay?"

When she nodded, he went on, "You must have subconsciously known Butler had uncovered the circle, but I think you had to see the event for it to enter your consciousness. Thus, the vision of the past. The reason his saying your name seemed real is that it was. Once you consciously acknowledged that he had the circle, you told him to bring it to you."

"I didn't tell him to bring it to me," she protested. "I didn't even speak to him."

"You didn't have to speak, Sarah. You mentally linked with him, and once you did, he was automatically drawn to you, just as I was."

She shook her head in bewilderment. "You have me completely confused, and I still don't see how any of this would make me the talisman's power source."

"Sarah, the reason I haven't connected with John Butler is because we're nothing more than pawns," he said. "The talisman is using us to bring the other pieces to you."

"But that's good!" she declared, her shoulders sagging in relief. "That means I'll be able to stop it from destroying my people."

"No," he said again. "It means the talisman has chosen you to act as its instrument of destruction. The question is, why has it picked you, the guardian, to destroy your people? And make no mistake—they'll be destroyed along with everyone else."

As the import of his words sank in, Sarah couldn't move. She couldn't even breathe. What he was saying wasn't true. It *couldn't* be true! She had conquered the triangle. If she hadn't, Leonard would have never given it to her.

Suddenly, John Butler's voice reverberated in her mind. *You're just like me.*

"No! It's not true!" she yelled, jumping to her feet and glaring at the *wicáhmunga*. "I would *never* hurt my people."

He gave her a compassionate look as he asked, "How long have you had the triangle, Sarah?"

"I'm telling you, I would never hurt my people!" she responded angrily, although it wasn't anger mushrooming inside her. It was absolute terror. He had to be lying to her. If he wasn't . . .

"How long have you had it, Sarah?" he repeated, interrupting her horrifying thoughts.

"That has nothing to do with this," she answered belligerently.

"It has everything to do with it," he stated. "John Butler has had the circle no more than a day or two, and from what you've said, he's already killed two people, maybe even more. I've had my triangle less than twenty-four hours, and the talisman has been manipulating my emotions. It made me sexually demean you. It made me so angry at you that I somehow burned you. If it has gained that much power over me and Butler in such a short time, what has it done to you?"

"It has no power over me!" she declared frantically. "I spent my life overcoming the triangle's evil, and I mastered it. *It cannot corrupt me.*"

"Your *entire* life?" he said, his expression shocked. "No wonder it has chosen you!"

"It has not chosen me!" she screamed at him, taking a step back as she shook her head.

"Sarah—"

She wouldn't—couldn't—listen to what he had to say. She spun around and ran toward the cave door, telling herself that he was lying to her, trying to confuse her, so she would give him her triangle. What he was saying wasn't true. She would never hurt her people. Never, never, never!

But as she burst from the cave into the night-shrouded forest, John Butler's voice began to reverberate in her mind. *You're just like me.*

"Wanága, help me!" she cried as she raced into the trees, swiping at tears that blurred her eyes.

She was already terrified, but it was nothing compared to the dread that rushed through her when Wanága didn't answer.

As Sarah ran out of the cave, Sebastian sprang to his feet and raced after her.

Damn! Why had he let her maneuver him into sitting behind the fire, allowing her clear access to the cave's opening? Because he'd needed answers, and he'd hoped that by giving her that edge she'd cooperate.

When he dashed outside and saw her heading into the trees, he muttered a curse and followed her. She hadn't had much of a head start, but she darted through the moonlit forest with an agility bred of familiarity. Sebastian realized that if he didn't catch her quickly, she'd escape. If his suspicions about her were true, he couldn't allow that to happen. She'd hook up with Butler, who had the circle. Ulrich Morgret had buried the circle rather than one of the triangles because he was convinced it was the talisman's primary force. Sebastian's instincts said that if Sarah possessed both the circle and her triangle, she'd be unstoppable.

At the thought, urgency rushed through him, prodding him to run faster. He forced himself to maintain a steady lope. There were too many rocks and fallen trees on the ground, and, unlike her, he didn't know the terrain. If he tripped, he'd lose her for sure.

A few minutes later, he saw Sarah cast a quick glance back at him. When she did, she stumbled, landing on her hands and knees. She quickly regained her feet and resumed running, but before she could pick up full speed, he closed the gap between them.

Knowing she'd ignore him if he asked her to stop, he didn't waste his breath. Instead, the moment he got within reach, he wrapped his arms around her slender waist and lifted her off her feet.

"Let me go!" she screamed, squirming frantically against his hold as he slid to a stop and pinioned her back against his chest.

He cursed when one of her heels connected solidly with his shin. When an elbow slammed into his side, he gasped in pain and almost lost his hold on her.

"Dammit, Sarah! I am not going to hurt you!" he yelled, trying to evade her flailing limbs.

"Let me go!" she repeated, landing a few more kicks and punches.

Without even thinking, he mumbled an incantation that would temporarily render her immobile. Spell lightning encircled her and she went limp. Elation shot through Sebastian. His magic was back!

His elation switched to alarm, however, when Sarah started trembling violently and gasping for breath. He quickly hooked an arm beneath her legs and gently laid her on the ground, kneeling beside her. Her eyes were closed, but one look at her tortured expression assured him her distress was real. What in hell was wrong?

"Your magic is killing her, *wicáhmunga*. Remove your spell or she will die."

Sebastian's head shot up. The spirit he'd encountered in the cave stood in front of him, and Sebastian had no doubt that he was indeed a spirit. His feet hovered several inches above the ground, and Sebastian could see the landscape through his incorporeal image.

"That's ridiculous! It's a harmless spell specifically designed for mortals." Sebastian declared, automatically glancing down at Sarah, his alarm increasing. She still gasped, and her trembling had increased to the point that it was almost convulsive.

"Sarah is not a mortal," the spirit said.

"Not a mortal?" Sebastian echoed, glancing back at him in disbelief. "Then what the hell is she?"

"If you are meant to know all, you will understand. Remove your spell," he reiterated as he disappeared.

Sebastian returned his attention to Sarah and immediately chanted the words to withdraw the spell. The instant it was gone, her trembling decreased. Her eyes were still closed, and she continued to gasp. He could tell, however, that she gulped in air rather than fighting for it.

As he waited for her to recover, he sat back on his heels. Staring at her in confusion, he considered the spirit's assertion that she wasn't a mortal. Again, he wondered if she could be part witch but quickly rejected the idea. The spell he'd cast was as harmless to his race as it was to mortals.

But if she weren't a witch or a mortal, then what was she? A spirit? He discarded that idea, too. A spirit was already dead, so there was no way his magic could kill her.

Before he could ponder the matter further, she opened her eyes. Since she'd been fighting him when he'd cast the spell, he expected her to at least start railing at him. Instead, she stared up at him, her expression confused, disoriented. Worriedly, he leaned forward and brushed the back of his fingers against her cheek. She felt like silk, and, unexpectedly, desire stirred inside him.

He jerked his hand away. What in hell was the matter with him? Now was *not* the time for libidinous pursuits! Unfortunately, that didn't calm his libido, particularly when she chose that moment to run the tip of her tongue across her lips.

His fingers itched to follow the sensuous path her tongue had taken. With an inward curse, he firmly planted his hands on his thighs and gruffly asked, "How do you feel?"

She answered him, but her voice was so soft that he couldn't hear her.

Leaning toward her, he said, "What did you say?"

"I don't know."

"You don't know what you said, or you don't know how you feel?"

"Both," she said, raising her hand to her forehead and grimacing as though in pain.

"Does your head hurt?"

"Yes," she said, closing her eyes.

He started to cast a spell that would take her headache away, but stopped himself. She'd already responded badly to one supposedly harmless spell. He didn't dare expose her to another one.

"Well, you just rest. I'll carry you," he said, standing.

Again, he expected her to fight him, and he frowned when she passively let him lift her into his arms. He'd known she was small, but her slight weight startled him. Why hadn't he noticed how light she was when he'd caught her? Because she'd been struggling so frantically that she'd felt heavier.

As he cradled her against his chest, she rested her head against his shoulder and laid a hand against his chest. He glanced down at her face. Her eyes were closed and her brow furrowed in obvious pain.

Sympathy stirred inside him, and he wanted to brush his hand across her forehead to smooth out the lines. Instead, he headed for the cave, thankful that his magic was back. It functioned as an internal compass, and without it, he knew he would have been lost.

As he walked, he thought about the spirit. Who was he? And what part did he play in this drama?

More importantly, was he good or evil? Sebastian hadn't picked up on any evil vibrations, but that wasn't surprising. Both times he'd encountered the spirit, it had appeared to protect Sarah. In a protective role, the spirit's aura would emanate honorable intentions. Once Sarah felt better, he'd have to question her about her ghostly companion.

Now that his magic was back, he also needed to contact Lucien, he reminded himself. He'd alert him to the problems with the triangle and tell him that if it returned, he wasn't to put it on.

As they neared the cave, Sebastian glanced down at Sarah. She hadn't moved a muscle during the walk back, and he thought she'd fallen asleep.

The moment they entered the cave, however, she raised her head and asked, "Where are we?"

"Home," he answered, walking to the fire. "Can you stand on your own?"

"I think so."

He dropped her to her feet, keeping his arm linked around her waist until she steadied herself. Then he released her, took a step back, and stuffed his hands into his back pockets, saying, "How's your head?"

"It hurts," she replied, raising a hand to her temple as she glanced around the cave. Finally, she looked at him, her eyes narrowed in confusion, as she asked, "What happened to me?"

"You don't remember what happened?"

She shook her head, and then grimaced at the action.

"What's the last thing you do remember?"

"Waking up."

A shiver of unease tracked its way down Sebastian's spine. "Do you remember who I am?"

"No."

His uneasiness increased. "Do you know who you are?"

She stared at him for a long moment before confirming his worst nightmare. "I have no idea."

8

Evil Manipulated

✛

As the troubleshooter, Sebastian had come to think of himself as omnipotent. And rightly so, he assured himself as he walked to the cave door and stared outside. He was the most powerful warlock alive, which, in effect, made him the most powerful human being alive.

Of course, that didn't make him invincible, he admitted. It did, however, give him a better chance to defeat the evils—both supernatural and natural—that preyed upon the covens around the world. Or, at least, it had until now.

He turned back to face Sarah. She stood in front of the fire, staring at him. As he took in her perplexed expression, he raked a hand through his hair, feeling damned perplexed himself. From the moment he'd arrived on this mountaintop, she'd thwarted him. Now, when he needed answers the most, she'd developed amnesia.

Wondering if she was faking it, he let his mind brush against hers. Since he'd only been able to mentally link with her during their sexual fantasy, he expected to be blocked from her thoughts. Surprisingly, her mind was open to him, verifying that she told the truth.

"Well, hell," he muttered, deciding that her reaction to the spell had caused her memory loss. But how long would it last?

"What did you say?" she asked.

He smiled ruefully. "Nothing important. Why don't you sit down and rest? Maybe that will help your memory come back."

"Maybe," she said, but she made no move to sit. Instead, she rubbed a hand against her temple and asked, "Who am I?"

"Sarah."

"Sarah what?"

"I don't know your surname," he said, surprised to realize that was true. They'd never formally introduced themselves, and the triangle had only provided him with her first name. "We only met a few hours ago."

Her brow furrowed in puzzlement. "Then why did you say we were home?"

He blinked, confused by the question. Then, he recalled that when he'd carried her into the cave and she'd asked where they were, he'd said home.

"It was just a figure of speech. You brought me to this cave earlier tonight, but from what you said, you don't actually live here."

"Oh," she said, looking around the cave curiously, still massaging her temple.

They both started at the sudden rattling from the back of the cave. Sarah spun toward the sound, and Sebastian quickly cast another protective spell over himself. The spell lightning no more than encircled him than the rattler slithered out of the shadows.

"What a beautiful rattlesnake!" she said, walking toward it.

"Yeah, well, as the old saying goes, beauty is in

the eye of the beholder," Sebastian stated dryly. "She's your pet."

Sarah glanced back at him. "Really? What's her name?"

"You called her Willow."

"Willow. A perfect name," she said, dropping to her knees in front of the snake. She lifted the reptile and brought its head close to her face, crooning, "You're as slender and supple as a willow branch, aren't you?"

Sebastian grimaced when the beast flicked its tongue against Sarah's lips. Sarah, however, laughed. As grotesque as Sebastian found the sight of her fondling the snake, her laughter enchanted him. It was rich and wholly sensual.

Desire again stirred inside him, and he muttered an inward curse. Even if he wanted to get involved with Sarah—which he didn't—she was the enemy. Not only that, according to the spirit, she was neither mortal nor witch. So what *was* she?

Suddenly, Sarah swiveled her head toward him, and Sebastian felt as if he'd been punched in the gut. Her lips were curved in a smile, her golden eyes agleam with delight. While serious, she was beautiful. Smiling, she transcended beauty to something so extraordinary he couldn't even describe it. He wanted to walk across the cave and sweep her into his arms, and then he'd . . .

He cut off the fantasy abruptly and asked, "How's your headache?"

He hadn't meant for the words to come out harshly, but they did. When her smile died and she eyed him warily, he wanted to kick himself. She needed to be reassured, not frightened. She had amnesia, for pity's sake.

"Sorry," he muttered. "I'm not fond of snakes, particularly those of the poisonous variety. They make me nervous, and that makes me curt."

"Oh," she said, her expression still wary. She placed the snake back on the ground and murmured something inaudible. The snake slithered back into the shadows.

Sarah watched until it disappeared, then she returned her attention to him. "My headache is better. Who are you?"

"Sebastian Moran."

"Sebastian," she said, as though testing the word. "I like it. It sounds solid, reliable."

Sebastian shrugged, uncomfortable. It was the first time she'd spoken his name, and the way she said it in her soft, throaty voice didn't make him feel solid or reliable. It made him horny as hell.

Get your mind off sex! he ordered himself impatiently.

Aloud, he said, "It's just a name."

"How do we know each other?"

It was a question he'd expected but didn't know how to answer. In her condition, he couldn't dump the story of the talisman on her. Yet he was averse to lying to her. She would, hopefully, regain her memory shortly. Instinct said that if he lied to her now, when she did remember she'd be even less cooperative.

"I came here because I needed your help, but it's a complicated story," he finally said. "I think we should save it for later. So why don't I gather some wood to stoke the fire? While I'm doing that, you can unroll the sleeping bag that's over there next to the trunk and lie down. You should get some rest."

"What are you hiding from me, Sebastian?"

He closed his eyes against the blunt question and rubbed his fingers against the bridge of his nose. He was getting a headache of his own.

He dropped his hand and opened his eyes. "I'm not hiding anything from you, Sarah. I just don't think you're in any condition to listen to my story right now. As I said, it's complicated. After you've had some rest, we'll reevaluate the situation, okay?"

She tilted her head and regarded him for a long moment. "Can I trust you, Sebastian?"

Involuntarily, Sebastian's gaze slid from her head to her feet, taking in her alluring feminine curves. He knew that wasn't the context of her question, but his body chose to interpret it that way.

Forcing his gaze back to her face, he saw her watching him with a strange, speculative look. Automatically, he let his mind touch hers, startled to discover that she too felt the stirring of desire. That realization caused a sharp tug of lust in his groin.

"Yeah," he stated gruffly, knowing he had to get out of here before he acted on his baser instincts. "You can trust me. I'm going to get some wood."

He left the cave, walking until he was out of sight of the opening. Then he leaned against a nearby pine tree, closed his eyes and drew in several deep breaths, forcing his body to calm.

Why was she suddenly having such a strong physical effect on him? Granted, she was gorgeous, but his response to her was more than plain, old-fashioned sexual chemistry. More importantly, why had she suddenly become sexually aroused? Considering her condition, sex should have been the last thing on her mind.

Was it a residual effect from the fantasy lovemaking they'd shared earlier? Or was it something more ominous? The talisman had taunted him into sexually debasing her. Could it be stimulating their libidos now? But if so, to what purpose? Sarah had no memory. Of course, he knew that didn't negate her connection to the talisman. Memory or no memory, it could—and would—continue to use her.

Suddenly, Sebastian wondered if his spell had caused her amnesia, or if the talisman had used the event to induce it. In a horrible macabre way, it made sense. Sarah called herself a guardian and considered herself a protector. When he'd told her that the talisman had chosen her as its instrument of destruction, she'd fiercely denied it, declaring she'd never harm her people. That meant she had a conscience. For the talisman to use her, it needed to override her ethics and that would take time. But with amnesia, she didn't remember her established moral code, and that explained why the talisman would choose sexual manipulation.

Sebastian knew there were three basic, primitive human emotions: Anger, fear, and sex. Of the three, sex was the most primitive. The genetically encoded need to procreate overrode intellect and could make people perform acts that they'd never commit otherwise. Indeed, lust that wasn't tempered with conscience was a highly dangerous emotional state.

"So if I'm right, the talisman wants Sarah and me to copulate so it can connect with her baser instincts," he said, needing to hear the theory aloud. "Once it has a primeval hold on her, it can prevail over her morals and mold her into whatever monster it wants. To stop that from happening I can't make love to her, but as long as I'm wearing the triangle, I'm susceptible to the talisman's machinations."

Of course, he could be wrong, he told himself. It

was possible that Sarah had a simple case of amnesia. He knew, however, that if there were even the slightest possibility that he was right, he only had one option. He had to take off the triangle and let it return to Sanctuary. Thankfully, his magic had come back, and he could contact Lucien, tell him what was going on, and warn him about the triangle.

He stepped away from the tree and looked up at the sky. The moon's position assured him it was only a couple of hours after midnight, which made it around three in the morning in Sanctuary. Since his race's power was at its zenith during nighttime hours, they were primarily nocturnal. Lucien would still be up.

He sat beneath the tree and cast an invisibility spell over himself for protection. To connect with Lucien over so many miles, he had to use astral projection, and his body would be vulnerable.

Closing his eyes, he breathed deeply and focused inwardly until he reached a trance state. Then he willed his soul-mind to leave his body.

Sebastian wasn't a novice to astral projection, but he'd never become accustomed to the giddy sensation of leaving his body. And giddy was the right description. He always felt dizzy, as though the world spun at a crazy speed, yet it wasn't an uncomfortable sensation. Indeed, it gave him a sense of freedom that he imagined a bird must feel as it soared through the air.

He wasn't aware of moving upward, but suddenly he hovered above the treetops. He glanced down, startled to see his body sitting beneath the tree in suspended animation. As many times as he'd done this, it still unnerved him to see his physical self so lifeless. Was that what death would be like? The soul-mind soaring, while the body remained grounded forever? Would it still startle him to be separated from his body in death?

Although the questions intrigued him, he knew that now was not the time to indulge in them. He had a mission and he needed to take care of it quickly. Sarah waited for him, and her memory might come back at any moment.

He no more than completed the thought than he found himself in Sanctuary. He stared at his surroundings in surprise. He'd willed himself to go directly to Lucien, and he'd expected to find him at home with his mate Ariel and their twins.

Instead, Lucien stood in the crystal cave, where the coven met for the nightly rituals. Kendra Morovang, the coven's youngest narrator, was with him. As Sebastian studied Kendra, he noted that she looked as if she carried some horrible burden.

Sebastian wasn't surprised. The narrators were the coven's historians. They committed to memory everything of significance that had occurred within their race from the beginning of time. He knew that their job was not only onerous, but terribly limiting. They were condemned to live as observers, never actively participating in historical events. Sebastian couldn't imagine anything worse than a life that made you sit idly on the sidelines with no chance of making a personal mark. He also knew it was hardest on the young narrators like Kendra, and it wasn't unusual for Lucien to be counseling—or, more accurately, consoling—her. He hated to interrupt them, but he didn't have a choice.

"Lucien?" he said to make his presence known.

"Sebastian?" Lucien gasped, spinning around, his silver-blue eyes searching for him. "Where are you?"

"Here," Sebastian answered, concentrating on making himself materialize, though he knew he'd appear as incorporeal as a ghost.

"Thank God, you're here," Lucien said, raking a hand through his shoulder-length shaggy, black hair.

Sebastian arched a brow. "Thank *God*? You've been spending too much time with Ariel, Lucien. You know we don't believe in God—or at least not the concept of a single spiritual being."

"All belief is relative, isn't it?" Lucien answered with a wry smile. "Who or what you worship isn't as important as the precepts your religion imposes on you. As long as those precepts are for the betterment of mankind, how can you go wrong?"

"Touché," Sebastian said with a chuckle, needing a taste of Lucien's sense of humor right now. But he knew a taste was all he could afford. He had to get down to business. Sarah waited.

Sobering, he said, "I have something important to tell you. I'm going to be removing the triangle, and when I do, it will return to Sanctuary. I'm here to warn you that under no circumstances should anyone—including yourself—put it on."

"After you hear what Kendra's revealed about Ragna and the triangle, you'll see that goes without saying," Lucien said, his own expression sobering, enhancing the cragginess of his stark features.

As Sebastian switched his attention to Kendra, he felt a shimmer of unease. Lucien hadn't been counseling her, but talking about the talisman. That put a different connotation on her burdensome look.

"What about Ragna and the triangle?" he asked, automatically lowering his voice to a quiet, non-

threatening tone. With her long brown hair, large
brown eyes, and cupid-bow mouth, Kendra was one
of the most beautiful witches Sebastian had ever
met. But she looked so ethereal that he always felt
that if he touched her, his hand would pass right
through her. Everyone in the coven treated Kendra
like fragile porcelain, but Sebastian suspected there
was nothing fragile about her. He couldn't confirm
his suspicions, however, because a narrator's mind
could only be read by another narrator.

"Shana told you everything she found in the journals?" she asked.

"Yes," Sebastian answered.

Kendra nodded. "What the journals don't report is
that Ragna took her own life within a month of
Seamus's banishment."

"What?" Sebastian gasped. "That's impossible!
She had a daughter. Her maternal instincts never
would have allowed her to resort to such a desper-
ate act, unless she feared she'd bring harm to the
child."

"That's exactly what she feared," Kendra replied,
folding her hands in front of her in a lecturing
pose. "Ulrich underestimated the power of the talisman. He thought that once it was broken up and
a piece buried, it would be rendered powerless. But
soon after Ragna put on the triangle, she began to
change."

"Change how?" Sebastian questioned, the shimmer of unease growing stronger.

"She began to subconsciously perform evil spells,"
Kendra answered. "For instance, if someone irritated her, she'd think, 'I hope he breaks a leg,' and
he would. At first she dismissed it as coincidence,
but after several instances of wishing ill and having

it come true, she realized something was wrong. Then her daughter got the croup and cried all the time. When Ragna found herself on the verge of wishing harm on the child, she went to Ulrich and told him what was happening to her.

"Ulrich was upset, but he didn't feel she'd been permanently corrupted," Kendra went on. "She had, after all, only performed small, albeit malicious, spells. He told her to take off the triangle, sure that would solve the problem. But when Ragna tried to take it off, she couldn't."

"Are you saying she was spellbound by the triangle?" Sebastian stated in disbelief.

"Yes. Ulrich tried every spell he could think of, but nothing broke the enchantment. When Ulrich couldn't help her, Ragna killed herself."

"Why wasn't the council told about this? Even if, for some insane reason, Ulrich decided to keep it a secret, the narrators were obligated to report such an ominous incident to the council," Sebastian stated angrily, though he wasn't mad at Kendra. He was furious with himself for not consulting with the narrators before running off to South Dakota.

Then again, they probably wouldn't have told him any of this. They lived under a spell that prohibited them from speaking of anything that might affect the outcome of history in the making. If they violated that code, the spell governing them would instantly destroy them. The talisman's resurrection was definitely a historical event, and telling him about Ragna's fate would have influenced his decision on how to deal with the triangle. Once he put on the object, however, he'd exercised his free will. Divulging Ragna's experiences now wouldn't affect the outcome, because the die was cast.

"Both Ulrich and my ancestors tried to make a report to the council, but the information wouldn't transmit," Kendra replied, shifting uneasily from one foot to the other. "Every narrator in my family since then, including myself, has tried to mentally communicate the story to the council, but no one ever receives it. Grandfather Oran even went to Europe several years ago to tell them in person. By the time he got there, he'd forgotten why he'd gone, and he didn't remember the talisman until he returned. It's as if there's some spell or power inhibiting us from reporting the information."

"That doesn't make sense," Sebastian said, frowning. "If you can't communicate the information to the council of high priests, how can you tell Lucien and me the story?"

She shrugged. "Grandfather Oran thinks . . ."

"Thinks what?" Sebastian prodded, when her voice trailed off. Oran Morovang was the oldest warlock on this continent. He'd soon be celebrating his one hundred and twentieth birthday. Sebastian respected the insight that came with such an advanced age.

"I know it sounds crazy," she said, looking at him with a bemused frown. "He thinks the reason the information can't be transmitted to the council of high priests is because the talisman was created on this continent. Thus, the knowledge of the talisman's true purpose is limited to persons residing here. But Aodán Morpeth had the talisman nearly five hundred years before Christopher Columbus discovered the Americas, so Grandfather Oran has to be wrong."

"Not necessarily," Lucien said. "There is archeological evidence that the Vikings discovered the Americas around the year 1000 A.D."

"You're not suggesting that Aodán was here with the Vikings?" Sebastian asked incredulously.

"That not only fits with Aodán's time period, but his coven was on the Norwegian coast," Lucien replied. "And remember, Aodán disappeared for five years. When he returned with the talisman, he couldn't remember where he'd been. It's possible that he did make the trip with the Vikings."

Sebastian felt dizzy, and it had nothing to do with his astral state. "That's conjecture. Let's focus on what we know for sure. The triangle corrupted Ragna. She tried to take it off and couldn't, so she killed herself. Neither Ulrich nor the narrators could communicate the information to the council of high priests, so Ulrich—at least I assume it was Ulrich—sealed the triangle into a dome and stored it in the repository. What can we honestly speculate from that information?"

"That you are now wearing the triangle, and it has you spellbound," Kendra answered.

Sebastian jerked his head toward her. He knew that what she said was true, but he couldn't bring himself to admit it. Instead he said, "Not necessarily. Ragna was Seamus's mate, and he also wore a triangle. The mating bond is so strong that that's probably what stopped her from removing it. Also, Seamus was permanently corrupted by the talisman. It stands to reason that through the unbreakable emotional bond between them, he'd transfer his evil to her."

"Unless Oran is right and the talisman was created here," Lucien rebutted. "Then the geological energies of this continent would have empowered the talisman, even when it was broken up. It could have been ruling over both Seamus and Ragna through their triangles."

"Again, that's conjecture, and you don't have one shred of evidence to support it," Sebastian argued, refusing to acknowledge the fear erupting in his mind. They were wrong. He *could* take off the triangle, and as soon as he returned to his body, he would do exactly that.

"But we do have evidence to support it," Lucien countered. "Aodán couldn't remember where he'd gotten the talisman. When you combine that fact with our narrators' inability to transmit the information off this continent, it lends credence to the theory it was created here."

"It still doesn't make sense," Sebastian contended. "There are dozens of objects in Sanctuary that were created in Europe. They are no longer within the purview of their source energies, but they not only work, we know everything about them."

"But our race originated in Europe," Kendra interjected. "We spent thousands of years dealing with the energies there, so we knew them intimately. When our ancestors came here with the Pilgrims, they had to learn the idiosyncrasies of this continent's forces."

"Exactly," Lucien said. "Also, for nearly seven hundred years after Aodán showed up with the talisman, no one in the Morpeth family could put on the triangle, because they had an innate fear of it. That type of fear is generally caused by a subconscious recognition of evil forces. When Seamus's father inherited the talisman in Europe, his fear was instilled there. Once the fear was implanted, he wouldn't have gone near the talisman.

"But Seamus's first introduction to the object was in Massachusetts," he continued. "Seamus was afraid of it, but Ragna said he was also beguiled by it, and he put it on despite his fear. That tells me that the talisman's energy was at its peak, or it wouldn't have been able to override his instinctive fears. The only way for it to reach that stage is to be aligned with the continental energies under which it was created."

"That's insane!" Sebastian automatically objected. Unfortunately, he knew Lucien's premise had too much potential to dismiss out of hand.

"We're veering from the point," Kendra said. "It doesn't matter where the talisman originated. It must be stopped."

"You're right, Kendra," Sebastian said. "And I've already spent too much time here. I need to get back."

"Before you go, is there anything else we should know?" Lucien asked.

"I suppose I should give you a brief outline of what's going on. There's a Native American involved. Her name is Sarah, and she has Seamus's triangle. On the surface she appears innocent. I believe, however, that the talisman has chosen her as its instrument of destruction. There's also a man named John Butler, who has the circle and is on his way to South Dakota. I haven't linked with him, but Sarah has. According to her, he's killed at least two people."

"That makes sense," Kendra murmured. "If, as Ulrich suspected, the circle is the talisman's primary force, then death would feed it, giving it more power to reach its goal."

"Maybe we could cast a spell that will stop this Butler," Lucien suggested.

Sebastian shook his head. "The talisman is shielding him, or I would have connected with him. So before we even tried something like that, we'd have to pinpoint his location. If we aren't there to take the circle from him the moment the spell takes hold, it will just latch on to some other unsuspecting person."

"Can't you get Butler's location from the woman?"

"No. She has amnesia."

"Amnesia?" Lucien repeated in disbelief. "How did she get amnesia?"

"It's too long a story to go into now. I need to get back and try to remove the triangle. If I succeed, it will return within the hour. If I can't remove it, I'm bringing Sarah to Sanctuary."

"If the talisman has chosen her as its destructive weapon, bringing her here will put the coven in extreme danger," Kendra pointed out.

"If I don't stop the talisman, all of mankind, including the coven, is doomed," Sebastian rejoined. "And I don't think having her here will be as dangerous as you think. When she mentally connected with me, she waited outside the magic circle surrounding Sanctuary. That suggests the talisman can't penetrate our protective magic, and that gives us an edge. If I bring her here, it will force the talisman to bring John Butler and his circle to us and we may be able to defeat it."

"I hate this, Sebastian," Lucien muttered furiously. "My life is finally getting on an even keel. I have a mate. I have children. I have every reason to believe that because I'm half mortal our race has a chance to survive. Now we may be wiped out because of a damn magical object that's almost a thousand years old, maybe older."

"I know, Lucien, but I have to honestly say I'm not surprised by this. Visit the repository. There are literally hundreds, perhaps thousands, of objects in there that could be potentially catastrophic, and there are three more repositories in Europe."

"The sins of the father," Lucien quoted softly.

"What?" Sebastian said, confused.

"It's a mortal saying," Lucien explained. "It goes something like 'The sins of the father are visited upon the son.' And that's what's happening with us. While practicing the Old Ways, our people made objects that threaten our existence centuries, sometimes millennia, later."

"That's a sobering thought," Kendra said.

"It's also an absolute truth," Sebastian stated grimly. "But I don't have time for philosophical discussions. I have to get back to Sarah. If the triangle isn't here shortly, prepare for the worst."

Before either Lucien or Kendra could respond, Sebastian let his image fade and willed himself back to South Dakota. His return was almost instantaneous, and his soul-mind entered his body with such ease that he was barely aware of the transition.

The moment he opened his eyes, he grabbed the chain around his neck and tried to jerk it over his head. When he couldn't even lift it away from his skin, fear coiled in his belly. The talisman had turned Seamus into a malevolent fiend and caused Ragna Morpeth to kill herself. Now it had its hold on him.

At that moment, Sebastian knew he would never

get out of this mess alive. But before he died, would he end up like Seamus? Or would he find the moral strength to follow in Ragna's footsteps and commit suicide before the talisman turned him into some monstrous killing machine?

9

Evil Enticed

Sarah unrolled the sleeping bag in front of the fire and frowned down at it. Sebastian had told her to rest, but she knew there was no way she could rest when she didn't know her identity. So instead of lying down, she prowled the cave, waiting for his return.

After several minutes passed with no sign of him, she walked to the opening and glanced outside. How long could it take him to pick up a few sticks of wood? She listened for some sound that would tell her his location. All she heard, however, was the scurry of small animals and the hoot of an owl. When she heard a coyote's lonesome howl, she shivered. The howl emphasized her own aloneness, and she wanted to call out to Sebastian.

She squelched the impulse, because she knew he'd probably run back, thinking something was wrong. She'd feel like a fool confessing that she felt lonely, abandoned, even if it were the truth. He'd be back shortly. She just wished he'd hurry.

Deciding that she needed something to occupy her until he returned, she glanced toward the old, battered trunk that sat against the far wall. Did it belong to her? If so, maybe its contents would prod her memory.

She walked to the trunk and opened it, discovering a meager pile of clothes. Kneeling in front of the trunk, she removed a pair of denims and a fringed leather shirt, identical to the one she wore. Laying them aside, she lifted a long-sleeved, leather dress. Like the shirts, it laced up the front. Fringe hung from the sleeves and the hem. The bodice was ornately beaded in symbols that looked familiar, but she couldn't recall their meaning. Withdrawing the dress, she found a pair of knee-high, buckskin moccasins, also elaborately beaded, and two changes of underwear. The remaining items were a stack of red cloth, cut into one-inch squares, a ball of twine, and a large tin of tobacco.

"Prayer ties," Sarah murmured, a memory stirring as she stared at the squares of cloth. She could see herself sitting on the cave floor. As she said a prayer, she placed a small amount of tobacco in the center of a fabric square. Then she folded up the corners to form a pouch and tied it with a section of twine. She repeated the process until she had a long, continuous string of pouches.

The memory ended at that point, but Sarah knew that after completing the prayer ties, she would take them to a sweat lodge. During an Inipi ceremony—an ancient ritual of purification—she would offer the bundles as prayer offerings to the Great Spirits.

"I'm Lakota!" she gasped, elated by the revelation.

You are not Lakota.

Sarah let out a startled yelp and pivoted on her knees to glance around the cave. She didn't know why she searched for a person. The voice came from inside her. Yet she knew that it wasn't a part of her, but someone—some *thing*—that communicated mentally. Was it a spirit?

"Who are you?" she demanded, her tone quavery, as she stood and continued to search the cave. When there was no response, she changed tactics by asking, "If I'm not Lakota, then what am I?"

Retrieve the triangle. It will tell you who you are.

At the declaration, her mind conjured up an image of herself kneeling on the ground in a small meadow. She dug a hole in the dirt with her hands and buried a silver triangle attached to a silver chain. The image was so real she knew she'd performed the act, but she didn't recognize the meadow. How could she find the triangle if she didn't know where to go?

Go outside. I will lead you to the triangle. It is time for you to know all.

Sarah frowned. She'd heard those words before, but this time there was something different about them. Something that made her uneasy, distrustful. She waited for the voice to respond to her doubts. When it didn't she again walked to the cave opening and stared outside. Where was Sebastian? He'd been gone close to a half hour, maybe longer. It couldn't take *that* long to find firewood.

He's abandoned you.

Sarah spun around, again glancing around the cave. This time the voice seemed to come from behind her, but there was still no one there.

"*Dammit!* Answer me. Who *are* you?" she stated, refusing to acknowledge the fear its charge evoked. Sebastian hadn't abandoned her. He'd gone to get wood, and he *was* coming back.

No. He's abandoned you.

Sarah tried to reject the words, but they clung tenaciously. As her fear increased, she turned and looked outside. What if the voice were right? If Sebastian had abandoned her, what would she do? She didn't know who she was. She didn't know *where* she was. Without him, she was lost and alone.

"Sebastian?" Where are you?" she called, deciding that she didn't care if she ended up looking like a fool. She needed to know he was out there, that he was coming back.

He didn't answer, and she felt a knot of panic form in the pit of her stomach. Maybe something had happened to him. Should she look for him? No. When he came back and found her gone, he might leave for good.

He's already left. He's abandoned you.

"Stop it!" she cried, spinning around to again face the cave's interior. "He is coming back! He is!"

Retrieve the triangle, or you'll be alone forever.

Again she tried to reject the words, but they'd struck a painful chord inside her. She wrapped her arms across her chest and rubbed at her upper arms, trying to alleviate a chill that crawled from the inside out. She still didn't know who she was, but she did know that she was alone. Had always been alone.

Abandoned. By everyone.

"Who are you? Why are you tormenting me?" she yelled, more frightened than angry, because she knew deep in her heart that the voice spoke the truth.

Retrieve the triangle, or you'll be alone forever.

"I'm not going to listen to you," she said, clamping her hands over her ears.

Alone. Forever.

As the words reverberated in her mind, she again cried, "Stop it!"

But the voice ruthlessly reiterated. *Alone. Forever.*

With a sob, she raced out of the cave. As she fled into the forest, she paid no attention to where she headed and she didn't care. She had to get away from the voice.

But no matter how fast she ran, its foreboding words stayed with her. Alone. Forever.

Tears filled her eyes. Why did everyone abandon her? Why did they leave her alone?

Retrieve the triangle, and you will never be alone again.

"Yes," she whispered hoarsely, as the image of the meadow again formed in her mind's eye. This time she knew its location, and she veered in that direction. "I'll get the triangle, and I'll never be alone. Never."

Absorbed in the mind-reeling ramifications of what he'd learned about the talisman, Sebastian took several steps into the cave before glancing around the chamber. He saw the sleeping bag unrolled in front of the fire, which had nearly burned down to embers. It still cast enough light, however, for him to see that the trunk had been opened. A small pile of clothes lay on the ground in front of it.

As his gaze roamed the remainder of the cave, he suddenly realized that Sarah was nowhere in sight. He dropped the wood he carried to the floor and glanced around the cave again, refusing to believe she was gone. But she was.

"Sarah? Where are you?" he yelled, spinning around and running to the opening.

She didn't answer, and he tried to connect with

her mind. When nothing happened, he felt a stirring of panic. Was his magic malfunctioning again?

He quickly chanted a short, nonsensical spell and flicked his fingers toward the ground. Spell lightning shot from his fingers and created a tiny whirlwind at his feet. As it dissipated, he frowned. If his magic worked, why couldn't he connect with her?

He knew there were a half dozen possibilities, but his instincts said it was because the talisman shielded her from him. A frisson of alarm raced through him, because he suspected the talisman had led her away from here.

Damn! When he'd left the cave, he should have cast a spell over the opening, trapping her inside. So why hadn't he done that?

Because he'd been so caught up in the sexual chemistry igniting between them that he'd had only one thought on his mind. To get the hell away from her before he lost control and made love to her.

After muttering a violent curse, he cupped his hands around his mouth, bellowing, "Sarah! Answer me! Where are you?"

He started when a voice said behind him, "She cannot hear you, *wicáhmunǧa.*"

Sebastian swung around. The spirit hovered in front of the fire, his outline so faint Sebastian could barely see him. "Where is Sarah?"

"In the forest."

"I know she's in the forest," Sebastian said, exasperated at the spirit's literal interpretation of his question. That was the major problem when dealing with spirits. They took everything literally. "Where, *exactly,* in the forest is she?"

"I do not know."

"What do you mean, you don't know? Aren't you in contact with her?"

"No."

"Why not?"

"Sarah does not remember me, so she refuses to acknowledge me."

"Then how do you know she can't hear me calling her?"

"It is the way."

"The way of what?"

"If you are meant to know all, you will understand," the spirit said, disappearing.

Sebastian considered summoning him back. He knew, however, that even if he could conjure him up, the spirit wouldn't—probably couldn't—say any more than he already had. His words implied that destiny was at work here. Even if a spirit wanted to, he couldn't reveal a human being's destiny.

"But whose destiny are we talking about?" Sebastian mumbled as he stepped outside and studied the woods, looking for some sign of Sarah. "Mine? Sarah's? Butler's? Or are all three of our fates tied together in some magical continuum?"

He knew that only time would give him the answer, so he couldn't waste it pondering the problem. He had to concentrate on finding Sarah. It was critical that he get her to Sanctuary before Butler arrived. But if he couldn't connect with her mind, how was he going to find her?

As he considered his options, he raked a hand through his hair. He couldn't cast a spell because it would physically affect her. A minor spell had almost killed her; a major one like he'd have to use to find her might destroy her instantly. He could, he supposed, go looking for her, but he didn't know in

which direction she'd headed, or even how long
she'd been gone. He could wander for days and
never find her.

"So that leaves me with only one choice," he said,
with a fatalistic sigh. "Try to find her in the same
way I initially found her. Touch the triangle."

Even as he made the statement, he knew that by
touching the triangle, he flirted with danger. The
more he touched it, the more control the talisman
would have over him. And the more control it had,
the quicker it would corrupt him, make him as irrevocably evil as Seamus Morpeth.

"I am *not* like Seamus. I've encountered evil
before, and I've not only endured those confronta-
tions, I've been made stronger because of them.
That's why I'm the troubleshooter—the most powerful warlock alive," he declared, needing to hear
the encouraging words aloud.

Unfortunately, they didn't assuage his fears, but
they did put the situation into perspective. He
was the troubleshooter, and this was his job. He
raised his hand to the triangle.

The moment he touched it, he heard a soft whirring sound overhead. He looked up, and his jaw
dropped in shock. Spinning above him was a wreath
of lightning, just as Sarah had described to him
earlier. Why hadn't he seen it before? Why was it
choosing to reveal itself now?

Because he'd consciously chosen to use the triangle to find Sarah. By doing so, he'd acknowledged
the talisman's existence and its power. He had, in
effect, given it permission to lay claim to his soul.

When a lightning bolt broke free from the wreath
and flew toward him, he shuddered in terror and
tried to pull his fingers away from the triangle. Be-

fore he could, the lightning struck the back of his hand. His body convulsed from the electrical jolt, and he screamed in agony as he fell to his knees.

But, oddly enough, as excruciating pain inundated him, he also felt tremendous physical energy surging through him. He'd never felt so alive, so vigorous.

When the lightning finally released him, he felt as if everything masculine in him was magnified, strengthened. The sensation was so intense, so potent, that he didn't even care that his vision was blurred.

As he closed his eyes and basked in the glory of male puissance, he acknowledged that he'd been wrong about the talisman. It wasn't out to destroy mankind but to purify it. It had chosen him and Sarah to create a new race—a pure and extraordinary magical race—that would cleanse the earth of the weak masses. Through the talisman, they would restore the world to its natural order.

He smiled and stroked the triangle. His eyesight would clear momentarily, and then the triangle would lead him to Sarah. Once he found her, he'd do what he should have done the moment he met her. Stake his carnal claim upon her.

When Sarah reached the moonlit meadow, she raced to the spot where she'd buried the triangle. Dropping to her knees, she clawed at the dirt with her fingers. She knew that if she didn't dig up the triangle quickly the voice would abandon her, and she'd be alone forever.

When she finally uncovered a piece of chain, she grabbed it and jerked it out of the ground. Holding it up, she stared at the silver triangle dangling in front of her.

She gasped, startled, when the object suddenly glowed, emitting a white-hot light. When she heard a strange whirring sound overhead, she glanced up and her jaw dropped in shock. Above her circled a wreath of lightning bolts.

Put on the triangle, the voice suddenly commanded.

"No," she whispered, terrified. The wreath circled faster, and she knew instinctively that lightning would erupt from it and touch the triangle. When it did, she would writhe in excruciating pain.

As panic surged through her, she tried to throw the triangle to the ground, but its chain adhered to her skin like metal to a magnet. With a moan, she grabbed the chain with her other hand and yanked, but it continued to cling to her flesh.

Put on the triangle or be alone forever.

As the voice issued the portent, a lightning bolt broke free of the wreath and struck the triangle. Electricity zipped up the chain. As it arced through her body, Sarah screamed in agony.

The pain disappeared a moment later, and Sarah gazed around her surroundings in bewilderment. She no longer knelt in the meadow, but stood in a shabby motel room. A full-size bed nearly filled the small space, and a threadbare, red chenille bedspread covered a mattress that dipped deeply in the center. A badly scarred pine nightstand was crammed into the corner below a minuscule window, whose red curtains were as shabby as the bedspread. A shadeless wall lamp was bolted to the wall above the nightstand. However, its bare bulb only provided a dim circle of light that didn't stretch the length of the bed. Except for a coin-operated television set chained to a shelf on the wall, there were no other furnishings.

Where is this place? Why am I here? she wondered, confused.

"Ah, Sarah, I see you've finally arrived," a man drawled.

Sarah jerked her head toward the sound of his voice. He stood in the darkened bathroom doorway across the room. The bare bulb beside the bed didn't put out enough illumination for her to see his face.

When he swaggered toward the bed, Sarah noted he was short for a man. He was also shirtless, revealing a wiry physique that, when clothed, would look deceptively scrawny.

"Deceptively scrawny is right," he said, suddenly flexing a muscular biceps.

Sarah stared at him in shock. My God, he'd read her mind!

"Of course I read your mind," he stated impatiently as he reached the bed and threw himself down on the mattress. Placing his hands behind his head, he stared up at her impassively. "That's part of our power, Sarah. Or at least it was until *he* inhibited you and made us weak. But I'm going to tell you how to get your power back, and then we'll be stronger than ever."

As Sarah listened to him, she studied his face. His hair was short and dark, but it was wild, unkempt. Obviously, he hadn't shaved in a couple of days, giving him the scruffy look of a bum. But the image of a bum was not reflected in his eyes. They were a clear and cunning ice blue, and she could see his malevolence in their frigid depths. She knew intuitively that he lacked a soul, so why did he enthrall her? What *drew* her to him? And "drawn to him" was the only way she could describe the feelings moving through her.

"You are drawn to me because we are the inheritors of the power," he said, suddenly sitting upright and lifting his hand toward a circle hanging from a chain around his neck.

As he caressed the circle, Sarah frowned. She knew she'd seen the object before, but no matter how hard she tried, she couldn't bring the memory into focus.

"You can't remember because *he* inhibited your power," the man reiterated bitterly.

"Who inhibited my power?" she asked, returning her attention to his face.

"Sebastian Moran."

"Sebastian abandoned me," she said, anger stirring inside her. He'd told her he'd be back, but he'd lied. He'd left her alone in the cave, not knowing who she was or where she was.

"No, he wants you to *think* he's abandoned you," the man corrected, interrupting her thoughts. "Then, when he returns, you'll be so happy to see him you'll give him anything he wants. And he wants your triangle.

"But you can't give it to him," the man stated urgently. "Moran's a demon who wants to steal our power. Once he has it, he will kill us."

"A demon?" she repeated dubiously. She wasn't sure if she doubted the existence of demons, or the concept of Sebastian being one. Both concepts seemed preposterous.

"Believe me, Moran really is a demon, Sarah. He suppressed your power and took away your memory because you were too powerful for him to fight. That's why you must put on the triangle. It will restore our power, and we can defeat him."

"I can't put on the triangle," Sarah whispered fearfully. "It draws the lightning, and—"

"The lightning is a part of our power, Sarah. It hurts us because you fight it. Embrace it and it will make us all-powerful.

"Now you must return," he said, his voice again urgent. "Moran is near the meadow, and you must put on the triangle before he can take it away from you. Trust in it, and it will protect you from him until I arrive. Then you'll no longer be alone."

As the room disappeared and Sarah found herself again kneeling in the meadow, the man's words repeated in her mind. *You'll no longer be alone.*

She knew his statement should reassure her, but for some odd reason it frightened her. Before she could analyze her fear, she heard a noise behind her. Knowing it was Sebastian, she leaped to her feet and spun around to face him.

When her gaze landed on him she tried to scream, but it came out as a terrified whimper. He stood in shadow at the edge of the meadow and his eyes glowed so brightly they looked like two brilliant, pulsing moons hovering in the air. At that moment, she knew the man in the motel room had told her the truth. Sebastian Moran was a demon.

With another whimper, she turned and sprinted toward the trees. She had to get away from him before he killed her. She'd run no more than a few feet when she heard Sebastian shout some indistinct words. An instant later, she saw a small flash of lightning fly past her and hit the ground. It immediately burst into a tower of flames that quickly swept the length of the meadow, cutting off her escape route.

She veered to the right, but the flames leaped down that side of the meadow. She then turned to the left, but the same thing happened. With a cry born as much from frustration as fear, she slid to a stop and pivoted to face Sebastian. He stood where he'd been when she'd first run, his arms crossed over his chest. As impossible as it seemed, his eyes glowed more brilliantly than ever, pulsing in the same eerie rhythm of a strobe light.

"You cannot escape me, Sarah," he said, raising his hand and flicking his wrist. The fire instantly spread across the area behind him, enclosing them inside the inferno.

Sarah frantically searched the flaming perimeter for some weak spot that would allow her to break out. It was as if the fire read her mind, because it grew denser and flared higher whatever direction she turned. Casting a glance back at Sebastian, she wondered if it would be better to plunge into the fire and burn to death than to stay here and die at his hands.

You don't have to die, Sarah. Put on the triangle. It will protect you, the man from the motel murmured in her mind.

As he spoke, she looked down at her clenched fist. She didn't remember gathering the triangle and its chain into it, but she could feel the triangle's sharp edges cutting into her palm. If the man was right, all she had to do was put it on and she'd be safe. So why did she feel hesitant about donning the object?

Put it on, Sarah. Hurry!

At the man's urgent prodding, Sarah glanced up.

Sebastian walked toward her, his long stride eating up the distance between them. Within moments, he'd reach her, and then he'd kill her.

He'll kill us, Sarah, because if you die, I'll die too. You can't let that happen. You are the guardian, and you've sworn to protect your people. I am one of your people, and you must protect me.

Guardian. As the word echoed in Sarah's mind, she saw an image of herself standing in this very meadow. It was spring, and the air was filled with the scent of wildflowers. An elderly, stooped man held the triangle out to her. His voice had the hoarse rasp of old age as he declared, "You are now the guardian, Sarah. Protect the triangle, and through it, your people, from the curse of the evil *wicáhmunġa.*"

"I remember!" she whispered in awe, as the vision faded. "Sebastian is the evil *wicáhmunġa*, and he wants to destroy my people."

Yes! Now put on the triangle and protect us!

Sarah uncurled her fist, grabbed the triangle's chain and opened it into a circle. Hastily, she dropped it over her head.

As the chain settled around her neck, she heard the whirring sound overhead. She looked up, shivering as she spotted the lightning wreath, but she quickly thrust aside her fear. The man in the motel had told her to embrace the lightning and it would not harm her. His advice had been echoed by the old man, who'd given her the triangle and told her to protect it, and through it, her people.

Still looking at the wreath, she raised her arms toward it, palms turned upward, and said, "Come to me."

Three lightning bolts broke free of the wreath and

arced toward her. As one bolt struck the triangle and the other two her upraised palms, thunder exploded with such intensity that Sarah felt the ground shake beneath her feet. Then everything faded to black.

10

Evil Transformed

Sebastian was halfway to Sarah when she suddenly lifted her arms toward the lightning wreath and said, "Come to me." At her summons, three lightning bolts broke free and shot toward her. As they struck her, an earth-shaking clap of thunder nearly knocked him off his feet.

As he fought to maintain his balance, he gaped at the scene taking place in front of him. The wreath descended over Sarah, elongating itself until it encompassed her in a whirling, electrified cocoon. He gave a dazed shake of his head. What in hell was the wreath doing to her?

When the ground stopped shaking, he eyed the cocoon warily, trying to see Sarah, but it whirled too fast.

Come to me, Sebastian.

Sebastian started. It was Sarah's voice murmuring in his mind, but it was different—huskier, more sensual. So sensual, in fact, that it reignited his lust with such intensity that his groin ached with need. If she wasn't enshrouded by the wreath, he knew he'd rush into her arms to assuage his passion. But she was in there, and he wasn't going near her until he figured out what was going on.

Come to me, Sebastian. You know you want me.

He gave an adamant shake of his head, though not denying her claim. She was right. He did want her—was meant to have her. They were the chosen, and their child would liberate his race. Witches and warlocks would no longer be forced to live in hiding. They would again live openly, as they had before the Romans marched into their world and started the first wave of witch hysteria that escalated through the Inquisition and threatened their survival to this very day. So why did he suddenly feel as if mating with Sarah were wrong?

He tried to analyze his doubts, but his mind kept short-circuiting, scattering his thoughts.

Now is not the time to think, Sebastian. It is the time to feel. So come to me. Touch me. Kiss me. Lose yourself inside me. It's what you want. What I want.

As Sarah's seductive words crooned in his mind like a siren's lure, two lightning bolts broke free from the bottom of the wreath. Sebastian shuddered as they slithered along the ground toward him. Their sinuous movement reminded him of Sarah's rattlesnakes, and he intuited that the lightning bolts were just as deadly to him as the vipers.

He chanted a spell to protect himself from them, but when he finished the incantation and flicked his wrist to activate the spell, nothing happened. His heart skipped a terrified beat. His magic was gone again!

Run! his survival instincts yelled, but he could only stare at the bolts in fatalistic mesmerism.

When they reached him and coiled around his ankles, he closed his eyes and gritted his teeth, preparing for the pain he knew would come from their touch, the torturous death that was sure to follow.

Instead of pain, however, he felt one foot tugged forward, and then the other.

As the bolts pulled him another two steps ahead, he opened his eyes and looked down at them in disbelief. They didn't want to harm him. They were taking him to Sarah!

As he tried to kick his feet free, two more lightning bolts broke away from the wreath. These streaked through the air, wrapping themselves around his wrists and pulling him forward. He attempted to jerk his hands from their hold, but they were as secure as manacles.

"Tell them to let me go," he stated, anger surging through him as he glared at whatever monstrosity Sarah had become. He welcomed his rage, encouraged it, because without it, he knew fear would overwhelm him. He'd never encountered anything like this, and with his magic malfunctioning, he couldn't fight it.

You don't want the lightning to let you go, Sebastian. You want to come to me. You want to be with me. I can feel the lust pulsing inside you, making you hard and eager for me.

"I'm aroused," he ground out between clenched teeth, still struggling against the lightning bolts, which dragged him inexorably closer to her. "But I want to make love to a woman, not an . . . obscenity."

But I cannot become a woman until you transform me. Come to me, Sebastian. Change me into a woman so that I can evolve fully into my powers.

Sebastian stared at the cocoon in uneasy bemusement. What did she mean she wasn't a woman? Did she no longer exist on a physical plane? Had the wreath absorbed her, turned her into electrified en-

ergy? If he did her bidding would that also happen
to him?

He realized that his questions would be answered
soon, because the lightning bolts had hauled him to
within a few feet of her. Again, he tried to see Sarah
through the wreath, but it still moved too swiftly.

Change me into a woman, Sebastian, Sarah's siren-
voice coaxed, as more lightning shot from the cocoon. It wrapped around his body and drew him
toward the whirling mass.

Sarah! his mind screamed in agony when his body
came into contact with the wreath. He'd suffered
pain from its lightning touch, but it was nothing
compared to the torment he now endured. He felt
as if he were being slowly roasted alive and stabbed
with a thousand needles at the same time. But as it
dragged him into its center, his pain disappeared
and instantly changed to lust. The passion grew inside him until he felt nothing else, thought of nothing else. He had to make love to Sarah, but where
was she?

I'm here, Sebastian. Open your eyes.

He didn't realize he'd closed his eyes until she issued the command. Slowly, he opened them. At
first, everything was out of focus, but after blinking
a few times, he saw his surroundings. He sucked in
an awed breath. Why had he been afraid to come in
here?

Lightning swirled around him, reflecting glittering light. He imagined that this was what it would
be like to stand inside a diamond. The space around
him wasn't large; he could stretch out his arms and
touch the sides of the wreath. He sensed, however,
that if he wanted it larger, all he had to do was wish
for it to expand and it would accommodate him.

As he watched the spectacular light show, he became aware of the hushed silence. All he could hear was the sound of his own breathing, or rather, his and Sarah's. But where was she?

"I'm here," she said behind him.

Before he could turn, she slid her arms around his waist and molded her soft body to his back and buttocks. As her warm flesh brushed against his, he jumped, startled to realize they were naked. What happened to his clothes?

"Do you always worry about such mundane things in the throes of passion?" Sarah murmured, pressing a kiss to his shoulder blade.

He opened his mouth to respond, but groaned instead as she trailed her fingertips down the narrow line of hair running from his navel to his groin. When she stopped to toy with the tight curls cloaking his penis, his entire body tensed in anticipation of her more intimate touch.

"Do you really want me to touch you, Sebastian?" she teased in a sultry voice that sent shivers of excitement racing up and down his spine.

But despite his excitement Sebastian's temper stirred at her question. He didn't know why he was angry, but when she slid her hand toward his jutting erection, he caught her wrist before she could cup him.

Maintaining his hold on her, he swung around to face her. As his gaze landed on her, he felt as if he'd been kicked in the gut. Her extraordinarily long black hair was no longer braided, but hung down her back in a rippling, silken fall that reached the backs of her knees. His gaze flicked down her, taking in her high, firm breasts, narrow waist and flaring hips. When he finally reached her shapely legs and the dark thatch of hair veiling her femininity, his penis quivered, urging him to throw her to the ground and ravish her.

"So do it, Sebastian," Sarah murmured, stepping up to him so that her pebbled nipples brushed enticingly against his chest. She stared up at him, her eerie golden eyes glowing with hot enticement. Then she parted her lips and slid her tongue invitingly across her lower lip. "Throw me to the ground and take me as hard and as fast as you can."

Sebastian frowned at her words, but he couldn't figure out why they disturbed him. He wanted to do exactly what she suggested—throw her to the ground and take her ruthlessly, selfishly—and she'd just made it clear she wanted him to do so. So why did he feel so reluctant to touch her?

Because she wasn't asking him to make love to her. She was encouraging him to rape her, he realized with a jolt.

Suddenly, he recalled what she'd said when he'd stood outside her cocoon. *I cannot become a woman until you transform me. Change me into a woman so that I can evolve fully into my powers.*

At the time she'd made the statements, he'd thought the wreath had absorbed her. Now he understood that her meaning was literal. Sarah was a virgin, and for the talisman to bestow her with its powers, she had to lose her virginity—be transformed into a woman. But the talisman thrived on violence, so it wouldn't be satisfied with Sebastian making love to her. He had to take her brutally, because only through pain could the talisman lay claim to her soul.

Thrusting Sarah's hand away and spinning around to face the talisman's whirling lightning wreath, he yelled, "Everything you told me was a lie, wasn't it? You played upon my fears for the extinction of my race. Sarah and I aren't the chosen, and our mating won't result in a special, magical race that will free the covens. You lied to trick me into deflowering your chosen consort, so she could inherit your power. Well, I'm not going to do it. Do you hear me? *I won't corrupt her for you!*"

"Sebastian, what is wrong with you?" Sarah cried.

He pivoted toward her, scowling. "Dammit! You can read my mind, so you know exactly what's wrong with me."

"That's crazy. People can't read each other's minds," she said, her expression so bewildered that Sebastian knew it wasn't an act.

He frowned, confused. Obviously, the talisman inhibited her mental abilities, but why? As he stared at her, the answer came to him. The talisman knew that because of the procreation problems within his race, one of the most primal emotions a warlock possessed was protectiveness toward females. Right now, Sarah looked tiny, fragile, in need of protection. He wanted to rush to her, pull her into his arms and shelter her from harm. And the talisman counted on him to do just that.

Sebastian took a step back. He couldn't go to Sarah, no matter how vulnerable she appeared. His attraction to her was too strong. If he touched her, he'd succumb to his desire, and the talisman would win.

"I want you to listen to me, Sarah," he said, "and I want you to listen very carefully. The triangle you wear matches the one I wear. Both are pieces of an evil talisman that wants to destroy mankind, and the talisman has chosen you as its instrument of destruction. But before it can fully bestow you with its powers, you must lose your virginity. Once that happens, you'll be evil, Sarah. Horribly and irrevocably evil. The only way to stop that from happening is for you to remain pure."

"Sebastian, if you don't find me desirable, then just say so," she said, her expression wounded. "You don't have to make up bizarre stories."

"The problem is I do find you desirable, and I'm not making up bizarre stories," he said impatiently. "The reason you don't believe me is because the talisman has taken away your memory. It did that so it can latch onto your baser instincts and erode your moral code."

When she eyed him skeptically, he raked a hand through his hair. "Look, Sarah, from what you've told me, you spent your life training to protect your people from the talisman's evil. Unfortunately, you were in constant contact with your triangle. I've recently learned that the triangles themselves are capable of corrupting their possessors. And the more contact you have with them, the more at risk you are.

"You've gone beyond the risk stage, Sarah. You're on the brink of losing your soul, but I can help you. Send the lightning wreath away and come with me to Sanctuary—a town in Pennsylvania where my people live," he added when she looked confused. "We're a magical race, and if anyone can save you from the talisman, we can. So, listen to me—*trust* me. *Let me save you.*"

If she'd looked bewildered before, she now looked positively befuddled. When she crossed her arms and rubbed at her upper arms as though cold, Sebastian knew she suffered an emotional chill. The temperature inside the wreath was uncomfortably hot. Why hadn't he noticed the unrelenting heat before?

Because he'd been so aroused, he'd been a hundred times hotter on the inside. Even now, as he waited for her to respond, he could feel his internal temperature rising, and, to his chagrin, his penis stirred. He might be determined to keep his hands off Sarah, but she was so damn beautiful that he couldn't stop wanting her. He feared that if she didn't make a decision soon, he'd lose control and take her, regardless of the consequences.

Suddenly she frowned at him, while shifting from one foot to the other. Sebastian, sensing she wanted to believe his story, said, "Sarah, please. Everything I've said is the truth. Send the wreath away before it's too late."

She still looked indecisive, but then she whispered, "I don't know how to send it away."

"You summoned it, so you have to be able to dismiss it," he stated encouragingly.

"I . . . don't remember . . . summoning it," she stammered, looking at the lightning spinning around them.

Sebastian also looked at it, frowning worriedly. Was it his imagination, or was the wreath starting to close in on them? If it was, it would force them together. Once they came into physical contact . . .

He cut off the disturbing thought and said, "When you summoned it, you said, 'Come to me,' and it came. Try saying, 'Leave me.'"

She arched a brow dubiously. "That sounds so . . . simple."

"Magic usually is simple, and that's what we're

dealing with here. Magic. Just say the words and see what happens."

She clasped her hands in front of her and hesitantly said, "Leave me."

"Say it with meaning," Sebastian ordered, when, instead of lifting, the wreath definitely moved in closer to them, confirming his fears. "It has to *believe* you want it to go away."

"If you aren't happy with the way I'm talking, then why don't you send it away?" she retorted.

"Because I didn't summon it; you did," he shot back angrily, though he knew his temper was only a defense mechanism to hold his fear at bay. "Now, get rid of it!"

She glared at him, and for a moment he thought she'd defy him. But then she stated forcefully, "Leave me!"

Sebastian clenched his hands at his sides and stared at the gyrating walls, willing the wreath to lift. They *had* to get out of here. If they didn't . . .

Sarah suddenly let out a pained yelp. Sebastian jerked his head toward her. The wall nearest her bumped against her, and he could see small flares of lightning striking her, prodding her in his direction.

He opened his mouth to yell at her to stay where she was, that it was too dangerous for her to come near him. But when he started to utter the words, he cut them off, recognizing the futility of his warning. The talisman would not release them until Sebastian took her virginity. There was no way he could stand by and watch it torture her when he knew that, in the end, he'd be forced to succumb.

As the lightning continued to abuse her, Sarah turned toward him, her eyes wide and frightened as she whimpered, "Sebastian?"

"Come here, Sarah," he said, opening his arms and accepting the inevitable.

With a sob, she rushed to him. As she threw herself into his embrace, he closed his eyes with a defeated shake of his head. Already, the lust was consuming him. Within minutes, maybe even seconds, he would be responsible for the loss of Sarah's soul.

Sarah clung to Sebastian, her mind muddled. She knew he'd just explained something to her—something important—but she couldn't remember what. Indeed, she couldn't remember anything beyond their names, and she supposed that should frighten her. But with Sebastian's strong arms linked around her, she didn't feel afraid but . . . She frowned, unable to identify the strange restlessness stirring inside her.

"Sarah, look at me," Sebastian said gruffly.

She glanced up at him and shivered, but it wasn't fear that made her tremble. It was the restlessness inside, which grew more intense as she looked at him. His expression was taut, almost angry, and his eyes glowed with an unearthly light. He reminded her of a ferocious predator, and she was his intended prey. Again, she knew she should be frightened, but heaven help her, she *wanted* to be his prey.

"I'm sorry, but I can't help myself," he said, his voice a guttural rasp as he cupped her face in his hands and his lips swooped down to hers.

His kiss was bruising, as though he had some overwhelming need to punish her, and she welcomed his castigation. It fed the restlessness, which made her feel hot and quivery and ravenous, though

she couldn't name her hunger. When Sebastian slid
a hand beneath her hair, cupped her buttock and
pulled her tightly against his erection, her restlessness exploded into a conflagration. At that moment,
she knew the source of her hunger and her heat.
Pure, unadulterated lust.

With a moan, she twined her arms around
Sebastian's neck and returned his punishing kiss
with one of her own. As their mouths battled, she
ground her pelvis against his. He groaned and
caught her hips in both hands, lifting her so that
she was forced to wrap her legs around his hips.

As she did, her womanhood opened to him, and
she gasped, "Take me, Sebastian. Take me *now*."

At her command, the whirling walls closed in,
clinging to them like blankets. Then the walls tilted,
moving their bodies into a reclining position and
cradling them in the air.

She gazed up at Sebastian, who was positioned
between her thighs. When the tip of his erection
probed against her, she raked her hands down his
back and arched up to him, eager to complete their
union. She felt his hips flex, and she closed her eyes
in anticipation. He was going to take her—
transform her into a woman—and then she'd be . . .

Her eyes flew open in confusion when, instead of
entering her, Sebastian jerked away from her. He
knelt above her, and the wreath's walls pelted him
with small bolts of lightning as he struggled to
stand.

She knew the bolts attempted to force him back
into her arms, and his grimace assured her he suffered acutely from their assault. So why didn't he
come back to her to escape the pain? Why had he
left her in the first place? She knew he wanted

her as badly as she wanted him. It didn't make sense.

She raised her arms encouragingly toward him. "Please, Sebastian. Come to me. Take me."

"No," he said with an adamant shake of his head. "I will *not* take you like a damn rutting animal."

She frowned. "You don't have a choice. You *have* to take me. It's the only way we'll be released."

"No."

"Why are you being so stubborn?" she asked, bewildered. "I know you want me, Sebastian, and I want you so badly that I'm burning up inside. So please. Come to me and put out the fire."

He shook his head again. "You're burning for sex, not me."

"It's the same thing!"

"No it's not, and I'm going to prove that to you."

He leaned forward and sealed his mouth over hers. But instead of the punishing kiss she expected, his lips moved over hers lightly, tenderly. A shimmer of fear raced through her. What was he doing? Why wasn't he just taking her?

"Sebas—"

He took advantage of her parted lips to slip his tongue into her mouth. As he indulged himself in a ravishing exploration that sent tingles of excitement racing through her, he cupped her breasts in his hands, kneading them lightly.

When he brushed his thumbs over her nipples, making them hard and taut, she felt a strange yearning ache low in her abdomen. The ache wasn't as hot or as needful as the fire that raged inside her. Oddly enough, however, it was stronger, more potent, causing another shimmer of fear to sweep through her. She tried to pull away from his kiss, but he caught her face in his hands and held her captive.

Fight him! a voice screamed in her mind. *This is not the way it's supposed to be!*

She immediately placed her hands on Sebastian's shoulders and gave him a frantic push. He didn't budge. Panicked, she gave him another push. This time, he broke away from the kiss and lifted his head, looking down at her.

Sarah shuddered as she stared at his face. His eyes again glowed with that unearthly light, and he'd again assumed the look of a predator. This time she didn't find the thought of being his prey appealing. Indeed, it terrified her.

"Why do you want to torture me?" she whispered.

"I don't want to torture you," he said, caressing her cheek. "I want you to want more than a mindless coupling to satisfy your lust."

"But there isn't *supposed* to be more than that," she said plaintively.

"And that's exactly why there has to be more."

"I don't understand what you're talking about, Sebastian."

"You will."

She started to respond, but he cut off her words by settling his lips over hers. As his tongue danced with hers in a slow, seductive dance that made the yearning ache return to her abdomen, she clutched at his shoulders and moved agitatedly beneath him.

"That's it, Sarah," he murmured, pulling away from the kiss and rotating his pelvis against hers. "Feel."

"I don't want to feel!" she cried hoarsely. "I just want this to be over."

"But I've only just begun."

She gasped when he suddenly lowered his head to her breast and laved his tongue across her nipple. Then he drew it into his mouth, and she could only cling to him while shock waves of pleasure coursed through her.

Fight him! the voice screamed again. *This is not the way it's supposed to be! He will steal a piece of your soul!*

She wanted to heed the voice, but Sebastian moved to her other breast. As he licked and sucked it, he lightly pinched the nipple he'd just released.

"Sebastian, please!" she cried as the yearning ache grew to unbearable proportions. "Take me!"

"Soon," he said, trailing his lips from her breasts down to her navel. He paused and circled his tongue around it, and then he headed unerringly south.

"No!" Sarah gasped, trying to wriggle away from him when she realized his intentions.

"Yes," he muttered huskily, catching her hips in a firm hold. Then he treated her to the most intimate of kisses. As he teased her clitoris with his lips and his tongue, the yearning ache coiled inside her womb until it felt like a bomb ready to detonate.

"Sebastian! Please!" she cried as she burrowed her fingers into his hair and clutched it.

"Let yourself go," he urged, replacing his mouth with the heel of his hand and massaging her. "Feel the pleasure, Sarah."

"I can't," she whimpered, shaking her head from side to side. "This isn't the way it's supposed to be."

"This is exactly the way it's supposed to be," he countered, increasing the pressure of his hand. "Lovemaking is pleasurable, not painful. So let yourself enjoy the pleasure, Sarah."

"I can't. I can't. I can't!" she chanted frantically, even as she rocked against his palm involuntarily.

"You can, Sarah," he murmured. "You can."

As he spoke, he reached up with his other hand and lightly tweaked her nipple. It was as if he'd lit a fuse, because pleasure arced from her breast to her womb and the bomb exploded.

"Sebastian!" she sobbed as her world spun out of control.

"I'm here," he said, coming over her and enfolding her in his arms. "I'm here, and I'm sorry, Sarah, but I can't hold back any longer. At least I was able to open your eyes to the pleasure before I had to cause you pain."

Before Sarah could assimilate his words, she felt the tip of his penis slide between the folds of her womanhood and probe at the entrance to her womb. Then he flexed his hips and entered her.

Sarah cried out at the sharp, tearing pain, and the voice cried triumphantly, *This is the way it's supposed to be! Hold onto the pain. Don't let him steal a piece of your soul!*

But as the voice issued its advice, Sebastian stopped moving.

"What are you doing?" she demanded, anger stirring inside her as she glared up at him. "Take me!"

"Not without pleasure," he stated softly, slipping his hand between them and tenderly stroking her clitoris. "Never without pleasure, Sarah."

"But I don't want pleasure," she whispered breathlessly, trying to ignore the yearning ache that again coiled inside her.

"Of course you want pleasure, and I want to pleasure you," he said, continuing his provocative caress.

Sarah closed her eyes tightly and fought against his seduction, but her body refused to ignore the beguiling torment of his fingers.

"Sebastian!" she cried out again when the yearning ache reached explosive proportions.

"I'm here, Sarah," he murmured, dropping a kiss to her lips as he began to move against her in a slow, steady rhythm. "We're going to reach the peak together. Come on, Sarah. Give yourself to me, and let me give myself to you," he rasped, increasing his rhythm. "Come with me, Sarah. Do it *now.*"

"No!" Sarah gasped, because she knew that the raging storm inside her—the spiritual agony that wasn't really agony but devastating pleasure—would destroy her if she gave in to it.

But Sebastian made one final thrust, and her world again exploded and whirled out of control. A moment later, she felt Sebastian shudder his release.

As she lay there, waiting for the world to right itself, Sebastian gathered her into his arms and rolled so that he lay beneath her. When he began to stroke her back soothingly, she heaved an exhausted sigh, decided to worry about what had happened later, and let her body mold bonelessly to his.

She wasn't sure how much time passed when he murmured, "That's how lovemaking is supposed to be, Sarah. A beautiful, magical blending of bodies and an exchange of souls."

At his words, her mind flashed back to the voice that intruded during their lovemaking. *Don't let him steal a piece of your soul.*

But you didn't listen, the voice now said, its tone filled with doom. *You surrendered your soul to him and let him open your eyes to pleasure. Now, it is time for you to remember who you are and see what you have done by giving in to him.*

As the voice faded, a vision flooded into Sarah's mind. She stood on a mountaintop, surrounded by the dead bodies of the people she knew and loved— the people she had vowed to guard with her life— and every one of them, down to the tiniest infant, had had their eyes gouged out.

Noooo! she screamed in mental anguish, trying to shut out the image, but it remained entrenched in her mind.

Yes, the voice countered. *By giving yourself to him, you have granted him the power to do this. You are the guardian, Sarah, and you were supposed to protect your people from the evil* wicáhmunġa. *Instead you let him manipulate you into sacrificing them for a few moments of sexual satisfaction.*

But it's not too late to stop him. You are now a woman, and you've evolved fully into your powers. Use that power and kill the wicáhmunġa *before he can carry out this atrocious act.*

As Sarah's gaze traveled over the mutilated faces of her people, rage exploded inside her. The voice was right. She was now a woman who had evolved fully into her powers. She also knew the perfect weapon to destroy the *wicáhmunġa,* and she would make sure he suffered as agonizing a death as he planned for her people. She reached for her triangle.

11

Evil Fled

As Sebastian stroked Sarah's silken back, he decided he'd never felt so exhausted. It had taken all his physical and mental strength to make love to her rather than succumb to the mindless lust the talisman had instilled in him. He'd thought that by fighting the lust he'd thwart the talisman's plans and break its hold over them. He was wrong.

As the lightning wreath continued to whirl around them, he closed his eyes in angry defeat, shutting out the frustrating sight. *Dammit!* The talisman must have another scheme in mind. He just prayed he'd have enough time to gather his wits before it sprang it on them.

He no more than completed the thought when Sarah suddenly wrenched herself out of his arms. His eyes flew open, and he saw her climb to her feet beside him. As his gaze swept up her body, his heart skipped a fearful beat. She cradled her triangle in her right hand, and it emitted the same white-hot light his triangle had given off in the repository.

Cautiously, he sat up and raised his gaze to her face. His jaw dropped in shock. Her features had taken on a subtle sharpness that made her look cruel, inhuman. The image was fostered by her golden eyes, which glittered with malevolent hatred.

His lovemaking hadn't thwarted the talisman after all. Sarah was definitely under its spell.

"What's wrong, Sarah?" he asked, purposely keeping his tone light and ignoring the impulse to stand. He sensed that if he moved, she'd consider it an act of aggression.

"You know what's wrong, *wicáhmunga*," she drawled.

"Yes, but I'm not sure you do," he responded, barely able to keep from shivering at the tone of her voice. It vibrated with the same malevolence reflected in her eyes, making her sound positively demonic. "The talisman is exercising its power over you, but you can still turn away from its evil, Sarah. If you couldn't, it wouldn't keep us trapped in here."

"There is only one evil I need to turn away from, and that is *you*," she responded vehemently.

At her words, the air filled with a peculiar hissing sound that emanated from the wreath's walls. As Sebastian warily eyed them, he couldn't refrain from shuddering. The lightning bolts no longer whirled, but moved in a slow, sinuous snakelike manner. The hissing came from the lightning tips, which had taken on the shape of eyeless snake heads. The talisman couldn't have come up with a better way to scare the hell out of him and that assured him that his premise was true. She could still turn away from its evil, or it wouldn't need to play on his fears.

He returned his attention to Sarah. "I'd like to say that you're wrong about me, but I can't. Everyone has the capacity for evil, and the talisman has a hold on me. As much as I hate to admit it, I'm vulnerable to its manipulations, but I'm fighting against its evil, Sarah. That's why I made love to you instead of taking you like a brute as the talisman intended."

"Liar!" she declared shrilly. "You made love to me so you could steal a piece of my soul and destroy my people."

"You're wrong, Sarah. I made love to you so that the talisman couldn't steal your soul," he corrected. "The talisman gains its power from pain and violence, and it has to implant those emotions in you before it can use you. When I refused to rape you and gave you pleasure instead, I foiled its plans. Now it's working on your fears for your people to get you to commit a violent act. Once you do that, it will have a permanent hold on your soul. You can't let that happen, because once it corrupts you, you'll be evil forever."

When the sinister cast to her features softened in confusion, Sebastian knew he was making some headway. Quickly, he continued, "You told me earlier tonight that you spent your entire life overcoming the triangle's evil and that you mastered it. If you were able to do that, you're able to fight the talisman. So fight against its evil. If you can't find the inner strength to do it for yourself, then do it for your people. You are their guardian, Sarah. If you let the talisman corrupt you, it will make you destroy them. What kind of a guardian destroys those it's supposed to protect?"

Sebastian knew that her guardianship was her strongest emotional motivator. He'd hoped that by triggering that emotion, she would be more inclined to listen to his reasoning. By the time he finished his speech, however, he knew he'd made a mistake. Her features hardened, making her look crueler than she had before.

"You're lying to me. I would *never* harm my people," she stated fiercely. "I've seen the future. *You're* the one who wants to slaughter them. But I have now come into my powers, and I'm going to kill you in the same manner in which you would kill them."

Before Sebastian could respond to her charge, Sarah gripped her triangle more tightly and yelled, "Come to me! Take from him what he would take from my people!"

At her summons, two lightning bolts streaked toward her triangle. They hit it and rebounded toward him. Sebastian screamed in agony and terror, as, a moment later, the lightning bolts struck his eyes.

The pain was so excruciating that he was sure he would die, and then, as his anguish continued to build relentlessly, he feared he wouldn't die. Unable to bear the lightning's torture a moment longer, he closed down his mind and sought refuge in the haven of unconsciousness.

Sarah frowned in displeasure when the lightning disappeared and she stared down at the *wicáhmunġa*. He had fainted, but his eyes were open, and she realized the lightning hadn't obeyed her command. His eyes hadn't been gouged out, but had the opaque look of blinding cataracts.

She gripped the triangle, ready to recall the lightning and try again, but a familiar voice said, "Why is it not enough that you have blinded him, Sarah? Why must you take his eyes?"

"Wanáġa!" she gasped, spinning around. He hovered in the air behind her. Noting that he appeared in his leather breach clout, she scowled. This was her moment of triumph—the moment she'd trained for all her life. He should be showing his respect for her defeat of the *wicáhmunġa* by appearing in full battle regalia.

"I'm glad to see that you still recognize me," he said.

She frowned, confused. "What are you talking about?"

"That does not matter now, Sarah. My question does. Why must you take his eyes?"

"Before he dies, he must suffer as he would make my people suffer," she answered. "He would take their eyes and keep them from finding the spirit world. I have to make sure it is he who can never find the spirit world."

"He is blind. Is that not enough to stop him from doing that?"

"Why are you questioning me?" she demanded, her temper flaring. "As you've told me so many times, *I* am the guardian. *I* am the one who has to make the decisions."

"This is true. I simply wish to understand why you feel it necessary to remove his eyes."

"Dammit, Wanáǧa! I've already explained why, and I am not going to repeat myself."

He glanced around them. "Then perhaps you will explain this place that you are in?"

She also glanced at the lightning walls. "This is the source of my powers."

"And what will you do with these powers once you have destroyed the *wicáhmunǧa*?"

"I'll use them to help my people," she said, looking back at him.

"And if they don't want your help?"

"Of course they'll want my help," she replied impatiently. "I am the guardian, and I know what's best for them. If they don't listen to me, I'll . . ."

"You'll what?" he prodded. "Do the same to them

as you plan to do to the *wicáhmuṅga*? Take their eyes, and if they still fight you, their lives?"

"Of course not!" she cried, horrified, because that was exactly what she'd been thinking. But she'd never hurt her people, she assured herself. To reaffirm that assurance, she said, "That's what the *wicáhmuṅga* will do to them if I don't kill him. I know. I've seen the future."

"But did you see *him* in that future? Did you see *him* perform these atrocities? Did you see their blood on *his* hands?" Wanáǧa asked softly.

"Why are you doing this to me?" she said, raising her hands toward him beseechingly. "I am only doing what you trained me to do—to destroy the *wicáhmuṅga*."

"No, Sarah. I trained you to protect your people. Before you cause further injury to the *wicáhmuṅga*, journey back to the future. Confirm that what you believe is the truth."

Sarah wrapped her arms around herself, shivering, as she whispered, "No. I don't need to journey back to the future. I already know the truth."

But her denial didn't keep the encroaching vision at bay. As the vibrations of the future struck her and the image took form, she shuddered. She again stood on the mountaintop, her people's lifeless, sightless bodies spread around her. Forcing the horror to the back of her mind, she looked for the *wicáhmuṅga*. She knew he was the perpetrator of this carnage, but she had to see him here. Only then would Wanáǧa believe her.

But no matter how hard she looked, she couldn't see him. She drew in a frustrated breath. Where *was* he?

"Look at your hands, Sarah," Wanága suddenly instructed.

Understanding his insinuation, she gave a frantic shake of her head. He was wrong!

"Look at your hands," he repeated relentlessly.

"No. I'm not going to listen to you," she said hoarsely.

But her hands seemed to rise into her line of vision of their own accord. They dripped with blood.

"No, no, no, no, *nooooo*," she screamed, squeezing her eyes shut. "I would never do this. *Never!*"

But if she wouldn't do it, why was there blood on her hands? And why, even as she found the scene horrifying, was there a part of her that felt strangely aroused by it?

Suddenly, she remembered John Butler saying she was just like him. When she'd denied his claim, he'd said that when he arrived he'd prove it to her, because they shared the lust.

Sarah's stomach churned, and bile rose to her throat. At the time, she thought he referred to physical lust, but he'd replied that there were different kinds of lust. Now, she understood his meaning. He'd been talking about the blood lust.

"What kind of monster am I?" she whispered brokenly.

"You are not a monster, Sarah," Wanága said. "You are the last of your kind, and you are paying for my sins."

Sarah's eyes flew open. The vision was gone, and she stared at Wanága in bewilderment. "What are you talking about?"

"When it is time for you to know all, you will understand."

"Dammit, Wanága! You can't make a statement

like that and then follow it up with your stupid riddle. Tell me what you're talking about."

He gave a sad shake of his head. "I cannot do that, Sarah. All I can do is guide you and pray that you will make the right decisions."

"Wanága—," she started, but he disappeared.

She stared at the space where he'd been, feeling positively flabbergasted. What did he mean she was the last of her kind? She was Lakota!

Or was she? she wondered, suddenly recalling that when she'd seen the materials for prayer ties in the trunk in the cave, a voice had declared that she wasn't Lakota. But if she weren't Lakota, what was she?

The *wicáhmunga* groaned, interrupting her frustrated musing. She turned to look at him, startled to see that he wasn't naked but dressed. She immediately glanced down at herself, stunned to see that she too wore her clothes. Quickly, she raised her head to confirm what she'd already subliminally recognized. The lightning wreath was gone.

"I imagined it all!" she said, relief flooding through her. "It was just some kind of horrible dream."

Not everything was a dream, Sarah, Wanága whispered in her mind. *Look at the wicáhmunga's face.*

Realizing what Wanága intimated, her heart skipped a beat. She instinctively balked at his instruction, but she knew she had to face what she'd done.

Slowly, she moved her gaze to his face, trepidation shuddering through her. When she saw that his eyes were closed, she fervently whispered, "I can't have punished him for a future that is really mine. *Please, don't let him be blind.*"

It was as if her words were a command for him to awaken, because his eyelids lifted. She clapped her hands over her mouth and let out a horrified gasp. His eyes were completely white.

Pain and darkness. The two sensations swept over Sebastian in endless waves. The pain he could handle, but the darkness nearly suffocated him. Where was he? Why was it so damn dark?

"Sebastian? Are you awake? Can you hear me?"

"Sarah?" he said, turning his head toward the sound of her voice. He frowned, confused when he couldn't see her. Impulsively, he reached up and touched his eyes. They were open. So why couldn't he see her? he wondered, panic knotting his stomach. What was going on?

"I'm right here," Sarah said, brushing her fingers against his cheek.

He started at the contact. If she were close enough to touch him, he should be able to see her. As she withdrew her hand, he grabbed it, needing the firm contact to reassure himself that she was real. When she curled her fingers around his, he sighed in relief. She was real. Now he needed to figure out where they were and why it was so damn dark.

"I am so sorry, Sebastian," Sarah suddenly said.

He frowned again. She sounded so distraught. What had happened? Why was she sorry?

Because she touched your eyes with the lightning. Now you are blind forever, the talisman's voice stated with cold maliciousness.

As its statement sank in, Sebastian's heart raced and his pulse sounded. It wasn't true. He *wasn't* blind. The talisman was toying with him, trying to rile him. They were inside the wreath, and the talisman had created this impenetrable darkness to force them into a violent confrontation so it could capture Sarah's soul.

But even as he offered himself the excuse for the darkness, he knew it wasn't true. Sarah had summoned the lightning and made it strike his eyes.

"No!" Sebastian gasped, bolting upright. He couldn't be blind. He was the troubleshooter. He needed his eyes to do his job!

"Sebastian, I don't know if you should be moving around."

"I'm blind," he said, more to himself than to her. He sounded so calm. How could he sound calm when desperation clawed at his insides?

"I'm sorry," Sarah whispered mournfully, laying her hand on his arm.

He jerked away from her, fury erupting inside him. "Don't say you're sorry! I tried to save your soul, and you *blinded* me."

"I know, but you have to understand," she said, a tearful catch in her voice. "I had a vision of the future, and I thought that you were going to gouge out my people's eyes and kill them. I was trying to protect them from you, but now I know it wasn't your future I saw. It was mine. You were right, Sebastian. The talisman has chosen me for its instrument of destruction. What am I going to do?"

"You're asking me, a *blind* warlock, for advice?" he rasped, his temper escalating. He'd done everything he could think of to save her. He'd even made love to her when every atom of his being demanded he take her ruthlessly. But instead of being grateful for his efforts, she'd turned the lightning on him.

He wanted to grab her around the throat and

throttle her, but he couldn't see her throat to grab it. Unable to act on that desire, he wanted to leap to his feet and pace, but how could he pace when he couldn't see? How could he do *anything* without his sight?

"Sebastian, you said earlier that your people might be able to help me. Maybe if we go to them—"

"Forget it," he broke in furiously. That's why she sounded so pitiful. She and the talisman were after the coven! "You may have robbed me of my eyesight, but I haven't lost my mind. I'm not taking you to Sanctuary so you can destroy the coven."

"But if you don't take me to them, who is going to help me and my people?"

"Help you and your people?" he repeated incredulously. "Didn't you hear anything I told you before you burned out my eyes? To be saved, you had to refuse to commit a violent act, and blinding someone is definitely violent. Now the talisman owns you lock, stock, and soul. Even if the coven managed to stop the talisman, we can't help you because you are forever corrupted. You're just like Seamus Morpeth."

He heard her suck in a harsh breath. It seemed to be forever before she released it and said, "Then I guess that only leaves me with one option. I'll have to kill myself before I hurt anyone else."

Sebastian gave a disgusted shake of his head. "Forget the contrite act, Sarah. Even if you are sincere—which I doubt—the talisman now owns you. The only way you could kill yourself is if it decides that you aren't of any further use to it, and then I'd wager that it won't let you take the easy way out. It will find some way to make you suffer through a slow, torturous death."

"Then you kill me," she said fervently, grabbing his hands and pulling them up to her neck.

When he felt her soft skin and delicate bones beneath his palms, he wanted to do as she asked. She had *blinded* him. But as his fingers flexed, itching to curl around her neck, he snatched his hands away. The talisman wouldn't let him kill her, and by hurting her, he'd be feeding its appetite for violence, giving it more power over her and possibly him.

"That's a great plan," he told her derisively. "I wring your neck, and then what am I supposed to do? I'm blind, remember? How the hell would I get off this damn mountain?"

"I didn't think about that," she said, sounding defeated. "I've really messed everything up, haven't I?"

"That's the best understatement I've ever heard."

Despite his anger, Sebastian felt a pang of sympathy for her. When he'd made love to her, he'd learned firsthand how difficult it was to fight against the talisman's manipulation. Because he'd managed to do so, he'd expected her to do the same. Now, he realized that not only had his expectations been unrealistic but impossible. Sarah had been under her triangle's influence since childhood. She'd been lost from the beginning.

He wanted to reach out and touch her, tell her that it wasn't her fault. He refrained, knowing that his words would be as little comfort to her as hers had been to him when she'd said she was sorry for blinding him.

So instead of consoling her, he raked a hand through his hair, trying to decide what to do. His mind raced through a dozen possibilities, but he finally concluded that he had to do what she'd suggested in the first place. Take her to Sanctuary.

"I've changed my mind," he told her. "We're going to Sanctuary."

"No!" she objected. "If I go there, I might hurt your friends, and I've already caused enough damage. Besides, you said that no matter what happens, you can't help me. I'm forever corrupted."

"I'm not taking you there to help you," he shot back, flinching when she sucked in another harsh breath. Realizing how cruel he'd sounded, he considered rephrasing the statement, but he knew it wouldn't take the sting away. "I'm taking you there because the talisman has to be stopped, and I need the support of the coven to fight it. I also have to make sure that you don't hook up with John Butler. You're dangerous now, but if you get hold of his circle, you'll be unstoppable."

"I'll be a lean, mean, killing machine, huh?" she said with a harsh laugh. "Maybe I should join the military. I also see a major problem with your plan. What if the talisman doesn't want me to go to Sanctuary? Won't it stop us?"

"It won't stop us," he said, suddenly understanding why the talisman had only made her blind him rather than kill him. "To achieve full power, all three pieces have to be reunited. If I die, my triangle will automatically return to Sanctuary, so you'll have to go there to retrieve it. But if I take you there, you'll be granted automatic entrance onto coven land. Otherwise, you'll have to go there by yourself. The coven will be waiting for you, and you'll have a hell of a fight on your hands."

"There's a big hole in your theory. Even if I go with you, the coven will be waiting for the talisman, so it will still have to fight them. It seems more logical that I just give you my triangle. Then you can return alone and let me stay behind."

"Now that it has a firm hold on you, it won't let you remove the triangle," he said. "And even if you could remove it, I can't leave you behind. You're corrupted. Since the talisman was introduced into mortal society by Seamus Morpeth, we are responsible for your actions, and we have to make sure that you're controlled.

"But more significant is the talisman's need to get you onto coven land," he continued. "That tells me that we either know something or have something that makes it vulnerable, and it wants you on coven land so you can neutralize whatever threatens it. The only way to discover its vulnerability is for me to take you to Sanctuary and let the coven members watch you. Eventually, you'll lead us to the answer."

"I see," she said. "I wonder if this is what a laboratory rat feels like."

He felt another sympathy pang toward her. "I'm sorry this has happened to you, Sarah. It must seem unfair."

"That's nothing new," she said, another tearful catch in her voice. He heard her rise to her feet as she went on, "Most everything in my life has seemed unfair. So now that we have a plan of action, I guess we'd better get out of here. Do you think you can stand?"

"I've lost my eyes, not my legs," he snapped, though he wasn't irritated with her but with the situation. He hated the resigned tone of her voice. Worse, he despised himself for not saving her. He knew, however, that now was not the time to dwell on the matter. He needed to get her to Sanctuary. He could wallow in regret once they were there.

He pushed himself to his feet. When he stood, he swayed and would have fallen if Sarah hadn't suddenly grabbed his arm to steady him. He cursed violently. Without the perspective of sight, he felt disoriented, dizzy. How would he grow accustomed to this unyielding blackness?

"Are you all right?" Sarah asked, concern vibrating in her voice.

"I'm fine," he muttered. "Let's get the hell out of here."

"Okay. We need to stop by the cave so I can get a couple changes of clothes."

"We'll get you clothes in Sanctuary," he said, remembering the meager pile of garments he'd seen in front of the trunk. If that was all she had, it was hardly worth the effort to get them.

"It will only take a minute. Hold onto my arm, and watch your step," she said, as she led him across the meadow. "I'll warn you of anything in your way."

Sebastian scowled at the sudden realization that because he couldn't see, he was basically helpless and would always have to depend on others.

You are not helpless, he quickly upbraided himself. *Blind people all over the world lead self-sufficient lives.*

The pep talk didn't work, because he wanted to lead *his* life. He wanted to be the troubleshooter.

He had no idea how long it took them to reach the cave, but it seemed like hours. When they got there, Sarah said, "Why don't you wait here? I'll grab my things and be right back."

"Sure," Sebastian said, though he found the

thought of standing here alone intimidating as hell. Pride, however, kept him from telling her that. Besides, he needed to get used to this, he told himself as she released his arm and walked away from him. He'd be like this for the rest of his life.

But it won't be a very long life, the talisman suddenly whispered in his mind.

Sarah paused inside the cave entrance. The fire had burned down to glowing embers, and she needed a moment to let her eyes adjust to the dark interior.

When she could finally see enough to make out the general details of the walls, she let her gaze travel over them. She didn't know why she surveyed them. They were really unremarkable, but they had given her a haven for most of her life, and she would miss their familiarity.

Finally, she stepped further into the chamber and said, "Willow?"

The snake instantly rattled, and Sarah turned her head in the direction of the sound and watched her pet slither across the ground toward her. She dropped to her knees, tears flooding her eyes, when the snake reached her. Picking her up, Sarah stroked her head, and then rubbed her face against Willow's, letting the tears fall when the snake flicked her tongue against her cheek.

"I wish I could take you with me," she said. "But they don't allow Prairie rattlers on airplanes, and you're way too big to stuff into my pocket and sneak aboard. But I couldn't leave without saying goodbye and telling you to take care of yourself."

Willow rattled softly as she again flicked her tongue against Sarah's cheek. Sarah barely held back a sob. She'd had Willow on her lap the day Leonard had found her, and the snake was the only true friend she had left in the world.

She wanted to sit and hold Willow for hours, but Sebastian was waiting. Gently, she placed the snake back on the ground. Then she stood and walked to the trunk. Carefully, she folded her clothes into a small bundle and tied them together with the twine for the prayer ties.

Tucking the bundle under her arm, she walked to the cave entrance. She glanced around it one last time, and then looked down at Willow, who'd coiled herself in the spot where Sarah had placed her.

"Goodbye, my friend," she whispered. "I love you."

Willow rattled again, and Sarah turned and walked out, knowing she'd never see her pet again. Once Sebastian and his coven did manage to stop the talisman—and she refused to believe that they wouldn't be able to stop it—she would somehow find the strength to kill herself. It was the only way to make sure that she never harmed anyone again.

Part Two

✣

The most momentous thing in human life
is the art of winning
the soul to good or to evil.

—"Pythagoras,"
from Diogenes Laertius,
Lives of Eminent Philosophers,
Bk. VIII

12

Evil Arrives

Lucien Morgret's gaze swept over his sleeping wife's beautiful face. As she did every afternoon, she napped on the daybed positioned between the cribs of their four-month-old twins. While he watched her sleep, he felt an odd mixture of love and anger. Of course, only the love was directed toward Ariel. She was his mate, the very essence of his soul, and he would give his life to protect her and their children.

And it looked as if he might have to do that.

With a heavy sigh, he walked to the crib on the right and looked down at his sleeping daughter, Deirdre. He stroked the crown of black curls framing her sweet, tiny face, which already resembled her mother's. As he did, his mind spun back to the source of his anger—Sebastian's predawn astral visitation.

His ire flared higher at the memory, and Deirdre's small face immediately puckered into a frown. Realizing his daughter, whose mental powers were already strong, had picked up on his unruly emotions, Lucien quickly tamped them down.

When her features relaxed, he crossed to his son's crib. He smiled wryly as he studied Derek. Like his sister, the boy had a crown of black curls, but he didn't resemble either of his parents. He'd inherited a composite of Ariel's wholesome beauty and Lucien's stark, craggy features that, even at this young age, could only be described as handsome. Ariel said that when he grew up, he'd be a heart-breaker.

Lucien suddenly shuddered, as though touched by an ominous portent. If the coven didn't stop the talisman, neither of his children would grow up.

"We *will* stop it," he murmured quietly, fiercely, as he stroked his son's head.

"Stop what?" Ariel asked.

Lucien started and swung his head toward her. As she sat up, he automatically smiled. Her long blonde hair was in disarray, and her green eyes peered at him sleepily. She covered a yawn with her hand, and then returned his smile with one so filled with love that Lucien's heart twisted. He wanted to grab her and the twins and run as far away from Sanctuary as possible. He knew, however, that the only way to keep them safe was for him to stay and fight.

"We need to talk," he said, crossing to Ariel and sitting beside her.

She eyed him worriedly. "What's wrong?"

"As you so often say, it's one of those witchy things," he replied, smoothing her hair. "I'm afraid, however, that this time it's bad. Very bad."

An anxious frown creased her forehead, but her voice remained calm as she said, "So tell me about it."

"Let's get out of here first," he said. "I don't want to wake the twins."

She nodded and rose, heading for the kitchen.

Lucien followed. When they got there, she sat at the table. Lucien, however, was too tense to sit. While he pulled his thoughts together, he paced.

Finally he began, "Early yesterday, Shana discovered a glowing triangle in the repository, and she summoned Sebastian. They learned that it's a piece of an ancient talisman." He stopped and looked at her. "Do you know what a talisman is?"

"Not really."

Lucien wasn't surprised. Ariel was a mortal and hadn't had much exposure to the occult before meeting him. Since they'd mated, she'd started studying magic, but there was so much to absorb that it would be years before she'd have a good understanding of it.

"A talisman is a magical object with supernatural powers, and it can imbue its possessor with those powers," he explained.

"I see," she said. "Since this talisman has you so upset, its powers must be evil."

"They're more than evil, Ariel." He leaned his head back and looked at the ceiling, trying to think of a way to explain the situation so that it wouldn't frighten her too badly. He soon realized that there was no way to soften the revelation of the talisman's purpose.

He looked at her and said, "We think the talisman is a doomsday device, that its purpose is to destroy mankind."

Her mouth dropped open and she stared at him in shock. Then she closed her mouth and swallowed hard. "You can stop it, right?"

He raked a hand through his hair and resumed pacing. "I honestly don't know if we can stop it. As I said, the triangle is a piece of the talisman. There are three pieces all together—two triangles and a circle. Sebastian put on our triangle, thinking it would lead him to the other two pieces. He planned on gathering them and disposing of them to stop the talisman, only . . ."

"Only what?" she prodded, her voice quavery.

He stopped again and stared at her, hating the terrified expression on her face. For a moment he considered not telling her the rest of the story, but he knew he had to tell her everything. If he didn't, she'd never agree to his plan to keep her and the twins safe.

"Sebastian paid an astral visit to Kendra Morovang and me last night," he replied. "Apparently, he only connected with one piece—the other triangle. A Native American woman in South Dakota has it. He went there and . . ."

"Please, Lucien. Just tell me everything and get it over with," Ariel stated impatiently when he stopped speaking. "I can handle the truth better than I can handle the suspense, and your hesitancy is driving me crazy."

He nodded and resumed pacing. "Kendra's information suggested that once Sebastian put on the triangle he wouldn't be able to take it off because he'd be spellbound by the talisman. He said he'd go back to South Dakota and try to remove it. If he succeeded, the triangle would instantly return to Sanctuary. That was nearly twelve hours ago, and the triangle never arrived."

"So you have to assume that he's spellbound," Ariel said. "What do you do now?"

"Sebastian thinks that the talisman can't penetrate the protective circle surrounding Sanctuary," he answered. "He said that if he couldn't remove the triangle, he'd bring the woman here."

Ariel frowned thoughtfully. "Why? What's her part in all of this?"

"Sebastian believes the talisman has chosen her as its instrument of destruction," Lucien answered. "There's also a man who has the circle, and he's killed at least two people. Sebastian is bringing the woman here to draw that man to us. He hopes that once we've brought the three pieces into close proximity, the coven can find a way to stop the talisman."

Ariel gaped at him, horror slowly spreading across her features. "Are you saying that Sebastian is bringing a killer—no, *two* killers—to Sanctuary?"

"One killer and a potential killer," Lucien corrected. "As far as I know, the woman hasn't harmed anyone yet."

"But if the talisman is in control of her, it's only a matter of time."

"Yes," he replied grimly. "We also have to be concerned about Sebastian. There's a chance that he too is capable of harming us."

"That's ridiculous!" she declared ardently. "Sebastian would *never* harm a member of the coven."

"I'd like to believe that, too, Ariel, but after what happened to Seamus and Ragna—"

"Seamus and Ragna?" she interrupted, her expression now confused. "Who are they?"

Lucien spent the next few minutes telling her the story of Seamus and Ragna. When he finished, she gave a dazed shake of her head and buried her face in her hands. She sat that way a long moment, and then she looked up at him.

"This is a nightmare, Lucien."

"I know," he said. "That's why I want you to take the twins and go to your brother's until it's over."

She shook her head. "No way."

He frowned. "Ariel, it isn't safe for you and the twins to stay here."

"From what you've just said, if you don't stop the talisman, we aren't going to be safe at my brother's, either."

"We *will* stop it," he stated just as fiercely as he had earlier.

"Then there's no reason for us to leave."

"Ariel, I'm not going to argue this point with you."

"Good," she said. "What would you like for dinner?"

"Dammit, Ariel! You have to take the twins and leave," he declared, his temper flaring.

She frowned at him. "Tell me something, Lucien. Do you plan to send the witches and their children away?"

"You know I can't do that," he replied with an impatient wave of his hand. "In the first place, they aren't familiar with the mortal world. They wouldn't know where to go or how to take care of themselves. Secondly, Sebastian and I may need to draw upon their power to defeat the talisman."

"In other words, you may need every ounce of the coven's power to defeat the talisman, even the children's magical powers."

"Yes," he agreed grimly.

"And what about our children? They've been tested, and they have magical powers. I know they're too small to personally offer you the use of their powers, but you can draw upon it anyway, right?"

"Yes, but they're just *babies*, Ariel. Their power is

so weak at this point it's almost negligible," he said, growing more impatient.

"Well, what if that tiny oomph of power is all you need to make a difference?" she said. "And even if it isn't, have you considered the consequences of sending me away? Many of the coven members still haven't accepted me because I'm mortal. If I run at the first sign of trouble, they're never going to accept me."

Before he could respond, she went on, "You're the high priest, and the coven members look to you for guidance. If you send the twins and me away, they'll think that you either don't believe the coven can beat the talisman, or that you expect most of them to die. You can't do that to them, Lucien. To win, they have to believe that winning is possible. You can't instill defeat in them before the battle even begins."

Lucien scowled, but he wasn't angry with her. He was furious that every damn point she'd made was right. Still, he said, "If you stay, you and the twins could die. Don't you want to protect our children?"

"Don't you dare try and lay a guilt trip on me," she stated, surging to her feet. She propped her hands on the tabletop, leaned forward, and glared at him. "You know I will do everything within my power to protect my children. If I thought running with them was the solution, I'd pack their things so fast you'd think I had magical powers myself. But if the talisman isn't stopped here, we're going to die anyway. If that's the case, then we'll die as a family, not apart, just like every other coven family in Sanctuary."

She paused to draw in a breath and finished, "Now, what would you like for dinner, and should I prepare enough for Sebastian and the woman he's bringing with him?"

As she stared at him, her chin raised a determined notch, Lucien couldn't decide if he wanted to yell at her or kiss her. He compromised by giving her a reluctant smile. "You're a damn stubborn woman."

"That's one of the reasons you love me," she quipped, returning his smile.

"Yeah, it is," he murmured, walking to her and pulling her into his arms.

As she cuddled against his chest, he rested his chin on top of her head and tried to quell the fear churning inside him. His efforts failed, because he couldn't purge the feeling of doom that had hovered over him since Sebastian's astral visit.

It isn't fair! he railed inwardly. *Ariel and I have only had each other for a little over a year. We have a family now, and we should be looking forward to the future, not contemplating the end of the world!*

But he'd learned long ago that life wasn't fair, and he knew that no amount of railing would change that.

He continued to hold Ariel for a few minutes. Finally he released her from his embrace, dropped a quick kiss to her lips, and said, "Surprise me with dinner, and make enough for Sebastian and his guest."

Then he headed for Sanctuary's boundary to wait for Sebastian and the woman who'd been chosen to destroy mankind.

As Sarah turned the rental car onto the highway exit leading to Sanctuary, she glanced nervously toward Sebastian. He sat in the passenger seat, facing straight ahead. Even with his two-day growth of beard, she could see that he clenched his jaw. He looked angry and dangerous, and not necessarily in that order.

She heaved an inward sigh and returned her attention to the road. Other than giving her directions, he hadn't spoken a word in the two and a half hours since they'd left Philadelphia's airport. Actually, he hadn't spoken more than a few dozen words since they'd left the mountain in South Dakota, and his sullen silence grated on her nerves. Not that she blamed him for not talking to her. She had, after all, blinded him.

Guilty tears stung her eyes, but she quickly blinked them away. Remorse wouldn't change things, and she didn't have the right to indulge in it. She'd had the choice between good and evil, and she'd chosen evil. Now, she had to face the consequences.

It would be easier to do that, however, if she knew more about the coven. What were the people like? Were there any special formalities she needed to know when dealing with them? She wanted to ask Sebastian those questions and a dozen more.

But most of all, she wanted to know how they'd react when they learned what she'd done to him. Not knowing what to expect from them was eating her up inside.

"I'm at the turnoff for Sanctuary," she told him when she reached the stop sign at the top of the exit. "Did you say that I'm supposed to turn left?"

He swiveled his head toward her, and she involuntarily caught her breath. On the way to the Rapid City airport she'd stopped at a convenience store and bought him a pair of mirrored sunglasses. Every time she saw herself reflected in the lenses, she felt as if he could see her. Knowing it was only wishful thinking didn't lessen the impact.

"Yes, left," he confirmed, turning to face forward again.

"There's a gas station here, and we're down to a quarter tank," she said. "Should I fill up?"

"No."

She turned onto the narrow, two-lane road running west of the gas station. After she'd driven through the thick woods for several miles without seeing another car, a house, or any other sign of life, she couldn't stand the silence any longer.

"Sebastian, I know you don't want to talk to me," she said, "but—"

"You're right," he interrupted coldly. "I don't want to talk to you."

Anger stirred at his curtness, and she gripped the steering wheel tightly, telling herself to do as he asked. But the uncertainty of what lay ahead continued to torment her, and she knew that if she couldn't ask her questions, she'd go nuts.

"I'm sorry, Sebastian, but I can't be quiet," she said after they'd traveled another mile. "I need some answers to some questions, and I expect you to give them to me."

"You *expect*?" he drawled derisively, jerking his head toward her. "After what you've done to me, you don't have the right to *expect* anything from me. So shut up and drive."

Sarah told herself not to lose her temper, but it flared anyway. Impulsively, she steered the car to the shoulder of the road and slammed on the brakes. The car skidded to a stop so fast that they were thrown forward against their seatbelts.

"What the hell do you think you're doing?" Sebastian yelled as she threw the gear shift into park and turned off the ignition.

"Taking a walk," she snapped, wrenching her seatbelt free and tossing open the car door.

Before he could respond, she jumped out of the car, slammed the door shut, and strode across the road. Standing on the embankment, she stared at the woods in front of her, her emotions as thickly tangled as the forest's undergrowth. She was angry and afraid, but most of all, she felt so utterly alone.

"If I had an ounce of sense, I'd just walk into those woods and disappear," she muttered.

"So do it. I sure as hell can't stop you," Sebastian rasped.

With a startled cry, she spun around. He'd climbed out of the rental car and stood with one hand braced on the open door and the other on top of the roof. Even from this distance, she could see the flash of images against his mirrored sunglasses. Suddenly, she felt as if he could see right down to the depths of her soul. She shivered and wrapped her arms around herself, unnerved by the sensation.

As she continued to regard him, she decided that for him to have heard what she'd said from across the road, he had awfully good hearing. Either that or he was able to read her mind again.

She considered brushing her mind against his to see if that was the case, but his expression was so hostile she decided against it. Facing his anger on a physical level was intimidating. Mentally connecting with it would probably scare the daylights out of her, and she was already scared enough.

"You're right. You can't stop me," she said, her temper flaring again, but it wasn't anger sparking it.

It was her fear of the unknown and the hopelessness of this entire mess. "So, give me one good reason why I shouldn't just walk away and leave you sitting on the side of the road?"

"You don't want me to give you a reason," he replied harshly. "You want me to reassure you, to tell you that everything is going to be all right, and we both know I'd be lying. Is that what you really want? For me to give you meaningless platitudes?"

"Yes!" she cried hoarsely, the tears returning. She swiped at them impatiently. "I want you to lie to me, and . . ."

"And?" he urged, his voice suddenly softening.

"Never mind. It doesn't matter," she stated miserably, looking down at her moccasins. She hated him being mean to her, but, conversely, after what she'd done to him, she didn't want him to be nice, either.

"It must matter a great deal, or we wouldn't be standing here having this conversation. What is it you want from me, Sarah?"

"I don't want you to despise me," she confessed so softly she knew he couldn't hear her.

Obviously, his hearing was more acute than she'd imagined, because he sighed heavily and said, "I don't despise you, Sarah. I despise myself for not saving you, and I detest being blind and feeling so damn powerless. I'm furious, and even though this isn't really your fault, I can't help blaming you. It's taking all my willpower to keep from striking out at you, and I know that's unjust. But it's going to take me some time to gain some perspective."

"Well, I guess that answers one of my questions," she replied, the last remnants of her anger dissolving as she raised her head to look at him. "The rest of the coven is going to feel the same way about me, aren't they? They're going to hold me accountable for you and the talisman, and they're going to want to strike out at me. Don't get me wrong. I don't blame them for that. I made the wrong choice, and now I have to pay for that decision. Unfortunately, you're paying, too. I'd give anything to bring your sight back."

"I know that, Sarah," he said, sighing again. "But as the old saying goes, what's done is done. You also don't need to fear the coven. No matter what they think or how they feel, they aren't going to harm you in any way. Now it's time for you to make a decision. Are you coming with me to Sanctuary and fight against the talisman? Or, are you going to surrender to it and let it turn you into a monster?"

Though he made it sound as if she really had a choice, Sarah knew she didn't. She had to go to Sanctuary. She was the guardian, and working with Sebastian and his coven was the only way she could protect her people.

She gave a defeated shake of her head. "Get in the car, Sebastian. We're going to Sanctuary."

"If it's any consolation, you're making the right decision," he said.

"Yeah, I know," she mumbled as she watched him carefully—blindly—ease his way back inside.

She waited until he closed the door before she walked back to the car. As she pulled her door open, she had a flash of a horrifying vision. She stood in the center of a strange town, whose buildings were constructed in the Gothic architectural style with slender towers, pointed arches, and flying buttresses. Littering the street were the bodies of strangers, and they'd all had their eyes gouged out.

The vision ended so abruptly that Sarah tried to

tell herself she'd imagined it. But she knew it was real, and her knees shook so badly she was barely able to climb into the car.

When she was seated, she gripped the steering wheel and drew in a deep breath, telling herself that just because she'd had the vision didn't mean it would come true. After all, the future was not engraved in stone, and the people in Sanctuary were going to stop the talisman. When they did, she'd kill herself, so whoever those poor people were in the vision, they'd be safe.

Despite her effort at reassurance, she shuddered again, because she knew in her heart that her visions of the future always came true.

As Sarah started the car and they began to move again, Sebastian slowly released the breath he'd been holding. Until she'd turned the ignition and put the car in gear, he'd feared that she'd change her mind and run. And it would have been his fault.

Why had he ignored her rising anxiety? He'd known she was upset. The growing tension in the car had been palpable.

You ignored her because you were too busy feeling sorry for yourself, his conscience charged.

With an inward curse, he leaned his head against the seat rest, deciding his conscience was wrong. He hadn't been absorbed in self-pity. As he'd told Sarah, he'd been wallowing in anger. Ever since Sarah had blinded him, the emotion had been prowling inside him like a wild beast. He'd felt as if he'd go mad if he didn't release his fury.

But he'd known he couldn't give his temper free rein. The velocity of the wind that accompanied a warlock's temper was in direct proportion to his fury. He was so enraged over his blindness that he'd probably cause a tornado. The only way he could safely release that much anger was if he could focus his eyes on the person with whom he was angry. Once he made that physical connection, he'd be able to contain the wind, and it wouldn't cause any damage.

But he couldn't see Sarah, so he couldn't focus his eyes on her. Of course, if he could see her, he wouldn't be angry.

Frustrated by that simple paradox, he readjusted the sunglasses Sarah had bought him. Then he breathed deeply and forced himself to concentrate on the hum of the car's tires against the pavement. Sound was the only thing that oriented him in the unremitting darkness surrounding him. The ponderous gloom that made time seem to stand still. The utter blackness where every sound, every movement, was unexpected and seemed threatening.

His stomach knotted, and fear commingled with his anger. How would he survive without his sight?

Thankfully, Sarah saved him from having to answer that question by nervously saying, "I think we have a problem, Sebastian. There's a huge, golden barrier ahead of us. It's like the one I saw in my vision of you when you first put on the triangle, and I can't see through it. What should I do?"

"That's the protective energy barrier surrounding Sanctuary. It won't hurt you, so just drive through it," he said, startled by her words. Although she'd seen the magic circle in a vision, she shouldn't have been able to see it in reality. It was invisible to mortals. Only the Indian spirit said Sarah wasn't a mortal. So what *was* she?

"Sebastian, I have to stop the car," Sarah said, again interrupting his thoughts.

"Why?" he asked, swiveling his head toward her.

"I feel . . . funny."

"Funny how?"

"I . . . don't . . . know," she stammered. "Just . . . funny."

"Have we passed through the barrier?" he asked, wondering if the talisman were up to something.

"No," she answered. "It's . . . still . . . a ways . . . off, but . . . Oh, God!" she suddenly cried, and Sebastian felt the car lurch. Then it slammed to a stop and the engine died.

"Sarah? What's wrong?" he demanded, panic flowing through him when he heard her begin to wheeze.

"Your magic is killing her, *wicáhmunga*."

Sebastian started at the Indian spirit's voice, which seemed to come at him from every direction.

"What the hell are you talking about? I'm not using any magic!"

"The golden wall, *wicáhmunga*."

Sebastian felt the color drain from his face. Of course! The energy barrier was not only pure magic, it was also some of the most powerful magic in existence. It also cast a spell over any mortal who came within a quarter mile of its proximity.

Only Sarah wasn't a mortal, and the harmless spell he'd cast over her last night had nearly killed her. The energy barrier would surely do so.

"Sarah, you have to find enough strength to back up the car," he said, reaching out for her.

When his hand came into contact with her body, panic erupted inside him. She shook so badly that if she wasn't convulsing, she would be at any moment.

"Dammit, Sarah! Wake up and back up the car!" he yelled, even though he knew she couldn't hear him. He also knew he had to get her out of the car and away from the barrier.

Frantically, he released his seatbelt, and then he leaned over to search for the button that would release Sarah's. When his fingers couldn't find it, he cursed violently. She was dying, and because he was blind he couldn't help her.

Suddenly his door flew open and he heard Lucien say, "Sebastian? What's wrong?"

Relief flooded through him. He didn't know why Lucien was here, but thankfully he was.

"I don't have time to explain. Get Sarah out of the car and away from the protective circle," Sebastian ordered, continuing his search for the release on Sarah's seatbelt. "Hurry! Its magic is killing her."

Thankfully, Lucien didn't waste time questioning him, and Sebastian no more than found the button and pressed it when he heard Sarah's door open.

"Take her away from the circle, not through it," he instructed. "Understand?"

"I understand," Lucien stated tightly.

Sebastian listened to the sounds of Lucien lifting Sarah out, and he knew when he'd succeeded, because her agonized gasps for breath faded. But instead of hearing Lucien run away from the car, he heard him exclaim, "What the hell is that?"

Sebastian didn't need to ask Lucien what he was talking about. He could hear the familiar whirring sound of the lightning wreath. He also knew why it was here. The talisman wouldn't let Sarah die, and it had sent the wreath to protect her. He knew instinctively that it would cocoon her, just as it had on the mountain.

"Put Sarah down on the ground and get away from her!" he yelled at Lucien, not sure what would happen to Lucien if he got trapped in the wreath with her. He wasn't wearing a piece of the talisman, so the lightning wreath might kill him.

Lucien didn't respond to his order, and Sebastian cursed the fact that he couldn't see what was going on. He listened for something—anything—that would tell him what happened, but the only sound he could hear was the wreath's whirring.

"Lucien? Are you all right?" he called out.

Lucien didn't answer.

13

Evil Attacks

✛

When Sebastian opened his mouth to yell for Lucien again, he stopped himself. If Lucien were able to respond, he would have done so. Sitting here bellowing for him wouldn't accomplish anything. But he was blind, so what the hell else could he do?

"*Dammit!* Why isn't my magic working so I can summon help?" he declared angrily.

"Your magic is working, *wicáhmunġa*. You have just been too angry to let yourself feel its return."

Sebastian started so badly at the sudden sound of the Indian spirit's voice that he nearly fell out the open car door.

Grabbing the seat back to steady himself, he asked, "Are Sarah and Lucien okay?"

"Sarah is safe."

"And Lucien?" he questioned hoarsely.

"He is not yet ready to enter the spirit world."

Did he mean that Lucien wasn't on the immediate verge of death? Or that it wasn't his time to die?

Sebastian decided that he couldn't waste time finding out. Lucien was alive. Now that the spirit had opened his eyes, so to speak, to the fact that his magic was back, he could feel it thrumming through him.

He tried to connect with both Sarah's and Lu-

cien's minds to establish their conditions, but both
were closed to him. In Sarah's case, he was sure it
was because she was cocooned. As for Lucien, he
could be cocooned or lying on the ground unconscious. The only way Sebastian could make contact
with an unconscious person was if he could look at
them, or if he was communicating through someone
else who looked at them. It was an idiosyncracy of
magic he'd never understood, but it was the case
nonetheless.

But regardless of Lucien's predicament, he
needed to summon help, and he needed to do it
fast.

His first impulse was to send out a general alarm.
Thankfully, his common sense surfaced first. A general alarm would bring the entire coven running,
and then they'd all be outside the protective field of
the energy barrier. That might be exactly what the
talisman wanted—to lure the coven members outside that sphere of safety so it could attack them.

Even if that weren't its goal, Sebastian knew he
couldn't alert the entire coven to Lucien's situation.
He was their high priest, and they depended upon
him to lead them. Ordinarily, if something happened to Lucien, they'd turn to Sebastian for direction until a new high priest was installed. But they
couldn't turn to him, because he was not only corrupted by the talisman, he was also blind. Once
they learned that, they'd panic.

So he had to be selective about who he contacted. He needed a warlock with excellent magical
proficiency, as well as courage, because the warlock
might have to battle the wreath. It also needed to be
someone whom he could trust to quietly fetch Ryan
Alden, the mortal doctor who'd mated with Shana,

and bring him here. Sebastian didn't know if Ryan could do anything for either Lucien or Sarah, since their difficulties involved magic. It was, however, better to have him at hand in case he was needed.

Knowing that every moment might make a difference in Lucien's survival, Sebastian quickly ran through the list of warlocks in Sanctuary. He finally, albeit reluctantly, settled on Zachary Morcombe.

Drawing in a deep breath, he let his mind connect with Zachary's. *Zachary, it's Sebastian.*

Sebastian? What can I do for you? Zachary responded, and Sebastian could feel the warlock's startlement at the unexpected connection.

Lucien has been injured. We're outside the boundary on the road leading to the interstate. Get Ryan Alden and bring him here quickly. Don't let anyone else in the coven know what's going on, and before you get here, cast a protective spell over both yourself and Ryan. There's magic at work here—magic we've never encountered before—and you could be in danger.

I'm on my way. We're both in town, so we should be there in ten or fifteen minutes, Zachary responded instantly.

Sebastian was tempted to maintain his contact so he could follow their progress. He realized, however, that his emotions were running too high, so he wouldn't be able to shield his monitoring from Zachary. At best, his presence would distract the warlock; at worst, it would make him feel as if Sebastian didn't trust him, and that would make him resentful. When he arrived, he needed his full attention focused on the wreath, not split between his wounded pride and dealing with unknown magic.

"I hope I made the right choice by selecting him," Sebastian muttered, breaking off contact and leaning back in the seat. He liked Zachary, and outside of Lucien and himself, Zachary was the most powerful warlock in Sanctuary.

However, Zachary wasn't endowed with courage as much as an uncommonly daring nature. Ariel Morgret had once used a mortal saying to describe him. She'd said he was the type to rush in where angels feared to tread. Sebastian didn't believe in angels, but he had to agree with the sentiment of Ariel's saying. He just prayed that Zachary would maintain a cool head and not treat this situation like an exciting adventure.

Stop doubting your decision, he quickly upbraided himself. *Zachary is the best choice, and you know it.*

But despite the chastisement, he couldn't rid himself of the uncertainty, because his blindness affected his confidence. He knew it was irrational, but he felt physically weak and magically ineffective, and that made him feel intellectually incompetent.

As soon as he made that admission, he realized that since Sarah had blinded him, he'd been using Lucien as a crutch. He'd been telling himself that all he had to do was get back to Lucien. Then he would lead the battle against the talisman and everything would be okay.

But it wasn't okay, because the talisman had just kicked his crutch out from under him.

"So get your act together," he stated, balling his hands into fists and slamming them against his thighs. "You may be blind, but you're still the troubleshooter. Stop sitting here feeling sorry for yourself and do something productive."

Taking that advice to heart, he again tried to connect with Sarah and Lucien. When he still didn't link with either of them, he contemplated casting a spell to see if it would locate Lucien.

He quickly squelched the idea. Magic was meticulous, and for him to perform at a precise level, he needed to either see or be mentally linked with the person on whom he cast an enchantment. If he sent out a random spell, it might hit Sarah. He doubted it would harm her. If the wreath were powerful enough to protect her from the barrier, the spell he'd use would be about as annoying as a gnat. But the wreath might consider it an assault on her and strike out in defense, causing more harm to Lucien and possibly to himself.

With that option dismissed, he considered getting out of the car and looking for them. He realized, however, that would be as reckless as a random spell. If he didn't fall and break his neck, he might get caught up in the wreath. It could cocoon him, and then there'd be no one here to advise Zachary and Ryan when they arrived.

He released a frustrated breath and mumbled, "There has to be *something* I can do. If I have to just sit here in the dark, where each minute seems like hours, I'll go insane."

But no matter how hard he racked his brain, he couldn't come up with a plan of action that would make him feel useful. All he could do was sit here and worry and wonder. It wouldn't be so bad if he knew what was going on with Lucien and Sarah, but without a mind link, that was impossible.

Or was it? he suddenly wondered, as an idea struck him.

He straightened in his seat and said, "Spirit, are you here?"

"I am always with Sarah," the spirit answered instantly.

"How are Sarah and Lucien?"

"They are the same."

Sebastian knew he should be relieved that Lucien's condition hadn't worsened, but he couldn't relax until he found out if the worst possible scenario had occurred. "Is Lucien inside the wreath with Sarah?"

"Yes."

Sebastian shuddered as a feeling of doom crept over him. His voice was again hoarse as he asked, "Can Lucien survive in there?"

"His time is short."

"Do you know how to make the wreath leave them?" he asked next, ignoring the panic writhing in his belly. If anything happened to Lucien . . .

He abruptly cut off the thought as the spirit replied, "It will leave when Sarah goes behind the golden wall and your magic can no longer hurt her.

"Are you saying that if we take her onto coven land, the wreath will leave her and Lucien?"

"Yes."

"Is it safe for us to touch the wreath?"

"Only you. You must use your tipi."

"What's a tipi?" Sebastian asked, confused.

"Hurry. His time is short. I must go. Sarah calls for me."

"No! You can't leave until you tell me what a tipi is," Sebastian said frantically.

But before he finished the statement, he knew the spirit was gone.

"*Dammit!*" he bellowed. "What in hell is a tipi?"

The spirit, of course, didn't answer, and he muttered a string of vitriolic curses. By the time he finished, he was out of breath, and he still didn't know what a tipi was.

Before he could contemplate the matter further, he heard the sound of a car. He sat forward in his seat, surprised. It seemed as if he'd contacted Zachary just minutes ago, but he now realized it had probably been more like ten or fifteen minutes. He muttered another curse. Help had arrived, and he didn't know what to do.

Easing himself out of the car, he turned to face toward the direction they'd come, clutching the open door. Moments later the car stopped, and he heard doors open.

"Oh, my God!" a male voice Sebastian recognized as Ryan Alden's suddenly declared in horror.

Zachary said excitedly, "What the hell is it?"

"It's a lightning cocoon, and stay away from it," Sebastian ordered.

"You don't need to worry, Sebastian," Ryan replied, and Sebastian heard the sound of footsteps running toward him. "I wouldn't get near it with a ten-foot pole. Zachary said that Lucien's hurt. Where is he?"

"In the cocoon," Sebastian answered.

"What?" Ryan gasped.

"Well, I'll be damned," Zachary said, his tone still excited. "Where did it come from?"

"It's a long story, and I only have time to tell it once, so listen closely," Sebastian said, hating to waste the time. But if anything happened to him while handling the cocoon, the coven would need the information to deal with the talisman.

He gave them a capsulized account of everything

that had happened since Shana had found the triangle glowing in the repository.

When he got to the part about Sarah blinding him, Ryan gasped, "My God, Sebastian! Did you go to an emergency room and see a doctor?"

"I was hit in the eyes by magical lightning, Ryan," Sebastian stated grimly. "Your doctors couldn't have done anything for me."

"You don't know that," Ryan stated impatiently. "If you'd gone right away, they may have been able to help you, and—"

"Dammit, Ryan! Now is not the time to worry about me," Sebastian interrupted. "Lucien and Sarah are in the cocoon. The Indian spirit who accompanies her says that Sarah's safe but Lucien's time is short. He also said that the cocoon will leave them once they're on coven land, but according to him I'm the only one who can move them. The trouble is, he said I have to use my tipi, and I don't know what the hell a tipi is. I'm sure it's some kind of Indian word. Do either of you have any idea what it means?"

"Not me," Zachary said, his voice now subdued. "You know that our knowledge of Native Americans is limited."

"Ryan?" Sebastian said hopefully.

"I'm afraid that us mortals are almost as ignorant of Native Americans as you are," he answered. "But are you sure he said tipi?"

"Yes. Why?"

"Well, when you first said it, I thought you meant tepee."

"Tepee? As in the tent?"

"Yes."

Sebastian shook his head in frustration. "That can't be it."

"Are you sure?" Zachary asked. "Maybe he's telling you that you need to put a tent over the cocoon, and it will magically transport itself."

"I don't think so," Sebastian said. "He specifically said I needed to use *my* tipi, and I don't have a tent. Of course, he is a spirit, and my guess is he's been one for a long time, so it's possible he might assume that everyone has a tent."

"Or he doesn't understand our vocabulary and he's using symbolism to communicate," Ryan stated thoughtfully.

"I'm not following you," Sebastian said, frowning as he turned his head in the direction of Ryan's voice.

"Well, he sees something, but he either doesn't know our word for it, or he isn't comfortable using it, so he uses a word familiar to him to describe it. So, if he saw something that had the shape of a tepee, it stands to reason that he would call it a tepee. And a tepee is shaped like—"

"A triangle," Sebastian finished, raising his hand to the triangle resting against his chest. "*Damn!* I should have realized that immediately. In order to move the cocoon, I have to use the triangle."

"From what you've told us about the talisman, that isn't safe," Zachary pointed out. "The more you use it, the more power it will have over you."

Sebastian jerked his head in Zachary's direction. "If I don't use it, Lucien is going to die, and we can't afford that sacrifice. I'm already tainted by the talisman, which means I can't be trusted to act in the best interests of the coven, and even if I could, I'm blind. My condition is going to upset the coven members, but if they lose Lucien on top of it they'll panic. With a situation like that, the talisman is sure to destroy the coven, and once we fall, the rest of mankind is doomed."

"And I thought Moira was the worst thing I'd ever have to face in my life," Ryan bemoaned, referring to the evil spirit-witch that he and Shana had fought and defeated only a few months before.

"As you mortals say, Moira was a picnic compared to this," Sebastian replied gravely. "But now is not the time to stand around comparing evils. We have to get Lucien out of that cocoon."

"So Ryan, I want you to drive back onto coven land and wait," he instructed. "Zachary, you'll have to lead me to the cocoon, but keep your distance from it. If you see lightning leave it, run like hell, and don't stop for anything, not even me. Once I'm in position, I want you to join Ryan, and don't, under any circumstances, interfere, even if you think it's killing me. If the worse does happen and both Lucien and I are lost, you're going to have to hold the coven together and fight the talisman. Any questions?"

"No," they said in unison.

Sebastian nodded. "Then let's get moving."

Ryan left without another word, and Zachary moved to Sebastian's side. Sebastian placed his hand on the warlock's arm and let him lead him.

After telling him that they were rounding the back of the car, Zachary declared, "Damn, that cocoon is the most terrifying and yet the most spectacular thing I've ever seen, Sebastian. Do you think it's a product of the Old Ways?"

"I don't know, but wherever it came from, it's

pure evil," Sebastian replied, frowning at the new excitement in Zachary's voice.

He considered reminding Zachary of his instructions, but decided against it. Zachary was adventurous, but he was smart enough to realize the seriousness of the situation. Sebastian did decide, however, that if they got out of this mess alive, he'd recommend that Lucien send Zachary out into the mortal world for a few months. It would give Zachary a chance to appease his yearning for adventure, and, with any luck, he might even find a mortal mate. Sebastian suspected that only mating would cure him of his proclivity to go where angels feared to tread.

"Okay, the cocoon's about five feet ahead of you," Zachary said, breaking into Sebastian's musing. "Do you want me to lead you closer?"

"No. Just give me an idea of how large it is," Sebastian replied, dropping his hand from Zachary's arm when they stopped.

"Well, it's as long as Lucien is tall, so about six feet four or five inches in length, and it's just about that wide. Much too large for you to lift. So how do you think the talisman will move it? By levitation?"

"Most likely," Sebastian replied. "How far are we away from the boundary?"

"About a quarter of a mile. I'd say we're right inside the edge of where its spell begins."

Sebastian nodded. "Okay. I want you to join Ryan, and when you're there, let me know."

"Are you sure you don't want me to stay closer?" Zachary asked. "We won't be able to clearly see what's going on, and if you need help—"

"No, I don't want you closer," Sebastian interrupted. "As I said, you aren't to interfere, and you need to be safe. Now go and let me know when you've reached Ryan."

Sebastian felt Zachary's hesitation, but then he said, "I'm on my way."

Sebastian heard Zachary run away from him. As he waited for his message, he shuffled forward until he figured he'd moved to within a couple of feet of the cocoon. He knew he risked the wreath also encompassing him, but since the talisman needed him to get Sarah onto coven land, he didn't think that would happen.

I'm here, Zachary finally communicated.

Sebastian didn't bother responding, but reached immediately for the triangle, muttering to the talisman, "Okay, you bastard. Do your thing."

At first nothing happened, but then the wreath's whirring sound increased until it was an ear-shattering, high-pitched whine that culminated in a burst of thunder so strong it knocked him off his feet.

As he fell to the ground, he cursed, and then he screamed as his body was hit from head to toe with what felt like a hundred searing knives. When his body began to convulse from the electrical energy surging through him, he knew it was the lightning tormenting him. He felt as if he would die, but he knew in his heart that he wouldn't be that lucky.

It was as if the talisman waited for him to make that acknowledgment, for its voice suddenly said, *Look at your future!*

No! Sebastian mentally yelled in anguish as a vision flooded into his mind. He was standing with Sarah in the center of Sanctuary. Her face was so sharpened with evil that it looked cadaverous, and her hands dripped with blood. But more horrifying than her visage was the sight of the coven members' bodies littering the street. They'd all had their eyes gouged out.

Suddenly, Sarah smiled maliciously at him and said, "Look at your hands, Sebastian."

He shook his head in frantic denial, but his hands rose of their own accord.

Noooo! he screamed when he saw the blood on them.

As Sarah felt the crushing weight leave her chest, panic flooded through her and her eyes flew open. Her panic changed to confusion as she watched the lightning circle her. What had happened to her? How had she ended up in here? And where was Sebastian?

She turned her head to look for him. When she saw the man lying next to her, her confusion increased. It wasn't Sebastian but a stranger. Who was he, and how had he gotten in here with her? She tried to touch his mind for the answers, but she met the void of unconsciousness. Indeed, his mind was so empty that if she hadn't heard the shallow rasp of his breathing, she would have thought he was dead.

She shuddered, and panic again erupted inside her. Before it could take root, however, the lightning closed in on her. Suddenly its whirring sounded like a lullaby to her ears, and it began to stroke her with the gentleness of a mother's touch.

Or at least it was what she'd always imagined a mother's touch would feel like, she thought, sudden tears flooding her eyes. She had no memory of her mother. Indeed, she had no memory of her life before the moment Leonard found her on the mountaintop. All she'd known was that her name was

Sarah, she was five years old, and Wanága had come to her and told her she was to be the new guardian.

Why did my mother abandon me? she wondered forlornly, as the sense of aloneness—abandonment—that had tormented her since childhood flared up inside her. *Why did she leave me beneath a tree on an isolated mountaintop? Why, when it was the middle of winter, did she leave me wearing nothing more than my underwear? Didn't she love me? Did she want me to die?*

It doesn't matter why she did what she did, John Butler's voice suddenly whispered in her mind. *I am here, and you'll never be alone again.*

At his words, the lightning walls began to shimmer and blur. Sarah knew she was still cradled within the lightning's embrace, but it was John Butler's shabby motel room she now saw. He sat in the center of the bed, his legs folded into a lotus position. She was surprised he was still at the motel. Whenever she'd connected with him, he'd seemed to be moving closer to South Dakota.

"I let you believe I was on my way to South Dakota," he said, his expression impassive as he watched her. "It was the only way to fool the *wicáhmunga.* But I've always known you'd come to Sanctuary, and I've been waiting close by for you to arrive."

Sarah knew she should say something, but she could only stare into his ice-blue eyes and marvel at the dichotomy of emotions reflected in their chilling depths. Malevolence and, oddly enough, compassion. She shivered, suddenly feeling as if she were staring into a mirror and seeing the reflection of her own soul.

"You are seeing your own soul," he said bitterly.

"We are the same, Sarah. No one wants us. No one loves us, but they will use us to get what they want and then try to destroy us. And that's what the *wicáhmunġa* plans to do to you. He wants our power, and he'll do whatever it takes to make you trust him enough to surrender it to him. But once you give it to him, he will destroy you—*us*, and then he will destroy your people."

"You're wrong!" Sarah declared, but she didn't know if she denied his premise that they were alike or his comment about Sebastian's plans. "I have seen the future, and I am the destroyer."

"That's a lie. A trick played on you by your other enemy."

"My other enemy?"

"The spirit who calls himself Wanáġa and claims to be your spirit guide—your mentor. But even as we speak, he collaborates with the *wicáhmunġa*, just as he collaborated with another *wicáhmunġa* nearly a millennium ago.

"Summon Wanáġa, Sarah," he urged. "Ask him what he and the other *wicáhmunġa* did to the Thunderbeings so very long ago."

Sarah frowned, confused, but before she could question him, he and the room disappeared.

As she again watched the lightning encircle her, she tried to make sense of what he'd said about Wanáġa. She knew about the Thunderbeings, of course. The superior god, Inyan—the Rock—had created the associate god, Wakinyan, who was also known as the Thunderbeing to the Lakota and the Thunderbird to many other tribes. Wakinyan was a great bird who flew through the sky without eyes, mouth or ears, because no one was ever allowed to see him as a whole. He was the earth's electricity, and he controlled the substance and movement of storms. His voice was thunder and his glance, when he deigned to reveal it, lightning. But what did Wakinyan have to do with Wanága?

Summon him, Butler whispered in her mind. *Tell him it is time for you to know all.*

I don't want to know all! Sarah mentally cried, suddenly frightened by his parody of Wanága's maddening riddle. All her life she'd wanted to know its meaning, but she now intuited that it held some hidden horror.

Then make him tell you what you are and ask him why he's here.

She shook her head, but, on its own volition, her mind called out, *Wanága! Who am I?*

You are the last of the people known as the Thunderbeings, and, because of me, you became the most evil people to walk the earth, Wanága replied.

As Sarah's mind reeled with the information, Butler whispered insidiously, *Now, ask him why he's here.*

Again, Sarah shook her head, but it didn't stop her from asking, *Why are you here, Wanága?*

He didn't answer, and his silence caused fear to swell up inside her. *Please, Wanága, you must answer me. Why are you here?*

He sighed heavily and said, *To destroy you.*

14

Evil Invades

✛

To destroy you. Wanáġa's words raced through Sarah's mind with the speed of a rabbit fleeing a coyote, and fear erupted inside her. It was quickly followed by confusion and hurt, and, finally—thankfully—anger.

She latched onto the anger, mentally clutching it as tightly as a drowning man clinging to a lifeline. Oddly enough, she wasn't as furious with him for betraying her as she was at his betrayal of Leonard. Leonard had devoted his life to being the guardian, and, because of Wanáġa, he had trusted her to do the same.

She clenched her hands into fists. How could Wanáġa have done that to Leonard? Why had he convinced Leonard that she was supposed to be the new guardian when he'd known all along that she was the true curse? All those years Leonard had spent training her to overcome the triangle's evil had been nothing more than a cruel deceit, because he'd unknowingly taught the person fated to destroy their people.

But they are not your people. You are a Thunderbeing, her conscience reminded.

Sarah shivered. A Thunderbeing. Only she wasn't a real Thunderbeing. The real Thunderbeing oversaw and assisted the caretakers of the earth. The real Thunderbeing was the force of truth, striking down anyone who lied while holding the Sacred Pipe. The real Thunderbeing was a single deity. He was good. Pure. Holy. A god.

She might be known by the same name, but she was the last of the most evil people who ever walked the earth.

She wanted to scream at Wanága for wasting Leonard's time and her life. Why hadn't Wanága just killed her when he found her in the woods? Why had he let her live so she could carry out Seamus Morpeth's curse?

And she knew she would carry it out, for she had now come into her power and the lightning was hers. She couldn't walk away from her heinous destiny, because the talisman would never let her go.

Why, Wanága? she finally beseeched angrily. *Why didn't you destroy me before I came into my powers?*

For the very reason that you ask that question, Sarah, he replied.

Dammit! Don't play your riddle games with me. Tell me why!

He didn't respond, and the lightning suddenly emitted a high-pitched whine that made the unconscious man beside her groan in pain. Sarah blinked, startled. The sound didn't cause her distress. It was music to her ears, but she wasn't commanding the lightning, so who was?

Sebastian. She could sense his presence, could feel him summoning the lightning, and a new surge of anger rushed through her. Sebastian claimed he wanted to stop the talisman and save mankind. John Butler said Sebastian wanted her power. Since Butler had been right about Wanága, she had to believe he was right about Sebastian. Like Wanáǧa, the *wicáhmunǧa* was a deceiver and her enemy.

For a moment Sarah considered refusing to let the lightning respond to him. Then she decided that if he wanted the power, she'd give him a good taste of it.

Staring at the lightning, she ordered, "Obey him. Give him what he wants, and then strike him. Let him feel the pain of the power he so desires."

A moment later the lightning whirled around her so fast it was no more than a blur, and she felt the cocoon lift and fly forward. Suddenly there was a sound like two cars colliding at high speed. She caught her breath fearfully, sure that the lightning cocoon would burst apart.

But then the cocoon drifted back to the ground without so much as a jerk. Sarah drew in a relieved breath, but before she could release it, the lightning disappeared.

She expected to see Sebastian, and she again blinked in startlement when she found herself staring up at two strange men. One of them was a good-looking blond with warm brown eyes and a worried, albeit wary, expression. The other had shoulder-length, mink-brown hair and a face that looked like a chiseled sculpture. Sarah would have described him as devastatingly handsome if his eyes hadn't been pulsing with that odd glow she'd seen in Sebastian's eyes.

Sensing his hostility, she scrambled to her feet and took several steps back, saying, "Stay away from me."

"There's no reason for you to be frightened," the blond told her. "I'm Dr. Ryan Alden, and this is

Zachary Morcombe. We're Sebastian's friends. Are you all right?"

She nodded, eying them warily as she took several more steps back. Where was Sebastian?

Before she could ask, Dr. Alden dropped to his knees beside the man who'd been cocooned with her.

"Is Lucien okay?" the man called Zachary asked, although he never removed his pulsing gaze from Sarah's face.

"I don't know yet," the doctor replied grimly. "Have you connected with Sebastian yet? Is he okay?"

"He says he's fine. He's asking about Lucien."

"Well, it's going to take me a few minutes to figure out what's wrong with him, so go get Sebastian. By the time you're back, I should have a better idea of what's going on."

Zachary didn't respond for a moment, but then he said, "Sebastian says I'm not to leave you alone with her."

The doctor glanced up at him impatiently. "Well, tell Sebastian he's being ridiculous. You've cast a protective spell over me, so I'll be fine for the few minutes you're gone. Besides, if Lucien is suffering from some type of magical problem, I'll need his help. If that isn't enough to convince him, tell him that Lucien's crystal is pulsating like crazy, so Ariel has picked up on the fact that something's happened to him. If Lucien doesn't regain consciousness and reassure her, she'll start looking for him. When she does, the entire coven will know something's wrong, and I don't think Sebastian wants that to happen."

Zachary continued to stare antagonistically at

Sarah, and she took another few steps back. She started to brush against his mind to learn what he thought, but he suddenly murmured some indistinguishable words and flicked his fingers.

Sarah let out a yelp as lightning shot from his fingers and hit the ground in front of her. A shimmering, golden barrier, much like the one she'd seen while in the car, suddenly surrounded her. Only this barrier she could see through.

"What in hell are you doing?" Dr. Alden questioned, his expression shocked. "Sebastian said your magic will kill her!"

"Sebastian says it won't hurt her unless she tries to walk through it," Zachary answered. "Besides, it's what he told me to do—cage her so she can't harm you while I'm gone."

With that, he turned and jogged away, and Sarah wrapped her arms around herself, shivering. But it wasn't fear that made her tremble. It was anger so intense that every cell of her body vibrated with rage.

She hadn't done anything but stand here, and Sebastian had ordered her caged like an animal. Any remaining doubts she had about John Butler's claim that Sebastian was her enemy disappeared, and she vowed that she'd make Sebastian pay for this. If he wanted her power, she'd share it with him. Or, at least, she'd give him enough of a taste of it to make him destroy everything and everyone that mattered to him. And she knew that making him kill his people would be a far better form of revenge than if she made him watch her do it.

Then, after he'd completed the task, she would destroy him.

* * *

As Sebastian's horrifying vision of Sarah and him on the streets of Sanctuary disappeared, he heard a screeching metallic crash and then a silence so total he could hear his racing heartbeat. They'd been wrong! The spirit hadn't been talking about the triangle, and when the cocoon had hit the barrier, Sarah and Lucien must have been killed!

You were right, Sebastian! Zachary suddenly communicated triumphantly. *The cocoon came through the barrier, and the moment it landed, it disappeared.*

How are Sarah and Lucien? Sebastian questioned in relief, deciding that the noise must have been some kind of clash of magics as the cocoon encountered the barrier.

The woman says she's fine. Ryan is checking Lucien now. How are you?

I'm fine, he lied, sitting up. He felt as if he'd been put on a spit and roasted. Every inch of his body burned, and he was sure if he could look at himself, he'd see nothing but charred flesh. But his physical pain was nothing compared to his mental anguish. He shuddered, recalling the vision of Sarah and him standing in the streets of Sanctuary with the coven members' bodies scattered around them.

But that vision isn't going to come true! he told himself firmly. The talisman is tormenting me, trying to keep me off balance so I won't figure out what we have in Sanctuary that will stop it. And we *will* stop it.

His determination didn't alleviate his fears, but it gave him the mental fortitude to push them aside. Worrying wouldn't accomplish anything. He needed to come up with a battle plan, but first he had to find out about Lucien.

How's Lucien? he asked Zachary when the warlock didn't give him a report.

When Zachary explained it would take Ryan a few minutes to figure out what was wrong with Lucien, and he wanted Zachary to come get Sebastian, Sebastian refused. After the vision he'd had of him and Sarah destroying the coven, he wouldn't leave her alone with any coven member, and certainly not with only Ryan—a powerless mortal—to guard Lucien.

He frowned when Ryan insisted Zachary fetch him. Every argument Ryan presented was valid, particularly the one about Lucien's mate, Ariel.

Sebastian knew that because Lucien was half mortal, he had to use a crystal to augment his powers, and Ariel wore a matching crystal that connected them. She obviously felt his distress, and, as Ryan said, if Lucien didn't contact her soon, she'd panic and start looking for him. All she had to do was tell one coven member that something was wrong and the general alarm Sebastian had avoided earlier would be raised.

But, dammit, he didn't know what had happened to Sarah in the cocoon! If that violent vision he'd had was any indication, he was sure the talisman had corrupted her further. Leaving her alone with Ryan and Lucien could be catastrophic. Then, again, he was blind, and he couldn't make it onto coven land on his own. He could summon someone else to help them, but it would take time for whomever he chose to get here. Every minute might make a difference to Lucien's survival.

He felt a twinge of guilt at the sudden thought of having Zachary invoke a spell that would cage Sarah within a barrier and protect Lucien and Ryan while they were alone with her. Sebastian knew she wouldn't react well to being confined for no reason. However, Ryan and Lucien's safety had to take precedence over Sarah's feelings.

Thrusting away his guilt, he instructed Zachary to cast a confining spell. He continued to monitor the warlock's thoughts, again relieved when the spell was cast and Sarah didn't have any negative reactions. Assured that Sarah was all right, he cut off his connection with Zachary and struggled to his feet.

While he waited for the warlock's arrival, he began to outline a plan to deal with the talisman. The first matter of business was to bring Lucien back to consciousness. After they'd accomplished that, he'd have Lucien contact the council of high priests and tell them they needed to send a new troubleshooter to Sanctuary. He'd contact them himself, but he doubted the talisman would let him get through to them. Even if it did, he couldn't take the risk, because he wore the triangle and that might give the talisman some kind of foothold into the other covens.

Of course, after what Kendra said earlier, the talisman might not let Lucien communicate with them either. That's why Sebastian would instruct him not to give any explanation; just tell them it was urgent that a new troubleshooter be sent here immediately. The council would find Lucien's request strange, but they'd do as he asked. Hopefully, they could find a replacement for Sebastian and get him to Sanctuary within the next twenty-four hours. In the meantime, he and Lucien would call a meeting of the coven. They'd explain what was going on and ask them to watch Sarah so they could figure out what information they had to stop the talisman.

He also decided to summon Sarah's Indian spirit. The spirit might have information that could help them. However, questioning him would be tricky. He'd already suggested that this was a matter of destiny, so he'd be limited in what he could reveal directly. But Sebastian knew from his experience with the narrators, who were also limited in what they could tell, that oftentimes what *wasn't* said was more important than what was. It would be his job to present questions to the spirit that would help him fill in those critical blank spaces.

By the time he heard Zachary's running footsteps, he felt back in control. They *were* going to stop the talisman, and no visions it presented to him would convince him otherwise.

When Zachary arrived, he gasped, "Sebastian! What happened to you? You look as if you've walked through a forest fire."

"How bad are my burns?" Sebastian asked, again becoming aware of the pain. He'd been so busy making plans that he'd managed to shove it to the back of his mind until now.

"Physically, you've only got a few red spots on your face and hands, but your clothes are full of burn holes."

Sebastian stood there, stunned. He'd been sure he was burned to a crisp, and he was shocked to hear that only his clothes were the worse for wear. But if his burns were so minor, why was he in so much pain?

He didn't know, and he didn't have the time to figure it out.

"We need to get back to Ryan and Lucien, so help

me into the car," he told Zachary. "While you drive, you can tell me what happened when the cocoon came through the barrier."

Zachary led him around the car. By the time he fastened his seatbelt, Zachary had climbed into the driver's seat and the engine roared to life.

As the car began to move Zachary said, "When the cocoon first hit the barrier, there was this blinding light and it sounded like two cars hitting head-on at high speed. I was sure the cocoon had exploded, but then there was this strange whine that reminded me of a drill boring through metal. A moment later the cocoon shot through the barrier and landed at our feet. Then the wreath disappeared."

Sebastian didn't respond to Zachary's account, because he could feel them entering coven land. As they drove onto it Sebastian frowned. He sensed something different about the atmosphere, but he couldn't pinpoint what it was.

"Do you feel anything . . . strange about the magical energy in here?" he asked Zachary.

"Strange? In what way?" Zachary asked.

"I don't know," Sebastian said, his frown deepening. The feeling was so subtle that he couldn't describe it. But whatever it was worried him.

Before he could pursue it, the car stopped and Zachary announced, "We're here."

Zachary needn't have bothered telling him they'd reached the others. Sebastian could sense Sarah, feel her presence and her unmitigated fury, but when he tried to connect with her, her mind was closed to him. He knew her anger was due to her confinement, but what else could he do? She could destroy his friends—their world.

"Should I release the woman?" Zachary asked.

Sebastian vacillated, feeling torn again. Keeping Sarah confined would only make her angrier, but he might need Zachary's help with Lucien and the warlock wouldn't be able to keep an eye on her. After seeing that damnable vision, Sebastian knew her every movement had to be monitored closely. For that matter, so would his, because he was also corrupted. But he'd deal with that after reviving Lucien.

"Don't release her yet," he replied reluctantly.

As he climbed out of the car, he tried to connect with Lucien, but there was nothing. It was as if Lucien's mind had simply disappeared, and Sebastian muttered an inward curse. What had the wreath done to Lucien?

"My God, what happened to you?" Ryan gasped when Zachary led him to where he waited with Lucien. "Are you all right?"

"The cocoon's lightning got a little carried away, and I'm fine," Sebastian said. "So, what's your diagnosis on Lucien?"

"Outside of a few minor burns on his face and hands, I can't find anything physically wrong with him," Ryan answered. "There's no sign of a head injury, so I thought he was in shock, but his vital signs are strong. Medically speaking, he should be awake."

"So whatever's wrong with him is magical," Zachary said.

"Probably," Sebastian murmured, turning his head toward Sarah, or, rather, toward the incensed vibrations coming off her. "What can you tell us about Lucien's condition, Sarah? What did the wreath do to him?"

When she didn't answer, he said impatiently, "Look, Sarah, I know you're angry with me for having you confined, but you'll be released as soon as we wake up Lucien. So if you have any information that could help us do that, it would be in your best interest to share it."

She still didn't answer, and he wanted to yell at her, but he knew his anger would only fuel hers. Instead, he drew in a deep breath and said, "Please, Sarah. Help us."

When she didn't respond right away, he thought she would continue to ignore him, but then she said, "I don't know what happened to him, but his mind is displaced. He needs to link with someone who can lead him back here."

"How do I connect with him to do that?" Sebastian asked warily. He'd never heard of a mind being displaced, and if, as she claimed, she didn't know what happened to Lucien, how could she know what was wrong with him, let alone how to help him?

"You can't do it by yourself," she answered.

Sebastian's internal warning signal went on red alert.

"Who has to help me?" he asked, instinctively knowing the answer.

She confirmed his suspicion. "Me."

"I see," he said.

"What's the matter, *wicáhmunǵa*? Don't you trust me?" she scoffed.

About as far as I can see you, he thought grimly. Aloud, he said, "Is there any reason I shouldn't trust you?"

"There must be. Why else would you have me caged like an animal?"

He inwardly cringed at her words. "I was merely taking the safest route for all of us, Sarah. I didn't want my friends hurt, but I'm also concerned about you. The talisman has its hold on you, and you were just in its cocoon. I have no idea how that affected you, and I didn't want you to do something you might regret later."

She let out a bitter laugh. "So you caged me for my own good. What amazes me is that you really think a few walls can control me. Well, you're wrong, *wicáhmunǧa*. I don't need to be free to summon the lightning and have it do my bidding. I can stand right here in your metaphysical prison cell and destroy you and every one of your people. Would you like me to prove that to you? Would you like me to strike down one of your friends right here and now?"

"No," Sebastian said, the hair rising on the back of his neck. Her voice had a sinister edge that was positively chilling. Suddenly, he recalled how, just before she'd blinded him, her face had taken on that cruel, almost inhuman, cast and her large golden eyes had glittered with malevolent hatred. He knew that's how she looked now. He also knew that she was on the verge of carrying out her threat. Somehow he had to talk her out of it.

"I believe you can do exactly what you say," he said. "However, I have to wonder why you didn't kill Ryan and Lucien while Zachary came to get me. For us to return and find them dead would have carried far more impact than you standing there telling us what you can do. Is it that you require an audience while you exhibit your power? Or is there a part of you rebelling against the urge to kill?

"I think it's the latter," he went on before she

could respond. "I think that during your training to be the guardian, you developed a strong moral code that the talisman hasn't been able to erode completely. It can push you into performing a violent act like blinding me, but I don't think it's yet reached the point where it can incite you to murder. In fact, I believe that so strongly that I'm going to have Zachary release you."

Again, he didn't wait for her to respond, but ordered, "Zachary, remove the confining spell and set Sarah free."

As he heard Zachary murmur the words, he started to mentally instruct the warlock to be ready to reinvoke the spell if Sarah exhibited combative behavior once it was gone. He refrained, because if she told the truth, confining her wouldn't make a difference.

When he felt the energy from Zachary's spell dissipate, he said, "Okay, Sarah. You're free, and I won't have anyone confine you again. However, I'm not sure that the talisman has let you in on the fact that our magic has a deadly effect on you. That's why you passed out in the car and the lightning cocoon had to come and save you. You were reacting to the magic emanating from the energy barrier surrounding Sanctuary. It won't affect you as long as you're on coven land, because the magic flows outward, not inward. But if you try to leave, you'll never make it through the barrier alive. If you think that killing all of us will alleviate the barrier, you're wrong. The spell will remain even if we're dead."

When he finished speaking, she laughed again, and again the hair on the back of his neck stood on end as she drawled, "Oh, *wicáhmunga*, if you could see your magical energy barrier, you'd realize what a fool you are. When my cocoon came through it, it put a crack in it. Even as we speak, your barrier is beginning to disintegrate. By the time I'm ready to leave here, it will be gone."

Shocked, Sebastian stood there while her words ricocheted through his mind. *When my cocoon came through it, it put a crack in it. Even as we speak, your barrier is beginning to disintegrate.*

That's why the magical energy felt strange when he came onto coven land! The protective barrier had been disrupted, and once it was gone Sanctuary would never again be safe from the mortal world.

At that moment, he understood the talisman's plan. It had used Seamus Morpeth to instill the witch hysteria in the mortal population, and then directed that hysteria toward the coven. If Ulrich Morgret hadn't figured out what Seamus was up to, the coven would have been destroyed. But Ulrich had figured it out, and he'd broken up the talisman. Then the coven fled to here, where they erected the energy barrier to protect themselves.

Now, once the energy barrier was gone, the talisman would use Sarah and Butler to again instill the witch hysteria in the mortals and direct them toward the coven. The coven couldn't fight them because they weren't allowed to use their magic against mortals, even to defend themselves. Of course, once the mortals were filled with fear, most of their spells wouldn't work against them anyway.

To escape the hysteria, they could flee to the covens in Europe. But according to Kendra, once they left this continent, they wouldn't remember anything about the talisman, so they wouldn't be able to warn the covens there of impending disaster.

Meanwhile, the talisman would just wipe out the population here and follow them.

A shiver of doom crawled up Sebastian's spine, but when he felt panic knot in his stomach, he quickly tamped it down. He'd brought Sarah here and endangered the coven, and now he had to save them. The only way to do that was to repair the barrier, and he'd need Lucien's help to do that. But according to Sarah he needed her help to bring Lucien back to consciousness.

Could he trust her to do that? Or was this just another of the talisman's tricks to cripple the coven?

He didn't know, but he had to make a decision fast.

15

Evil Seduces

As Sarah told Sebastian about the disintegrating barrier, she was so focused on him that she started when Zachary stated, "Sebastian, the woman's lying to you. I'm looking at the barrier, and there's nothing wrong with it."

Sarah jerked her head toward Zachary. He stood with his back to them, staring at the barrier. She glared at him, anger surging through her. How dare he call her a liar!

Impulsively, she reached for the triangle, ready to summon the lightning and make him pay for defaming her, but Wanága suddenly whispered in her mind, *How would Leonard feel if he could see you now?*

Don't you even think Leonard's name! she fumed, her anger escalating to fury. *You lied to him, betrayed him.*

Is that why you now betray him?

I am not betraying Leonard!

You prepare to strike down a man for saying what he sees with his eyes. Would Leonard approve of that?

I will not listen to you! You want to destroy me.

I did not say I want to destroy you, Sarah. I said I am here to destroy you.

Dammit! It's the same thing, so go away and leave me alone. You are my enemy!

I am not your enemy, and I cannot go away. But I will not contact you until you call for me.

I will never call for you again.

You will call. Don't wait until it's too late.

Before Sarah could come up with an appropriately scathing remark, she felt his presence leave her. Again, she reached for the triangle, but Leonard's image formed in her mind's eye, his eyes filled with disappointment and his lips pursed in disapproval.

New fury flared inside her. She was sure Wanága created the vision of Leonard, that it was one of his tricks to protect Sebastian and his friends. After all, John Butler had said that Wanága collaborated with the *wicáhmunga*.

Despite that knowledge, she couldn't touch the triangle with Leonard's reproachful visage so fresh in her mind.

With an inward curse, she crossed her arms over her chest and, still glaring at Zachary, said, "Is your friend calling me a liar, *wicáhmunga?*"

"Are you lying?" he rejoined.

She snapped her head toward him. When she saw her image reflected against the mirrored lenses of his glasses, she shivered involuntarily. Again she had the sensation that he could see her, was peering into the depths of her soul.

Giving an impatient shake of her head at that ridiculous notion, she countered, "What could I possibly gain by lying?"

"I can think of many possibilities," he replied, reaching up to adjust his glasses. The action reinforced the feeling that he could see her, and, to her irritation, she shivered again.

"Such as?" she challenged.

He smiled grimly. "The first rule of war, Sarah, is never reveal what you know to the opposition. And that's what the talisman is doing, isn't it? Declaring war on the coven."

"You are the one who declared war," she shot back. "You want to steal the lightning's power, and it doesn't belong to you. It belongs to me."

"You're wrong, Sarah. The power belongs to the talisman, and it grants its use to whomever it chooses. For now, it has chosen you, but John Butler and I are in possession of its other pieces. If it decides that one of us is more corruptible than you, it will transfer its fealty without hesitation. So if it's the feeling of omnipotence that's binding you to it, you'd better face up to the fact that your powerful days may be short lived."

Sarah opened her mouth to argue with him, but closed it when she recalled John Butler saying, "The lightning is a part of our power, Sarah. It hurts us because you fight it. Embrace it and it will make us all powerful."

Our power. It will make *us* all powerful.

Suddenly, she realized that John Butler spoke as if they shared the power and perhaps at this time they did. But Sarah knew deep down that once the three pieces came together, only one person would control the lightning. Since she was the last of the Thunderbeings, who, according to Wanága, were the most evil people who ever walked the earth, she knew she would be that person. So why was the talisman deceiving Butler, making him believe he would share her control over the lightning?

She knew the question was important, but she couldn't come up with the answer. Out of habit, she started to call for Wanáġa so she could ask him, but she caught herself before she gave in to the urge. She couldn't trust him to tell her the truth, so she would have to figure it out on her own.

"So, Sarah, where do we stand here?" Sebastian asked, breaking into her troubled musing. "Are you going to work with us or against us?"

Sarah shifted from one foot to the other, deciding that she'd never felt so confused in her life. Butler said Sebastian was her enemy. Sebastian said the talisman was her enemy. Wanáġa said he *wasn't* her enemy but admitted that he was here to destroy her. Who should she believe? Who told her the truth?

Suddenly, she recalled something Leonard had said to her many years ago. *All our lives we face enemies, Sarah, but in the end we discover that the true enemy lies within ourselves. Face the inner enemy first, and then you will know for sure who your outward enemies are.*

Deciding to take Leonard's advice, she looked at Sebastian and said, "For now, I will not work against you."

Sebastian frowned at Sarah's response. He was relieved that she wasn't going to fight them. However, she hadn't said she'd work with them, and he needed her help to bring Lucien back.

But what if Lucien's condition is another of the talisman's tricks? his conscience continued to nag.

Sebastian knew his doubts were valid, but he couldn't see any other choice. To restore the barrier, the coven would have to combine their magic. But the only way they could do that was to channel it through either their high priest or the trouble-shooter.

Sebastian's magic worked at the moment, but the talisman had taken it away from him before, and it could do so again. If that happened in the middle of the channeling, the coven's magic would rebound on them and that would destroy them all in an instant.

So he either had to bring Lucien back or ensure his death. Unless Lucien had broken coven law, which he hadn't, the coven members could only be released from their allegiance to him through death. But if the worst did happen and Lucien died, then the coven would be free to select a new high priest and join with him to repair the barrier.

Knowing that Lucien would gladly sacrifice himself to save the coven didn't make Sebastian's decision more bearable, and he wanted to rail at the unfairness. He refrained because he knew they'd run out of time. At this moment Ariel could be out spreading the alarm, and Sebastian couldn't contact her to stop her. As a mortal, she abhorred the coven members' abilities to read her mind when she couldn't reciprocate, so Lucien had cast an enchantment over her that blocked her mind from everyone but him. Sebastian decided that if Lucien did come out of this alive, he'd make him revise that spell. Ariel might be a mortal, but she was now a coven member, and in an emergency she had to be accessible.

But that was a problem to worry about later, he reminded himself.

Drawing in a deep breath, he said, "I'm glad you won't fight us, Sarah. Now, I need to know if you will help me bring Lucien back."

"That depends on whether you're willing to do what must be done," she replied.

"And what's that?"

"Join the power of our triangles and summon the lightning."

"Why do we have to join our triangles when you can summon the lightning on your own?" he asked suspiciously.

"I already explained that, *wicáhmunǧa*. He must link with someone who can lead him back here."

"So he can link with you, and you can lead him back."

"He doesn't know me, so he doesn't trust me. Without trust, he won't cooperate."

"Well, why don't you try it anyway? If it doesn't work, then we'll join the triangles."

"I'm afraid that isn't possible," she said. "When the lightning touched him, it created what, for lack of a better term, I'll call a negative polarity that displaced his mind. Once we use the lightning it will reverse that polarity and he will have a small window of time to return. Once that window is closed, it can't be reopened, which is why he needs to link with someone he trusts to draw him back before it's too late."

"Earlier, you said you didn't know what happened to him," Sebastian noted. "I find it damn suspicious that you now not only know what happened but exactly how to fix it."

"First your friend calls me a liar, and now you call me one," she said irritably. "I was telling you the truth earlier. I don't know what happened to him, or, rather, I don't know *why* it happened to him. As for knowing how to fix it, I just know that this is what we need to do."

As he considered her words, Sebastian rubbed a hand against his stubbled jaw. Magically, what she was saying made sense. His doubt lay in her knowledge of what had to be done to reach Lucien. He was sure the talisman fed her the information, but was it accurate or a deception?

"Assuming that we join the triangles, what will prevent us from being displaced by the lightning?" he finally asked.

"I cannot be displaced," she replied. "I control the lightning."

"That assures your safety, but what about mine?" When she didn't respond, he said, "Isn't it possible that we'll pull Lucien back, only to have me replace him?"

A long moment passed before she said, "I don't know."

"That's what I thought."

He turned in the direction where he knew Ryan and Zachary stood, and said, "Ryan, I want you to get in your car and go to Ariel. Explain to her what's going on, but keep her at the house. Under no circumstances are you to let her come here."

"I don't think I should leave," Ryan answered. "Both you and Lucien may need medical attention when this is over."

"If we do, you'll only be a short drive away. It's more important that Ariel have someone with her, and you know that's exactly what Lucien would want."

"Yeah, I know," Ryan said with a heavy sigh. "Is there anything else you want me to do?"

"Yes. Drive Zachary about three miles up the road and leave him there."

"Dammit, Sebastian! I'm not leaving you and Lucien here alone with *her*," Zachary declared.

"Yes, you are," Sebastian stated firmly. "If anything happens to Lucien and me, you're the most powerful warlock in Sanctuary. You'll become the new high priest and will have to lead the fight against the talisman."

"But—"

"Look, Zachary, I know that your allegiance to Lucien demands that you stay here to protect him," Sebastian broke in impatiently. "I also know that Lucien would be the first one to remind you that the safety of the coven comes first. If we die, the coven will need you, and you can't put yourself at risk. You know I'm right, so don't argue with me."

He heard Zachary draw in a deep breath, and he expected the warlock to argue with him anyway. But then Zachary released the breath and said, "Okay. You're right, but I don't like it."

"Join the club," Sebastian stated. "Now go with Ryan and let him drop you off about three miles up the road. You can connect with me and follow what's going on, but do *not* interfere under any circumstances.

"Once this is over if your connection with me is broken, try to connect with Lucien," he went on. "If you can't connect with him, get to Sanctuary and call an emergency meeting of the elder warlocks. Tell them what happened, and they'll be able to determine if Lucien is dead. If he is, they'll take the appropriate steps to make you the new high priest.

"While they're doing that, you summon the Narrators, Kendra and Oran Morovang, and ask them how to contact the high council to get a new troubleshooter. They'll probably balk, so be sure to tell them that you know everything that I know about the talisman. Explain that you aren't asking them to advise you, but to instruct you on the mechanics of making the contact, because they're the only ones who'll be left to know how to do that. Get in touch with the council first, and then unite the coven's power and try to mend the barrier. Do you have any questions?"

"A million, but you don't have time to answer them."

"No, I don't. Now go."

He sensed Zachary's hesitation, but then the warlock said, "Good luck."

"Thanks," Sebastian said, turning back toward Sarah as he listened to Zachary walk away.

The moment he heard the car start, he said, "Okay, Sarah. What do we need to do to help Lucien?"

"Are you sure you want to go through with this?" she asked. "By saving your friend, you may end up lost forever."

"Like you, I'm the guardian of my people. We both know the guardian is expendable."

She was silent for a long moment. "Why, *wicáh-munga*, are you trying to convince me that you're self-sacrificing rather than self-serving?"

"No," he muttered. "I'm just doing my job, so let's get started."

He heard her walk toward him, her moccasined feet a soft rustle against the ground. Even though he knew she approached, he still started when she suddenly touched the triangle on his chest. Energy coursed through him, and he cursed silently when that energy promptly shifted to desire, centering itself in his groin. As he felt his penis swell to life, he wanted to jerk away from her. Conversely, he wanted to grab her and haul her into his arms. He almost succumbed to the latter urge, but then remembered that Zachary would be connecting with him. The warlock wouldn't be able to see what happened between Sarah and him, but he would pick up on Sebastian's physical and emotional feelings.

"Zachary is going to connect with my mind at any moment, if he hasn't already done so," he told Sarah. "I don't know about you, but I'm not into voyeurism, even if it is only cerebral."

She laughed softly, seductively. "Don't worry, *wicáhmunga*. In a moment he'll be cut off from everything but your heartbeat."

Before he could respond, she said, "Come to me!"

Instantly, he heard the lightning wreath's whir, and he braced himself for the ensuing pain of its touch. It came swiftly and with such searing magnitude that he couldn't breathe, let alone scream. And then, as quickly as it arrived, the pain was gone, leaving in its wake a quivering, tumultuous lust so voracious it consumed him.

"You don't need these any longer," Sarah suddenly murmured, and he felt her remove his sunglasses.

Until then he didn't realize his eyes were closed. Slowly, he opened them, and he gasped, stunned, as he saw the whirling walls of the wreath's cocoon surrounding them. He could see!

"Only in your mind, *wicáhmunga*," Sarah said, taking a step back from him.

Sebastian's gaze automatically flicked over her. She was naked, and her black hair was again loose, swirling around her slender body like a cape. The sight of her feminine curves incited his lust to such intensity that he wanted to grab her and take her violently, painfully.

"Then do it," she encouraged, stepping toward him again and trailing her hand down his chest.

"No!" Sebastian declared furiously, grabbing her wrist as her hand began to slide toward his erection. "We've played this game before, and I am *not* an animal."

His fury was nothing compared to the rage that leapt into her eyes, turning them into golden flames of hatred as she spat, "You have no choice, *wicáhmunga*. Take me as you were meant to take me before, or I will torture your friend until you do."

She raised her free hand and pointed to the left. Sebastian immediately swiveled his head in that direction and gasped in horror. What seemed like hundreds of lightning tendrils left the walls and slithered onto Lucien's body, which lay on the cocoon's floor.

As Sebastian stared at the tendrils their tips transformed into eyeless snake heads, just as they had when he and Sarah had been cocooned on the mountaintop, and they began to writhe and hiss. He knew that they were waiting for Sarah's order to strike. He also knew that when they did, Lucien would suffer the torture she promised.

He shuddered and forced his gaze back to Sarah's face, which had again sharpened into inhuman cruelty. He knew the change in her was due to the cocoon. Every time it encased her, it changed her, stealing another piece of her humanity. But apparently it had to force Sarah and him into a brutal coupling to complete her transformation into its evil minion, or she wouldn't be demanding that he rape her. But why did it need her to be sexually victimized to accomplish that goal, when there were any number of equally vicious means it could use?

He didn't have the faintest idea. If, however, it was that important to the talisman, he knew he couldn't go through with it.

"I am not going to rape you, Sarah," he said, steeling himself against the knowledge that he could be condemning Lucien to a horrible, torturous death. "So if you're going to kill Lucien, get it over with."

"Oh, I will not kill your friend," she drawled. "I will leave his mind trapped in the darkness where it now exists, and his only company will be the lightning snakes."

Sebastian shuddered at the image her words conjured up. Lucien was trapped in darkness, just as blind as Sebastian would again become once he was released from the cocoon. He looked at Lucien, not even wanting to imagine what it would be like to be lost in that murky void with those monstrosities.

"He can hear the lightning snakes, *wicáhmunga*," Sarah said in a strangely crooning voice. "He can feel them crawling over his body. But he can't see them. He can't touch them to knock them away. He knows they will strike, but he doesn't know when or how often. It will always be a surprise attack."

"Stop it!" Sebastian yelled, jerking his head back to glare at her.

"What's the matter, *wicáhmunga*?" she mocked. "If you can choose to condemn your friend to a nightmare, surely you should be willing to know how he will suffer."

He balled his hands into fists. It was the only way he could keep from wrapping them around her throat and strangling her. He knew, however, that the talisman wouldn't let her die. It would just use the violence to sink its claws deeper into both of them.

Through gritted teeth, he ordered, "Release Lucien. Now."

"I can't," she replied, her lips lifting into a taunting smile. "The only way to open the window to where he is is if you take me, and if you don't do it soon, it will be too late."

As the impact of her statement hit him, Sebastian trembled with new fury. The talisman had maneuvered him into a no-win situation. If he didn't take Sarah, Lucien would be trapped alive. And as long as he was alive, the coven couldn't elect a new high priest without a special dispensation from the high council. That would take time—time they didn't dare risk, because he had no idea how fast the barrier was disintegrating.

However, if he did take Sarah with brutal ruthlessness, he was sure she'd turn completely evil. So even if that act would bring Lucien back, they'd not only have to contend with the barrier, but with Sarah's transformation. Even a child warlock could figure out that she'd use the talisman's power to stop them from their repair work.

Sebastian muttered a violent curse and raked a hand through his hair. He loathed the thought, but his only logical choice was to sacrifice Lucien—let him remain in that dark, nightmarish world with the lightning snakes—rather than give in to Sarah's demand. After all, there was no guarantee that if Lucien did come back his magic would work. The talisman could have taken away his powers, just as it had Sebastian's so many times.

Except if Lucien came back powerless, he could voluntarily step down as high priest, and Zachary

could be put into the position immediately. The only
other solution was to send for a new troubleshooter,
but there was no guarantee that they could get
through to the high council to make the request.
Even if they did, he might not make it here in time
to save them.

Dammit! Why was it so important for Sarah to be
sexually assaulted? If he just knew the answer to
that question, he might be able to fight back.

The question is not why, wicáhmunga, the Indian
spirit suddenly murmured in his mind. *It is who.*

What in hell does that mean? Sebastian demanded.

If you are meant to know all, you will understand.

16

Evil Gathers

✠

The question is not why. It is who. As Sebastian mentally repeated the spirit's words, their meaning suddenly hit him. He shook his head, irritated that he hadn't seen the answer before. The sexual assault wasn't important. It was *who* performed it, and obviously, that *who* was him.

But why him specifically? he wondered as he regarded Sarah's evil countenance warily. The only reason he could think of was that he wore a piece of the talisman. But if that were the case, why hadn't the talisman chosen Butler for the job? According to Sarah, the man had killed at least two people, so he wouldn't think twice about rape.

Dammit! There's something I'm not seeing. What the hell is it?

"Your time is running out, *wicáhmuŋġa*," Sarah said. "Are you going take me as you were meant to take me? Or do I tell the lightning snakes to attack your friend?"

As if to add emphasis to her words, the lightning tendrils hissed louder. Sebastian told himself to ignore them, but he couldn't resist looking at them. They'd wrapped themselves around Lucien's body so that he now resembled an electrified mummy. As Sebastian watched them writhe and quiver, they

suddenly raised their illusionary heads toward
Sarah, as if eagerly awaiting her permission to begin
their torture.

Bile rose to Sebastian's throat, and he returned
his attention to Sarah. Every ounce of decency in
him screamed that he should do what she wanted
and save Lucien. No one should suffer through
what she planned to do to him.

But the credo for his race was inviolable. No single person's life was more important than the safety
and survival of the coven. And it wasn't just the
coven at risk, he reminded himself. It was all of
mankind.

"What is it going to take to make you reach a decision?" Sarah demanded. "Do you want to see the
lightning snakes strike your friend? Do you want to
hear his screams of agony? And you will hear them.
His mind is displaced, but his body functions as if
it were whole, so his vocal cords work just fine."

As Sebastian listened to her diatribe, he felt a
sense of déjà vu. He'd heard a variation of this
speech before. Why did it sound so familiar? Why
did he feel it was important that he remember?

"This is your last chance, *wicáhmunġa*," Sarah
warned. "Give me your answer now, or I will prove
to you how badly your friend will suffer."

The moment she said *prove,* Sebastian realized
why her words were familiar. She was threatening to
harm Lucien, just as she'd threatened to harm
Zachary or Ryan to prove that her powers worked
from within the confines of Zachary's spell. Then, as
now, she *told* him what she could do, when *showing*
him would have had a greater psychological effect.

As the significance of that hit him, he stared at
her in amazement. Outwardly she looked like evil

personified, as if she didn't have one shred of humanity left, but perhaps she hadn't lost her humanity. If she had, she wouldn't refrain from torturing Lucien to coerce Sebastian into doing what she wanted.

The instant he came to that realization, he understood why the talisman wanted him to rape Sarah. Three people wore pieces of the talisman—Sarah, Butler and himself—and he knew instinctively that all three of them had to be debauched before the pieces could come together. But so far the talisman had only managed to fully corrupt Butler, as evidenced by the fact that he'd committed murder.

Sebastian was sure that the taking of a life was the final, irrevocable step all of them had to take for the talisman to reach its full power. It had pushed Sarah into blinding him, but he wore a piece of the talisman. It couldn't let her kill him, because it needed him alive and corrupted or the pieces couldn't reunite.

So for Sarah to fall victim to its corruption, she had to kill. The talisman gave her the chance to do that while confined in Zachary's spell. But she'd resisted because, as Sebastian had told her then, her strong moral code was still intact. She'd been furious at being unfairly confined, but no one had done her any actual physical harm, so her morality wouldn't let her commit murder.

But rape was one of the most brutal, degrading crimes that could be committed upon a woman. If he assaulted Sarah, he would cause her both physical and emotional trauma. She'd have reason to strike out in revenge against him, and what better revenge than to kill someone important to him— Lucien. Once she did that, her soul would belong to the talisman. And by raping her, he'd have taken the first step toward losing his own soul.

At the moment he knew the talisman was lying to Sarah. His sexually debasing her wouldn't open a window to release Lucien's mind. Indeed, he doubted there was any window involved. The talisman had simply used Lucien as bait to draw him into the cocoon with Sarah, and to give her a victim to kill once he'd raped her.

But if he didn't go along with the talisman's plans, would Lucien's mind be restored? Hopefully, he could trick Sarah—or, rather, the talisman—into answering that question.

"If I refuse to do what you ask, will the talisman release us, or will it just force us together as it did before?" he asked her.

Her lips twisted into a malevolent parody of a smile. "Very good, *wicáhmunga*. It's true that you will take me one way or another. Your decision lies in whether you will save your friend before you do."

"How can I be sure that having sex with you will save Lucien? How do I know you aren't lying to me?"

"I have no reason to lie. As I said, you will take me, regardless of your decision."

He nodded. "How does the magic work? Is it the act of copulation that opens the window to Lucien's mind or something else?"

She scowled at him. "You don't need to know how it works. You only need to do what you were meant to do."

"Oh, come on, Sarah," he cajoled. "I'm a warlock and magic is my stock-in-trade. Satisfy my curiosity and tell me how it works. After all, it isn't as if I can get out of having sex with you, so why would it matter if I know how the magic works?"

Her scowl deepened and she eyed him warily. "You're trying to trick me, but it won't work. I can read your mind, and I will make you do what you must do."

"You haven't been reading my mind, though, have you?" he countered, startled to realize it had to be the truth. Otherwise, she'd have tried to persuade him his conclusions about the talisman's scheme were wrong. "Why, Sarah? Are you afraid to read my mind for some reason?"

"I have no reason to fear you!" she declared angrily, "and the time for talking is over. Do you choose to save your friend or not?"

"I choose to save him, but I still want an answer to my original question. Is it the sex act itself that opens the window?" Sebastian replied, knowing by the vehemence of her response that she *was* afraid to read his mind. But why? Was the talisman instilling her fear? Was it afraid that if she followed his deductions, she'd realize it was a trap and fight against it?

"It doesn't matter how it opens, only that you do what you were meant to do so that it will," she said, breaking into his musing.

Her refusal to answer the question convinced Sebastian that he was right. There was no window involved. Lucien was nothing more than bait for him and a convenient victim for her. Since the talisman wouldn't let them out of the cocoon until they'd had sex, he'd have to thwart it as he'd done before—make love to her and pray that by resisting the talisman's scheme, Lucien would be freed.

Even as he made the decision, Sebastian knew

making love to Sarah wouldn't be as easy as it sounded. His fear for Lucien had quelled his desire, or, at least, quieted it. But now, as his gaze flowed down her beautiful, naked body, lust streaked through him like a bolt of white-hot lightning.

Before he could make a grab for self-control, Sarah walked to him, dropped to her knees and took him into her mouth. As her lips closed over him, he lost the ability to think. All he could concentrate on was satisfying the overpowering needs of his body.

He must take you as he was meant to do. You must not fail this time.

Sarah shivered, fear gnawing at her insides. The words were an insistent chant that had echoed through her mind from the moment the cocoon descended over them. She knew Sebastian desired her; his magnificent erection proved that. But he'd wanted her before and refused to take her as he was supposed to take her. She couldn't let him do that again. She had to make him want her so badly that he'd take her as he was meant to do.

When he paused in his questioning, she decided that it was time to stop talking and take action. Instinctively, she walked to him, dropped to her knees, and drew his erection into her mouth. He gasped and she felt a tremor race through his body. But though she could sense the lust coursing through him, he stood unnaturally still.

At first she thought she had done something wrong, that she wasn't providing him enjoyment. But then he tangled his fingers in her hair and groaned deeply, gutturally, while moving his hips so that he slowly slid in and out of her mouth in a provocative parody of lovemaking.

Sarah shivered again, but it wasn't from fear this time. It was from a seductive sense of feminine power, the certain knowledge that her intimate kiss could drive Sebastian to the brink and beyond. She wanted to continue her teasing torment and bring him to a shattering climax, just as he'd used his lips and tongue and hands to do the same to her when they'd made love on the mountaintop.

No! don't let him bewitch you, a voice inside her protested vehemently. *You must deny him satisfaction, or he will not take you as he was meant to take you. You cannot fail this time!*

The words flashed through Sarah's mind with the force of a shout. She immediately released Sebastian from her oral intimacy, and he muttered a curse. Slowly, she let her gaze travel up his muscular body to his face. His eyes gleamed with that incandescent light, and his expression was taut with lust. But the triangle on his chest glowed red with anger.

She regarded him warily. Lustful anger was the emotion she wanted to provoke in him. She needed him to want her so badly that when she refused him, he'd take her anyway. However, she knew that he'd again managed to separate his lust from his anger, just as he had on the mountain. Somehow she had to make him unite the two emotions or she'd never conquer him.

His fingers were still tangled in her hair, and he flexed them against her scalp as he drawled derisively, "What's the matter, Sarah? Lose your nerve?"

"No," she said, running a hand up the inside of his thigh to his testes. As she cupped him, he sucked in a harsh breath and closed his eyes tightly. Again, the seductive sense of feminine power surged through her. While she gently kneaded him she drew the tip of his shaft into her mouth, circling it with her tongue. His entire body went rigid and his fingers again flexed in her hair. She knew he was on the verge of ejaculation, and she immediately pulled away from him.

His eyes flew open, and he scowled down at her as he rasped, "It isn't going to work, Sarah. You can't tease me into raping you."

"Well, you aren't going to deny me the pleasure of trying, are you?" she responded throatily.

His scowl darkened to a glower. "That depends on how brave you are."

"I can be as brave as necessary."

"I doubt it."

She dropped her hands away from him and eyed him suspiciously. "What is it you think I'm not brave enough to do?"

He uncurled his fingers from her hair and crossed his arms over his chest. "Truly seducing me—not just physically, but mentally. And that's what it will take for you to drive me into mindless lust."

At his blatant challenge, Sarah told herself to ignore him, that whatever he was up to was a trick. Curiosity, however, got the best of her, and she asked, "And just how do I conduct this mental seduction?"

"Open your mind to me," he answered. "Let yourself connect with me and let me show you how I feel—how my body responds—when you arouse me."

"No," she stated hoarsely, an erotic shimmer of excitement stirring low in her abdomen at his words. She knew she couldn't do as he asked. He was a *wicáhmunga* and could take control of her mind, and she couldn't let that happen.

That didn't stop her from wondering what it would be like to feel what he felt when he was aroused.

His lips lifted in a taunting smile. "I told you you weren't brave enough, so you might as well give up now. Without the mental seduction, you'll never get what you want from me."

Sarah frowned, retorting, "You would think that by now you'd know I won't fall for your tricks, *wicáhmunga.*"

Instead of responding, he dropped to his knees in front of her, caught her chin in his hand and studied her face for a long moment. Then he gave an amazed shake of his head.

"You look so . . . wicked, but I know the talisman's distorting your image. I also know that deep down you're fighting its evilness, and that's why it doesn't want you to connect with my mind. It's afraid you'll learn it's lying to you, that it's been lying to you all along."

She opened her mouth to object, but he quickly went on, "I'm convinced that there is no window to release Lucien, Sarah. The talisman used him to get me into this unholy cocoon with you. It wants me to brutalize you so you'll turn on me, and then it's going to make you kill Lucien to avenge me for raping you."

"That's a lie!" she declared, jerking her chin out of his hand and climbing to her feet. She glared down at him, her hands balled into fists at her sides.

"It's not a lie, Sarah. It's the truth, and I can prove it to you."

Before she could reply, he reached down and

snatched the sunglasses off the floor of the cocoon. As he lifted them toward his face, a wave of terror swept through Sarah. She didn't know what he planned to do, but it was a trick and she couldn't fall for it. She had to make him take her as he was meant to take her. *She couldn't fail again!*

He slid the glasses onto his nose and said, "Look at yourself in the mirrored lenses, Sarah. See what the talisman is doing to you."

"No!" she yelled, spinning around and burying her face in her hands before she could focus on the image of herself.

She didn't hear him stand, and she jumped when he placed his hands on her shoulders. She tried to move away from him, but he forced her to turn around so that she faced him.

"I *won't* look," she said fiercely, keeping her hands over her face.

"Of course you'll look," he murmured softly, compassionately. "Your scruples are too strong to let you turn your back on the truth."

"I know you lust for me, so why won't you just do what you're supposed to do?" she whispered brokenly.

"Because it's wrong."

Sarah wasn't prepared for such a simple statement, and the sincerity with which he delivered it rocked her to the core.

He lies! the voice inside her screamed.

If the voice had made the claim earlier, Sarah knew she'd have listened to it. But its charge was too loud and sharp in contrast to Sebastian's quiet delivery.

Slowly, fearfully, she lowered her hands. Her gaze was centered on Sebastian's chest, and she stared at the triangle nestled in the dark curls covering its muscled expanse. The triangle no longer glowed red. Indeed, it no longer glowed at all but had returned to normal.

Drawing in a deep breath for courage, she raised her gaze to his face. As she focused on the image reflected in the mirrored lenses, she gave a frantic shake of her head. That . . . grotesque *ghoul* wasn't her. *It couldn't be her!*

But it was her, and she knew that no amount of denial would change it. Worse, she knew that Sebastian was wrong. The talisman wasn't distorting her image. It portrayed the true essence of her soul.

As the horror of that hit her, her entire body began to tremble and her legs went weak. She wanted to scream and cry and rail, but she couldn't find the strength to release a whimper let alone an angry word. Instead, she sank to her knees, wrapped her arms around herself, and cursed Wanága for not destroying her before she'd come into her powers. Now it was too late. She'd become a horrible monster, and she'd remain that way for the rest of her life.

"Sarah?" Sebastian questioned gently as he again knelt in front of her.

"Go away," she stated dully, refusing to look at him.

"I'm afraid that's not possible. We're stuck in this damnable cocoon, remember?"

Reluctantly, she raised her head. She'd expected to again confront the demonic caricature of herself in his glasses, and she was both surprised and grateful to see he'd removed them.

"I don't know how to make it go away without

hurting you," she said, tears suddenly blurring her eyes. "I would if I could, but I don't know how."

"I do," he said, reaching out to stroke her cheek. "Open your mind to me, and then make love with me."

She flinched away from his hand. "How can you touch me when I look like this?"

"Because I can see beneath the surface to the real woman inside. She's good and kind and brave and strong. She's a fighter, and she isn't going to let the talisman defeat her."

She gave a miserable shake of her head and glanced down as she confessed, "What you see is the real woman. It's the other that's a fake."

"That's what the talisman wants you to believe, but I know it isn't true."

She didn't respond, and he again caught her chin and raised her head, forcing her to look at him. His eyes stared deeply into hers, and she shuddered, horrified to think of the ogre he must see in their depths.

She tried to pull away from him, but he held her fast and whispered, "Let me help you."

"Why would you want to help me?" she asked, her tears spilling down her cheeks. "All I can bring to you and your people is death."

He released his hold on her chin and dropped his hand to his lap. "If that were true, the talisman wouldn't keep trapping us in here. That has to mean we still have control of our souls, and as long as we maintain control, we have a fighting chance."

"You may have a fighting chance, but as you said on the mountain, I'm corrupted. Even if we defeat the talisman, I'm doomed."

She almost expected him to deny her assertion.

When he didn't, she couldn't decide if she felt disappointed or relieved. A part of her wanted—*needed*—his reassurance, but she didn't think she could bear him lying to her.

"Will you do it, Sarah?" he asked instead. "Will you open your mind to me and make love with me?"

"The talisman will fight us," she said, wiping at her tear-stained cheeks. "In fact, I'm surprised it isn't fighting us right now."

"The fact that it isn't fighting us tells me that we still have free will. It can try to tempt us away from our choice, but it has to let us make the choice in the first place. That means we can fight back."

"It won't be as simple as you make it sound."

"We can do this, Sarah."

"How can you be so confident?"

"Because I know you want to fight the talisman as much as I do. I trust you to help me win this battle."

I trust you to help me win this battle. She closed her eyes, his words vibrating warmly inside her. His trust was the last thing she was worthy of, but he was giving it to her anyway. He was a fool. But so was she, because she wanted his trust, even though she knew he'd regret giving it to her.

"I'll do it on one condition," she said, opening her eyes and cursing when they again filled with tears. She quickly blinked them back, because she knew that he wouldn't take her request seriously otherwise.

"If it's within my power, I'll do anything you ask," he said.

"It's within your power." She had to pause and draw in a deep breath before she could find the fortitude to continue. "When this is over and we've defeated the talisman—and I know we'll defeat it—I want you to promise you'll help me kill myself."

He frowned and shook his head. "My race doesn't believe in suicide, Sarah, and even if we did, there's no reason for you to kill yourself. The coven released the talisman into your society, so we're responsible for what's happened to you. We would never punish you for that, and I swear we'll take care of you. You'll have to be confined, but you'll never want for anything."

"I'll be confined, but I'll never want for anything?" she repeated with a bleak laugh. "I know you mean well, but listen to what you're saying, Sebastian. In the first place, you're assuming you can keep me confined. What if I still have some power after the talisman's gone? And even if I don't, what if, somewhere down the road, someone accidentally releases me? I could end up like Seamus Morpeth, running off to torture innocent people."

He opened his mouth to respond, but she held up her hand. "Maybe neither of those scenarios would ever happen, but I'm twenty-five years old. I've spent the past twenty of those years doing nothing but training to be the guardian. I'm not about to exchange that prison for another that could last fifty or more years. If I can't lead a normal life, possibly have a husband and a family, then I don't want a life at all. I'll do anything you want, and I'll fight against the talisman as hard as I can. But you have to make me this promise. You have to swear that when this is over, you'll help me kill myself."

When he looked hesitant, she said, "Sebastian, before you say no, I want you to understand that I'll do this with or without your help, it's just . . ."

"It's just what?" he prodded when she couldn't continue.

"All my life I've been alone," she said, hating it when she again felt the sting of tears. She rubbed her hands across her eyes to erase them. Then she stared at him pleadingly and said, "Please, Sebastian. Don't abandon me at the end. Don't make me die alone."

"Oh, Sarah," he whispered hoarsely.

He started to say more, but she knew he wanted to console her, to try to talk her out of her plans. But she also knew that nothing he said would change her mind, so she threw herself into his arms and sealed her lips over his. She'd worry about getting his promise later. For now, she'd make love with him, and with any luck, she'd bind him so tightly to her that he'd never be able to say no to the only thing she'd ever ask of him.

17

Evil Spawns

As Sarah threw herself into Sebastian's arms and pressed her lips to his, he decided that the talisman didn't know a damn thing about using seduction as a means of corruption. Her kiss, given willingly and honestly, was far more lust inducing than the oral pleasure she'd given him earlier.

When she slid her tongue into his mouth and began a shy game of thrust and parry, he suddenly recalled that when they'd made love on the mountaintop, she'd been a virgin. He knew it was ridiculous, but possessiveness surged through him at the knowledge that no other man—or, in his case, warlock—had ever made love to her.

And now it was time to introduce her to another first. He wanted—*needed*—to make love to her with his mind. Burrowing his hands into her thick mane of hair, he started to ease away from the kiss.

"No," she murmured in protest when he finally managed to pull his lips away from hers. As he looked at her, she stared back, her golden eyes filled with hot, urgent passion as she whispered, "Please. Don't stop."

"I have no intention of stopping," he said gruffly. "I just want to make it more pleasurable. Open your mind to me, Sarah. Let me show you how you make me feel; then, you can show me how I make you feel."

She closed her eyes tightly and shivered. Sebastian wanted to believe it was a sexy reaction to his words. Her tense features, however, told him that it had nothing to do with him. He suspected that the talisman bedeviled her, and he frowned, feeling a strange jab of jealousy. He didn't want her attention on the talisman or anything else, for that matter. He wanted her focused on him and him alone, and he was tempted to crush her against his body and plunder her with kisses until she shut the damnable object out of her mind.

He knew, however, that if they hoped to beat the talisman, she had to make this choice on her own. And, if she decided to open her mind to him, he would have to be the submissive partner in their lovemaking, letting her take the lead and maintain control. Otherwise, the talisman would twist everything he did to her, even sexual penetration, into an act of aggression.

He drew in a deep breath, shaken by that realization. He wasn't bothered by the thought of letting Sarah take control of their lovemaking. He knew from experience that playing the passive role could be highly satisfying. But what he felt toward her was not the normal manifestation of desire. It was barbaric lust sparked by the talisman, and he wasn't sure he could remain acquiescent while she made love to him.

Sarah suddenly opened her eyes and announced, "I'll open my mind to you."

Her capitulation was too swift, and Sebastian warily searched her face, looking for an answer to his unease. When he noted the overtly libidinous gleam in her eyes, his own libido went on a rampage. Once their minds joined, the desire simmering between them would explode into passion so intense it would consume them.

At the thought, he suddenly knew why her agreement disturbed him, and he drew in a shaky breath. The talisman had used reverse psychology on him. It had made him think that it didn't want Sarah's and his minds to connect, but that was exactly what it wanted. It knew that once they linked, Sarah's every look, every touch, every kiss, would be magnified to unnatural proportions. The talisman would use that amplification to heighten his desire for her and fuel his lust until he was sexually reduced to the same level as a caveman. There was no way he'd be able to refrain from tumbling Sarah to her back and taking her just like the talisman wanted. He couldn't go through with this! He had to keep his mind closed to her!

Except I have to go through with it, he told himself, angry at letting the talisman dupe him. *If I tell her I changed my mind, she'll think I set out to humiliate her by making her agree to my terms only to turn her down. Any measure of trust she has in me will be destroyed.*

He closed his eyes and inwardly cursed. How could he have been such a fool? Why hadn't he seen the talisman's scheme? Why . . .

He stopped himself. Self-castigation wouldn't solve anything. He'd walked into the talisman's trap, and now he had to ensure that he escaped the snare. And he *would* escape. He was not a caveman, and there was no way he would lose this battle because he couldn't control his hormones.

Opening his eyes, he said, "I'm ready whenever you are."

As Sarah drew in a deep breath, preparing to connect with Sebastian's mind, the voice inside her cried, *You can't do this! He doesn't want to help you. He wants to control your mind so he can learn your secrets and steal the power of the lightning. Then he will destroy you.*

Sarah's survival instincts flared to life at the declaration, and it took all her willpower to squelch them. She knew that everything the voice said might be true. But after seeing the image of herself in Sebastian's sunglasses, she also knew that, regardless of his motivations, she couldn't allow herself to survive. If he told her the truth, they'd defeat the talisman and he'd help her die. If he lied to her, then he'd destroy her, and she'd be spared seeing herself fully evolve into the monster she now knew she was.

Knowing the voice would continue to torment her, she didn't give it a chance. She stared deeply into Sebastian's eyes and opened her mind to him.

All her life she'd read others' minds, but this was the first time she'd actively joined with one, and she started when his psyche suddenly meshed with hers. His thoughts and feelings overwhelmed her, jumbling her own thoughts and emotions, so that she couldn't separate her personality from his. It was disorienting and frightening, and she immediately began to withdraw.

"No. Don't pull away. Give yourself a few minutes to adjust," Sebastian said. She was looking at him, but she was so muddled she wasn't sure if he actually spoke or mentally communicated with her.

"I'm speaking," he told her. "I know this is a new experience for you, and until you become accustomed to it, the sound of my voice will help you maintain your own autonomy."

"I don't feel autonomous," she replied shakily. "I feel . . . swallowed up."

"You're not being swallowed up. You have complete control over your mind, and you can break this link at any time simply by deciding to do so. But you're feeling confused right now because you're trying to absorb everything at once. Focus on one thought or feeling until you're anchored. Once you've done that, you'll automatically begin to filter our thoughts and feelings, and you'll know which is yours and which is mine. Then you can pick and choose which ones you want to pursue. So pick a thought or feeling and focus, okay?"

"What thought or feeling should I focus on?" she asked, still feeling shaky but intrigued by his premise.

He flashed her a grin. "You mean, *whose* thought or feeling. It can be yours or mine. All that matters is that you're comfortable with it."

Sarah nervously flicked her tongue across her lips. She was tempted to choose his mind as an anchor, if, for no other reason than the novelty it presented. But she knew that she'd be playing with fire. She might feel overwhelmed, but she was very conscious of his physical desire. Indeed, it was so uppermost in his mind that it nearly swamped her own senses.

Instead, she concentrated on looking at him, letting herself absorb the details of his face. For the first time, she saw the tiny lines that flared out from the corners of his eyes, the small scar that rode high on his left cheek. How did he get that scar? she wondered, barely resisting the urge to touch it.

"I fell out of a tree when I was seven years old, and you can touch me anywhere at any time."

"I don't think I like you being in my mind," she said, frowning at him. "It makes me feel—"

"Vulnerable," he finished for her. "I'm in the same boat, Sarah. Everything I think, everything I feel, is open to you. My natural inclination is to pull away from you, to hide from you."

"So why don't you?"

"You know the answer to that."

"Yes," she murmured as she reached up to touch his scar. "You want to defeat the talisman and . . ."

"And?" he encouraged, catching her hand as she began to pull it away. He brought her palm to his lips and pressed a kiss against it. Then he laved his tongue across it.

Shivers of excitement shot through her, and she suddenly had trouble breathing. "And you want me to . . . make love to you," she answered hoarsely, as he kissed her palm again. "You're confusing me, Sebastian."

"I'm arousing you," he corrected. "Or, rather, the thought of your making love to me is arousing you. It's having the same effect on me. Can you feel what's happening to my body, Sarah?"

"Oh, God, yes," she gasped, closing her eyes as his lust suddenly inundated her. It pulsed heavily through his veins, gathering in his groin until he was hard and quivering in anticipation of burying himself inside her. Her own womb contracted in need, and heat shot down her inner thighs.

"Touch me, Sarah."

Her eyes flew open at his gruff request. His eyes

had taken on that spooky, internal light, but this time it didn't frighten her. By melding with his mind, she realized that it was a physical quirk of his race. Extreme emotion, ranging from anger to lust and anything in between, created the glow.

And right now they glowed from the lust he felt for her.

Again, her womb contracted from the sensation of feeling what he was feeling, the intimate knowledge of understanding what she was doing to him. Could anything be more arousing? She was bound and determined to find out.

"Touch you where?" she asked, although she knew exactly where he wanted her to stroke him.

"Anywhere. Everywhere," he replied, surprising her. "Draw out the anticipation. Tease me. Taunt me. Torment me. Make me want you in a way I've never wanted anyone."

Sarah drew in a shallow breath at his suggestive words. Could she do that to him? Could she make him want her that badly?

"Believe me, Sarah, you can do it," he rasped.

His reassurance gave her courage, but she wasn't sure how to proceed. They still knelt in front of each other, and she raised her hands to his face. Gently, she traced his strong, rugged features, reveling in the different textures of his taut skin and his stubbled jaw.

When she reached his mouth, she outlined his lips with her fingertips, and she trembled at the passion that swept over him. She could feel his need to draw her fingers into his mouth and suck on them. She could read his thoughts of how he'd then release her fingers and transfer his lips to her breasts. She lost her ability to think, to breathe as he envisioned himself drawing her nipple into his mouth, licking it and sucking it until it was pebble hard. And then he'd move to her other breast. After he'd treated it to the same pleasure, he'd trail his lips down her body until he reached her mound. He'd taste and tease her clitoris, while plucking at her sensitive nipples, until she writhed beneath him with need.

As his imaginings of how he'd touch her and taste her sent a new wave of desire rushing toward his groin, she gasped and closed her eyes. He'd been hard before his fantasy, but now his penis was so engorged that he felt as if he'd explode. His need fueled her desire, making her entire body burn and ache with lust. She wanted to throw herself onto the ground and order him to take her, and then . . .

"Touch me, Sarah."

Her eyes snapped open at his hoarse request, and she caught her breath sharply. The glow in his eyes had intensified, and as his thoughts wove themselves through hers, she knew that he had meant what he'd said earlier. He wanted her to tease him, taunt him and torment him until he wanted her more than he'd ever wanted anyone.

Flicking her tongue over her lips, she lowered her gaze to his chest and decided to take a page from his book of erotic pleasures. She ran her hands down his shoulders and over his chest. When she reached his nipples, she stroked her fingers against them. He gasped and his pectoral muscles leaped beneath her touch.

Emboldened by his reaction, she leaned forward and flicked her tongue over one small, flat nub. His entire body went rigid, and she could feel his need to bury his hands in her hair and urge her mouth downward. To her amazement, he refused to let himself touch her, balling his hands into fists at his sides instead.

Confused by his determination not to touch her, she pulled away from him and studied his face, letting her mind entwine more intimately with his. It wasn't long before she realized what he was up to. He intended to remain totally passive and let her dictate their lovemaking. Desire coiled tautly inside her, but it wasn't the thought of being in control that intensified her lust. It was the challenge of making him so hot for her that he'd break his vow.

"Lie down," she ordered him.

As he did as she instructed, the light in his eyes flared brightly and pulsed. When he lay on his back, she straddled his hips so that her femininity barely brushed his erection. He trembled and again balled his hands into fists to keep from grabbing her hips and pulling her down so he could sheathe himself inside her.

"I think I like this game," she murmured, leaning forward to place a hand on either side of his head. "How long do you think you can hold out?"

"As long as it takes," he answered between clenched teeth.

"Mm," she hummed, lowering herself so that her breasts touched his chest. Then, she rocked so that her taut nipples brushed against his chest, and as her body moved backward, her womanhood opened just enough so that the tip of his shaft could graze her heat and her wetness.

The desire that erupted inside him hit her with such force that she closed her eyes and cried out at its intensity. She wanted to sink onto his erection and pull him deep inside her so she could experience the heat of herself surrounding him, the clench of her muscles holding him. But if she did that she'd be surrendering to his need, and he'd win his game of self-control. Instead, she opened her eyes and gazed down at him, deciding that it was time to give him a sample of her own desire. She slithered up his body until her breasts were suspended above his face.

Then she reached down and stroked one of his clenched fists that rested at his side. When his fingers relaxed and opened, she lifted his hand and brought it to her mound, ordering, "Touch me and taste me, Sebastian. Let me show you how you make me feel."

Her words caused another wave of desire to roll through him, and he drew in a deep breath. Then, he released it and closed his mouth over one of her nipples. As he teased it with his tongue, he slipped his fingers into her soft, womanly folds and began to stroke her clitoris.

Desire roiled through Sarah like a mounting thunderstorm. She leaned her head back and closed her eyes, letting the passion sweep over her in undulating waves, while projecting every erotic sensation her body experienced into his mind.

Suddenly, he switched his attention to her other breast, while using his free hand to pluck at the nipple he'd just released. At the same time, he increased the pressure of his fingers against her clitoris, stroking her fast and then slow and then fast again.

But the pleasure he gave her body didn't compare to his mental seduction. She could feel his mind stroking against hers, intermingling her lust with his until their desire was one hot, burning flame that threatened to incinerate them both.

"Sebastian! I need you inside me!" she gasped, burying her face against his shoulder as she slid her hips back down so that his erection again brushed against her. "Please."

He arched his hips and rubbed himself against her provocatively, but he made no attempt to enter her. Frustrated, she raised her head and frowned at him. His eyes pulsed with his lust, and his jaw was clenched so tightly a muscle twitched along its length. She knew he needed to lose himself inside her as much as she needed him there, but he was still determined to remain passive.

Inexplicably, his refusal to initiate their joining frustrated her. He was *supposed* to take her, and she was going to make him do so.

She shifted and settled herself against him so that his shaft was poised at the entrance to her womb. He drew in a deep, shuddering breath, and she could feel his body trembling against hers as he struggled to keep from surging into her. She lowered her lips to his and kissed him with all her pent-up passion as she moved her hips, drawing the tip of his penis into her. He groaned gutturally, and his tongue began to thrust in and out of her mouth in a frantic mimicry of lovemaking, but his hips remained still.

Her frustration intensified. He needed to be inside her so badly he was ready to explode. So why wouldn't he take her as he was supposed to take her?

She was so focused on trying to figure out a way to make him enter her that when he suddenly slid his hand between their bodies and stroked her clitoris, she was unprepared for his touch. Her own desire exploded, and with a startled, passionate cry, she flexed her hips and sank onto him, completing their union.

She automatically began to move against Sebastian, reveling in the feeling of his manhood stroking the most intimate part of her. In a tiny corner of her mind, she knew he still didn't move his hips. But she didn't care, because her mind was still joined with his. She knew that his inactivity was only temporary, that as she hurled toward climax, he hurled with her, and within moments he wouldn't be able to hold back.

As the pleasure-pain of release coiled inside her womb, she increased her tempo, whispering hoarsely, "Please, Sebastian. Come with me. I need you to come with me."

"I thought you'd never ask," he rasped, grasping her buttocks and lifting her up his length, then pulling her back down as he surged up to meet her.

The sensation was so exquisite that Sarah couldn't speak again, but she didn't need words to express her feelings. Sebastian's mind again entwined with hers, stroking it with his need and pleasure, while absorbing her need and pleasure, until they were again united into one hot, burning flame.

Now! he mentally cried.

Yes! Sarah mentally answered as their bodies came together and her world exploded and spun out of control. She collapsed against Sebastian, her head buried against his neck as she gasped for breath.

He wrapped one arm tightly around her and stroked her back with his other hand, mumbling, "We beat the talisman again, Sarah."

That's what he thinks, Sarah, John Butler suddenly whispered in her mind. *You have done what you were supposed to do. You are no longer the last of the Thunderbeings.*

Suddenly, the vibrations of the future settled over Sarah, spinning her mind ahead in time. She couldn't breathe as she saw herself heavy with child. Before she could fully fathom that, the picture altered and she saw herself holding a naked child in her arms. He was a boy who looked like Sebastian, except he had her golden eyes.

As she stared into his eyes, she saw that they were lit with the same strange inner glow she'd seen so often in Sebastian's gaze. But even the glow couldn't disguise the evil that lurked in their depths, and she knew what horror she looked upon. She was holding the devil's spawn.

Suddenly, Sarah understood that this must have been the same horror her mother had felt as she gazed into Sarah's eyes. She also suspected that that was why her mother had chosen to abandon her in the woods to die. She must have known that she had to destroy her child but she hadn't had the courage to do it herself, so she'd left it up to nature to do it for her.

When Sarah further realized that the talisman had effectively foiled her plans, panic surged through her. Her maternal instincts were strong— she could feel them flaring up inside her already— and now that she was pregnant, she knew she'd never be able to kill herself. She'd do everything she could to stay alive, even kill, to protect her child and give it life.

"*No!*" Sarah screamed, wrenching herself out of Sebastian's arms and leaping to her feet. She clenched her hands into fists and waved them at the cocoon's walls. "It isn't true! *It isn't true!*"

"Sarah, what is it? What's wrong?" Sebastian asked, suddenly grabbing her shoulders and spinning her around to face him. His bewildered expression told her he could no longer read her mind, and she knew that was more of the talisman's handiwork. It had cut him off from her so he wouldn't know the horrible truth of what they'd done.

"You have to kill me," she sobbed, grabbing his upper arms and shaking him, or at least attempting to. He was so big, so solid, that he didn't even move. "You have to kill me now!"

"Sarah, you're not making sense," he said, reaching up to thread his fingers into her hair. "What is the talisman doing to you now?"

"It tricked me—*us*," she said, tears welling into her eyes and spilling down her cheeks. "You have to kill me before . . ."

"Before what?" he prodded.

She looked down and shook her head, unable to say the words. How could she tell him that they'd just conceived a child so evil that even she, its mother, had only seen the devil when she'd looked into its eyes?

"Dammit, Sarah! What's wrong?" he demanded, breaking into her tormented thoughts as he cupped her face in his hands and forced her to look at him.

Before she could come up with an answer, there was a deafening clap of thunder, and she gasped as the lightning in the cocoon began to spin around them at a dizzying speed. Then it lifted until it whirled above their heads in its original wreath shape. Suddenly, two bolts broke loose and shot toward them. One hit the triangle on Sarah's chest; the other the one on Sebastian's chest.

Sarah saw their clothes magically appear on their bodies, and she watched in horror as Sebastian's eyes immediately started turning back to white. He'd soon be blind again, and she was . . .

Sleep now, Sarah, Butler ordered in a hypnotising drone. *Sleep.*

She fought against the blackness descending over her, knowing that if she gave in to it, she'd forget about her pregnancy. And she *couldn't* forget until she told Sebastian what they'd done. She had to tell him about the child. She had to warn him before it was too late!

Sleep, Butler repeated, and no matter how hard she fought, her eyes closed of their own volition.

As she sank into oblivion, she knew that the talisman had won. It would destroy Sebastian and his people, but it would keep her safe until its true instrument of destruction—hers and Sebastian's child—was old enough to destroy the world.

18

Evil Torments

✛

Sebastian had known that his eyesight's return was only temporary, but when the lightning struck him and his vision faded, panic swept through him. He couldn't stand the thought of again existing in that unrelenting black hole where he felt helpless and inept. However, his panic was cut short when, a moment before he plunged back into darkness, he glanced toward Sarah and saw her eyes close and her body slump. He made a blind grab for her and caught her, but her limp body dragged him down. He had to sink to his knees to keep from dropping her.

"Sarah?" he said anxiously, when he pulled her against his chest and her head lolled against his arm. He cursed the fact that he couldn't see her and tried to connect with her mind to find out what was wrong. But her mind was again closed to him. All he could determine was that she was alive. What had happened to her?

He started when he heard a groan off to his right, and he jerked his head in that direction. Lucien! Between his and Sarah's lovemaking and the ensuing events, Sebastian had forgotten him. He quickly brushed against Lucien's mind and let out a relieved sigh. Other than some aches and pains, Lucien was okay and should regain consciousness shortly. In the meantime, Sebastian had to summon help.

Zachary, it's Sebastian, he thought, establishing contact with the warlock's mind. *It looks like Lucien's okay, but there's something wrong with Sarah. Go get Ryan and—"*

Ryan's already here, Zachary interrupted. *We're waiting for you to give us the okay to come to you.*

Sebastian scowled. *I told Ryan to stay with Ariel.*

Ariel wanted Ryan to be able to get to Lucien as soon as possible if he needed medical attention, so she sent him back. Should we come?

Yes, Sebastian answered.

We'll be there in a couple of minutes.

Sebastian cursed as he cut off the connection, irritated that Ryan hadn't obeyed him. As a mortal, he couldn't protect himself against magic. If Zachary had had to battle the talisman, his attention would have been torn between it and protecting Ryan. That could have cost all of them their lives. But he couldn't summon up the anger Ryan's disobedience warranted, because he was relieved that Ryan would be able to examine Sarah right away.

It seemed to take forever before he finally heard the car. When it braked to a stop and he heard a door fly open, he called out, "Zachary, you stay with Lucien until he wakes up. Ryan, I need you over here."

There was a flurry of footsteps, and then Ryan said, "What happened?"

"I'm not sure," Sebastian answered, tilting his head up toward Ryan's voice. "She was—"

"My God! Your eyes!" Ryan broke in disbelievingly. "You said you were blind, but you didn't say that your eyes have turned solid white!"

"Forget my eyes," Sebastian snapped. "Sarah's the one you need to worry about."

"Of course." Sebastian heard Ryan kneel across from him as he continued, "It's just that you wore sunglasses when I saw you before, so I was shocked when I saw your eyes. What happened to the woman?"

"We were struck by the talisman's lightning, and—"

"You were struck by *lightning*?"

"It was *magical* lightning," Sebastian explained impatiently. "It shouldn't have made her pass out."

"Yeah, well, let's lay her on the ground so I can examine her."

When Ryan started to shift Sarah out of Sebastian's arms, he found himself reluctant to let her go. Something inside him insisted that as long as he held her she'd be safe, but if he let her go, something would happen to her. He knew the feeling was absurd, so he forced himself to release her.

"How's Sarah?" he finally asked when several seconds passed without any comment from Ryan.

"She's asleep."

Sebastian frowned, sure he'd misunderstood. "Asleep? She's completely out of it. If she were just asleep, couldn't we wake her up?"

"If we really tried, we might be able to, but I suggest we leave her alone," Ryan replied. "I've seen a few cases like this, and generally, the person is escaping from some emotional trauma she isn't ready to face. I suspect the lightning frightened her so badly that she's retreated for a while. When she's ready to deal with what happened, she'll wake up on her own. By the way, here are your sunglasses. You might want to put them on in case someone else shows up. Your eyes are ... startling, to say the least."

Sebastian took the glasses and slipped them on while considering what Ryan had said about Sarah. He knew the lightning wouldn't have frightened her, but she had been overly upset before it struck them. Indeed, she'd been so distraught that she'd told him he had to kill her before ...

Before what? he wondered, realizing she hadn't completed the sentence. What had she been trying to tell him? What had the talisman done to her to make her feel she had to die immediately?

He shuddered involuntarily, knowing that for her to beg for death and then fall into such a deep sleep, the talisman had either told her or shown her something horrible. If he'd learned nothing else about Sarah, it was that she was psychologically strong. Otherwise, she'd have surrendered to the talisman long before now.

"What?" he said, realizing Ryan had spoken.

"I said, why don't you let Zachary take you and the woman back to the clinic? I'll wait for Lucien to regain full consciousness and bring him in. Then I'll give all of you a good checkup."

"I don't need a checkup. I'm fine," Sebastian said, climbing to his feet.

"I want to look at your eyes, Sebastian."

"Forget my eyes. There's nothing you can do for them."

"You won't know that for sure until I look at them."

Sebastian started to argue, but decided to maintain his peace. If Ryan wanted to waste his time looking at something he couldn't fix, he'd let him look. For now, he'd get Sarah off the ground and into a bed. Maybe that simple comfort would encourage her to wake up so she could tell him what in hell the talisman was up to now.

But an hour later, Sebastian sat on the edge of an examining table, furious that he couldn't see so he could pace the room. Sarah slept soundly in the small bed in the corner, and he hadn't heard her move since Zachary had placed her there. Lucien, who was in another examining room, had awakened and was physically okay, but he was so disoriented he didn't even know his name. Zachary had just returned from the boundary to report that there was indeed a crack in the barrier, although it was so small you couldn't see it unless you were looking for it.

Sebastian wasn't reassured by the report. He knew the barrier's erosion would soon escalate, and the words *twelve hours* kept repeating themselves over and over in his head. He was sure the talisman was inserting that time frame into his mind to torment him. But was it telling him the truth about the barrier? If so, was it saying that they had twelve hours before the erosion accelerated, or twelve hours before it was complete? The only person who might know was Sarah.

"Dammit, Sarah," he muttered, turning his head in her direction. "Would you please wake up? I need your help."

When he didn't hear so much as a soft snore in response, he cursed. He'd never felt so frustrated or so ineffectual. Time was running out, and he didn't know what to do. Lucien couldn't start repair work on the barrier until his mind cleared, and Sarah, who might be able to give him some answers, was doing a damn good imitation of Sleeping Beauty.

"I can't believe this day," Ryan announced harriedly as Sebastian heard the door swing open and the man walk into the room. "For weeks I've sat here without a single patient coming in the door, and today, when I need to be concentrating on you and Lucien, I get two minor emergencies. But they're both taken care of and on their way home. I just checked on Lucien. He's still disoriented. So why don't you take off those glasses and let me look at your eyes?"

Sebastian scowled and reached up to push the sunglasses more firmly onto his nose. Earlier, he'd decided to let Ryan look at his eyes, but now that the time had come, he didn't want to go through with it. He was permanently blind, and he knew that Ryan couldn't do a damn thing about it. But there was a part of him that whispered that as long as his condition wasn't confirmed, there was a chance he'd see again.

Stop being a fool, he mentally chastised himself.

That didn't stop him from saying, "There's no need for you to look at my eyes. If you insist on doing something, check the burns on my hand and chest."

As he spoke, he held out the hand that had been burned on the mountaintop and lifted the triangle with the other one to reveal the burn beneath the object.

"Dammit, Sebastian!" Ryan declared irritably as he grabbed Sebastian's hand. "Why didn't you show me these wounds before? They're infected. How did you get them? No, don't tell me. Magical lightning, right?"

"You're starting to catch on, Ryan," Sebastian drawled facetiously, sliding the triangle along the chain so that it fell behind his shoulder. He didn't know if it would harm anyone if they touched it, but he wasn't about to take a chance.

Ryan released Sebastian's hand and probed at his chest. "These are third-degree burns, and I'm going to have to debride them. But with burns this bad the nerve endings are deadened, so you probably won't feel much discomfort."

"I can handle anything you dish out," Sebastian said, deciding that at this point he'd welcome physical discomfort to take his mind off everything else. "But before you get started on me, you should check Sarah. She had a burn on the back of one of her hands."

"When I examined her I didn't see any burn on her hand."

"Then check her again. You overlooked it."

"I wouldn't overlook something as obvious as a burn," Ryan responded indignantly.

"You overlooked mine," Sebastian shot back.

"I hadn't examined you yet, but if it will satisfy you, I'll check her hands again."

Before Sebastian could respond, he heard Ryan stalk away, and he cursed himself for being so combative. He knew he was taking his frustration out on Ryan, which wasn't fair.

"I was right," Ryan stated, walking back toward him. "Her hands are fine. There isn't even a mark to indicate she ever had a burn."

Sebastian frowned. "That doesn't make sense. I *saw* the burn." Even as he made the statement, he recalled that when he'd compared Sarah's and his burns in the cave, hers had appeared to be healing while his were getting worse.

"Well, it isn't there now," Ryan stated disgruntledly. "If you don't believe me, I'll ask Zachary to come in here and confirm it."

"Of course I believe you," Sebastian said, apologetic. "But she *was* burned. Maybe the talisman somehow accelerated her healing process. Or maybe it's an idiosyncrasy inherent to whatever she is. Remember, she isn't a mortal."

"Well, for whatever reason, she's okay, so I'd better get to work on you."

"I'm sorry for sounding as if I doubted you, Ryan."

"Forget it," Ryan mumbled, and Sebastian listened to what sounded like the rattle of instruments. Then he heard what he guessed was a table roll toward him. A second later, Ryan lifted his hand and placed it on a cold metal surface.

They were silent while Ryan bandaged his hand. When he turned his attention to Sebastian's chest wound, he said, "With you blind and Lucien disoriented, we're in serious trouble, aren't we?"

"Let's just say that we'd be a hell of a lot better off if you could snap Lucien out of his fog," Sebastian answered.

"Sorry, but I'm a doctor, not a miracle worker. Isn't there someone who can take over in Lucien's stead? Surely the coven has some contingency to handle emergencies if the high priest is incapacitated."

"They do. The troubleshooter takes over," Sebastian stated grimly. "Unfortunately, I'm also incapacitated. The only other way is to contact the council for permission to remove Lucien as high priest and temporarily grant his powers to someone else."

"So, why haven't you contacted the high council?"

"I don't think the talisman will let me get

through. If it did, I might give it a link to them, and that would put them in danger. The only other people who can contact them directly are the narrators.

"I sent Zachary to bring Oran Morovang here so I can ask him to contact them," he went on. "But what's happening would be considered a historical event. That means Oran can't tell the council about the talisman, because he'd be interfering with history in the making. All he can do is request that the council send a new troubleshooter as soon as possible."

"Well, at least we'll get some help," Ryan said.

"Yes, but it will be at least twenty-four hours before a new troubleshooter can arrive, and I don't think we have that much time," Sebastian responded grimly.

"Would waking the woman help you?"

"Her name is Sarah, and I'd appreciate you calling her that," Sebastian replied, not sure why Ryan's calling her "the woman" irritated him. "And you said she's probably fallen asleep because she's facing some trauma she's not ready to handle emotionally. You're the doctor, and you have more expertise than me in this area. Do you think waking her would traumatize her further?"

"It's a risk," Ryan admitted as he taped a bandage onto Sebastian's chest. "However, if you think this situation is worth taking the chance, I can inject a stimulant that will wake her."

"Why would you need to give her a shot? Why can't we just . . . shake her awake?"

"She's almost comatose, Sebastian. Unless she's ready to wake up on her own, rousing her through traditional means will be almost impossible."

"Would this stimulant be dangerous to her?"

"No drug is completely without risk," Ryan allowed. "There's always that one-in-a-million person who will have an adverse reaction. But she appears to be healthy, and I wouldn't use a large dose. It shouldn't cause her any ill effects."

"But Sarah isn't mortal, and our magic is deadly to her," Sebastian pointed out. "Knowing that, do you still feel comfortable giving her the shot?"

"I'm talking about pharmacology, not magic, Sebastian, and I'd feel comfortable giving the stimulant to anyone in the coven, including Shana, and she's pregnant. If it's safe enough for a pregnant woman, it shouldn't bother Sarah. Her physiology can't be that much different from your race or mine, for that matter."

"But you don't know that for sure," Sebastian countered. Despite Ryan's assurance that he'd give the stimulant to his own pregnant mate, Sebastian was still uncomfortable with the idea.

"No, I don't know that for sure. I'll tell you what. You think about it, and while you're doing that, I'll look at your eyes," Ryan said, reaching up and removing Sebastian's sunglasses.

Sebastian started to object, but Ryan caught his jaw and said, "Hold still and keep your eyes open." Several seconds passed before Ryan let out a low whistle. "I've never seen anything like this."

"Like what?" Sebastian asked with begrudging curiosity.

"As I said earlier, your eyes are completely white. When I first saw them, I thought they were covered with some kind of growth—something like a cataract. But whatever this is, it isn't organic."

Sebastian felt a spark of hope flare inside him. "You're sure it's not organic?"

"Positive. It almost resembles a contact lens, but it's definitely attached to the eye. Do you see anything at all? Even shadings of light and dark?"

"No. Everything is pitch black."

"Well, you were right," Ryan said, releasing Sebastian's chin. "There's nothing I can do for you."

"But you have helped me," Sebastian stated, letting that spark of hope grow a little brighter. "If it isn't organic, then it's magical. That means it can be reversed. It's just a matter of figuring out how to trick the talisman into doing it."

"Well, that's your bailiwick. Have you made a decision on the woman?"

"Her name is Sarah," Sebastian reminded him with a frown.

"Sorry. Sarah," Ryan said.

Sebastian nodded and then raked a hand through his hair, trying to decide what to do. With Lucien out of commission, he needed Sarah awake. She was the direct link to the talisman, and, hopefully, she could tell him how much time they had before the barrier disintegrated.

But what if she had as bad a reaction to the shot as she'd had to his spell? An injection couldn't be revoked. Then again, if the talisman thought the shot would hurt her, wouldn't it cocoon her to protect her, just as it had at the boundary? Or was he giving it too much credit for knowing what was going on? It was, after all, only an object—an *ancient* object. Did it have any understanding of modern medicine?

Damn! If he just knew exactly who and what Sarah was he'd know if this was a good idea. But he didn't know anything about her, and there wasn't anyone who could tell him.

Except that wasn't true. There *was* someone with whom he could confer. The Indian spirit.

"Ryan, take me over to Sarah, and then leave until I call for you," he stated, standing. He knew that the spirit wouldn't respond to him if there were an audience.

"Sure," Ryan said.

When they reached Sarah, Sebastian released his hold on Ryan and sat on the edge of the bed. After Ryan left, Sebastian said, "Spirit, I know you're here, because you said you're always with Sarah. Would you speak with me?"

"I would," the spirit answered.

"Thank you," Sebastian said, noting the formal response. Realizing the spirit was setting the tone for the interview, Sebastian knew he needed to keep his questions and responses formal if he wanted cooperation.

Keeping that in mind, he said, "I just realized that even though we've communicated several times, we haven't exchanged names. I am Sebastian Moran. Do you have a name you wish to be called?"

"Wanága."

"Well, Wanága, I have a problem. I need to speak with Sarah, but, as I'm sure you know, she's asleep and won't wake up. Can you tell me why she's sleeping?"

"Sarah sleeps because it is not yet time for you to know the future."

Sebastian frowned. "Don't you mean it's not time for *her* to know the future?"

"Sarah knows, but she must forget."

"I see," Sebastian murmured as a courtesy, while he mulled over Wanága's words. "So Sarah is asleep because she knows something about *my* future that I'm not supposed to know yet?"

"Yes."

"What will happen to Sarah if I wake her?"

"She will not remember."

"She will not remember my future, or she won't remember anything, like what happened to her on the mountain?"

"That is up to you."

The ambiguous response frustrated Sebastian, but he kept his voice even as he replied, "I'm sorry, Wanága, but I don't understand what that means. Can you explain it in more detail?"

"Why do you wish her to awaken?"

"I told you that already. I need to speak with her."

"But *why* do you wish her to awaken?"

Sebastian shook his head, confused. "Again, I'm sorry, Wanága, but I don't understand what you mean."

"Look at Sarah and you will understand."

"But I can't look at Sarah. I'm blind."

"It takes more than eyes to see, *wicáhmunga*."

"Yes, I suppose it does," Sebastian stated, although he still didn't know what the spirit was trying to tell him. He also knew that he wouldn't get any better explanation, so belaboring the subject wouldn't get him anywhere.

Instead, he said, "If I ask my friend to give Sarah a shot of medicine to wake her, will the medicine hurt her like my magic does?"

"It will not hurt her like your magic."

Sebastian frowned, disturbed by the answer. It took him a moment to realize it wasn't the spirit's words but his tone that bothered him. "Are you saying that the medicine won't hurt her like my magic does, but it will hurt her in some way?"

"Again, *why* do you wish her to awaken? Look at Sarah, *wicáhmunġa*. When you see her, you will understand. Now I must go."

Sebastian opened his mouth to object, but he closed it when he could no longer sense the spirit's presence.

"Well, hell," he grumbled. "I don't know any more than I did when I started."

But that wasn't true. As ambiguous as the spirit had been, he had provided Sebastian with answers. It was just a matter of interpreting them. However, that could take days, and if the talisman wasn't lying to him, he was dealing with hours.

"So what am I going to do?" he said in frustration.

He didn't know why he bothered asking the question, because he knew he only had one option. The safety of the coven was at stake, and he had to know just how long they had before disaster befell them. Only Sarah might know that answer, so he had to ask Ryan to give her the shot and hope for the best.

"Ryan?" he called.

"Yes?" Ryan said, coming back into the room.

"Give Sarah the shot."

While he listened to Ryan moving in the background, he reviewed his conversation with Wanáġa.

Look at Sarah. It takes more than eyes to see.

Impulsively, Sebastian let his mind travel back over the time he'd spent with Sarah. He saw her standing in moonlight, a snake curled around her arm as she threatened to kill him. But even when he'd escaped her bevy of rattlesnakes and ended up with Willow wrapped around his neck, Sarah hadn't given the snake the order to kill. From there, his mind flashed to the cave. He could see the proud tilt to her chin as she told him she was the guardian of her people. Her dedication to them was so strong that she'd lifted Willow to her neck to commit suicide so Sebastian couldn't get her triangle.

Now that he'd opened the dam, a flood of memories washed through him. He saw Sarah lying on the ground, her hand burned from the talisman's lightning. He remembered her horrified look when he'd informed her she was the talisman's instrument of destruction. He shivered as he remembered her attempt to escape him, and then he recalled her dying gasps when he'd cast a spell over her. He smiled at the memory of her smile when she'd had amnesia and had the momentary release from her duty. He frowned at the recollection of her look of terror when he trapped her in the meadow, and the lightning wreath cocooning her to draw him into the talisman's trap.

And then there was their lovemaking. Those images were so provocative that even the memories made him hard.

But it was the tearful tremor in her voice that cut at his heart as he remembered her saying, "When this is over and we've defeated the talisman—and I know we'll defeat it—I want you to promise you'll help me kill myself."

When he objected, she'd said, "Before you say no, I want you to understand that I'll do this with or without your help." Then she'd added, "All my life I've been alone. Please, Sebastian. Don't abandon me at the end. Don't make me die alone."

Finally, he recalled that when he told her the coven would confine her but she'd never want for anything, she'd said that she'd spent the past twenty years training to be the guardian. She'd further stated that she wouldn't trade that prison for another, that if she couldn't dream of having a husband and a family, then she didn't want a life at all.

Witches and warlocks were incapable of tears, but Sebastian would have sworn he felt their hot sting at that moment. Sarah—beautiful, brave, golden-eyed Sarah—had spent her life as a pawn. Her people had used her to be their guardian. Now the talisman used her to reach its evil goal. Even Sebastian used her in his fight to stop the talisman. Everyone took from her, and the only thing she asked for in return was that Sebastian wouldn't let her die alone.

At that moment, Sebastian knew that he'd just broken the vow he'd made the day he'd become the troubleshooter. He'd sworn that he would never fall in love because his job was too risky. He wasn't about to leave a witch mourning for him for the rest of her life if he were killed.

Well, he'd kept part of the vow, he admitted ruefully. He hadn't fallen in love with a witch, but he was falling in love with a woman who was neither witch nor mortal. She was also doomed for all eternity, and no amount of love would ever change that.

"I'm ready to give Sarah the shot," Ryan suddenly said.

"No! Get out of here until I call for you," Sebastian rasped, blindly swinging his arm out and starting in surprise when he felt it connect with Ryan.

But the contact wasn't enough to alleviate his agitation. If anything, it aggravated it, because he suddenly understood Wanága's ambiguities. He'd been trying to make Sebastian see that he was falling in love with Sarah. He'd also been trying to make Sebastian understand that though he said he wanted her awake to ask her questions, he really wanted her to awaken and reassure him that she was okay.

As soon as he made that admission, he understood what Wanáġa had meant about the shot. It wouldn't physically harm Sarah, but it would emotionally, because a shot was impersonal. By having Ryan give it to her, she would think that Sebastian didn't care about her, only about what she could do for him. She'd feel more alone—more *used*—and that would give her less reason to want to live. And he had to make her want to live, because no matter how hopeless their future was, he knew he couldn't face it without her.

But the only way she'd have a reason to live was if he let her know that she was wanted and needed for herself, not for what she could do for him. To give her that reassurance, he had to wake her up with his love.

"Sebastian, I don't understand what's wrong," Ryan said.

"You don't need to understand. Just get out," Sebastian snapped. "Now!"

Ryan didn't answer, but Sebastian listened to the door open and close. Then he leaned forward and let his hands slide across the sheet until he found Sarah's shoulders.

Gently, he pulled her up into his arms and cradled her against his chest as he hoarsely whispered in her ear, "Wake up for me, Sarah. Please, wake up. Somehow I'll find a way to fix everything so you can have the happiness you deserve. I promise. Just wake up for me. Please. Wake up. I need you."

Sarah knew she dreamed, but it didn't lessen the fear that coiled inside her. She stood in the center of a long, dark hallway, and she could feel the walls closing in on her. She had to escape before they crushed her, but she couldn't decide which direction she should go.

She glanced frantically toward one end of the corridor, where she saw an open door through which sunlight streamed. Then, she looked toward the other end. That door opened into murky blackness, but she could see a man's shadowy form standing there waiting for her. Although she couldn't see the man's face, his breadth and height assured her it was Sebastian.

Her instincts screamed at her to head for the safety of the light. Her heart, however, begged her to go to Sebastian. Unable to make a decision, she stood there frozen while the walls continued to close in on her.

Fool, John Butler suddenly said. *The* wicáhmunġa *stands in darkness. What more proof do you need that he is your enemy? If you go to him, he will destroy you, and you cannot let him destroy you. You are the guardian. You must protect your people.*

Wanáġa says they are not my people. He says I am the last of the Thunderbeings, she said, searching the lighted door for Butler. She knew that's where his voice came from, but he wasn't standing there waiting for her. He hid from her, but why?

But you are pregnant, so you are not the last of the Thunderbeings, Butler countered. *That alone should prove that everything Wanáġa has told you is a lie.*

However, he did not lie about one thing. He is here to help the wicáhmuŋga *destroy you, and when you die, so will your child. Will you do that to your son, Sarah? Will you abandon him to death, just as your mother tried to do to you? Or will you choose to live so that he may live?*

Sarah pressed her hand to her abdomen and shivered. She'd looked into her child's eyes, and she knew he was evil. She also knew he was the talisman's chosen, that it would use him to carry out its unholy goal of death and destruction until all of mankind was lost.

And among his victims would be the very people she'd spent her life training to protect—the people Leonard had entrusted into her care. If she let her child be born, their blood would be on her hands as surely as if she'd killed them herself. She'd have failed Leonard, the only person who'd ever loved her.

But the only way to stop the talisman was to sacrifice her child, and she knew she couldn't do that. Good or evil, he was a part of her. He was also a part of Sebastian, and, suddenly, she knew that the image of her son—the image the talisman had provided—wasn't exactly true. Yes, it had chosen her son as its instrument of destruction, and, yes, the child had the propensity for evil. But she knew in her heart—in her *soul*—that Sebastian could save their son from his heinous destiny. Sebastian could make the child good and kind and decent. He could turn him into a protector instead of a destroyer.

That's why you don't want Sebastian to know I'm pregnant! she gasped, staring at the lighted doorway. She suddenly understood why Butler hid from her rather than standing there waiting for her. He knew that if she saw him, she'd see through his lies to the truth! *Sebastian can change the future, can't he? He can save our son, and that will destroy the talisman, which in effect, will destroy you, because you have become its personification. It lives because you live, but if you die, it will die.*

Fool! John Butler declared again. *If you turn to the* wicáhmuṅga, *you will die. You will never hold your child in your arms. You will never hear him call you mother. You will end your life as you began it— abandoned and alone!*

You're lying to me! Sarah yelled, suddenly furious that she hadn't seen the truth all along. *I may die, but I won't be alone. Sebastian will stand by my side to the very end, and he will take our child and raise it as it should be raised. He will teach it right from wrong, just as Leonard taught me. But my son will be stronger than I am, because he won't be vying for the love of a stranger. He will be secure in the love of his father.*

You are not thinking clearly, Butler said, his voice now crooning. *Look at the* wicáhmuṅga, *Sarah. He exists in darkness, not light, and darkness is the habitat of evil.*

Sebastian exists in darkness because you made me blind him, Sarah shot back. *He saw the truth from the beginning, and you made me take away his sight so he would doubt himself. You made him blind so he would seem weak to me and I would doubt him. But you underestimated him, because even in darkness, he sees the truth and I am going to help him defeat you.*

She turned her back on the doorway of light and started walking toward the darkness and Sebastian. She knew she made the right decision. Sebastian existed in darkness, but he was the true light.

However, her confrontation with Butler had opened her eyes to a more momentous truth that filled her heart with a mixture of soaring joy and abject terror. Joy, because she knew she was irrevocably in love with Sebastian. Terror, because she understood exactly what the talisman planned. Sebastian was the real threat to its existence, because, as she'd told Butler, he could save their son from his evil destiny. That meant the talisman had to kill Sebastian to stop that from happening. She had to get to Sebastian and warn him!

Go to the wicáhmunġa *and you condemn yourself,* Butler screamed. *Your place is here with me. We are the power!*

There never was a we, and there never will be! Sarah screamed back as the walls started moving in on her at an accelerated speed. Recognizing her time was running out, she started running toward Sebastian as she added, *You are nothing more than a voice for the talisman, John Butler. It has never granted you its powers and it never will, because the power does not belong to you. It belongs to me and my son. You were born a nothing, and you will die a nothing.*

You're wrong! I am the power, and I'll soon prove that to you. I will kill you, your lover, and your son!

If you believe that, you're a bigger fool than I could ever be, Sarah rejoined as she neared Sebastian. *You can't kill me, because the talisman won't let you. It needs me alive so my son can be born. But I will make sure that you and the talisman are destroyed long before that happens.*

With that, she launched herself into Sebastian's arms, and she heard the corridor's walls slam closed behind her. But the reverberating sound didn't drown out John Butler's parting shot.

When you open your eyes, you will remember nothing you have learned here, Sarah. But before this day is over the wicáhmunga *will be dead, and you will be the one to have killed him.*

19

Evil Advances

✛

"Damn bitch!" John Butler yelled furiously as his eyes flew open. He lay on the bed in his ratty motel room, glaring at the sagging, water-damaged ceiling overhead. But it wasn't the ceiling he saw. It was a replay of the vision he'd just shared with Sarah.

As his mind relived those moments when Sarah walked away from him, her words resounded in his mind. *The power does not belong to you. It belongs to me and my son. You were born a nothing, and you will die a nothing.*

He bounded off the bed and paced the room, his rage mounting with each step. She was trying to steal the power and the glory from him, just as The Bitch had tried to steal the Middle East dig from him. Well, he'd taken care of The Bitch, and he'd take care of Sarah too. He knew exactly what to do with people who stole from him.

Stroking the circle hanging around his neck, he marched toward the door. "It's time I show you just how much power I have, Sarah. I'm on my way to you, and when I get there, I'll make you kill the *wicáhmunǧa*. Then I'll kill you and your bastard son. And it will be your fault, Sarah. I was willing to share my power with you. Together we could have ruled the world. Now I'll rule it alone."

* * *

Sebastian thought Sarah would wake gradually, and he was unprepared for the explosive way she came to life in his arms. One moment she was as limp as a rag doll. The next she flung her arms around his neck with such force that she nearly knocked them off the bed.

As he shifted his body to maintain his balance, he shook his head, dazed. Her volatile physical rousing was unexpected, but it was her mental state that stunned him. She'd awakened with her mind wide open to his, and the absolute terror racing through her engulfed him until he trembled as violently from it as she did.

Why is she so frightened? he wondered, wishing he could see her face. But he was blind, and he had to be satisfied with searching her mind for the source of her terror. He quickly determined that she didn't know why she was frightened, which didn't surprise him. According to Wanága, she'd fallen asleep because she wasn't supposed to remember Sebastian's future. A shiver of apprehension crawled up his spine. For her to be this afraid, the talisman must have one hell of a plan in store for him.

But that was the future, and he'd worry about it when it got here. Now he needed to reassure Sarah.

"It's all right, Sarah," he murmured, hugging her trembling body close. "I'm here, and I'm not going to let anything hurt you. Everything's all right. I promise."

She released a shuddering breath and rested her head against his chest. He stroked her back and murmured soothingly until he felt the tension ease from her body.

Several minutes passed before she raised her head. When she did, she let out a soft cry.

"What's wrong?" he asked in concern, raising his hands to cup her face.

"Your eyes," she whispered hoarsely. "How could I have done that to you? What kind of a monster am I?"

"You aren't a monster, Sarah. You're a victim of the talisman," he said, brushing his thumbs across her silken cheeks and feeling the dampness of tears. They tore at his heart, and he wanted to haul her back into his arms.

Before he could, she pulled away from him and scrambled off the bed, tearfully saying, "Victim or not, I'm still a monster. I wish . . ."

"Wish what?"

"I wish Leonard had never found me in the woods," she said as he heard her begin to pace. "Where are we?"

"At Ryan's medical clinic," he answered, trying to brush against her mind to learn what she thought. What did she mean by Leonard finding her in the woods? He frowned, frustrated, when he found that she was again closed to him, and he suddenly realized how little he knew about her.

"Why don't I remember coming here?" she asked.

"You were cocooned by the lightning wreath. When it released us, you . . . fell asleep. Ryan thinks that something frightened you so badly that you weren't ready to face it. Do you remember something scaring you?"

"No, but . . ."

"But?" he encouraged.

"I have this urgent need to tell you something important, but I can't remember what it is," she said, her tone frustrated.

"Well, I'm sure that whatever it is will eventually come to you, so don't worry about it," he said, sure that it was his future she couldn't remember. Deciding to divert her attention, he said, "You might be able to help me with something else. The protective barrier around Sanctuary is disintegrating. Do you know how long we have before it's gone?"

She was silent for a long moment, and then she said, "I'm not sure, but noon keeps repeating in my head."

Sebastian frowned. It was early evening, so noon was more than seventeen hours away, which didn't coincide with his twelve-hour time frame. If Sarah was right, why had the talisman been telling him twelve hours? Was it providing two times to keep him off base? Or was it predicting two separate events? Of course, it could be lying to both of them.

His musing was interrupted by a knock on the door, and he called out permission to enter.

"Sebastian, I hate to bother you, but Oran Morovang is here," Ryan said, opening the door. Then he declared, "Sarah! I'm glad to see you're awake. How are you feeling?"

"Fine," Sarah mumbled.

"I bet Sarah would like to freshen up, Ryan," Sebastian said, deciding that was the easiest way to occupy her while he met with Oran. "Why don't you ask Zachary to get her things from the car and show her where the bathroom is? Then you can ask Oran to come in."

"Sure. Come with me, Sarah. I even have a small shower if you'd like to use it."

"Um, that would be nice. Sebastian, you'll be here when I get back?" she asked hesitantly.

"Of course. My meeting will take a while, so you just take your time."

They left and a few minutes later Sebastian heard the tap of a cane and the shuffle of feet as Oran entered the room. Sebastian automatically conjured up the narrator's image. At one hundred twenty years old, Oran was the oldest member of the coven. He had long, silver hair that fell well below his shoulders, and a silver beard that hung almost to his waist. His body was stooped with the ravages of arthritis, and he used a gnarled cane to walk. But his dark brown eyes were alive and alert, leaving no doubt that his advanced age had not affected his mind.

As Oran's image solidified in his mind, Sebastian knew he had to find a way to trick the talisman into giving him back his sight. If he didn't, he'd never be able to add more images to his memory. He'd never see Lucien and Ariel's twins grow up. He'd never see what Shana and Ryan's baby looked like. He wouldn't see his own face grow old, or the faces of the people for whom he cared. He'd never be able to look into Sarah's beautiful golden eyes again.

Of course if he didn't stop the talisman, there wouldn't be anything to see.

He said, "Hello, Oran. Thank you for coming. As you can see, I couldn't come to you."

"Yes, your blindness is a fascinating complication to this event," Oran said in his quavering, raspy voice.

"Then you are aware of everything that's happened to me?" Sebastian asked, though he didn't know why he bothered. One of the narrators would have automatically connected with his mind the moment he first looked at the glowing triangle in the repository, and they would have stayed with him throughout his journey. However, the narrators were unobtrusive, so he wouldn't have been aware of the monitoring.

It was too bad that they weren't allowed to tell anyone what they learned until everything was over, he now thought. It might have saved Lucien from being trapped in the cocoon with Sarah. Instead of lying in the next room disoriented, Lucien would have been repairing the barrier.

"Of course I'm aware of what's happened," Oran said. "I've been particularly enthralled with the lightning wreath."

"Yes, it's an ... interesting anomaly," Sebastian stated. "But we can discuss it later. Right now, I need to discuss our situation. I know you can't interfere with what's happening, but knowing how serious things are, did you happen to contact the council for a new troubleshooter?"

"I tried, but I couldn't get through to them," Oran answered.

"Why not?" Sebastian asked warily. "You weren't telling them about the talisman, so you weren't interfering with history."

"That wasn't the problem, Sebastian. When the barrier started disintegrating, a strange electrical field formed around Sanctuary. Our magic can't penetrate it."

"What are you talking about?" Sebastian asked, confused. "Zachary's been checking the barrier for me, and he never mentioned any electrical field."

"That's because it's still too faint to be picked up

by casual observation. If I hadn't been specifically watching for abnormalities, I wouldn't have noticed it myself. But the more the barrier disintegrates, the stronger the field becomes. I suspect that within an hour or two it will be visible to everyone. I also think that when that happens, the field will completely disrupt our magic."

"Do you know the field's source?" Sebastian asked, although he had a sinking feeling he already knew the answer.

"As I said, it's still faint, so I can't confirm my suspicions, but I think the lightning wreath has surrounded us."

Sebastian shook his head in disbelief. "You can't be suggesting what I think you are!"

"Yes, I believe the wreath has cocooned us."

"But why?" Sebastian gasped, raking a hand through his hair. "No, don't bother answering that. That's why it wanted Sarah on coven land. To destroy the barrier and trap us here until it can put its plans to destroy us into motion. We need to evacuate the coven now, and—"

"The wreath has already cocooned us, so it's too late for that," Oran interrupted quietly. "Anyone who tries to pass through it will end up like Lucien or worse."

"*Damn!* I should never have brought Sarah here," Sebastian rasped as he climbed off the bed and paced its length.

"You didn't have any choice, Sebastian. You were blinded and your magic didn't function properly. If you hadn't brought Sarah here, she or this Butler would have eventually killed you. Your triangle would have returned to Sanctuary, and the talisman would have brought her here anyway. By then, she may have had two pieces of the object in her possession, and, like you, I believe that would make her an almost unbeatable foe."

"And you think we're in better shape now?" Sebastian stated angrily, though he wasn't angry with the old warlock. He was furious with himself for not figuring out what the talisman was up to. He was also tormented by the sudden recollection of that horrible vision he'd had after the cocoon bearing Lucien and Sarah had penetrated the barrier.

He and Sarah stood in the center of Sanctuary. Her face was so sharpened with evil that it looked cadaverous, and her hands dripped with blood. But it was the sight of the coven members' bodies littering the street that truly horrified him. They'd all had their eyes gouged out.

Sarah told him to look at his hands, and though he tried to ignore her order, his hands lifted into his line of vision on their own accord. He screamed when he saw the blood on them.

"Yes, we're in better shape this way," Oran said, snapping Sebastian out of the terrifying memory. "We know the talisman has been unable to fully corrupt Sarah."

"But every time the wreath cocoons her, it steals another piece of her soul. That's the cocoon's purpose—to transform her. Now she's going to be surrounded by it twenty-four hours a day. Worse, *I'm* going to be surrounded by it."

He paused and drew in a deep breath before continuing, "Oran, you've been connected with me, so you know how the talisman has tried to make me rape Sarah. I know the spell that governs you screens out the intimate details of our lovemaking, but you must be aware of how difficult it was for me to fight against the lust. If it becomes a continuous condition, I can guarantee that it won't be long before the talisman has its way. Once that happens, Sarah will strike out in revenge, and the talisman has given her an entire coven of victims to kill. And because I'll have raped her, I'll be fast on my way to corruption."

"I think you underestimate yourself, Sebastian," Oran said. "You've admitted to yourself that you're in love with Sarah. A warlock is incapable of harming the witch—or, in your case, woman—he loves."

Sebastian shook his head. "Remember what happened to Seamus and Ragna Morpeth. They were mates and had a child, and the talisman corrupted them. Sarah and I aren't mates, and we don't have a child. I don't stand a chance against it."

"So what are you going to do?"

"As soon as Sarah comes back I'm going to have Zachary cast another confining spell over her. Then I'm going to have him get me the hell away from her until I can figure out how to get us out of this mess."

"Before you put that plan into action, you'd better consider the consequences carefully. Sarah has already told you that she can use her powers from within the confining spell. Perhaps you should consider an aversion spell that will make her find you repulsive."

Sebastian shook his head again. "I'd have to cast an aversion spell over her, and she'd immediately go into distress. The only spell we can safely use is a confining spell, because it's the only type of spell that doesn't affect her directly. She'll be angry when we do it, but as long as no one hurts her, she won't hurt anyone," Sebastian assured.

"I don't know, Sebastian," Oran stated dubiously. "I'm unable to link with Sarah, but I have picked up on enough of her thoughts to realize she has a fear of abandonment. Right now, you're all she has to hold on to. If you have her confined and leave her, I don't think she'll handle it well."

Sebastian scowled. "I know what I'm doing, Oran, and you're dangerously close to interfering with history. I'd hate to see the spell that governs the narrators kill you for offering your opinion on such a trivial matter."

"I'm an old warlock, Sebastian. Death doesn't frighten me, but I will admit that I'd hate to die before I find out if Sarah is what I think she is."

"What do you think she is?" Sebastian asked expectantly.

"Now, that would be interfering with history," Oran said with a chuckle. "But I'll give you a hint. Think about the lightning. I'm sure that's why the talisman chose Sarah as its instrument of destruction. I'll tell Zachary to come in immediately."

With that, Oran shuffled out of the room, and Sebastian frowned in confusion. What did the lightning have to do with the talisman's choosing Sarah? He wanted to pursue Oran's statement but Zachary came in, saying, "Oran said you wanted to see me?"

"Yes," Sebastian said.

As he told Zachary his plans for Sarah, he recalled Oran's warning about confining Sarah and felt a stirring of uneasiness. But he couldn't think of any other way to handle the situation. If Oran was right and the wreath had encircled Sanctuary, then it was only a matter of time before the talisman filled him with lust. For both their sakes—for the salvation of their *souls*—he had to stay away from her.

But if he weren't around and she was allowed to move freely among the coven, the talisman might find some new way to complete her transformation to evil. As much as he hated it, Sebastian knew he had no choice but to confine her.

But the justification didn't alleviate his apprehension. When he had Zachary lead him out of the room, he couldn't help wondering if he was making a terrible mistake, particularly since he'd told Sarah he'd be here when she returned.

Again, he told himself he had no other option. Sarah would be unhappy with him, but she would be safe and so would the coven.

Sarah had hoped that a shower would rid her of the feeling of terror hovering over her. It hadn't. As she braided her wet hair, she stared at her image in the mirror, hoping it would provide her with a reason for her fear. It didn't.

"Why do I feel so scared?" she whispered in frustration. "And what is it that I need to tell Sebastian? I know it's important, so why can't I remember?"

Voicing the questions didn't provide the answers, and she sighed heavily as she untied her bundle of clothes. After donning clean underwear, she lifted the long-sleeved, leather dress from the pile. As she toyed with the fringe on the sleeves and then touched the elaborate beading on the lace-up bodice, she told herself it would be more practical to put on clean jeans and a shirt. But she wasn't interested in practical. She had a sudden urge to feel feminine.

You want to impress Sebastian, an inner voice whispered. *But that's ridiculous. He can't even see you.*

At the reminder, she buried her face in the dress. She knew why she'd blinded him. She'd thought he was going to kill her people—or, rather, Leonard's people. But she'd been wrong, and now Sebastian would never see again. Regardless of what excuse he gave her to justify her actions, she knew that she was a monster.

Tears stung her eyes, but she forced herself to blink them back. Crying wouldn't change anything. The only way she could achieve redemption was to help Sebastian stop the talisman. After she'd done that, she'd kill herself to ensure that she never harmed anyone again.

Quickly, she pulled on the dress and laced up the bodice. Then she sat down on the toilet and pulled on her beaded, knee-high moccasins. Standing, she smoothed the dress over her hips and retied her clothes bundle.

Sebastian had said his meeting would take a while, and she figured she'd been in here at least a half hour. Hopefully, that was enough time, because she was starting to feel claustrophobic. She'd go back to the examining room, and if he was still busy, she'd wait in the hallway. Tossing her braid behind her so that it hung down her back, she grabbed her bundled clothes, opened the door, and froze.

Zachary leaned against the wall with his arms crossed over his chest. As his gaze swept over her, Sarah could sense his hostility. She wanted to step back into the bathroom and slam the door closed.

Instead, she hugged the bundle to her chest and said, "Hello, Mr. . . . Morcombe, isn't it?"

"Just call me Zachary," he drawled as he raised his gaze to her face.

Sarah couldn't help shivering at the animosity reflected in their dark depths. She understood why he disliked her. Indeed, this was exactly how she'd treated Sebastian when he'd arrived on the mountain and she thought he wanted to destroy her—no, Leonard's—people. The difference was, she deserved Zachary's dislike. She truly was a threat to his people.

"I'm sorry. If I'd known you were waiting to get in here, I would have dressed faster," she said.

He shook his head. "I'm waiting for you. Sebastian asked me to escort you back to the examining room."

"Oh," she said, her spirits sinking at the realization that Sebastian didn't trust her. She didn't blame him. After all she'd done to him, she was amazed he still spoke to her. Unfortunately, that didn't make his actions hurt any less. "Is Sebastian finished with his meeting?"

"Yes," Zachary said, gesturing for her to precede him.

She headed down the hallway, refraining from looking back over her shoulder. She could feel his eyes boring into her, and she shivered. When she reached the examining room and stepped inside, she frowned. The room was empty.

"Where's Sebastian?" she asked, spinning around in alarm when she heard Zachary murmur some words behind her.

Instead of answering, he flicked his hand, and Sarah jumped back with a gasp as lightning shot from his fingertips and she saw a golden barrier fill the doorway.

"He's gone," Zachary said. "He told me to tell you that you're confined to this room. The door and the windows are sealed with a spell that will kill you if you try to leave. Meals will be delivered to you regularly, and someone will be here to provide you with anything you want or need, except release, of course.

"There's a bathroom over there," he continued, gesturing toward a closed door at the back of the room. "It doesn't have a shower, but Sebastian said you'd only be here for a day or two, so I'm sure you'll manage until we can relocate you. Is there anything I can get you before I leave?"

Sarah shook her head, too stunned to say anything. She told herself that Sebastian must have a good reason for doing this to her. But why wasn't he here to explain it to her?

"Wait! Is Sebastian all right?" she asked when Zachary turned to walk away.

He glanced over his shoulder, and she shrank back from the antagonism of his gaze. "No, he isn't all right. He's blind, and, from what I understand, he owes that handicap to you."

Before she could respond, Zachary stalked away, and, with a shudder, Sarah closed the door, hiding the barrier that sealed her inside the room.

However, the closed door didn't hide the barriers that shimmered against the windows, and she turned her back on them and trudged to the bed on which she'd awakened in the safety of Sebastian's arms.

She tossed her clothes to the floor and laid down, staring up at the ceiling. Sebastian had said he'd be here when she returned, so why hadn't he stayed to tell her why he was doing this to her?

Because you blinded him, and he hates you, her conscience supplied.

"It wasn't my fault," Sarah sobbed softly, covering her face with her hands. "I thought he was my enemy."

You're a monster. That's why your mother abandoned you. It's why Sebastian abandoned you. You'll always be alone. Forever.

"No!" Sarah cried, rolling to her side and curling into a fetal ball.

Alone. Forever.

"Why do you insist on tormenting me?" she wailed, realizing that it wasn't her conscience taunting her. It was the talisman. "Why don't you just let me die?"

Because if you die, your son will die.

Sarah's eyes snapped open and she stared at the wall as memory came flooding in. Pressing her hand to her abdomen, she gave a dazed shake of her head. That was the important thing she needed to tell Sebastian! She was pregnant!

So find him. Tell him.

"I can't!" she gasped, sitting up on the bed. "I'm trapped in here."

Their magic is not stronger than yours. You have the power, so use it.

"It's too dangerous," she said. "I could hurt my . . . son. Oh, God, I'm *pregnant*. I'm going to have a baby!"

You have to tell Sebastian. He's the father. He has a right to know.

"I'll wait until he comes back."

He isn't coming back. He's abandoned you. If you

don't go after him, you'll be alone forever. Your son will be alone forever.

"No!" Sarah whispered frantically as she bolted off the bed and ran to the door, throwing it open. "My son won't be abandoned. *I'll never let him be abandoned!*"

Instinctively, she reached for the triangle, closed her eyes and summoned the lightning. She heard it strike in front of her. and she opened her eyes in time to see the barrier Zachary had erected disappear.

"What do I do now?" she questioned as she stepped out into the hallway, waiting for someone to come rushing at her. But no one came, and she shivered as the silence assured her Zachary had lied to her. There was no one here. She was completely alone.

Find Sebastian. Your triangle will lead you to him, but you must hurry.

She clutched the triangle and ran outside. It was dark, but moonlight flooded the street. She rushed to the middle of it and glanced at the buildings surrounding her. As she stared at their slender towers, pointed arches and flying buttresses, a memory hit her with such force that she fell to her knees with a keening wail.

This was the strange town she'd seen in the vision when she'd stopped the car on the side of the road outside Sanctuary. Its streets had been littered with the bodies of strangers, whose eyes had been gouged out. And she had caused their deaths.

"You lied to me!" she yelled as she leaned her head toward the sky. "I am a monster!"

Yes, you are a monster. But the only way you can

*save your son is to find Sebastian, and your time is
running out.*

"Yes," Sarah whispered hoarsely as she climbed to
her feet. "Sebastian can save our son. I have to find
him and tell him he has to save our baby. *He has to
save him!*"

She struggled to her feet and started running to-
wards the woods. Everything inside her told her that
Sebastian was in the woods. And she had to find
him before the talisman claimed their son.

20

Evil Battles

✜

"Dammit, Sebastian! You can't stay out here in the woods alone," Zachary declared when they reached Sebastian's lean-to in the woods.

"As I've said for at least the dozenth time, I'll be fine," Sebastian replied impatiently as he braced his hand on the lean-to's roof to orient himself. "Ever since I came to Sanctuary, I've lived out here."

"Yes, but you weren't *blind*," Zachary shot back just as impatiently. "Not only will you be out here alone, but without your sight, you can't find your way out of the woods."

That's the whole point, Sebastian thought. Once the talisman filled him with lust, he'd be stranded out here and couldn't possibly find his way back to Sarah. He wasn't, however, about to share that information with Zachary. It was too . . . personal.

Aloud, he said, "If I want to come back to town, I'll connect with you and you can come get me."

"But—"

"Drop the subject, Zachary. I have my reasons for doing this. Get back to Sarah. I don't want her left alone for any longer than necessary."

"I think I should stay with you," Zachary persisted. "What if the talisman starts affecting you or tries to cocoon you with its lightning? You won't see it coming, so you won't be able to protect yourself. Let me contact one of the other warlocks and tell him to go to the clinic and guard Sarah."

"No," Sebastian stated firmly. "With Lucien disoriented, you're the most powerful warlock in the coven. Sarah's confined, but she can still use her powers. If she does, I need someone there who has a better than even chance of thwarting her."

"Come on, Sebastian. The way she reacts to our magic even a child could stop her. All they have to do is cast a simple spell over her."

Sebastian scowled. "I told you that a spell can only be used against her as a last resort. I'm serious, Zachary. Even the simplest spell could kill her. If for some reason you have no choice but to use one on her, revoke your spell the moment she collapses. Remember, Sarah's in this predicament because Ulrich Morgret let Seamus Morpeth take a piece of the talisman out into the mortal world. We are responsible for what's happened to her, and it's up to us to make sure that Sarah is protected and cared for for the rest of her life."

"I realize that," Zachary said, sounding frustrated. "But I just can't dredge up much sympathy for her at the moment. She may not be responsible, but she's still the reason the coven's in jeopardy. If you insist that I go back and guard her, I'll do so. However, let me at least send someone out here to be with you."

"Look, Zachary," Sebastian said. "I'm wearing the talisman's triangle, so I'm as potentially dangerous to the coven as Sarah is. We're even more dangerous if we're in proximity to one another. As long as Sarah and I are separated, the talisman won't be able to carry out its plans for us. That's why I want to be out here alone. If someone is with me, the talisman may persuade me to make that person take me to Sarah. If no one's here, then I won't be able to go to her. So go back to Sarah and protect her. *Now.*"

"Fine," Zachary muttered. "But if you need anything . . ."

"I'll contact you," Sebastian lied, knowing that the moment Zachary was gone he'd cast a spell over himself that would stop him from summoning anyone if the talisman was involved. He wouldn't allow himself even the slightest chance of getting back to Sarah. To ensure the spell was effective, he would add an incantation to make it irreversible until the battle with the talisman was over or he was dead.

"Well, I guess I'd better go," Zachary said, still sounding reluctant.

"Yes, and, Zachary, I do understand your feelings toward Sarah," Sebastian said. "I know it's hard for you to sympathize with her when the entire coven— hell, all of mankind—is in jeopardy because of her connection with the talisman. But try to put this into perspective. The talisman managed to corrupt Seamus and Ragna Morpeth beyond redemption, and they were not only mates, they had a child to protect. They were also in contact with the talisman for only a short time.

"Sarah has been in contact with the triangle her entire life, and she's alone in the world," he went on fervently. "Unlike Seamus and Ragna, she's bound to no one and has no compelling reason to fight against the talisman. Considering those circumstances, she should have caved in to the talisman the moment it focused on her. But she hasn't caved in, Zachary. She's fought against it every step of the way. Because she has, we still have a chance to survive. So keep that in mind when you're dealing with her."

"Hell, when you put it that way, I feel like an idiot for treating her like I have," Zachary stated gruffly. "I'll take good care of her."

"Thank you," Sebastian said. "Now please go to her. I don't want her to feel as if she's been abandoned."

"I'm out of here," Zachary replied.

Sebastian sighed in relief as he listened to the warlock leave. He also felt damn guilty about deserting Sarah the way he had, but at least he'd made sure that Zachary would give her the respect she deserved.

As soon as he could no longer hear Zachary's progress through the woods, he murmured the irreversible incantation that would keep him from summoning help from the coven. Once he felt the spell take hold he eased into the lean-to and groped around it until he found his sleeping bag. Unrolling it, he lay down and closed his eyes, wondering how long it would be before the talisman started tormenting him with lust.

His eyes flew open when a man suddenly drawled contemptuously, "That was a very touching speech you gave about Sarah. Am I crazy, *wicáhmunga,* or have you had the bad taste to fall in love with the conniving bitch?"

For a moment, Sebastian thought he was dreaming. But then he heard the man walking toward him. He bolted upright and pivoted his head toward the lean-to's opening. "Who the hell are you?"

"John Butler the third, but I have a Ph.D. in archeology, so you may call me *Doctor* Butler," the man replied. "I'm pleased to say we won't know each other long enough to get on a first-name basis."

"How did you get onto coven land?" Sebastian questioned harshly as the man's identity sank in. He'd fled Sarah, but he suddenly realized that lust wasn't what the talisman was going to use against him. It had brought him a cold-blooded killer, and now that Sebastian had cast the spell, he couldn't even summon help to fight him.

"I am *The Power, wicáhmunga,*" Butler replied with bravado. "Unlike you and Sarah, I'm not affected by the clash of magics. I can go where I want, when I want, and the wreath doesn't affect me."

"Clash of magics?" Sebastian repeated warily, latching on to that particular phrase.

"Why, *wicáhmunga,* you pride yourself on being the most powerful warlock alive," Butler taunted, and Sebastian barely refrained from scooting deeper into the lean-to. He knew that Butler knelt in front of it. He could feel and smell the man's hot, rancid breath against his face. It turned his stomach. "Are you telling me that you haven't figured out the problem with the magics?"

"No, I hadn't figured it out until now, but I suspect you didn't either. The talisman told you, didn't it?" Sebastian countered.

"How I know doesn't matter."

"It does when you make it sound as if your knowledge makes you superior to me, and we both know the opposite is true. If it weren't, the talisman wouldn't have kept you closed off from me all this time."

"You are *not* superior to me!" Butler yelled furiously. "The talisman has chosen me, and it is going to give me the power and the glory I deserve. As soon as the bitch gets here, I'll prove that to you."

As the implication of Butler's words sank in, Sebastian shuddered. Even though he knew to whom the man referred, he said, "Who are you talking about?"

"*Sar-ah,*" Butler said, drawing her name out in a lascivious drawl that made Sebastian's skin crawl. "She'll be here soon, *wicáhmunga,* and I'm going to show her what she gave up when she chose you over me."

Sebastian wanted to ask what Butler meant by Sarah's choice, but he sensed that was the response the man sought. Instead, he said, "Sarah's confined, Butler. She isn't going to get anywhere near this place."

"See! That proves that I'm superior to you," Butler declared with a malicious snicker. "Sarah's magic may be more primitive than yours, but with my help, she broke out of the magical cell in which you imprisoned her. She's on her way here to tell you her exciting news, and I bet you can't guess what it is."

"You're right. I can't guess," Sebastian said, determined not to play the man's game. He again cursed the fact that he'd cast the spell cutting him off from help. Zachary couldn't be that far off, but with the spell in place, he might as well have been a million miles away.

"Well, I hate to steal Sarah's thunder," Butler said. Then he let out another malicious chuckle. "No, that's not true. She's a Thunderbeing, and I have every intention of stealing her thunder, but I'm going to tell you her news anyway. You're going to be a father, *wicáhmunga*. Or I suppose I should say you would have been a father. I'm going to make Sarah kill you, and then I'll kill her and your bastard son."

Sebastian shook his head in disbelief. Sarah *couldn't* be pregnant! A warlock couldn't father a child until he mated. The talisman was trying to pull a scam on him, and he couldn't fall for it.

But what if Butler's right? his conscience prodded. *What if, by some unknown means, Sarah and you became mates? What if she really is pregnant?*

Sebastian rubbed his hand over his face, trying to decide what to do. Somehow he had to gain the upper hand with Butler, but how could he do that when he couldn't even see him?

Trick him into restoring your sight!

How? Sebastian wondered frantically, searching his mind for an answer.

"What's the matter, *wicáhmunga?* Is impending fatherhood too big a burden for you to bear?" Butler mocked.

At the question, Sebastian suddenly knew how to fight back, and he forced himself to shrug dismissively. "Do what you want with Sarah and the child. I'm blind and can't see what's happening, so why should I care what you do to them?"

Sebastian heard a horrified gasp at his words, and his heart skipped a beat. The gasp hadn't come from Butler, so who had it come from? Had Zachary disobeyed him and returned? He sure as hell hoped so.

But Butler dashed his hopes, and Sebastian shook his head in horror when the man let out a demonic laugh and drawled, "Why, Sarah. I see you've arrived in time to hear that your beloved *wicáhmunga* doesn't give a damn about what happens to you and your child."

* * *

As Sarah stared at Sebastian, who sat in a lean-to built against the side of a mountain, his words kept repeating in her mind. *Do what you want with Sarah and the child. Why should I care what you do to them?*

She knew she should feel anger or pain, but she felt oddly numb. She could understand him not caring about her. But how could he not care for his own child? How could she have misjudged him that badly?

"Sarah, listen to me," Sebastian suddenly said, jerking her out of her thoughts.

"Oh, yes, Sarah, *listen* to him," Butler mocked as he stood and swaggered a few feet away from the lean-to. "Now that he knows you're here, I'm sure he's going to tell you how he *really* feels about you. He'll probably declare his undying love and promise that if you join forces with him to fight against me, you'll be together forever. Of course, you're so damn gullible and emotionally needy, you'll probably fall for that lie, just like you've fallen for all his other lies."

"And of course you've never lied to me," Sarah said, anger suddenly flaring inside her. She welcomed the emotion. It was better than the empty, hollow feeling she'd had since hearing Sebastian reject their son. "You've always had my best interests at heart, haven't you, John Butler? That's why you plan to kill me and my son."

"I would have shared *everything* with you, but you want to steal the power and the glory from me," he rasped, glaring at her. "Well, you can't have it, because it belongs to me!"

"It doesn't belong to you. It belongs to me and my son, and I'll prove it to you!" she declared furiously.

"Sarah! No!" Sebastian bellowed, and she saw him crawl out of the lean-to and climb to his feet. He stumbled blindly toward her, saying, "Don't connect with the talisman or you'll be lost. Please don't do it, Sarah. *You have to save yourself.*"

Sarah hesitated at his urgent plea, but then she recalled that he didn't care about her or his son. He was only trying to save himself. Grabbing her triangle, she cried, "Come to me!"

The entire sky above them filled with the whirling lightning wreath. As three lightning bolts streaked toward them, there was a deafening boom of thunder. The bolts struck the individual pieces of the talisman and then arced between Sarah, Butler, and Sebastian so that they were joined in a continuous flow of electrical energy.

Sebastian and Butler screamed in agony and fell to their knees. Sarah, however, felt no pain. The lightning's touch filled her with euphoria, and she tossed her head back and laughed, reveling in the exhilarating sensation. Why had she fought so hard against something so wonderful?

"Sarah, please! You have to stop this," Sebastian gasped painfully. "You're killing me and Butler, and if we die, you really will be a monster. The talisman will make you destroy everyone, and when you're the last person alive, it will destroy you!"

She lowered her head and scowled as she glanced between him and Butler. Butler lay on the ground, writhing in pain as the lightning seared him. It also burned Sebastian, and though his tormented expression revealed his suffering, he still knelt.

"You can no longer fool me, *wicáhmunga*," she

stated derisively. "You're just like John Butler. You want my power. But the power belongs to me and my son. The son you were willing to let die!"

"That's not true, Sarah," Sebastian denied. "I was trying to trick the talisman into restoring my eyesight."

"Why do you insist on lying to me!"

"I'm not lying, and I can prove it. Link with my mind, Sarah. You know I can't hide the truth from you mentally. Please, Sarah. Link with me before it's too late."

"You're trying to trick me. You think that if I join with your mind, you can control me and steal my power."

His body swayed. Sarah was sure he'd collapse to the ground like Butler, but he managed to remain upright. "I don't want your power, Sarah, and deep down you know it. That's why you're afraid to touch my mind."

"I am not afraid!"

"Then prove it. Link with me and show me just how powerful you really are."

She continued to glare at him, knowing that he tried to trick her. But for some strange reason, she felt compelled to do as he asked. She opened her mind to him, but before she even meshed with him, she knew that he told her the truth.

That didn't stop his thoughts from hitting her with stunning force, and she fell to her knees with an anguished sob. But it wasn't pain that tortured her. It was the wave of undiluted love that washed over her as Sebastian mentally chanted, *I love you, Sarah. I love you.*

No! the talisman's voice bellowed inside her. *He is your enemy! You must destroy him!*

Sarah shook her head, confused. Every survival instinct she had screamed at her to kill Sebastian. But her heart, her *soul*, insisted she release him from the lightning. She knew, however, that to let him go she would have to turn the lightning on herself, and she and her son would die. She couldn't sacrifice her son for Sebastian! But she knew that if she didn't, her son would grow up to be exactly what she'd envisioned. The personification of evil.

Wanága, help me! she cried instinctively as she broke off her connection with Sebastian's mind. *I don't know what to do!*

You know, Sarah, Wanága responded. *But are you strong enough to make the right choice?*

Why do I have to make a choice? You said you were here to destroy me, so destroy me!

I cannot destroy you, Sarah. You are no longer the last of the Thunderbeings. It is up to you to decide if your son will walk in darkness forever.

Sarah automatically pressed her hands to her abdomen. She knew her son was no more than a microscopic bit of life, but now that she had her powers, she could feel him nestled within her womb. He trusted her to give him life.

She looked at Sebastian. His body was still wracked with pain, but his expression revealed his love for her. At that moment she knew that if she turned her back on love and sacrificed Sebastian for their son, she would not only lose her own capacity for love, but her child would be born without the ability to love. He wouldn't even care for her, his own mother, nor she for him. And what was life without love?

Nothing. She'd lived her life starved for love, and there was no way she would condemn her child to that kind of soulless existence. She had to destroy herself and her son to keep them from becoming the talisman's evil chattel.

Before she could lose her nerve, she clasped her triangle and cried, "Kill me!"

"No!" Sebastian bellowed. "You can't die! I love you!"

"I love you, too," she cried as the lightning wreath cocooned her for the last time.

"Sarah! Sarah, answer me!" Sebastian yelled, panicked as he heard the familiar whirring of the lightning wreath. "You can't die! I won't *let* you die! I love you, Sarah! Do you hear me? *I love you!*"

When she didn't respond, he lurched to his feet and stumbled forward. He had to get to her. He had to save her. He loved her. He *needed* her. She couldn't die. She *couldn't!*

He was so frantic that he'd taken several steps before he realized that his sight was back. He stopped walking and shook his head in horror as he stared at the cocoon that had enveloped Sarah. The lightning didn't whirl around her. It struck her unrelentingly, leaving no doubt in his mind that it would kill her.

"No! I won't let you kill her!" he yelled at the talisman as a combination of fear and rage surged through him.

Without even thinking, he murmured the words to the most powerful spell he could think of and flicked his hand toward the cocoon. Spell-lightning leaped from his fingers and shot across the small clearing. As it hit the talisman's lightning, there was an explosion of brilliant light.

Blinking frantically, he ran toward Sarah. He

reached her just as the last of the light faded and the cocoon disappeared. He dropped to his knees beside her and let his mind brush against hers. There was nothing, not even a tiny glimmer of life.

Where am I? Sarah wondered as she studied her surroundings. She hovered in a void that was neither dark nor light, but had the shadowy shading of dusk.

Wanáǧa suddenly appeared in front of her in his full battle regalia, "You are in the world between life and death, Sarah. It is here that you will make the final choice. It is time for you to know all." Before she could respond, he said, "You do not have much time, Sarah, so you must listen to my story without interruption. Do you understand?"

"I understand," she said.

He nodded. "I am your ancestor—a Thunder-being. This name was given to us because of our control of the lightning. When I lived, we felt as if we were gods, and we often made choices of life and death that only the gods should make.

"Our people lived beside the waters that you call the ocean. One day a big ship of wasičuns came to us across the water. With them was a *wicáhmunǧa* known as Aodán Morpeth."

"Morpeth?" Sarah gasped involuntarily, despite Wanáǧa's instructions to remain silent.

"Yes, he was Seamus Morpeth's ancestor," Wanáǧa confirmed. "We feared Aodán, because he had greater magic than we did. The braves of our tribe met to see how we should deal with him. Many wanted to kill him, but I felt we should try to steal his magic so that we would be more powerful."

He stopped speaking and shook his head wearily.

"I befriended Aodán, and I learned that his people were not allowed to kill, even to defend themselves. I told him that we had to kill, because many tribes were jealous of us and wanted to destroy us. Aodán said it was still wrong for us to kill people less powerful than us. We argued about this often. One day Aodán suggested we combine our magics and create a talisman that would protect the Thunderbeings from harm so we would not have to kill.

"I agreed to do this," Wanága went on, "but I did not want a protective talisman. I wanted to make one that would steal Aodán's power and give it to us. When we made the talisman, I deceived him, and then I took the talisman and used it to destroy our greatest enemies."

He stopped and shook his head again. "What I did not know was that by using the talisman for death I made the magics fight each other. It changed the talisman from good to evil, and instead of protecting my people, it made me destroy them. When Aodán found out what happened, he came to me. By then there was only a handful of my people left. When Aodán made me see what I had done, I was horrified, but the talisman had gained so much power it could not be stopped. Aodán tried to reverse the magic, but it was the Thunderbeing's magic trapped within the talisman and he could not release it. He said that the only way he could stop it was to take it back to his world. I gave him the talisman and he left with it. Then I killed myself for punishment of what I had done.

"But I was not allowed to move on to the spirit world. I thought it was because of the curse I placed on my people. Only when you were born was it revealed that I could not rest because the talisman was back and you were the last of the Thunderbeings. Through you it would unleash our magic and destroy the world. That's why I came to destroy you."

"So why didn't you destroy me?" Sarah asked, confused.

"I could not bear to see our people no longer exist because of what I had done, and as long as your mother, who was also a Thunderbeing, lived, you were not the last. But when you were five years old your parents were killed, and I knew I had to act. But I still could not bring myself to kill you, so I brought you to Leonard. He had a piece of the talisman and he had not been made evil by it. I hoped that Leonard could teach you how he did this so that I would not have to destroy you."

"Then my mother didn't abandon me?" Sarah gasped.

"No, Sarah. That was the talisman's way of hurting you to make you turn to it. Your mother loved you as deeply as any mother can love her child.

"But our time here is almost out, and it is time for you to make your final choice. Both John Butler and the *wicáhmunga* live, and by your refusal to kill for the talisman, you have destroyed it. Its evil will no longer torment you, but you carry the *wicáhmunga's* child. This child will have both the *wicáhmunga's* magic and the magic of the Thunderbeings. He is the beginning of a new race—the most powerful race that has ever lived.

"If he is born, his destiny will be a tormented one. Because of his extraordinary powers, he will constantly be faced with the choice between good and evil. If he chooses the path of good, he will bring great change to mankind. If he chooses the path of evil, he will destroy the world. The choice you must make is whether to let him live, which means you will also live, or let him die, and you will also die."

"Why are you giving me this choice?" Sarah asked in bewilderment.

"It is not I who gives it to you, Sarah. It is the great spirits of the universe. You chose the right path and redeemed yourself when your destiny dictated that you fail. You did this because the love you share with the *wicáhmuŋġa* is so strong and pure it gave you the strength to make the right choices. Now you must decide whether you want to give this same choice to your son."

"But if I make the wrong choice about him . . ."

"I'm sorry, Sarah. Your time is gone. You must make the choice now."

Sarah stared at him in bewilderment. She wanted to live, and she wanted her son to live. But knowing the adversity his future held, would it be fair to give him life?

Suddenly, Sebastian's voice echoed in her mind, *I love you, Sarah. Please come back to me!*

Tears filled her eyes at the heart-wrenching pain in his voice. It also wiped out her doubts. Sebastian loved her, and she loved him. At that moment she knew that together they could save their son.

"I choose to live," she told Wanáġa.

"I'm glad," he said. "Now it is time for me to go. I can finally rest in peace."

Before she could tell him goodbye, Wanáġa disappeared. She wanted to call out to him, to beg him not to leave her. He was her friend and her mentor. How could she survive without him?

As the question tormented her, she felt Sebastian

hug her close and say, "You're alive! Sarah, open your eyes. Please, open your eyes and tell me you're all right!"

Sarah opened her eyes and gazed up into his beloved face and knew that she no longer needed Wanága. She had Sebastian.

"I love you, Sebastian," she whispered.

"I love you, too," he said hoarsely and lowered his lips to hers.

When he raised his head, she said, "I'm sorry for everything I did to hurt you."

"Sarah, there is no reason for you to be sorry, and no pain you subjected me to could hurt more than the thought of losing you. Somehow I'll find a way to free you from the evil the talisman implanted in you so we can be together for the rest of our lives."

Tears welled into her eyes and she reached up and touched his face. He thought she still suffered from the effects of the talisman, but he loved her anyway.

"Wanága says that by defeating the talisman, I freed myself from its evil," she said. "Of course, your people will want more than my word as proof, and I'll do whatever they ask as long as I have you by my side."

"You couldn't get rid of me if you wanted to," Sebastian rasped. "You're bound to me forever."

As he again lowered his lips to her, Sarah knew that her final choice had been the right one.

Epilogue

Assured Sebastian slept soundly, Sarah slipped stealthily from the bed and headed for the nursery. She knew Sebastian would scold her for being overprotective of their three-month-old son, Gabriel, but she couldn't help herself. When she stepped into the nursery, Willow, who lay on the floor beside the crib, raised her head and rattled softly.

"Hello, Willow," Sarah whispered as she walked to the snake, picked it up, and brought it close to her face. "I see you're still on guard duty."

Willow flicked her tongue against Sarah's cheek, and Sarah laughed softly.

She started and spun toward the door as Sebastian grumbled, "I still can't believe I let you bring that damn snake to Sanctuary."

"As I remember, when we went to get my possessions, you were the one who said I should bring her with me. You said a Thunderbeing should never be separated from her familiar," Sarah pointed out, still finding it strange to refer to herself as a Thunderbeing and not a Lakota. She'd done extensive research, trying to find out more about her race, but there was no record of her people. What exactly was she? she wondered. Since her powers involved lightning and the coven's powers involved spell-lightning, Oran Morovang, the Narrator, felt she might be a primitive form of their race. Unfortunately, only Wanága could have confirmed that theory, and he was gone.

"Yeah, well, it just goes to show that even the troubleshooter has lapses of good judgment when he's in love," Sebastian said, breaking into her musing. "What are you doing in here? I didn't hear Gabriel cry."

"He didn't," she said, lowering Willow back to the floor and then turning to stare down at her son. "I just wanted to check on him."

Sebastian walked to her. When he wrapped his arms around her, she leaned back against his chest. As she continued to regard their son, she found it hard to believe that a year had passed since she had defeated the talisman. Thankfully, none of its evil had harmed the coven. Lucien Morgret's disorientation had cleared the moment the talisman was destroyed. The protective barrier surrounding Sanctuary was repaired shortly thereafter. The talisman's pieces now rested in the repository, although there was no need for them to be guarded. The coven had tested them and concluded that the pieces no longer had any magical properties.

"Gabriel's okay, Sarah," Sebastian murmured against her hair. "You need to stop worrying about him,"

"I can't stop worrying," she said with a heavy sigh. "You know what Wanága said about him. He's going to be constantly tested with choices between good and evil."

"Sarah, he's just a baby. Right now the only choices he's faced with are whether he wants to eat or sleep. And when the time comes for him to face the other choices, we'll make sure he makes the right ones."

"You make it sound as if it's going to be easy, and we both know it isn't."

"He's your son. He'll rise above the adversity, just as you did."

"Speaking of adversity, I visited John Butler today," she said, angling her head so she could look up at Sebastian. "Are you sure he needs to be confined in that cabin in the woods? His mind is gone, and he's no more than a child. It seems cruel to keep him isolated."

"Sarah, you have to stop feeling guilty about him," Sebastian chided. "Butler didn't lose his mind because of you. He lost it because when the talisman released him from its hold, he couldn't live with what he'd done while under its influence."

"I know, but it's been a year, and he hasn't done one evil thing. Can't he be allowed some freedom?"

"He killed two people, Sarah. If we turned him in to the mortal authorities, he'd be caged in a mental institution for the rest of his life. At least here, he has room to move around, and he gets fresh air and sunshine. And he isn't alone. People visit him all the time, including yourself. As time passes, we may give him more freedom. But before we ever consider that, we have to know beyond any doubt that he no longer has the capacity for evil. Now come back to bed."

"Let me kiss Gabriel first," she said, easing away from him. Leaning over the crib, she adjusted Gabriel's blanket and tucked his favorite teddy bear close to him. Then she kissed his cheek, murmuring, "I love you, baby."

He stirred, and Sebastian wrapped an arm around

her waist and tugged her away from the crib. "Let's get out of here before we wake him up. He'll demand that we play with him, and I'd like for us to have a little adult play time."

"Why, Sebastian, are you suggesting what I think you're suggesting?" she said, smiling up at him.

"You bet," he growled, dropping a quick, hard kiss to her lips.

She laughed softly and let him lead her out of the baby's room. As they walked down the hall, she thought she heard Gabriel and almost turned back. But when he didn't cry, she decided she was being overprotective.

Little did she know that by not going back, she missed her son's first display of magic. Willow was the only witness when Gabriel levitated his teddy bear above his head.

LOVE THAT SPANS TIME

☐ **TOUCH OF MAGIC by Carin Rafferty.** The moment Shana Morland met Ryan Alden, she was torn between sacred love and its darkest power. She wanted him—but the source of this overwhelming attraction lay veiled in mystery. This love could mean magic or menace for Shana. But only the fates she had so recklessly tempted held the tantalizing answer. (405153—$4.99)

☐ **SKYPIRATE by Justine Davis.** Captain Califa Claxton, once the Coalition's top battle strategist, wears the notorious golden slave collar. Dax, the skypirate hunted to the ends of the universe by the cruel interstellar Coalition, possesses the controller which can break her will. But his touch alone arouses her passion, and if she can gain his trust, a chance to destroy the Coalition together awaits them among the stars. (404912—$4.99)

☐ **TO CATCH THE WIND by Jasmine Cresswell.** Between two worlds, and across time, a beautiful woman struggles to find a love that could only mean danger. (403991—$4.99)

☐ **A DREAMSPUN CHRISTMAS Five Stories by Marilyn Campbell, Justine Davis, Carol Nelson Douglas, Edith Layton, and Emma Merritt.** These wonderful, heartwarming Christmas stories, written by five highly acclaimed authors, have happy holiday endings brought about by good ghosts, minor miracles, anxious angels, twists of time, and other kinds of divine intervention. (405277—$4.99)

*Prices slightly higher in Canada

Buy them at your local bookstore or use this convenient coupon for ordering.

PENGUIN USA
P.O. Box 999 — Dept. #17109
Bergenfield, New Jersey 07621

Please send me the books I have checked above.
I am enclosing $_____ (please add $2.00 to cover postage and handling). Send check or money order (no cash or C.O.D.'s) or charge by Mastercard or VISA (with a $15.00 minimum). Prices and numbers are subject to change without notice.

Card #_____ Exp. Date _____
Signature_____
Name_____
Address_____
City _____ State _____ Zip Code _____

For faster service when ordering by credit card call 1-800-253-6476

Allow a minimum of 4-6 weeks for delivery. This offer is subject to change without notice.

WE NEED YOUR HELP

To continue to bring you quality romance
that meets your personal expectations,
we at TOPAZ books want to hear from you.
Help us by filling out this questionnaire, and in exchange
we will give you a **free gift** as a token of our gratitude.

- Is this the first TOPAZ book you've purchased? (circle one)

    YES   NO

    The title and author of this book is: _____

- If this was not the first TOPAZ book you've purchased, how many have you bought in the past year?

    a: 0 - 5   b 6 - 10   c: more than 10   d: more than 20

- How many romances in total did you buy in the past year?

    a: 0 - 5   b: 6 - 10   c: more than 10   d: more than 20 ____

- How would you rate your overall satisfaction with this book?

    a: Excellent   b: Good   c: Fair   d: Poor

- What was the main reason you bought this book?

    a: It is a TOPAZ novel, and I know that TOPAZ stands
       for quality romance fiction
    b: I liked the cover
    c: The story-line intrigued me
    d: I love this author
    e: I really liked the setting
    f: I love the cover models
    g: Other: _____

- Where did you buy this TOPAZ novel?

    a: Bookstore   b: Airport   c: Warehouse Club
    d: Department Store   e: Supermarket   f: Drugstore
    g: Other: _____

- Did you pay the full cover price for this TOPAZ novel? (circle one)

    YES   NO

    If you did not, what price did you pay? _____

- Who are your favorite TOPAZ authors? (Please list)

- How did you first hear about TOPAZ books?

    a: I saw the books in a bookstore
    b: I saw the TOPAZ Man on TV or at a signing
    c: A friend told me about TOPAZ
    d: I saw an advertisement in_____magazine
    e: Other: _____

- What type of romance do you generally prefer?

    a: Historical   b: Contemporary
    c: Romantic Suspense   d: Paranormal (time travel,
       futuristic, vampires, ghosts, warlocks, etc.)
    d: Regency   e: Other: _____

- What historical settings do you prefer?

    a: England   b: Regency England   c: Scotland
    e: Ireland   f: America   g: Western Americana
    h: American Indian   i: Other: _____

- What type of story do you prefer?

    a: Very sexy
    b: Sweet, less explicit
    c: Light and humorous
    d: More emotionally intense
    e: Dealing with darker issues
    f: Other

- What kind of covers do you prefer?

    a: Illustrating both hero and heroine
    b: Hero alone
    c: No people (art only)
    d: Other_____

- What other genres do you like to read (circle all that apply)

    Mystery   Medical Thrillers   Science Fiction
    Suspense   Fantasy   Self-help
    Classics   General Fiction   Legal Thrillers
    Historical Fiction

- Who is your favorite author, and why?_____

_____

- What magazines do you like to read? (circle all that apply)

    a: *People*
    b: *Time/Newsweek*
    c: *Entertainment Weekly*
    d: *Romantic Times*
    e: *Star*
    f: *National Enquirer*
    g: *Cosmopolitan*
    h: *Woman's Day*
    i: *Ladies' Home Journal*
    j: *Redbook*
    k: Other:_____

- In which region of the United States do you reside?

    a: Northeast   b: Midatlantic   c: South
    d: Midwest   e: Mountain   f: Southwest
    g: Pacific Coast

- What is your age group/sex?   a: Female   b: Male

    a: under 18   b: 19-25   c: 26-30   d: 31-35   e: 56-60
    f: 41-45   g: 46-50   h: 51-55   i: 56-60   j: Over 60

- What is your marital status?

    a: Married   b: Single   c: No longer married

- What is your current level of education?

    a: High school   b: College Degree
    c: Graduate Degree   d: Other: _____

- Do you receive the TOPAZ *Romantic Liaisons* newsletter, a quarterly newsletter with the latest information on Topaz books and authors?

    YES   NO

    If not, would you like to?   YES   NO

Fill in the address where you would like your free gift to be sent:

Name: _____

Address: _____

City:_____   Zip Code: _____

You should receive your free gift in 6 to 8 weeks.
Please send the completed survey to:

Penguin USA•Mass Market
Dept. TS
375 Hudson St.
New York, NY 10014